PARIS NOIRE

PARIS NOIRE

Francine Thomas Howard

PUBLISHED BY

amazon encore

The characters and events portrayed in this book are fictitious. Any similarity to real persons, living or dead, is coincidental and not intended by the author.

Published by AmazonEncore
P.O. Box 400818
Las Vegas, NV 89140   MAR 0 9 2012

ISBN-13: 9781935597971
ISBN-10: 1935597973

This one's for you, GDS, the second of my three grandmothers. I've tried to honor your dream—a dream for
which you paid a heavy price. Through Glovia Johnson,
your golden voice has now sung throughout Paris.

CHAPTER 1

Outside, somewhere, the next gun blast thudded through the air, rattling the mahogany-framed photograph of Papa. Another shower of plaster shook loose from the foot of the haloed cherub guarding the far corner of her ceiling and floated down the blue-peony wallpaper. Marie-Thérèse shuddered at the sight of her daughter standing just five feet from the *appartement*'s front window, its vanes only half closed. Didn't that girl know by now that bullets—either German or Free French—could kill?

"*Maman!*" Collette called out. She waved an arm, sprinkled with plaster dust, toward the window. She covered her ears, but her eyes danced.

"*Mon Dieu*, girl!" Marie-Thérèse squeezed her eyes shut for a second. "How many times I tell you this? You have twenty years on you. You keep at the window and you will not have twenty-one."

"Oh, Maman." Collette dismissed her with that look that said, *You're doing a poor job of hiding your worry.*

Marie-Thérèse turned her back to her daughter and busied herself twisting the knob on the stove in the kitchen, measuring in her mind how far she could stretch the few liters of fuel she had left. She picked up the barley grounds, now three days used, dumped them onto a clean square of

1

cheesecloth, and lowered the whole thing into the boiling pot.

She couldn't help how she reacted when she was nervous.

That was a lie. She lapsed into the patois that was Martinique because it allowed her to relax into herself. She could speak proper French if she took a mind to the task. It wasn't even difficult. After all, it was De Gaulle's French she spoke every time she left her apartment and strolled the winding streets of Montmartre. Even General LeClerc could speak no better French than she when she taught her sixth grade class. Not that those ruffians from Morocco, Senegal, and Algiers would know the difference anyway. She sighed. Who was she to think such thoughts? Wasn't she born and bred in Martinique, herself?

Zing. Tat. Tat. Tat. The small-arms fire sounded just houses away now.

"*Mon Jésus.*" Marie-Thérèse tried to swallow back her outcry as her heart and stomach wrestled one another. She grabbed the broom, crouched next to the front room window, and extended the handle to push the shutters fully closed. One of the flat vanes, loose for months now, clattered down the three stories to the pavement of the rue de la Bonne. *Mon Dieu.* Marie-Thérèse frowned as she clutched at the front of her nightdress. She balanced against the broom and helped herself to her feet.

"Maman." Now Collette gave her that "soothe the old lady" look. "The bullets. The blasts. Yes, they've been coming every day for seven days. But today is the last day!" Collette closed her eyes and tapped the front of her gray work blouse. "I can feel it. Here." She lifted her chin toward the ceiling. Another light dusting of plaster floated down, this time from the cherub's belly.

"I know the calendar, girl." Marie-Thérèse looked at the sheet of paper tacked to the pantry door, its blue paint peeling. August 25, 1944. "What you feel is the bullet through your heart. I tell you again. No window for you." She heard the lilt in her own voice. Marie-Thérèse turned toward the missing vane. The pink-orange light filtering into her living room announced the dawning of another hot Paris day. But this day was like none other in her sixteen years in the City of Light.

"Where is the hot comb, Maman?" Collette ran her fingers through her wavy hair, and her voice sounded of lightness. "I tell you, Paris is free! There will be dancing in the streets this day!" She tapped her feet against the parquet floor.

Marie-Thérèse stared at the front door to her apartment, then turned toward the window just as another blast rattled the picture on the sideboard and loosened the last of the plaster from the cherub's foot. The rosary beads swayed against the wooden picture frame.

"It's pray you should do. Pray that your brother is safe in this war. Pray that Christophe…" She stood the broom in its corner.

Tat. Tat. Tat.

"The *comb*, Maman." Collette's voice feigned patience. "Christophe is not in the war, and he's home when the last loaves come out of the oven. You know that, Maman."

"I know the time of your brother's quitting better than you. Full dawn, and he's home from the *boulangerie*. And, missy, you do not know for sure who is Resistance and who…"

3

What for you want the comb? A little bit of frizz in the hair makes for a pretty face on a girl with tan skin like yourself. You don't need to make the straight hair like the French girls. You—"

"I am a French girl!" Collette's brown eyes blazed defiance for the whisper of a second.

"You watch that mouth on you, my girl. I, for sure, don't like all this *boom-boom* and the *zing-zing*, but I am your *mère* and I tell you what is true." Marie-Thérèse walked past the half wall that separated the kitchen from the family's living space. She bent down and parted the frayed blue gingham curtain covering the two shelves holding her cooking pots and utensils. From the top shelf she pulled out the pressing comb Glovia had given her.

"*Café*, Maman?" Collette kept her eyes downcast and her voice soft as she nodded toward the pot on the stove.

A blast that sounded more dull thud than whopping thunder swept the room. Marie-Thérèse's eyes went to the photograph of her long-dead Frenchman father. This time the rosary didn't move and the ceiling cherub lost no more body parts. "We are in France since you are four years old, that is for sure, but you are a girl of Martinique."

"My father was born in France, for the sake of God, Maman!" That look of defiance flashed from Collette's eyes again.

"Who you talk to like this, miss? I know who your father is." Marie-Thérèse shook the straightening comb in her daughter's direction. "I married the man, though my papa tell me this is a fool's thing to do. I marry him because he was a Frenchman. A white man, and maybe I can come

4

to Paris." She shook her head as she reached for her last un-chipped china cup. "I'll never do that thing again."

"I don't think you *can* do that thing." Collette directed her giggles into the steam coming off the pot of coffee. "You are fifty years old, after all."

"I hear you there, girl." Marie-Thérèse glowered as she handed the comb to Collette. She touched her own crinkly, dark hair. Maybe she needed a touch-up herself, especially that patch of gray in front. "You got nothing better to do than talk bad about your mother? You stand there, telling me you are a French girl. Well, French girl or girl from Martinique, you be dead either way when the Germans burn this city to the ground. Now talk to me no more about French girls."

Tat. Tat. Tat...tat.

"Yes, Maman." At least Collette sounded as though she almost meant her words. She laid the comb across the grate over the open flame. "When Christophe comes home," she sidled a glance towards her mother, "then you'll see."

"I'll see my hand laid to you for your sassiness."

"Maman! Maman!" Christophe's shout rang through the *appartement* door. "Open. Open."

Marie-Thérèse hurried to the door and fumbled with the chain fastening it shut. She wished she had listened to her son. What good was a chain against a Nazi jackboot? She slid the metal free, pushed back the locking bolt, and swung open the door. Christophe, his golden-skinned face wreathed in smiles, burst into the room.

"Christophe! Christophe!" Collette crossed the scratched floor in three strides and leaped into her brother's arms, her legs encircling his waist, her arms tight around his neck. "It's true. I knew it. Paris is free!"

He twirled her around. "With this news, even you feel light." Christophe set his sister down.

"No bullet holes in you?" Marie-Thérèse crossed herself. "I hear them all night. The Germans. There is fighting everywhere. I…"

"*Non,* Maman. That's just it. The sentries…the sentries…they…" Christophe crossed over to the kitchen table with its four still-sturdy chairs, and dropped the baguette. He reached for the mug Marie-Thérèse always left there for him after he returned from his night shift.

"Tell me. Tell me. Tell me." Collette's voice rose to a squeal as she rushed to the stove to retrieve the now-smoking straightening comb. She licked her index finger and laid it quickly against the comb.

"Collette. Maman. The sentries. The ones that always march by the *boulangerie* at least twice a night to make sure we're all inside the bakery and not sneaking out to help the Resistance. They…"

"Yes? Yes?" Collette slanted the small mirror against the wall and touched the comb to her hair, all the while keeping sight of her brother.

"Collette," Marie-Thérèse warned, "you watch that comb. Why you want your hair as straight as a stick I do not know. Christophe. The sentries. Tell me, what they do?" Marie-Thérèse looked from son to daughter and back again. Her heart raced. Was her world about to fall apart, or were they all going to live again?

"Today is the day!" Christophe strode across the floor and threw open the shutters.

"Oh!" Marie-Thérèse sucked in a breath and marveled that the old frame still held together. Her shutters had been open at no more than half-mast for over four years.

Her son turned the casement handles and flung open the windows. "This is the look of freedom!"

"I knew it. I knew it! *Ow!*" Collette winced as the hot comb sizzled too close to her ear. With each swipe, her brown hair fell in soft, straight cascades to below her shoulder blades.

"How can you be so sure this is true, son? All night, the *boom-boom*. The *zing-zing*. The Germans...they will never leave Paris untouched. They..."

"Maman." Christophe encircled her in his arms and squeezed.

She pushed against his chest for release and stepped away.

"Louis-Philippe," her son chattered. "You know him. At the *boulangerie*. His uncle's wife's cousin is Free French. He has a radio. They are on the blessed march!" Christophe's brown eyes twinkled.

"The Germans? The Germans are on the march? I knew it. Tell me where they go!" Marie-Thérèse fought back a fresh wave of worry.

"It's the Americans, Maman. *They* are on the move...to Paris!" Christophe's laugh filled the room. "Today. They will be here today!"

"I told you so, Maman!" Collette tossed the comb toward the stove, missed, and the implement clattered against the tile floor.

"What you say?" Marie-Thérèse wrapped her arms around her chest. "The Germans...they leave? No." She shook her head. "Not without a fight."

"Louis-Philippe. I told you, Maman!" Christophe's words ran atop one another. "On the radio. The Resistance. The sound of the trucks. This morning the Americans are no more than ten kilometers outside of Boulogne."

Swish. The sound came through the window like a deflated balloon. Marie-Thérèse walked over to Papa's photograph. The rosary beads hung limp. She ran her fingers over the old beads and gave thanks to her father who educated his mulatto daughter despite her illegitimacy.

"You tell me, Christophe," Marie-Thérèse lifted the rosary to her lips, "the Germans will leave and not burn Paris?"

Her son's laugh rocked the room again. "Maman. You do worry! The Germans are not leaving because they want to. They're leaving because they have to. The shots you hear? That's our side, Maman...the Resistance. Le Maquis. They don't mind giving the *ennemi* a little reminder that they've overstayed their welcome in Paris." Christophe punched a fist into the air.

Collette ran into the room and sped back, her purse slung over her shoulder. "Don't stand here talking to Maman. She can hide in the corner. Let's go!"

"Go? Where you think you take yourself, missy?" Marie-Thérèse turned to Christophe. "I am not the worried old crone that one would have you think." She jerked her head toward Collette. "Your eyes still have the sight in them, and your ears can carry the sound. I can hear the Germans. I can see what they do to my *appartement*."

Christophe gave Marie-Thérèse a quick peck on the cheek, as though he thought she was indeed the same old crone that Collette believed. "*Oui,* Maman. There is still shooting on the streets." He held her shoulders. "But listen to the sound. The Germans are blocks and blocks from here. Just stay away from the windows until we come back and you'll be fine."

"Foolish children! It's not for myself that gives my heart the worry, it's—"

"Yes, Maman," Collette and Christophe chorused in unison as they closed the door behind them.

Marie-Thérèse heard their whooping laughter as they clattered down the first of the three flights of stairs.

CHAPTER 2

Marie-Thérèse ran a hand along the side of her face to wipe away the perspiration. She fought her way uphill against the crush of people surging down Montmartre. She puffed her way toward the big oak door announcing Glovia's apartment and let out a sigh. The gray-white spires of the Sacré-Coeur, bathed in midmorning light, loomed just a half block ahead. She took a few more cautious steps along the rue de la Bonne and surveyed the crowd. Young and old looked giddy with joy. It was true, she admitted, that the throngs of people pouring out of their apartments and racing toward the Champs-Élysées had all assured her that today was the day Paris would be freed. Still, it was impossible not to see the fresh bullet holes blasted into the sides of the buildings. Suppose it was a Nazi trick? Only Glovia would know for sure if the German *monstres* had really gone.

She stared at the big brass handle on Glovia's front door, paused to arrange herself into something presentable, and gave the lion's head knocker a tentative rap. Inside the apartment she heard nothing. Was that good or bad? Marie-Thérèse swallowed hard. Had she made a mistake? Madame Johnson had always been welcoming, warm even, but she was an American, and the cleverest woman Marie-Thérèse had ever known. She rapped the door a second time. This time, louder.

The muscular Frenchman who served Glovia as butler, bodyguard, and saxophone player opened the door. "Madame Brillard?"

"Forgive me, *monsieur*. I know that the hour is early…that *madame*…" Marie-Thérèse stuttered. "I mean, the blasts last night. It has been difficult for any of us to sleep. Is Madame Johnson receiving at this hour?"

"Receiving?" Glovia's voice called out from somewhere in the interior. "Gaston, whoever it is, send her in."

Marie-Thérèse let the jack-of-all-trades lead her into the room Glovia called her study, even though she knew perfectly well how to get to the space by herself. Right before Gaston turned her down the hall to the left, she passed the room where Glovia used to hold court every Tuesday night— the salon. That is, until that German colonel entered the premises.

"Oh, Marie-Thérèse, it's you. What brings you to see me?" Glovia walked to the *étagère* and picked up a pack of cigarettes. "I don't do it often." She looked apologetic. "Bad for the voice, you know." Glovia stood wrapped in a silk dressing gown, even more striking because the green in the floral print set off her hazel eyes. She turned her face, bereft of makeup at this early hour, toward Marie-Thérèse.

"I heard the fighting all night." Marie-Thérèse struggled to hide her nervousness. Her French had to be correct even though this American spoke with the most atrocious accent. That is, when the *chanteuse* bothered to speak French at all. Still, she was one of them, and all Paris loved that accent coming out of the mouths of America's black *émigrés*. If only it were so for the Africans and the West Indians.

"You want me to set you up with a croissant and butter?" Glovia glanced out her window toward the church at the top of the hill. The shouts from the crowd blared through her open first-floor window.

"Oh?" Marie-Thérèse caught herself. While almost everyone else in Paris had been juggling dwindling rations these past four years, Glovia had been awash in eggs, fresh milk, chicken, butter, and the occasional beef. "*Non merci,* Madame Johnson."

"Honey, how many times do I have to tell you to call me Glovia?" She shot a coy look at Marie-Thérèse. "Mr. Johnson and I never did exactly hit it off." Glovia tapped the cigarette on the edge of the *étagère* before she lit up. "Pay me no mind. Sometimes this mouth of mine just goes on and on. Sit yourself down." She'd switched to English.

"I don't want to take up your time, Mad—Glovia. I just wanted to check on those in the neighborhood, with all the noise last night." Marie-Thérèse sneaked a quick glance around the room. Nothing seemed amiss. No empty champagne glasses. No cigar butts in the ashtray.

"Uh-huh." Glovia sprawled on the pale blue chaise longue, the front of her night wrapper falling away to show one well-shaped leg. She quickly rearranged the dressing gown. "That fuss last night scared you, did it?" A smile curved Glovia's lips as she puffed on the cigarette.

"You think we'll have many more like it?" Marie-Thérèse let the question ride the air as she peeked into the hallway and caught a glimpse of the open bedroom door.

"Honey," Glovia exploded in laugher, "it's a damn good thing you didn't play poker at my soirees back in thirty-nine. My guests would have made enough money off you to charter a private plane to take the whole kit and caboodle of us back to the States."

"Madame—Glovia." Marie-Thérèse felt her face flush beneath her cocoa-brown skin. "I only meant that..."

"I know what you meant, sugar. He ain't here. Left night before last. Scared as one of those French aristocrats being led to the guillotine." Glovia squinted at the white enameled clock on the marble mantelpiece. "Can't see a thing without my glasses. Does that damn thing say ten thirty?"

Before Marie-Thérèse could respond, Glovia called out, "Gaston. Honey. Go break it out." She sent a sly look toward her guest. "It's never too early when you got something to celebrate."

Marie-Thérèse darted her eyes from Glovia to a grinning Gaston as he slipped past the open door. "He's not here?" Marie-Thérèse ventured. "Forgive me, Ma—Glovia. The Nazi is not here?" Her heart thumped in her chest.

"Nope. You need to do a better job of pretending that a German colonel didn't visit me, so to speak, on a regular basis."

Gaston stepped back into the room carrying a bottle and three glasses. Glovia stubbed out the cigarette as she moved to her feet. She gestured for the container.

"You fixin' to join us, Gaston?" Glovia held up the dust-covered bottle and traced a finger over the label. "Veuve Clicquot, nineteen thirty-five." She held the champagne bottle against her cheek. Her eyes flickered closed for an instant. "You know that Kraut gave me this so we could celebrate the end of the war. Said thirty-five was a vintage year. Said he knew all about that stuff because he was like one of your aristocrats—a count of some sort." She sucked in her upper lip and the dimples in her cheeks deepened. "And that's just what I'm gonna do." Glovia sashayed around the room, head thrown back, hips swaying in exaggerated motion. She called out in singsong over her shoulder. "Only that no-count don't know the victory I'm gonna celebrate is his misbegotten ass laying dead somewhere in a French ditch."

"*Madame* will be the toast of Paris again." Gaston wiped the rim of the champagne glasses with a white cloth.

"Sure, sure, Gaston. We all did what we had to do for France, and I don't want no more talk about it. Pour that bubbly. Marie-Thérèse, you and me will be the first to celebrate."

"It is true, then? I see all the people, but I am afraid to believe." Marie-Thérèse felt the sting of relief puddling her eyes. "It is over? The Germans really are gone? Paris is truly free?"

Gaston poured champagne into the three flutes and handed one to Marie-Thérèse. "To *les Americaines*." The sax player kept his eyes on Glovia. "All of them."

"I'm staying low for a while. Having a German officer pay his respects three nights out of the week doesn't sit well with everybody in this neighborhood, you know." Glovia held her glass aloft.

"But what you do...what you did for France...the sacrifice," Marie-Thérèse managed.

Gaston let the liquid slide down his throat. "*C'est magnifique.* The wait has been long in coming, *madame*, but the aftermath is nectar." He backed out of the room.

"We know you here in Montmartre, Madame Johnson... Glovia." Marie-Thérèse held her glass toward her hostess.

"The help you gave, whatever it might have been, all Montmartre knows you sacrificed for our country. *Vive la France.*" She took a hearty swallow.

"And you didn't do the same to get yourself to France?" Glovia switched back to French. "Sacrifice for your kids?" She pushed up the sleeves of her gown, showing off the pale gold tones of her skin. "We women have to put up with a lot to get a thing done, eh, Marie-Thérèse?"

"*Mais oui.*" Marie-Thérèse closed her eyes and let the champagne trickle down her throat. She wanted no more of this topic. "*Mon Dieu.* My son, my daughter, they are gathering to see the liberators...the Americans march into Paris. Will they be safe?"

"The Champs-Élysées? Your kids are going to the boulevard? With thousands of soldiers pouring into Paris? I'd keep your daughter close, but sure, they'll be safe." Glovia finished her glass and poured herself another. "Word is the troops are rolling in a few hours. What do you say we leave that kind of celebrating to the young folks? You stay here with me. I've got a few friends coming over. Just like the old days."

"A soiree? In the salon?" Marie-Thérèse clutched her glass. "And it isn't even Tuesday. Who will come? Your friends are all so...so *intriguing.*"

"That's right. I did talk you into sitting in on a couple of my parties back in the old days. You came over and offered to help me out with the serving." Glovia took a swallow of champagne. "You never struck me as a timid one when I saw you around the neighborhood, but, Marie-Thérèse, you sure avoided my soirees."

"You forget, Glovia, I am from Martinique. With the likes of your friends...the Americans, the poets and artists who come to your parties, I have nothing to contribute."

"Contribute? Sugar, what are you talking about? *Contribute*." She humphed. "The folks who come to my house like to talk about anything and everything, that's for sure. Martinique would have put them on a roll for hours. The plight of black folks in the West Indies. Lord, Lord, that would have set Jimmie Lee Hudson up for weeks."

"If it were only that simple. Your friends do more than talk. They write beautiful poetry. Novels that stir the soul and wake the mind. They paint. They—"

"Yeah. They can do all that. You remember Langston, don't you? Langston Hughes? Now that man could write. 'The Weary Blues.' James could paint like nobody's business. You remember him, don't you?"

"Umm," Marie-Thérèse stumbled. "I remember Madame Bricktop quite well, though."

"Ada? Now that woman was as funny as they come." Glovia sent a wistful look toward Marie-Thérèse. "She got out in thirty-nine." She brightened. "No, I'm talking about James. James Van Der Zee."

"Ahh. *Oui*. The photograph about the basketball team. I remember him now." That usual wave of intimidation swept Marie-Thérèse as she recalled the brilliance of Glovia's soirees. "That's what I'm saying. So many talented people."

"You forget that I can barely write a straight sentence, and I sure as hell can't paint no still life like Laura Waring." Glovia aimed her glass in the direction of the cathedral.

"Write? Paint? You don't need any of that. You've got the most beautiful singing voice. Your man…Gaston was right. You were the toast of Paris."

"Maybe the crust off the toast of Paris." Glovia let out a snort. "Josephine always got in my way."

"Another great talent. Madame Baker."

"Mind you, I did have me some looks back then. Honey, I had legs up to here." She smoothed a hand over her hip. "Tits ridin' *high*." A small laugh escaped those full lips. "Now, I'm forty-eight years old."

"With the look of thirty-three. You still enchant Montmartre and Pigalle."

Glovia brightened. "With the Nazis out of here, Le Chat Noir can jazz it up one more time. No more Nazi officers ogling me. Hallelujah!"

Marie-Thérèse watched the legendary Noire-Americaine. If she could be called that. Glovia, with her caramel-colored hair, looked more French than Marie-Thérèse's own quadroon children. Whether she admitted it or not, Glovia Johnson had changed little since her heyday in Paris. No wonder that Kraut let every Nazi secret slip out of his mouth and onto her pillow.

CHAPTER 3

Christophe counted his six-foot height a blessing. Though he didn't tower over his fellow Frenchmen, he had a decided advantage in a crowd. But not on this steaming August day. He could barely feel his feet underneath him amid the surrounding throng. Shouts, screams, yells came in bursts, crescendoing louder and louder. Word passed in waves along the crowd on the Champs-Élysées.

"What did he say?" Christophe shouted into the ear of a beret-wearing stranger standing next to him, the Arc de Triomphe towering nearby.

"They can hear the roar of the trucks. Hundreds. Thousands!" The excited man almost jabbed Christophe in the eye with the staff of the Noveau Petit Larousse Illustré flag he carried. "Tell the others."

Christophe turned to his right and toward a middle-aged man in an ill-fitting uniform from the Great War. "They are just blocks from—" The words caught in his throat when he felt a slender body thud into his back.

"*Scuser, monsieur.*" The female voice sounded dizzy with excitement, not apology.

Christophe turned to stare into the dancing amber eyes of a Frenchwoman who looked little older than his own twenty-two years.

"It has happened at last. Paris is free!" She tried to hoist her own red, white, and blue flag, only to jam it into Christophe's shoulder. "Oh, *monsieur*. Forgive me again." She smiled at him, flashing even, white teeth.

"They're here. I can see them!" The beret-wearer elbowed Christophe as he jumped to better his view of the events on the broad boulevard. In the crush of the crowd, he tromped down on Christophe's foot. Christophe staggered into the young woman, feeling the firmness of her breasts brushing his arm.

"My turn to apologize," he laughed as he pushed away her neck scarf, which fluttered across his cheek.

"This is a day most *magnifique*. Please, sir, what can you see? I..." Her words drowned in the sound of trumpets, trombones, and drums drifting up the Champs-Élysées.

Christophe used the shoulders of the beret-wearer to give himself a quick boost over the heads of the crowd now swaying with the first faint strains of a familiar song: "*Allons Enfants de la Patrie.*"

"I can see them." Christophe could barely hear his own voice as the crowd grunted its recognition of its most sacred words—"La Marseillaise." A man's voice here, a woman's there. Then a dozen, a hundred, a thousand voices joined in unison. "*Le jour de gloire est arrivé!*" He felt the woman's small fists pound a tattoo on his shoulder blades as her tear-filled voice swelled the air. "Marchons! Marchons!" He turned to her. The afternoon sun caught in her tawny-brown hair as the swaying crowd jostled the woman against his chest. As he bent in closer, the faint smell of verbena wafted off her skin.

"What?" she called to him. "Who do you see?" Her lips, with their blush of red, pressed into his ear.

"The first wave. It is...they are...the Free French!" Christophe shouted back.

"Oh!" The woman tried to jump her five-foot-five-inch frame into the air, gave up, and squeezed his shoulder. "*Monsieur*, please, can you lift me? I must see." The sparkle in her eyes faded, replaced by a flash of concern.

Christophe grabbed her around the waist and raised her as high as he could. "Can you see them...the Free French?"

"Oh, yes, *monsieur!*" The lightness in her voice returned. "Look. Behind them. I see...I believe...yes. For sure. It is the *Corps Afrique.*"

"The Senegalese? You see the *Tirailleurs Sénégalais?*" Christophe felt that quick rush as the woman adjusted her rounded hips against his shoulder. He lowered her to the ground and tugged at his sweat-stained shirt. He jostled to get a look at the *kepis*-wearing black regiment. Word had spread throughout the immigrant community about these fez-wearing fighting men whose bravery had made them the real heroes in the battle for France. He swallowed and remembered. He could have been one of the Africa Corps, if pride hadn't pushed him away.

As the strains of the French National anthem faded, the roar of thousands of wheels on the Champs-Élysées blasted into his ears and mixed with the near-hysterical shouts of the crowd. The Great War veteran suddenly jabbed his flag into the air—this time the red, white, and blue of the United States bolted high.

"I save it!" the Great Warrior shouted to the crowd. "I save it from the Argonne. If the Vichy catch me, they kill me for this." His waving arm repeatedly slapped the side of Christophe's face. "No danger too great to celebrate this hour." Tears streamed down the old man's face.

Christophe jumped into the air again, rewarded by GI jeeps swarming with tired but smiling American faces. He laid a hand against his cheek and wiped away his own tears. A car carrying a single large star on its side moved down the boulevard, and the crowd roared its approval for some American general or other. Americans leaning over the tops of open-backed trucks tossed items into the crowd. Gum? Chocolate bars? Christophe savored the almost forgotten taste of rich, dark chocolate in his mouth. Such luxuries hadn't been seen in France these four years. Celebrants behind him pushed forward and bumped those in front. The young woman stumbled and nearly fell under the feet of the surging crowd.

"*Monsieur!*" Her plea was half groan, half shout. "My ankle."

Christophe flailed his arms into the crowd to make space for the fallen woman. He helped steady her.

"I'm so sorry," she groaned in her breathy voice as she tested her foot against the sidewalk.

"Let's get out of here." He slipped an arm around her waist and looked for an opening through the jostling crowd. He clutched her tightly and threaded his way back to the pavement.

"Ow!" she grunted as she limped along.

"Your ankle." Christophe stopped. "*Mademoiselle.*" He swept her into his arms and marveled again at her lightness. The Germans had put even the *Parisiennes* on limited rations. The crowd parted enough to allow entry into one of the open doors lining the boulevard. Christophe forced his way into a bistro where patrons stood on tables and chairs, searching through the plate glass window to catch a glimpse of the parade of victorious troops.

"A drink for *mademoiselle*, if you please!" Christophe shouted above the din to the bartender. "She was almost crushed in this crowd." He sat the woman in a quickly vacated chair.

"Oh, *monsieur*." The woman's face flushed red. "Do not trouble yourself. This is the day we've all prayed for. A twisted ankle is a small price to pay. It will heal, but none of us will ever see the likes of this time again." She grimaced as she lifted her injured ankle to the wooden chair seat. She leaned forward to inspect the injury. "I declare you a gentleman of France." She peeked up at him as her long, unadorned fingers brushed back her hair. "Now, go. Celebrate."

"And celebrate I shall." Christophe dropped to his knees beside her as another patron brushed past. "I shall celebrate here with you." He smiled. "Let's take a look at that ankle." He slid his fingers along the swelling skin and allowed his eyes to drift up her leg as far as her modestly arranged skirt would allow. He sucked in a breath of approval when the trim extremity showed no signs of the nylon stocking that only women with special Vichy connections, like Madame Glovia, wore. Despite her beauty, this woman was no German's plaything.

"Are you a doctor, *monsieur*?" Her voice cut through his reverie.

"Christophe. Christophe Brillard, and actually, with the Germans gone, I will be a doctor soon enough."

"Oh?" Understanding beamed out of her eyes. "You are a conscript. We all know the story."

"Was. I was an *appele*. Yes, the Wehrmacht assigned me to the night shift at the bakery."

"To better keep you under their watchful eye, of course." She flinched as his fingers probed a sensitive spot on her ankle. "Less chance for you to join the Resistance."

"*La Resistance?*" The barkeep, hands full of wine-filled goblets, his white apron straps askew, bent down and pecked the woman on the cheek. "To the Maquis." He handed her a glass and a second to Christophe.

"*Merci, monsieur.*" She smiled her thanks.

"To victory, *ma Genvieve.*" The barkeep gulped down one of his own flutes of champagne before he moved on to a nearby table. Rousing choruses of "La Marseillaise" shook the Bistro Cloche.

"To France!" As the woman leaned toward Christophe, the top two buttons of her blouse splayed open, revealing an overflowing brassiere. She slipped her free arm around his neck.

Before he could respond, she pressed her lips against his, parting them. Christophe answered with his tongue. "Marchons! Marchons!" played over and over in his head. She released him and leaned back in the chair, her lips now smudged with lipstick. She turned an off-center smile in his direction.

"Genvieve Pa—" Her voice turned throaty. "Genvieve. My name."

Christophe took his time appraising the look of this woman, her head tilted to the side. "Let's get your ankle better." He grabbed a napkin from a nearby table and tightened it around her lower leg. "Thirty minutes or so and we can really celebrate this day in style."

"Ahh. *Mon*—Christophe. I am so happy that this day has finally come. For today, I can do anything." She laid her hand on his thigh. "Let's us drink in this moment." She squeezed his leg.

The barkeep swept by long enough to splash more red wine into their goblets as "La Marseillaise" gave way to "Boogie Woogie Bugle Boy of Company B."

If the bells of the Madeleine church rang out at midnight, Christophe had not heard them for the din in the Bistro Cloche. The café filled multiple times over with locals and Americans. Hours ago, he and Genvieve decided to share their one chair and a half dozen bottles of wine. Every time one of the now-off-duty American soldiers approached even a block close to the bistro, four or five of the locals rushed out to greet the man and steer him into the bistro where the barkeep and customers plied him with liquor. For the last half hour, Christophe held Genvieve on his lap as though she were Madame du Pompadour holding court. As the Americans made their way around the room, Genvieve reached up to kiss them on the cheek and returned to kiss Christophe on the mouth.

"I have emptied my cellars," the barkeep called out as he spun toward a black American standing next to Christophe and Genvieve, "but for you, our liberators, anything. Everything!" He drained the last of a bottle of red into the three glasses.

"Hey." The American scowled down at Christophe. "You ain't in uniform."

"*Non*. Sergeant, I am not American." Christophe looked up at the man.

"You Free French?" The American cast back a curious glance.

"*Appele*," Genvieve answered as she beckoned the man closer to plant a kiss on his cheek.

"Ah-who?" The man shook his head. "Don't rightly know what that is." He turned to Christophe. "You one of the black Frenchmen? One of them Africa Corps? I hear they fought like hell." He leaned in close and whispered to Christophe, "Ain't it always the way, man? They're the ones who run the Nazis out of the south of France, but the white Frenchies get all the credit." He smiled as he clapped Christophe on the shoulder.

"No. I'm not Afri—I mean, I was a conscript...I..." The sweat already beading Christophe's brow from the crush of the crowd began to streak down his face.

"Uh-huh." The distracted soldier was interrupted by another black American.

Before Genvieve could beckon the second man for a welcoming kiss, the two teetered off to another part of the bistro.

"The Africa Corps would not take the likes of you." Genvieve leaned in, a lopsided grin on her face as she drained the last of her wine. "I think my head is beginning to hurt." She held her middle fingers at her temples as she wiggled her foot. "But my ankle is better."

"Perhaps I can take you home." Christophe adjusted her in his lap, hoping his too-bold offer would make her forget the subject of the Africa Corps. "Do you live alone?"

Genvieve looked at him through glazed eyes. He moved her to her feet only to see her legs wobble. But, this time, the ankle was not the cause.

"I fear I celebrate too much. *Monsieur*, I fear that I am going to be ill." She clapped a hand hard over her mouth just as the barkeep passed by.

He grabbed the wrist of one of his barmaids and pointed to Genvieve, then turned to face Christophe. "*Merci, monsieur.* Thank you for joining us on this marvelous day." He looked through his open door and the darkened sky. "This marvelous *night*," he corrected. He watched as the barmaid helped Genvieve behind a much-patched green velvet curtain. "But as you can see, our Genvieve has enjoyed my wine a bit too much. She is local. We will see that she gets home." He nodded his head toward the door. "*Bonsoir, monsieur.*"

As Christophe fumbled for the key to the family apartment, he hoped he wouldn't wake Maman or Collette. Tiptoeing through the house as quietly as he could, he passed his mother's bedroom. It was empty.

CHAPTER 4

Marie-Thérèse smiled to herself as she hurried the pâté onto the serving trays in the green and tan tiled kitchen. It felt good to be back in Glovia Johnson's big apartment slathering duck liver pâté on toasted baguettes, even if the pâté had sat in a can for over two years.

"To the victor go the spoils." Monsieur Williams's big American laugh boomed out of Glovia's salon and down the long hall.

"To the victor go the spoils? That ain't even original." As usual, Glovia's melodious sound dominated the room. "If that's the best toast you can come up with, I swear I don't see how the French ever gave you the *Prix Goncourt*."

"Victory is for the just, the pure, the strong...and the lucky," Monsieur Williams retorted in that baritone of his that always sounded like he was keeping some inside joke.

A rougher American voice chimed in. "Hell, no. Victory is to the Red Ball Express—best damn truck brigade in this whole goddamn war!"

Marie-Thérèse jolted at the man's coarse outburst. In the ten years she'd helped out at these soirees, she'd never known Glovia to shy away from a good curse. In fact, the singer relished a clever turn of phrase, but the words could never be common or obscene. Marie-Thérèse lifted the platter of hors d'oeuvres, put her shoulder to the familiar swinging door leading from the kitchen, and walked toward the salon.

"Hey, buddy." Monsieur Crawford's voice went through the room. "I raise my glass to you, my colored brethren. You all sure did save our behinds, but we kind of watch our words around here, especially when a lady is present."

As she carried the tray down the hall, Marie-Thérèse couldn't see the face of the offending American, but she could guess the expression on Monsieur Crawford. He was a sculptor, after all, and knew just the right way to arrange features to get a point across in the most tactful manner. She looked for the bearded artist as soon as she stepped into the salon crowded with almost two dozen of Glovia's celebrating American *noir* soldiers. Marie-Thérèse did a quick calculation. Would there be enough food? With the entertainer's usual guest list of ten overwhelmed by these ravenous newcomers, she wondered.

"No fussing and fighting today. Not today, when we're all about celebrating." Glovia, her hair done up in a pompadour, a silver snood covering the back, nodded a greeting to Marie-Thérèse. "Meet my friend here. She's from Martinique." She spun toward a stout soldier with a fresh scar creasing one side of his face. "Now, don't be like me when I first met Marie-Thérèse. I asked her how close to Atlanta was Martinique." Glovia cocked her head, waiting.

The soldier looked confused. "Well, she's a fine-lookin' woman, and I don't care what little old Georgia town she hails from. I like my women with some heft on 'em." The soldier bumped his pelvis against Marie-Thérèse's hip as his army buddies guffawed. "What you got there for me,

Mama?" The tipsy soldier pointed to the tray as his eyes widened.

"Don't ask. Just take a bite." Glovia swept up a pâté-covered slice of toast and handed it to the American. "And, GI Joe," she wagged a finger under the man's nose, "none of that hip grinding in my house." She laid a protective arm across Marie-Thérèse's shoulders. "Gaston, see that our hero here gets some real coffee; then I want you to get your sax," she called over her shoulder.

"Sax? Somebody here play the sax?" The smooth-edged, low-toned voice came out of another American who was almost lost in the shadows at the far corner of Glovia's salon.

Glovia guided Marie-Thérèse toward the seated man. "Sure," she called to him. "You play anything?"

Marie-Thérèse pasted a smile on her face, glad that her flush of embarrassment didn't show through her brown skin. These new Americans were a different breed from Glovia's friends, that was for sure.

"I play a little piano." The man rose from his chair to his over-six-foot height as the women approached. "I want to thank you for inviting my men here tonight." He looked down at Glovia, but not before his eyes swept over Marie-Thérèse. "And I do apologize. My men have been on the move since Normandy."

"Apology accepted." In the soft light of the room, Glovia leaned in close to the American, peering at his uniform. "Are those lieutenant bars I see there, sir?"

"The Second Armored Truck Brigade, ma'am. The Red Ball Express." The tan-skinned soldier with the hazel eyes had yet to smile. "This is our first downtime in over two months."

"Honey, I understand." Glovia bestowed one of her patented smiles on him, the kind Marie-Thérèse had seen make men gush and do all sorts of silly things. "If you can play the piano and Gaston can riff on the sax, all we need us is a trombone player." Glovia gave the man one of her trademark shimmies in her tight red dress. "Get yourself on over here." Glovia jerked her head toward the grand piano that sat by the front window. "By the way, Marie-Thérèse here is not my maid."

"Thank you, ma'am, but I'm not really *that* good at the piano," he called after Glovia's departing back as she shouted out for trombone-playing volunteers.

Marie-Thérèse felt a jolt of boldness in this mixed crowd, where she wasn't the only one without artistic credentials. "Forgive me, Monsieur Lieutenant." She tried out her English. "My ear for American is not very good. Which part of the United States do you come from?"

"I'm from California, ma'am. San Francisco." He reached for a cracker, took a bite, and grimaced. "Umm... nice." He cracked a smile.

"Monsieur Lieutenant." She returned the smile. "The politeness comes too easy to your lips." She failed at suppressing her laugh.

"This is the worst da—darn pâté I've ever eaten." His laugh was low and private. "Not that I've eaten that much. I worked my way through college as a busboy at the Palace Hotel in San Francisco—thus the pâté."

Marie-Thérèse leaned in close. "It's from a can." A wave of disloyalty swept over her. She shot glances around the room searching for Glovia. "I am sorry, Monsieur Lieutenant. All Paris has been on near-starvation rations these past four years. Madame Johnson is fortunate to have pâté at all, even from a can." She smiled again. She couldn't help it. It was an easy thing to talk to this man, even in American.

"Hey, Lieutenant!" Glovia called from across the room. "Get that good-looking behind of yours over here. I've got us a trombone player!" Glovia lowered the top on the grand piano, jumped up, and struck the pose that had made her famous: one leg crossed over the other, her skirt hiked to mid-thigh, one foot dangling a strappy, high-heeled sandal over the edge of the piano, back arched, leaning on half-bent elbows. She'd slipped the low neckline of her red dress off one shoulder and let the light of the chandelier glisten off her creamy-gold skin.

Marie-Thérèse stepped aside as the American lieutenant headed toward Glovia like a moth drawn to the flame. That had always been the way with Madame Glovia Johnson ever since she first set foot in France in the 1920s.

"Aw, now. Get ready for Miss Glovia!" Monsieur Crawford let out that gleeful sound as the roomful of people turned toward the piano.

Marie-Thérèse, still holding her tray, moved around the edges of the crowd. She stopped at the gilt-framed mirror on the wall opposite the piano. Marie-Thérèse chanced a peek into the looking glass. She was no Glovia, that was for sure, but she wasn't all that bad. Yes, she carried an inch less in height and hoisted thirty more pounds than the singer, even though Glovia had more access to food these four years. But Marie-Thérèse had more bosom than her friend, though she needed the help of a good brassiere to keep things perked up. She laid a quick hand over her apron strap and sighed. She hadn't been able to afford a new brassiere since 1939.

"*Straighten up and fly right.*" The words floated on a wave of velvet mixed with an extra-smooth male tenor. Marie-Thérèse turned to see if she could identify the new singer, only to be met by a sea of gyrating GI backs, shouting and clapping hands.

"*A buzzard took a monkey for a ride in the air.*" The voice rose and fell to the notes of a pounding piano, a blazing trombone, and Gaston's heroic efforts to keep up with an unfamiliar tune.

Marie-Thérèse slid between the GIs and Glovia's soiree group.

"*Cool down, papa, don't you blow your top.*" The unfamiliar male voice rose over the din coming from the bobbing and weaving American soldiers.

"What is this song?" Monsieur Crawford shouted to one of the soldiers just as Marie-Thérèse elbowed her way next to him.

"'Straighten Up and Fly Right'!" The entire room of GIs chorused out the words.

A corporal snatched the tray from Marie-Thérèse and pushed it toward Monsieur Crawford. "Where you *been*, man?" the American shouted as he grabbed Marie-Thérèse's hands and pushed her backwards to an open space on the carpeted floor. "That's the King Cole Trio." The corporal pulled Marie-Thérèse toward him with a quick jerk of one hand, then pushed her back, all the while wiggling his hips and stomping his feet. "What's the matter, Mama? Don't you know the boogie-woogie?"

"*Le boogie…*who?" She lapsed into French as he repeated the pull-push movement. Marie-Thérèse struggled to keep her feet moving, and out of the way of this crazy American, before he broke her toes. He spun her under his raised arm. She gasped for breath. He twirled her into a group of khaki-colored backs. Panting, Marie-Thérèse couldn't get out a decent apology as her partner plunged her into a crowd of his comrades. For an instant, the men parted just enough to give her a quick look at the piano player. Monsieur Lieutenant, a hint of gray sprinkling his temples, boomed out the words as his fingers flew over the keyboard.

"Sing it in French, I dare you." Glovia stood, shoeless, on the top of the piano, watching the GIs, mimicking their foot movement. She added her shimmy, and one soldier scooped her shoe from the floor.

"Champagne! Maid. Over here. Champagne." He held out the shoe.

"Fool." Glovia raised her dress to the tops of her gartered stockings and dropped to her knees. "It's a sandal. That thing can't hold no champagne, but I'll tell you what I will do for you." She leaned toward Monsieur Lieutenant.

The rampaging corporal jerked Marie-Thérèse into the empty space behind the milling crowd just as Monsieur Lieutenant trilled the scales on the piano. The room quieted and Marie-Thérèse was free.

"You've got to forgive us," Glovia called, easing her knees apart, the dress riding high. "We haven't heard any new music since forty. Just 'Deutschland Über Alles.' We don't know what's what back in the States." She shifted her weight to one side and let one nylon-stockinged leg hang over the piano. "Tell you what. Here is one song that did get through. Courtesy of Miss Billie Holiday."

Monsieur Lieutenant adjusted himself on the piano bench and laid out the first notes.

Marie-Thérèse closed her eyes in gratitude. She didn't recognize the song, but at least it was not a rollicking "boogie-woogie." She looked over her shoulder and edged as far away from the corporal as the crowded room would allow.

"*To leave me like this alone.*" Glovia tilted her head and picked out a soldier in the back of the room. She fixed her hazel eyes on him as though he were the only man in the world.

Marie-Thérèse recognized the move so well, she could almost read Glovia's thoughts.

"*When you could make my life worth living.*"

Marie-Thérèse wrapped her arms around her own waist. It was finally here—that wave of joy in her belly that told her that Paris was really free and her children were safe. She felt the well of tears clouding her eyes. Glovia was in her element and the world would live again.

"*By taking what I'm set on giving.*" Glovia turned that iron gaze on Monsieur Lieutenant. "*I'm all for you, body and soul.*" She slid one arm slowly along the top of the piano, her fingers pointing toward the lieutenant. She shifted both legs to the ebony top, her scrunched-up red dress revealing a hint of the black lace edging her panties. Gaston's sax filled the air.

While the GIs hooted and stamped their feet, Marie-Thérèse dropped her arms. A wave of loss she couldn't explain washed over her, and she wasn't sure why. After all, Glovia was just being Glovia.

CHAPTER 5

Alain-Hugo crouched in the ditch behind the hedgerow, the moonlight playing a child's game with the wind-whipped clouds. He checked his watch. Eleven fourteen. He lifted his head just enough to see the trio's leader, the man code-named Courageux, lash together the sticks of explosives. He dared not chance a glance in the direction of the third man, Panthère, crouching in his own ditch twenty yards south of Alain. If all went as planned this night, the signal to move on the rail line would come precisely at eleven twenty-nine—nine minutes before the Nazi train ferrying guns, men, and ammunition from the retreating armies in the north moved them southeast.

"*Wie geht es?*" The voice of the German sentry drifted up the track and startled Alain-Hugo, though he knew the soldier was right on time. Eleven sixteen.

"*Alles geht gut,*" came the expected reply from the soldier guarding the northern end of the rail line.

Alain-Hugo smiled. That was the only good thing he could say about the Germans: they were prompt. All his team had to do was borrow that one German virtue and get their explosives in place before the train approached their van-tage point at eleven thirty-eight. Eleven twenty-nine to eleven thirty-eight. Nine minutes. Seven and one-half minutes to place their charges, and ninety seconds to run as far and as fast as they could manage.

He felt the sweat pop out on his brow. He was no Courageux, a man who must have been born without nerves. Alain-Hugo scooped up a handful of dirt and rubbed it over his face, dabbing at the places where perspiration had washed away an earlier application. Did he have time? He checked his watch. Seven minutes before the train would race toward them in the silent darkness. The two sentries, one moving north, the other south, would be two hundred yards down the tracks by then, one hidden by a stand of trees, the other by a tall hedgerow. The two were not scheduled to meet again until eleven forty-six. Neither would see the three Free French tie their explosives to the railroad track. If all went as planned.

A whistle that mimicked the call of a night bird sounded.

Alain-Hugo lifted his head to stare north across the twenty yards to Courageux. The leader nodded his head and gave the thumbs-up sign. The plan was on schedule and would show the Nazis that yesterday's liberation of Paris was just a prelude to the end of the Third Reich. Alain blew a strand of dark hair out of his beard-stubbled face. With a full five minutes to go, he would have time. He quickly unlaced his left shoe, peeled back the inner sole, and pulled out the scrap of paper.

He usually saved this ritual until after the job was done. A quick look at the photograph on the other side of that bit of paper would settle his nerves. It always brought him luck. He turned the folded sheet over. There she was. Just as she'd been when he bid her a quick good-bye in Paris eighteen months ago. He raised the photograph of the beautiful, tawny-haired woman to his lips.

Whoosh. Something rustled in the hedgerow yards to his right. Alain-Hugo froze, his hand on the photo. He inched his fingers toward his Mas 35. *Whoosh* went the sound again. A small boar burst out of the hedgerow and ambled toward the railway tracks.

Alain-Hugo swallowed and slipped the picture back under the inner sole. He laced his boot. He checked the time. Two minutes to go. He felt that sudden urge to urinate that had overcome him on each of the dozens of missions he'd carried out in the south of France. He gritted his teeth, raised his head a fraction of an inch to double-check the railroad tracks and the sentries. Not a German in sight.

"Hoot!" Courageux gave the signal to move.

Alain-Hugo looked again at the watch strapped to his wrist. Eleven twenty-nine.

"Zzit. Zzit," Panthère answered his commander.

As one, the three men crawled out of their ditches. On their bellies with explosives strapped to their backs, they moved along the hedgerows toward the pebbles lining the railroad tracks. As Alain pulled himself arm over arm, the larger rocks ground into his clothing, a few pricking his skin. Three yards from the railway ties, he moved to his knees and tugged loose the leather strap fastened at his belly. He looked up the track. Courageux worked quickly, with an almost effortless grace, pulling out a string of six explosives, all linked together. Alain-Hugo slid out his own first string. He dropped to his stomach and crawled to the opposite side of the metal track. He pulled out his knife and scooped away enough of the rock and dirt to push the rope holding one end of his string under the edge of the railway tie. He secured it.

The grunt of the boar now in the hedgerow closest to Courageux beat into Alain-Hugo's ears. His hand jerked and the knife slipped. *"Uhh."* He'd gashed his left hand between thumb and forefinger.

Alain-Hugo stuffed the wounded hand into his mouth to stifle another grunt. His sleeve rode up enough to allow him a glimpse at his wristwatch. Eleven thirty-three. Four minutes to go. Still on his stomach, he scooted backwards across the track. His breaths came harder as he reached for his second line of explosives. He pulled them out, pitched his knife deep into the gravel. With blood dripping over the rope, he worked to slip the knot from the explosives line under the railway tie. He missed.

The boar burst out of the hedgerow, lumbered onto the tracks, and moved past Alain-Hugo and toward Panthère.

The urge to urinate returned. Stronger this time. Alain-Hugo plunged the knife deeper into the soil, scraping into the earth as quickly as he could. Down the tracks, the sound of the boar drifted back into his ears. There. He'd done it. The explosives were secured. He turned to his left. The moon slipped out of a cloud and bathed the men in too much light. Courageux held up two fingers, one at a time, the signal to begin the run from the train, due in ninety seconds. Then a sudden head shake as Courageux took two steps toward Alain-Hugo.

Something was amiss. Alain-Hugo looked down the tracks to Panthère. The man still fumbled with the second tie. A quick shot of fear rumbled in Alain's stomach. He scrambled to his feet just as the snorts from the boar grew louder. Afraid to call out a warning to his compatriot, Alain dropped to his knees and began crawling toward Panthère just as the moon made its way to another cloud.

Bam! The bullet from the German Luger felled the boar, which went down without a sound. "*Wildschwein! Ich habe gerade ein wildschwein getötet!*" The German's laugh told Alain-Hugo that the Resistance fighters had not yet been discovered.

Breathing hard, and cursing the German for breaking the protocol the Free French mission relied upon, Alain-Hugo dropped to his belly, reached Panthère, and dug his knife deeper into the ground. Panthère slid the rope under the tie. Alain-Hugo knotted the strands just as the tracks began to shake with the first rumble of the German troop train.

Courageux stepped off the track and moved closer to the hedgerow as he steadily crept toward his men and the oncoming sentry. Alain began to slide back from the track. He tapped Panthère on the leg to follow. Panthère started his backward crawl, dislodging several of the bigger rocks.

They rolled against the metal of the track.

Ten yards to the south, the drawn Luger flashed in the flickering moonlight. "*Helmut, iss das Sie?*" A sliver of moonlight escaping from a cloud caught the German's pale face. The look of uncertainty, unmistakable. The man's eyes scanned the tracks. His mouth opened in surprise. He raised the Luger and aimed it at Alain-Hugo. A shot rang out. Courageux? Alain-Hugo blinked. The round hole in the German's forehead oozed something dark. The German dropped to the ground.

"Courageux!" Panthère screamed out.

Alain-Hugo turned from the dead German to see the second sentry stalking up behind the commander, his rifle at the ready, his pistol still holstered. Before Courageux could complete his turn toward the man, the German slammed the rifle butt down hard on the commander's gun hand. The Resistance leader staggered, but grabbed the barrel of the rifle and aimed it toward the ground. The German unsnapped his holster with his free hand and reached for his Luger just as Alain-Hugo stormed him.

The roar of the train, now only seconds away, silenced the gurgles of the sentry as Alain-Hugo's knife plunged between the man's ribs and straight into his heart.

"The ditch!" Panthère called out as all three men sped for the hedgerows and dived into the ditch.

Alain-Hugo lay on the bottom, Courageux and Panthère piled on top as the explosion thundered into the sky. The first charge, laid by Courageux, wobbled the engine off the track. The black lead car, spewing steam, traveled another fifty yards down the pebbled roadbed when Alain-Hugo's charge exploded its nose-stinging smell underneath the troop train. Men screamed and the earth rumbled as the engine rose off the roadbed, teetered, and toppled sideways to the opposite side of the tracks. The five following cars rammed into one another. Chunks of metal flew in all directions. Sound left Alain-Hugo's ears. He couldn't feel his legs. Tingling moved in and out of the place where his arms were supposed to be. He saw his compatriots scramble out of the ditch and run. His arms pumping, Alain followed, his legs bursting back into painful life. As he huffed his way to safety, he checked his wounded hand. The wristwatch read eleven thirty-eight.

The woman finished wrapping the bandage around Alain-Hugo's injured hand. She took the gun from Courageux and reached for the knife from Alain-Hugo.

"These will be returned to the stockpile, *monsieurs*." She nodded. "Without weapons, the Wehrmacht cannot accuse you three of killing their sentries or blowing up their train."

"I will keep the knife," Alain-Hugo announced, doubting that he'd ever find another with such a fine blade as this—his father's favorite boning knife. A blade tempered of the finest steel.

The woman nodded.

Too tired to do more than nod his appreciation, Alain-Hugo loosened his boot. He slipped out the photo, turned it over, and kissed the woman's likeness. "Genvieve. *Mon amour. Ma femme.*" With care, he slipped the photograph of his wife back into his boot.

CHAPTER 6

Marie-Thérèse stopped on the second-floor landing to retrieve the key from her purse. She glanced up at the last flight of stairs. The morning light forced its way through the little window in the third-floor garret, painting square, oblong, and rectangular patterns on the worn carpeting. As she stepped on the stair tread announcing the thirteen steps to her apartment, she squeezed the key. While two American soldiers had volunteered to escort her home last night, and Glovia assured her the city streets were now safe, Marie-Thérèse wasn't at all convinced that the German curfew had been lifted. When Glovia offered her chaise longue, Marie-Thérèse happily accepted. Besides, the soiree had been great fun. Except for the dancing. She turned the key in the lock.

"Maman!" Christophe's face flooded with a mixture of relief and annoyance. "Where have you been? I thought the Wehrmacht had hauled you off as a Resistance spy!" Relief won out as her boy stared at her from his perch on the arm of her living room settee.

"I don't need to tell you this." She switched to her comfortable patois as she hid her amusement from her son. "You tell me where you go every time you leave this house?" She turned her back to him as she fought down her smile. Let her children worry about her for once.

"But you were out all night." Christophe blended accusation with question.

"Maybe it is what you say." Marie-Thérèse went to the kitchen and noticed the boiling pot of chicory. She turned to her son. "But what of you? I think you out all night with feet jumping and fingers snapping. You think about me worrying, I ask you?"

Her son stood and followed her the short distance to the kitchen archway. "Maman. You know where I was. The Champs-Élysées. Paris is free! It was fantastic. I met the most amazing wo—" His look of glee turned into a frown. "Oh, no. This is not about me. This is *you*." The frown deepened. "Anything could have happened to you!"

Marie-Thérèse poured herself a mug of the four-day-old, warmed-over coffee. "I pray to the good Lord that your Americans bring real coffee with them." She sent a sly glance toward Christophe.

"Where were you all night?" he blurted.

"I'm here now. Safe and sound." She took a sip from the mug. "Who did you meet?"

Christophe faltered. "Americans, Maman. Dozens of them."

"They put that look on your face?" She lowered the cup and looked over the rim at her firstborn. "I think, maybe, Martine help you in your celebration." She grinned.

Her son dipped his head, and Marie-Thérèse startled. That move had alerted her to a Christophe version of the truth ever since he was a toddler. What was he up to now? She gave her boy a close look as she moved past him and into her living room.

"There were enormous amounts of people on the boulevard." His eyes brightened as he followed. "It really was amazing. Maman, I saw General LeClerc!"

"May the Lord's blessings fall full upon your head for the good fortune you find." Like always, she gave him a few seconds to let him come up with the real story. "Our Collette still sleeps?" Marie-Thérèse looked down the hall toward the second bedroom. The door her daughter always kept closed when she was home stood wide open.

"Everybody celebrated last night. Collette, too. Maman, I saw the *Tirailleurs Sénégalais*." He'd done it again.

Marie-Thérèse moved toward the hall.

"Collette stepped out for a minute or two," Christophe cried out in that way that confirmed his guilt.

"At this hour? Seven o'clock, you tell me your sister step out?" Marie-Thérèse stood halfway between her son and the bedroom she was sure was empty. "Just where is *ma fille*?"

"You worry too much, Maman. She's just fine." Christophe hurried to the kitchen, his eyes nowhere near her own. "I think she's with Martine."

"You *think*?" Marie-Thérèse stopped and faced her son, who conveniently kept his back to her in the kitchen. "Why aren't you with Martine?" That worried feeling crept into her stomach. "Christophe Deveraux Brillard, don't let the words come out of your mouth that your sister is with that man!"

"Maman." He tried his she's-too-old-to-understand voice on her this time as he poured a cup of coffee, his eyes down.

"Christophe, you go bring your sister home this minute." Marie marched into her daughter's bedroom. Her eyes confirmed what she suspected. "How many times I have to tell that girl?" she called out to the empty room.

"Collette is a woman now. Old enough to make her own choices."

"What fool nonsense you talk to me? She better not yet be a woman. I will give a good girl to the man my daughter marries." She turned back to the main room. "And that man will not be a *French* man."

"Here we go again," Christophe muttered.

"I hear your mouth."

He turned to face her, his hands cupped around the mug. "It's the same old story. French men are no good. French women are no good. They can't really love you because you're from Africa. You're—"

"I hear enough of that mouth on you, Christophe." She marched up the hallway. "Why you think I tell you these things? You think I talk just to be talking? No. I tell you these things because they are the truth."

Christophe moved into the living room. "Maman, just because my father was a bast—no good...Look at *grand-père*. He was a Frenchman. A white Frenchman." He jabbed a finger toward the photograph.

Marie-Thérèse felt a quick jolt of surprise. "Clement-Edouard Brillard was French, yes. But he was a Frenchman of Martinique. He—"

"That's worse." Christophe drowned the words in his mug of coffee. "A colonial. He didn't even marry your mother. We can call ourselves Brillard all we want, but under the law, that was never our name."

The slap she laid across his cheek brought fright to Marie-Thérèse faster than the surprised look spread across her son's face. "Don't say such words about your *grand-père*." She clenched and unclenched her fingers. "He was a man above all men. He needed no law to tell him to do right by his daughter." She felt the tears flood her eyes as she reached for the picture of dear Papa.

"Sorry, Maman." Christophe patted his cheek where not even a hint of redness showed. "I appreciate *grand-père*, though I barely remember him. I know that you brought us all to Paris because you inherited a little bit of money from him. That's just it, Maman. He was a white Frenchman, and you loved him."

She clutched the stiffly posed photograph of her father, dressed in all his colonial finery, to her chest. "Papa was nothing like the Frenchmen here." She turned back to Christophe. "And I will not allow Collette to have an affair with one."

"Jean-Michel is a good man. He helped the Resistance."

"And what does that tell me? Everybody fought the German the best way we can." Marie-Thérèse turned to the window. "That boy who lives on the rue de…you know the one…I forget the name…Gerard…"

"Gerard? On the rue Clichy. Maman, you know perfectly well that's Martine's cousin."

"Ah, is he that one? Well, he is a nice boy." She turned back to Christophe. "Your Martine is a sweet girl. Why don't you have her bring her cousin over here the next time she come?" Marie-Thérèse let a hopeful note sound in her voice.

"Maman. Stop playing matchmaker. Collette will make up her own mind." Christophe laid the cup on the kitchen table.

"How can the girl make up what is empty? All the time with that Frenchman." Marie-Thérèse watched as Christophe walked toward the door. "How can your sister choose the right man when she has only one in her mind? Collette needs more than one man. You tell Martine about the cousin. You'll see. I tell you nothing but the truth."

"*Mais oui,* Maman." Christophe walked out the door.

CHAPTER 7

Christophe stepped off the Metro Blanche at the Arc de Triomphe stop and climbed the steps to the street. Now he only had to determine where, in that crowd, he had stood yesterday. He recalled walking to his right past the fancy *boucherie* with its sides of beef that no ordinary Frenchman could afford. But did he travel two blocks or three when each step had felt like pushing along an elephant?

To recreate the day, he let his mind play the reason he'd taken the Blanche line this morning, though it was seven blocks out of his way. Martine. And that was Maman's fault.

"*Bonjour, monsieur,*" chorused a trio of men about his age coming toward him down the Champs-Élysées. "Isn't this day *magnifique?*"

"*Vive la France!*" Christophe joined in the laughter. Of course, it was a magnificent day, and not only because the sun spread its early afternoon light over the boulevard on this first full day of liberation. His mind rummaged back to his mother. Why did Maman choose today to fret about Martine? He would see his girlfriend tomorrow, or maybe the day after, but not to talk about her big-eared cousin. Was the blame his that he ran straight to the Champs-Élysées when he heard the news of freedom? There had been no time to search out his secondary school sweetheart. Besides, the idea of Martine and him as young lovers appealed more to Maman than to either of them. At least these days.

As he pondered the distance, a quartet of young people marched along the boulevard, nodding their jubilation at him. A man of middle years, hand in hand with a woman who must have been his wife, smiled his excitement as they passed, moving in the opposite direction. Christophe strode along, searching for anything familiar to jostle his memory of yesterday. Perspiration sprinkled his forehead in the heat. He quickened his pace, peering at the signs announcing the names of small shops and big stores. Was that the wavering, brown-faced image of Martine reflecting back at him from one plate-glass storefront? He bit his lip. He wasn't really being disloyal to Martine. Though she hadn't said, he was sure she was just as ready to meet new friends as he. Only Maman clung to the notion of them as a couple.

"La Maison de la Soupe," he muttered aloud, dismissing the image of Martine and Marie-Thérèse. The tangy smell of Gruyère cheese atop thick country bread and bubbling onion soup floated through the open front door. He spotted another sign. Le Pharmacie de Peter. He stepped across the street, and out of habit glanced up at the Arc de Triomphe. Something in the way the shadow fell across the pavement jammed his mind back to the throngs of yesterday. As he set foot on the patterned sidewalk, he turned toward the side street at his left. Three doors down the rue de l'Etoile, he saw it. Le Bistro Cloche. His chest swelled on a quick intake of breath as he raced toward the building.

"Is anybody in there?" Christophe banged on the door and peered over the white lace curtain half covering the front window. Then he found the handwritten note tacked to the front door. *Cet établissement ouvrira à cinq heures. Nous sommes à la célébration.*

"Gone to celebrate?" He spoke aloud. *Mon Dieu!* A shot of resentment rammed through his belly.

"Hey, man." An American corporal walked up beside Christophe. "When does this joint open? What you doin' out of uniform anyway?"

"Sorry, *monsieur*, I am not American." Christophe tried out the English Maman insisted he perfect.

"Sorry, buddy. Took you for one of us." The brown-skinned man smiled at him. "You speak much English? When does this place open?"

"Five o'clock." Christophe sounded more disappointed than he meant. "It is but two." He remembered his manners. "Corporal, let me buy you a drink."

"Now that's what I like to hear. The drink part, I mean. But let me be the one to buy you a drink. I didn't know they *had* any colored Frenchies." The American clapped an arm around Christophe's shoulder as he pulled him away from the closed door of the Bistro Cloche. "Let's go find us a joint that's open."

Christophe looked back at the receding awning as the American shepherded him along the rue de l'Etoile.

"Hey, how about here?" The American stopped in front of a café bustling with patrons and wafting out saucy scents of roasting chicken sprinkled with sage and tarragon.

Christophe glanced at the five or six white-clothed tables scattered in front of the little eatery, all occupied except one. He nodded his yes to the American as he took one last look in the direction of the Bistro Cloche. The corporal steered the pair to the empty table at the farthest edge of the allotted sidewalk space. The table was the only one that caught the full glare of the sun. Nearby, French and American voices chattered at one another. Christophe sat down, still keeping an eye toward the passersby moving to and from the direction of the bistro.

"*Bonjour, monsieurs.* Le Poulet Farsi welcomes you." The woman's voice brought Christophe's head up abruptly. "May we offer you a sip of Burgundy to help you celebrate?" He watched the waitress lean down to whisper into the ear of the American, strands of tawny hair flicking the man's cheek. "Our champagne is almost gone from last night, but I believe, for you, Monsieur Corporal, I can find..." Her amber eyes drifted to Christophe.

Her face flushed. She stood. Her hands fluttered over her apron.

"*Mademoiselle?*" Christophe stared. "Genvieve? Have I found you?" He felt the somersaults flipping around his stomach.

"I...uh...*monsieur*," she stammered.

"You two know each other?" the American interrupted. "Well, sugar girl," the man took a long, languorous look at the Frenchwoman, "if that's the case, I'll take that champagne you were about to find for me. Bring a glass for yourself, too." He squeezed her arm and aimed a wink at Christophe. "Sorry, man. Don't mean to mess with your woman."

The waitress scurried away. She bumped into a waiter carrying a tray of empty wineglasses and two bottles of red wine.

"That woman..." Christophe shouted to the waiter, who deftly righted his tray without losing a drop. "What is her name?" He jumped to his feet.

"That one?" The waiter began dispensing empty glasses and two bottles of red wine to the adjacent table. "That's Genvieve Papilion."

"When is she off duty?" Christophe demanded.

"Ask her yourself." The waiter moved two tables down.

"Look here, buddy." The American stood, reached for his wallet, and peeled off two American ten-dollar bills. "I ain't about to rain on your parade. Take this from one colored man to the next. Buy your girl some nylon stockings." He winked and walked away from the eatery.

Christophe moved toward the front door of the Poulet, but not before the woman appeared in the doorway carrying a bottle of champagne and two glasses. She looked startled when Christophe closed the distance between the two. "Genvieve, where's the third glass?" He waved an arm in the direction of the departing corporal. "The American wanted you to join us...him to celebrate." He watched her face turn pale, then flush and go pale again.

"I'm on duty," she whispered as she looked over her shoulder into the café's crowded interior.

"He's paid for your services." Christophe felt the blush sting his face. "No, I mean, he's paid for you to join us... me...him."

"I cannot do that, *monsieur.*" She sucked in her lips as she looked around.

"When are you off duty? And it's Christophe. Remember?"

"In an hour, but, *monsieur...*I..." She handed the bottle of champagne to him.

"I will sit here with this," he lifted the bottle, "unopened until you can join me."

"*Monsieur.*" The woman looked agitated. "It is not possible."

"Genvieve!" A man's voice crackled through the air. Its aproned owner appeared behind her. "Don't just stand there blocking the doorway, girl. Serve the customers." He gave her a little shove. She brushed Christophe's shoulder.

"*Monsieur,*" she whispered, "you must leave."

"Leave? I'm a paying customer." Christophe walked back to his table just as a couple in their sixties took two of the three empty seats. "Genvieve Papilion. For you, I shall wait."

More people swarmed past the Le Poulet Farsi, casting hopeful glances in the direction of one of the now fully occupied tables. Christophe checked his watch. Three o'clock. He watched Genvieve limp her way between tables. She showed no sign of removing her serving apron now that her shift was up.

"*Garçon.*" Christophe spoke as the waiter passed the table.

"Is *monsieur* ready for the bill now?" The server glanced over at the crowd of pedestrians who had stopped to read the day's menu on the signboard.

"*Monsieur* is waiting for Mademoiselle Papilion to get off duty." Christophe put out his annoyed voice.

"*Mademo...*Genvieve?" The waiter pulled out his watch. "Maybe she works double duty." He turned to Christophe. "This is a time to celebrate, you know."

The man's sarcasm was not lost on Christophe. "*Garçon,* if it would not trouble you too much, point out the owner of this establishment, if you please."

"I will alert Genvieve that you are ready." The waiter walked as slow as a snail toward Genvieve, who headed inside the café.

Christophe lost sight of the pair. Afraid to relinquish his seat, he smiled at the couple occupying the other two chairs.

"*Monsieur.*" Genvieve, still wearing her apron, approached. "I told you not to wait for me." She waved an arm toward the six tables. "Today, we are quite busy."

"I can see that, Genvieve, but I will speak to the owner. Surely he can spare you for two or three hours. I promise to have you back by the dinner hour." He grinned up at her.

He had not been wrong. Yesterday's champagne had not dulled his first impression of this woman's good looks. Her skin was creamy white with just a hint of rose petal blushing her cheeks. Her figure was slender, and best of all, accented with a bountiful bosom and rounded hips.

"Oh, no, *monsieur.*" She looked toward a beefy-looking man wearing both a beret and an apron. "Please do not trouble yourself." She reached to her apron tie. "I will join you shortly." Her eyes darted toward the big, apron-wearing man who served another table some ten yards distant. "My...my boss," she whispered.

"Think of the most wild and wonderful thing you ever wanted to do in Paris." Christophe smiled at her as they turned the corner of the rue de l'Etoile onto the Champs-Élysées, the sun warming his back. It delighted him that Genvieve was as tall as he remembered. "Let's have our own special celebration."

"*Monsieur*, I would like nothing better than to celebrate." She shifted her eyes from the pavement on the grand boulevard to his face and back again. "It has been so difficult... the sacrifices...so long since...forgive me, *monsieur*, these have been difficult times for us all." She frowned as she looked down at her low-heeled shoes strapped at the ankle. "I long to feel free and to be able to breathe again."

"We all long to feel free. After four years of hell, I think maybe we've forgotten how." Christophe wanted to wipe that note of sadness from her voice. "Your ankle? I see no limp." He turned, grabbed her around the waist, and swept her into the air.

"Ooh!" Her face moved from worry to surprise to pleasure with the magic of a kaleidoscope. Still held aloft, she wiggled her right foot. "As good as ever. I'm a quick healer. I want all the problems of this world to go away as quickly as the pain in my ankle." Her hands gripped his shoulders more tightly.

"So what is it to be?" He searched those eyes staring down at him for anything that might make them sparkle. "Pick the one thing you always wanted to do in the city but never did." He lowered her to the ground, his hands lingering on her waist for an instant.

She wrapped her arms around her chest, a faint smile fighting its way onto her lips. "You won't believe it."

"Try me."

"Le Tour d'Eiffel. I want to climb the Eiffel Tower." She laid a hand against her lips as she leaned in close. "I've never been to Le Tour d'Eiffel in all my life."

"What? Never?" Christophe feigned disbelief. Anything to make this woman smile. "And you call yourself a *Parisienne?*"

"All right, Mr. Christophe." The smile flickered wider. "How many times have *you* climbed the Eiffel Tower?" Her voice trilled the sweetest part of the musical scale as they headed toward the train.

"Hundreds. Dozens. Maybe ten…perhaps." Christophe guided her down the steps to the Metro, his attention so full on her his heel caught on the bottom step. "All right, then. I confess. Three times." On the train platform, he spun around to help her navigate the last stair. "But, still, I am ahead of you."

"Are you telling me, Mr. Tourist, that you've seen all the best spots in Paris while I've seen nothing but the inside of a drudge bucket all my life?" The lightness creeping into her voice turned into a full laugh as the two raced to board the Metro headed for the Eiffel Tower.

"Well, I…" he sputtered as they squeezed inside the train.

"Yes, Mr. I've-done-it-all, tell me that you visit the Louvre every Thursday…the one day when there is no discount for locals." The rhythm of her voice matched the swish of the Metro rumbling its way down the track. "As for the Seine, you must sail in the Bateaux Mouches four times a week." She bit on her lower lip, making the dimples in her blush-pink cheeks all the more adorable.

"Well, if the truth be known"—Christophe hung on as the Metro lurched to a stop—"I've never actually floated down the Seine." He put on his best sheepish grin.

"*Monsieur*," Genvieve gasped, "you speak blasphemy." She chucked him under the chin as they disembarked and headed toward the base of the tower. "And you call yourself a Parisian?" She flicked her tawny hair.

"I dare you to climb to the second landing," Christophe yelled as he held up the American ten-dollar bill, calculating how many French francs went into the conversion.

"How many steps is that?" she challenged.

"Maybe twelve hundred. Could be fourteen." He tilted his head as he spotted only one person ahead of him at the ticket window. "But don't fret. Then there is the elevator to the very top."

"And if I make it to the second platform—and I shall—what will you give me, Monsieur Christophe?" She twirled around on the pavement like dancers in the old days at the Moulin Rouge.

"Ah, but that is not the question, my girl." He completed the ticket purchase. "What will you give me when I leave you one hundred paces down and have to come back to carry you like a sack of rutabagas to the second platform?" He stuffed a handful of French francs into his pockets.

"Let's both be surprised when we get there." She raced toward the first elevator, her hair bouncing against her shoulders.

The look and sound of her warmed him faster than the sun.

"It will be no contest, of course. And when you pay up, you will owe me at least a gallon of Joy perfume. For starters." Her full-throated laugh carried the melody of a jaunty folk song he'd learned in primary school.

"Only a few more to go." Christophe looked six steps below him, his heart fluttering with more than the exertion of climbing Gustav's tower.

"You sound winded." Genvieve's voice called up. "I've yet to hit my stride." She bounded to the stair just below his.

"We can stop on this landing if you like?"

"Not on your life." She sped past him.

Christophe looked toward the top of the tower, the iron grid-work crisscrossing his view, and blew out a deep breath. Had that been the scent of lemon verbena he sniffed as her hair brushed his cheek? His eyes moved back to Genvieve, the hem of her skirt swaying against the back of her knees as she pushed ahead. He brushed past her as he pumped his legs up the next ten stairs.

"Another bet," she called out, a hint of breathlessness shading her words.

"Oh no. You see your perfume slipping away, and now you want to renegotiate?"

"It's obvious I'm getting to the second level." Her breathing came harder. "But this bet should not be about who can make the climb to the platform, but about the one who gets there first." Her laughter carried on short bursts of air.

Christophe arched his back and strained to catch a glimpse of his goal. He calculated another thirty steps. "When I get to the platform first, then you'll do my bidding?" He grinned as he crossed off another five stairs. He chanced a look down. A dizzying array of steel swept at his equilibrium. His stomach hinted protest. Christophe laid a hand on the stair rail and kept climbing.

"Ah, Monsieur Christophe. I will be...first." Now her breath came in quick spurts, but she was only six steps behind him. "And then we will see...who does whose bidding...this day. When the choice is mine to make...then I will decree that we...both march right back down again... without even a look around."

"We'll see about that." Christophe counted only ten more stairs to the second-level platform and the elevator that would take them to the top. He urged his legs to cooperate, but they signaled unwillingness. Genvieve was almost close enough to touch his back. An image of the woman's strong legs moving underneath that knee-length skirt steamed into his mind. He reached for the rail to steady his gait.

"Hmm." The sound of her breathing carried up to him.

Christophe chanced another glance over his shoulder. Genvieve, her head down like a charging lioness, poked her tongue to the side of her mouth. Her legs, free of stockings, churned a steady rhythm. She pushed herself within four paces of him. Oh no. This was one race he had no intention of losing. Christophe took two steps at once, the gray of the platform three treads ahead.

"Ooh." Her cry made him stumble at the stair edge.

"What?" He whirled around.

Genvieve slumped against the rail at her back and, with her right foot lifted in the air, pointed to her leg. "My ankle is not as good as I thought." She turned a plaintive face up to him.

"Are you all right?" Christophe shouted as he headed back down the stairs, stopping one tread above her. He reached out an arm.

Her eyes twinkled as she righted herself. "Not as bad as you think." She cocked her head as she quickly bounced to the stair tread where he stood, flashed him a smile, and pushed her body against his in a struggle to squeeze past.

"Oh no you don't!" Christophe smelled the verbena as he wrapped his arms around her shoulders and twisted her to his right. He wriggled free and raced the six steps to the platform. "I win!" he shouted as he raised his arms skyward.

"Monsieur Christophe," she panted as she leaned against the rail holding her side. "I would say...you cheated and caused me...me to stumble." She gulped in air as she walked to the platform. "I would say it...but you did not." The faux-serious face she turned to him dissolved into more peals of laughter. "Must I say good-bye to my gallon of Joy so soon?"

"Say good-bye to your gallon of perfume, your liter...not even an ounce remains."

She dashed away her disappointed face as he led her onto the elevator.

"Close your eyes," he ordered. "It's best to allow the view to surround you all at once." Christophe entwined his fingers into her hair and tipped her face against his shoulder.

"Ohh," Genvieve reacted as they moved upward. "I don't believe my tummy is enjoying this ride all that much."

The elevator at last glided to a stop. A gust of wind whipped around them as they alighted. He watched her shoulders shake in the ten-degree-cooler weather. She kept her eyes shut.

"I insist upon some consolation, *monsieur*, after a climb... and a ride like that."

"If you're sure you want to insist, then here is your first consolation." He slid a hand over her eyes and led her to the southern corner of the top platform.

The wind swirled against their faces. Christophe closed his arm around a waist that felt taut. He uncovered her eyes but held her tight. "Look. There." He nodded downward. "Les Invalides. The Pantheon. Paris at your feet."

"*Mon Dieu.*" She blinked and brushed a strand of hair from her face. She stared down at the postcard scene. "Oh, Christophe, it is..." She looked up at him, her eyes shining. "I don't have the words."

Another blast of wind racked the platform, and she shivered her body into his. She laid an arm around his waist.

"This is your first time to the Tour d'Eiffel, so you wouldn't know the custom." He grasped at strands of her hair blowing in the wind. "First-time visitors to the Tower must make their way to all four corners...and make love to Paris at each."

She looked up at him, her face balancing doubt against merriment. "And how long has this been the custom?" Her eyes danced.

"For many...many long..."—he pressed his cheek against hers—"...long..."—he let his lips find and linger over her cheek—"...minutes."

"Surely not minutes, sir. Perhaps seconds? All of them in your mind?" She laughed.

"But, *mademoiselle*, we are just beginning."

The laughter flickered for an instant.

"Take heart, Genvieve, there is much, much more." He moved to the southwest. "There, way below, is Swan Alley."

"It looks like a creek in Burgundy."

"To Burgundy and its Seine River, we must celebrate." He kissed her on both cheeks and swept his tongue over her mouth. She parted her lips in response.

"Dare I say that Burgundy is delicious." Her breath smelled of minted orange as she kept her eyes on the sight below.

He guided her along the platform, their bodies fighting a quick gust. "And now, the Sacré-Coeur." He swallowed. "Montmartre."

"My favorite place in all Paris." This time she reached a hand around his neck.

Christophe wrapped his arm around her shoulders and pulled her toward him. He stroked his hand up and down her back, lingering seconds over her bra hook. He slid his tongue from her cheek to mouth. But when he tilted her chin to kiss her full on the lips, she turned her head slightly away.

"Christophe." Her voice was lost in the swirl of a brisk breeze.

"More," he pleaded in her ear.

She pushed away. Her eyes seemed to stare into space. A rush of concern splashed over him. He grabbed her hand and led her toward the north pillar.

"It was just yesterday, Genvieve. Where we met. The Champs-Élysées. The..."

"Christophe. Do you think I could forget yesterday... and you so quickly?"

His mind emptied of everything except this mystifying woman. Before he could reclaim his brain, she reached her arms around his neck and pulled him to her. His heart quickened when she ran her tongue over his upper lip.

"Mmm." The sound of her tinkled through his ears.

She kissed his lower lip, and a shiver he couldn't control racked his body when she sucked his lip into her mouth. Her tongue captured his, and the swelling between his legs became unstoppable.

Far below, from the Sacré-Coeur, the thin sound of a pealing bell caught in his ears on a wisp of wind.

CHAPTER 8

The worm hole in the peach was the least of Marie-Thérèse's worries. She looked around at the sparse bins in the greengrocer's little stand off the rue de la Bonne. She poked a gentle finger around the hole and gave the fruit a little squeeze. As least no worm emerged. She supposed she should be grateful. Marie-Thérèse put the peach to her nose test and inhaled its sugary ripeness. She nodded her satisfaction.

"Madame Brillard," Martine's voice called out as the neighborhood girl stepped through the door, the morning sun at her back. "*Bonjour*. It is good to see you." The girl, with her white bobby sox in stark contrast to her cocoa-brown legs, didn't sound as though she meant it.

"I should *bonjour* you, *mon bonbon*. How long since you come to my house?" Marie-Thérèse almost swept into her Martinique patois around this girl who was sure to become her daughter-in-law. But each time she came close to disclosing her roots, one look at Martine's mop of springy hair jolted Marie-Thérèse's memory. This girl was the daughter of mixed-blood immigrant parents from Senegal. Both father and mother were the mulatto offspring of French fathers and Senegalese mothers. Martine's French, like her own when she cared to trot it out, could be impeccable.

"A while, *madame*." Martine busied herself with a scrawny head of lettuce.

"Is that shyness I see in you?" Marie-Thérèse teased. "I've always liked that about you, but do have my Christophe bring you around soon. You and your cousin. You know the one. Gerard."

"Christophe? You think I've seen him?" Martine blurted. "Your son has been hiding from me since before the day of liberation."

"The day of liberation? *Mon Dieu*, girl. That's been over a week. September has come. You two must have misconnected." Marie-Thérèse shook her head. "With him still working the night shift at the bakery, and you the day at the dress factory, I always marvel that you two ever find time for one another."

"Christophe always used to find time for me." Martine stared at her hands. "Has there been…is he seeing…?" Her nervous fingers plucked off one of the lettuce leaves.

"Seeing what? Seeing who?" Marie-Thérèse frowned. "You are a silly girl if you mean another woman." She clapped a hand over Martine's forearm. "You have no worries about Christophe. He is mad for you. Now, my Collette, on the other hand, that girl will…"

Martine poked her lower teeth over her upper lip in that way Marie-Thérèse wished she wouldn't. It wasn't that Martine was plain. She certainly was not. She just wasn't especially pretty. She had the pouty mouth of her African grandmothers, and that was good. But she had a face a shade too long like her Frenchmen grandfathers, and on her, that was unfortunate.

"Madame Brillard." The fresh voice broke her reverie before either she or Martine could speak. "I have been searching for you. Madame Glovia doesn't have your address."

"Gaston?" Marie-Thérèse managed. "Madame Johnson, uh, Glovia...is looking for me?"

"For several days now," Glovia's manservant answered. "She would like to invite you to her house. Tonight. Another soiree."

"Umm." Marie-Thérèse stumbled as she glanced at Martine. "Another soiree? I am happy to serve at Ma— Glovia's parties, but I had supposed to spend a bit of time with my son and his paramour." She smiled at Martine. "Perhaps if I come early to set up, then I can return home for an hour or so." She laid a hand on Gaston's arm. "Please tell Glovia that I'll be back in time for the cleanup. I believe the streets are finally safe at night."

Gaston turned an appraising eye toward Martine. "No, Madame Brillard, you do not understand. Madame Glovia does not want you to serve the party, she wants you there as her guest."

"Her guest?" Marie-Thérèse slapped her palm to her bosom. "Me? I'm not certain, but I'll be happy to serve."

"Madame Glovia insists that you come as a guest. But do come early. She expects you at seven o'clock sharp." Gaston bobbed his head to her, but ignored Martine. "She expects you to remain throughout the evening." He turned and walked away.

"I'm sorry to trouble you, Madame Brillard." Martine showed those irregular teeth again. "It's just that if you happen to see Christophe..."

"Nonsense, girl. I insist that you come to my house this Saturday. With your cousin, Gerard." She headed toward the door, her bag of peaches in hand.

"He's been asking after you." Glovia sat on her white boudoir chair, the one Marie-Thérèse admired because of the elaborate gold leaf scrolling over the legs. Glovia peered into the attached three-way mirror on her perfume-covered dressing table as Marie-Thérèse wielded the straightening iron.

"Of course he is asking of me. I served him your pâté." She ran the warm comb through Glovia's hair, wondering again why the wavy-haired woman wanted to press each strand as flat as a crêpe. "I doubt very much that Monsieur Lieutenant cares enough to ask about anything I might do."

"I wouldn't be so sure." Glovia cocked her head. "My pâté isn't all that good." She turned a mischievous smile on Marie-Thérèse, her hand bending one ear out of the way of the straightening comb. "Remember, that Kraut gave me those tins."

Marie-Thérèse waved the comb in the air to cool before she slid the iron back inside its metal box. She blew out the blue-tinged flame in the bottom of the housing and flicked her wrist to clear the smoke. Glovia stared in the mirror as she pouffed her hair into a pompadour now that the back was stick straight.

The singer more than held her own at these soirees, and not just because of that jazz-filled voice of hers. Glovia had a wit about her, and she sometimes trotted it out for a spin. Like tonight, and the teasing about the American army officer. What man was going to pay attention to Marie-Thérèse with Glovia around? Even back in the thirties, when Glovia's house swarmed with American *noir* literati and artists, every male who stepped into her salon turned his full attention to the hostess. Marie-Thérèse could have paraded as naked as one of Mr. Crawford's nude models across the salon floor, and Glovia, wrapped in a flannel nightgown, topped with a granny shawl, and her hair in a mobcap, would still have captured every eye.

"I think that'll do it." Glovia's voice brought Marie-Thérèse back to the boudoir.

Marie-Thérèse reached for the snood. Glovia shook her head as she rose from the pink-cushioned chair.

"Not tonight." Glovia reached into her armoire and retrieved a silver dress with a halter top. "I'm going to shimmer and shine this night." She flipped her fingers through her hair and stepped into the gown. "Here. Zip me up."

Marie-Thérèse tugged at the tight zipper and slid it slowly up Glovia's back, the folds of the dress stretching snug over the woman's considerable curves.

"Now get yourself on out there and act like a guest." Glovia picked up a powder puff and dusted it over her nose.

Marie-Thérèse, in her six-year-old Sunday best, walked into the salon, not surprised to see several guests already there. Three or four often came early to Glovia's parties, though they knew full well the hostess loved making a late entrance. Marie-Thérèse scanned the room. Monsieur Crawford had hauled in one of his bronzes—this one about two feet tall and of a zoot-suited American black man playing a saxophone.

Zaidie Mabry walked up to Marie-Thérèse, a sheaf of papers in her hand. "I'm reading tonight. Say, I've seen you here before. A time or two." Her eyes squinted. "What was your name again? Can't remember what you do."

Marie-Thérèse bobbed her head out of respect for the American even if Madame Mabry, with her marceled hair and deep brown skin, had never shone quite as bright as the other *émigrés* at Glovia's affairs. Before she could struggle out an answer for the woman, Gaston led three new arrivals into the salon. All American soldiers. One of them was Monsieur Lieutenant.

"Gaston, have you gotten everybody a drink?" Glovia, on time for once, swept into the room.

Marie-Thérèse chanced a glance at the American officer as he sucked in a breath. The man's eyes traveled down one side of Glovia, stopped to linger at a spot just below her hip, and drifted up the other. The singer's silver dress sported a short train and a slit that moved up one leg almost hip-high, flashing one garter-belt-secured nylon stocking. Marie-Thérèse glanced away. She could almost feel the heat steaming off Monsieur Lieutenant.

"Tonight, I've got champagne from Dom Pérignon. Rémy Martin cognac. Courvoisier. Good wine from Bordeaux. Name your poison." Glovia's eyes landed straight on Monsieur Lieutenant.

Zaidie Mabry sidled her way toward the soldiers. "I'm taking myself one of these good-looking men tonight." She zeroed in on Monsieur Lieutenant. "This one here. He's my poison."

Glovia and Zaidie Mabry, both with eyes on the army officer? The winner was obvious. For some silly reason, a wave of sadness swirled in Marie-Thérèse's chest. No woman could compete with Glovia Johnson over a man, not even another American.

Marie-Thérèse searched the far corners of the room where the tall and lanky poet, Jimmie Lee Hudson, usually sat—as antisocial as ever. While she might have to endure hours of the artist's doom and gloom, at least a seat beside the difficult-to-approach man would keep her away from all the sparkling banter coming from the Americans. With Jimmie Lee, there was no worry. Nobody expected the laconic man to make small talk. When the time came, and only Jimmie Lee knew when that time was, the poet would stand and begin his recitation about lynchings, rapes, burning crosses, and other cheerful subjects. The man had even interrupted Glovia in the middle of one of her songs. He was the one person to whom the hostess always relinquished the floor.

"*Bonsoir*, Monsieur Hudson." Marie-Thérèse scooted her chair closer to the potted palm in the back corner of the room. She moved as far away from the morose Jimmie Lee as she could manage while still keeping him as her safety net.

Jimmie Lee turned one of his angry stares in her direction. She took no offense. She'd figured out long ago that the deep lines between his eyes always made Jimmie look angry, even when what passed for happy played out around him. As usual, he didn't acknowledge her. But he never acknowledged anybody. Not even Glovia.

Zaidie sauntered over. "Jimmie Lee, take a look at my new manuscript." She held out the pages to him. "Maybe I can get it published now that I don't have to get approval from the Wehrmacht."

Jimmie Lee turned his face to the potted palm.

Zaidie frowned. "Guess he's not receiving just yet." She brightened as Gaston approached with a cognac. "*That* man knows what I like."

Marie-Thérèse's tongue searched for her teeth as Madame Mabry laid a scarlet-lipped grin on Gaston that looked just a shade short of a drool. Marie-Thérèse leveled her gaze at the American and snapped, "Know what you like? I thought you say that was the American Lieutenant, not Gaston." *Mon Dieu!* Marie-Thérèse's gasp rattled in her ears. What had made her say such a thing to one of them— the exalted Americans? Why hadn't she bitten down harder on her tongue? "Madame Mabry...I..." Marie-Thérèse turned to Gaston, hoping Zaidie wouldn't see her flustered face and lash into her. "A champagne, please?" She lowered her voice. "But make it just half a glass."

Madame Mabry shrugged her shoulders and sauntered off. She hadn't even given Marie-Thérèse that "now who is *this*" look.

"I know *madame*'s drinking habits," Gaston responded. "No more than four swallows for you." He winked as he handed her the glass with the least amount of liquid.

"Hey, everybody." Glovia stood in the center of the salon where the light from her chandelier glistened off the sequins in her dress. "Gather round. Morgan's gonna tell us all about his latest bronze."

"I call this piece *Black Man Rising*," Monsieur Crawford began. "See how the saxophone is tilted at a fifty-three-degree angle? That represents the black man's triumph over..."

A rustle in the corner where Glovia's prized potted palm stood caught her ear. "The drums beat the sound of death. The conch resounds the toll of defeat." The regulars swiveled their heads to the back of the room. He was at it again. Jimmie Lee, all six-foot-three of him, his suit jacket bagging about his skinny shoulders, made his wooden walk to the center of the floor. Like always, he expected anyone standing in his path to part and allow him passage. And, as always, they did.

Monsieur Crawford worked his mouth like he was going to speak, but kept quiet. He knew the rules.

Marie-Thérèse gave a quick look around the room as the crowd focused on Jimmie Lee. Now was the time to scurry into the kitchen, even though tonight she was not the official cook or server. There was only so much she could take of Jimmie Lee. Especially with this new, strange sense of emptiness threatening her.

"Their feet encased in the chains of despair. Their mouths spewing lamentations into the fetid air. The..." Jimmie Lee's look-of-stone face matched every somber word.

Marie-Thérèse kept her eyes on Glovia, hoping her hostess wouldn't notice the escape of just one guest. "Oops." She bumped into someone entering the doorway she tried to exit. "Gaston, *pardon. J'ai...désolé...*" She turned to look directly into the uniform collar of the American lieutenant.

"I don't know what you said, but I'm guessing it's sorry." He grinned down at her. "No apology necessary, Madame Brillard. I'm delighted to see you again."

"Madame Bri...? *Enchanté? Moi?*" Marie-Thérèse felt her tongue tie in knots.

The American's smile turned a little lopsided. She realized she'd spoken in French. He hadn't understood a word.

"I took Spanish at San Francisco State. Not French," the American answered. "I do apologize."

"Oh, Monsieur Lieutenant. I am the one. Forgive me. I did not mean…" She flitted her hands in the air as she tried her English. Marie-Thérèse fought back a wave of embarrassment and tried to squeeze past the man in the doorway. She brushed against his body and jumped back into the salon. Café-au-lait face or not, she was certain the American saw only beet red.

Jimmie Lee kept at it, his baritone voice booming even louder: "Down, down, they were sent, their hands tied, and their feet bent."

"He's a cheery one, isn't he?" The American stepped back into the hallway. "Is there somewhere in this house where we can escape for a moment until Gloomy Gus gets finished with whatever it is he's doing?"

"*Certainement.* Certainly." Marie-Thérèse took in a deep breath, glad that her chest loosened enough to allow her to breathe like a normal person. "On that, Monsieur Lieutenant, the minds…you and me…are the same."

He laughed and stepped aside. Marie-Thérèse walked down the hall toward the kitchen. He followed. She fidgeted with the belt of her dress as she stepped into the room nearest the garden.

Gaston, elbow deep in Brie, pâté, and phyllo, peered around his two Frenchwomen helpers to look at Marie-Thérèse. "Not tonight, Madame Brillard." Gaston shot glances between Marie-Thérèse and the American lieutenant. "Remember?"

"But, Gaston…" Marie-Thérèse looked around the bustling kitchen.

Gaston shook his head as he wiped his hands. He picked up his full tray of drinks and headed toward the swinging kitchen door. Marie-Thérèse stepped aside.

"*Madame* will not mind if you speak in her boudoir for a moment, Madame Brillard. For you, it is permissible." Gaston nodded toward Glovia's closed door, then headed up the hall and into the parlor.

"Here?" the American asked. He opened the door and peered inside. "Is this the lady's bedroom?" He smiled. "I promise to keep the door wide open."

"*Monsieur.* I…perhaps Monsieur Hudson is *se taire*…no more talk." Marie-Thérèse made sure she kept a decent distance between herself and the lieutenant.

"Are you kidding? I'd rather fight D-Day all over again than to hear that cat drone on like that." He stepped inside and headed across the floor toward Glovia's organdy-skirted dressing table. "See?" He pointed to the floor. "I'll stand right here. I'll even turn my back to the bed." He twisted sideways. "You can stand there. Just inside the doorway."

Marie-Thérèse laid a hand across her mouth to hide the smile she felt coming. She could see Glovia's pink and gold bedecked bed with its Empress Eugenie headboard as plain as day. Even turned sideways, Monsieur could see it, too. But he was trying. "I am silly. Give me forgiveness, please." She patted the gray streak in her hair. "I have too many years. Old."

"Ouch." He winced. "I admit I'm forty-eight, but I don't feel old…that is, not until you just told me I was."

"*Non!* No, no, Monsieur Lieutenant," she stammered. "Not you. You are not the one with the age. It is me."

"Well, let's sort this one out. I'm not drawn to older women. Or younger ones, for that matter. I just fancy a good-looking woman with that something special."

She felt his eyes take a slow roam over the frame that packed a little too much around the middle.

"Take two steps to your right," he ordered.

"Two steps, *monsieur*? To *ma droite*...my right?"

"Yeah. Go on."

She moved her feet, wearing the only pair of high heels she possessed.

"Now look in that mirror, there." He pointed to Glovia's three-way. "You see what I see? A fine-looking woman, for sure. She's got a quick brain and, I suspect, an exceptional heart. That's my kind of woman. Years don't count for much with me."

"*Monsieur.*" She felt that flush swamp over her again. "You mistake me. Words like that...they are for the ears of Madame Glovia."

"Now don't get me wrong." He held up his hands. "She's a swinging dame, all right." He gave an approving nod toward the parlor. "Just not my type. By the way, how did your English get so good?"

Even in the dim lamplight of Glovia's two boudoir lamps, Marie-Thérèse could see the handsome features of the American. Were those eyes hazel? He tilted his head, waiting for her answer. Marie blushed again. He'd just caught her staring at him.

"*Monsieur,* I wish only that my English was good enough. My father made certain that I receive lessons. But, of course, the schools in Martinique..." She couldn't decide if she wanted to smile or frown. "Then all the Americans here in Paris...at Glovia's."

"Yeah, I heard that a bunch of colored folks settled in Paris during the thirties. Something about not being appreciated in America. Never knew till now what happened to them after they left the States."

"Many returned home. Glovia, Monsieur Crawford, Madame Josephine Baker, even Jimmie Lee, they all stay. The passage was expensive, you see."

"I bet if they'd known what this war was going to be like, they would have hightailed it out of here somehow."

"But what of you, Monsieur Lieutenant? What of your San Francisco?" She took a step inside the doorway. This man, with his prizefighter build, was easy to talk to.

"San Francisco? It's a nice little town. Lots of hills. Cool weather. Got a couple of new bridges. A colored man's got a respectable chance there. Tell me, Marie-Thérèse, how long has Paris had colored people living in it? Besides the Americans, I mean."

"Oh, Monsieur Lieutenant. Forever, I am sure, but more people of color come to Paris from the colonies. You understand? French Morocco. French West Africa. I come from Martinique." She took another step inside the room.

The American pulled out the boudoir chair.

"Martinique, you say? I'm not sure I quite know where that is." He bobbed his head toward the cushioned seat. "Here. Take a load off."

"Load, Monsieur Lieutenant?" She walked across the floor and sat. Her breathing came much easier now. As she adjusted herself in Glovia's gold-inlaid boudoir chair, he moved closer to the door "Martinique. The West Indies." She waited. "You know Cuba, and perhaps Haiti? The Empress Josephine...Martinique...was born there." She waited for an acknowledgement that did not come. "The wife of Napoleon?"

"Oh, yeah. That Josephine. I heard she was part colored." He turned those eyes on her. "I bet Martinique is one swell place, or it could never produce such beautiful brown women."

"Beautiful? That I am not, Monsieur Lieutenant." She shook her head. She was coming back to herself. "You may tell me I have the good heart. That I want to believe. But the beautiful? I know that cannot be so." Marie-Thérèse laughed as she turned in the chair to stare at her unlined image in Glovia's three-way.

"Have it your way, but I bet some other man found you pretty good-looking, too. You married?"

Marie-Thérèse tugged at the hem of her dress as she turned back to face the American. Good. It properly covered her knees. "For one time, yes."

"Not now?"

"Never no more, Monsieur Lieutenant. And you?"

"She passed away two days after Christmas. In forty-one." Marie-Thérèse wished she could swallow back her words. "Something called sickle-cell anemia." A quick wave of sadness washed over his face as he stared at Glovia's pink-carpeted floor. "Figured I might as well join up. The army, I mean." He brightened as he lifted his eyes back to her. "That and my college degree got me to OCS down in Alabama."

"OCS?"

"Officer Candidate School...for colored."

"Monsieur Lieutenant, I am so sorry. Your wife. I can tell you have much love for her." Marie-Thérèse stood, walked over to the American, and laid a comforting hand on his shoulder.

"So this is where you got to." Glovia stood with both hands braced in the doorway and ducked her head into the bedroom. Her eyes swept from the American to Marie-Thérèse to the bed and back again. "Don't let me be the one to stop you," she announced as she stepped inside. She hooked her arm through the American's. "But I don't want you going too fast with my friend here."

The lieutenant tugged against Glovia's arm. "Is that poet fella through reciting the downfall of mankind yet?"

"Mr. Jimmie Lee has dazzled us all with his brilliance one more time. Now I want you in my salon." She winked at the officer. "You've got to play the piano. It's time for more boogie-woogie."

CHAPTER 9

"Collette. Serve young Monsieur Gerard a fresh cup of *café*." Marie-Thérèse sat on the kitchen chair she had pulled into her living room. She had reserved the small settee for Gerard and her daughter, the settee compact enough to force the shoulders of its occupants against one another. Martine sat quietly in the only other stuffed bit of furniture in the room. Christophe, who looked surrounded by a cloud of doom deeper than Monsieur Hudson's, sat apart from Martine in the second of the kitchen chairs. Marie-Thérèse suspected a lovers' spat.

"Maman," Collette groused, "you know perfectly well we have no coffee. But if you want me to boil up some more barley and throw in a handful of chicory, I can do that." Collette bounced off the settee too quickly for Marie-Thérèse to protest.

She sent a warning look toward her daughter and grimaced a smile at Gerard for good measure. "Gerard, now that Paris is free, what will you do?"

The big-eared youth looked at her. "But the war is not yet ended, Madame Brillard. I shall help France, of course."

"Well, most certainly you shall. But with the Americans here, surely this war will not last too long."

"You set great store by the Americans, Maman," Christophe growled from his corner. "Two weeks ago, you swore the Germans would never leave Paris, no matter how many of Eisenhower's troops flooded the streets."

"Martine," Marie-Thérèse called out, "this friend of your heart has turned quite sour." She sent her most damning scowl toward Christophe. "Please help him see that the Americans will prevail."

"With the considerable help of Gerard, no doubt." Collette stood against the half wall of the kitchen while the coffee pot simmered.

"In any case, Gerard," Marie-Thérèse plowed on, though both her children were being impossible today, "I'm sure you will make a brilliant future for yourself whenever the war is won." She nodded toward her son. "Christophe here will attend medical school. Have you much interest in medicine?"

"Uh, not really." Gerard looked down at Marie-Thérèse's parquet floor.

"Any form of science?" Marie-Thérèse added a hopeful note.

"Not for me." Gerard looked to the kitchen. "Collette, is that coffee ready yet?"

"In a minute, Gerard, and when it comes, you should drink it quick so it doesn't get cold. Aren't you due at work sometime soon?"

"Collette," Marie-Thérèse hissed, "Gerard knows the time of his work better than you." Marie-Thérèse put the blame for her lapse into patois squarely on the shoulders of her daughter. Why was this girl being so rude?

Gerard's face flushed. "Actually, Madame Brillard, I don't really need any coffee. Collette is right. I do have to be someplace." He bounded from the couch, brushed past

Collette, and reached for the front-door handle. "Thank you for your hospitality." The boy's hands shook.

"Collette? Martine?" Marie-Thérèse put on her accusatory stare. "What have you done to Gerard?"

"Maman, stop playing matchmaker!" Collette stormed.

"Forgive my cousin, Madame Brillard," Martine interrupted. "He is but twenty years old and has not shown much interest in girls. Aunt Bridgette says he is a late bloomer. *Ma mère* frets that he may not be the marrying kind."

"I, for one, am thrilled," Collette stormed as she stalked to her bedroom.

"What problem make your sister do this thing?" Marie-Thérèse quizzed her son as she glanced at Martine. "Gerard is a perfectly fine lad. Even if he hasn't settled his mind on his future just yet."

"Maman, you're doing it again!" Christophe exploded, his face reddening. "It doesn't work." He jumped from the chair.

"Set yourself right down," Marie-Thérèse demanded as she stood to confront him. "I see you and Martine have the fight, but talk to your *mère* like this? Never!"

Collette burst out of her room clutching her purse.

Marie-Thérèse crossed the apartment. "You go to say sorry to Gerard, I know this."

"Yes. Yes, Maman. Have it your way." Collette slammed the door after her.

"Now, *what* is in the mind of that girl?" Marie-Thérèse shook her head at her son.

"Agh," Christophe grunted as he headed toward the door after her.

"Wait just one damn minute, Christophe Brillard!" Martine jumped to her feet. "You're not leaving this apartment until you tell me a thing or two." She crossed the room to confront Christophe.

"Oh, oh," Marie-Thérèse whispered under her breath. She turned down the hallway to the fainting room she had converted to her own tiny bedroom. Best to let those two have their lovers' spat in private. She squeezed sideways into the room, where her double bed took up eighty percent of the floor space, and eased the door almost shut. She needed air in the room, she told herself, when her only ventilation came from the skylight.

"Martine, I'm sorry. It's just that Maman…she can be so…" Christophe lowered his voice, but not enough to avoid the practiced ear of a caring mother.

"I have not seen or heard from you in two weeks." Martine's usually soft voice bounded through the apartment.

"I know. And I'm sorry." Now Christophe was almost whispering. "With the Americans in town, the bakery has been working overtime."

"I know the Americans are in Paris." Martine's sarcasm bounced down the hall and straight into Marie-Thérèse's little bedroom. "No thanks to you, Christophe. Where were you when the Americans marched down the Champs-Élysées?"

"Oh no, Martine." Christophe's voice rose. "I passed by your house when I got the news! I didn't see you, so I hurried to the boulevard. Everyone did. I didn't want to miss a minute!"

"I heard the news at the factory, and I was on my way back to Montmartre…to meet you." Accusation dripped from her words. "How could there be a celebration without you beside me? And what of all the days since the liberation?"

"Martine, Martine." Christophe laid out his charming voice, the one Marie-Thérèse recognized as placating. "Let's not fight. You could have come here just as well as I could have gone to you. It is possible for the two of us to celebrate with other friends on occasion, is it not? You know you are special to me."

Marie-Thérèse bit her lip to stop herself from peeking through the crack in the door. If only she could see Martine's face. She had no need to look at Christophe. She knew her son was keeping something from his girlfriend. But what?

"I only want to celebrate with you." Martine sounded petulant.

"Let's do that right now." Christophe's voice scratched fake cheeriness. "Let's get out of here and find some real *café*. I swear I'll never let another drop of chicory run down my throat again. Not in this lifetime." He put out his soothing laugh as the door closed behind the two.

Marie-Thérèse arched one eyebrow as she reached for the metal pole to push open the skylight. What was her son up to now?

CHAPTER 10

Christophe tugged down the sleeves of his sweater as he stood in front of the *boucherie,* where Genvieve had directed him. The October day had been bright and even warm. But now, with the sun flailing out its last rays, the evening breeze off the Seine brought the hint of a slight chill with it. He turned his head in the direction of the Le Poulet Farsi, knowing full well that he wouldn't be able to see Genvieve leave the restaurant, since it was two streets over from where he stood. He looked back through the window as the butcher flipped out the last of the shop's lights after clearing his wares for the evening.

"*Bonsoir, monsieur.*" The butcher gave him a curious look as he turned the open sign to closed. "May I be of further service to you?" The man lent a pointed stare at the wrapped package in Christophe's hand.

"*Merci, non, monsieur.* This meat will work well. I thank you for it." He held up the parcel that had cost him far more francs than he was prepared to spend. "I am waiting for a friend, if that is all right with you." He turned in the direction of the rue de l'Etoile again. "She should be along any moment."

The butcher grunted as he locked the door to his shop and walked toward the Metro stop on the corner. Before he descended the stairs, he gave one last look behind him.

Christophe pasted on his most innocent smile and wondered again why Genvieve had insisted upon meeting him here. He had offered to pick her up at the Poulet after she'd completed her shift, but she had suggested the butcher shop instead. In fact, in all their outings since that first one, he had never picked her up at her workplace.

"Had you given up on me?" Genvieve's voice, full of rushed excitement, sprang out at him as she swung around the corner. "I had to inventory the wine cellar." She slipped her arm through his. "What shall we do tonight? Another trip to the Tour d'Eiffel? That boat ride down the Seine?" She sounded breathless.

"You're kidding, right?" Christophe was only half joking. Genvieve had a way of getting him off track. "I see you only once a week because, you tell me, the next day is your time off. That way, you can spend the entire evening with me."

"Ahh, you are so perfect, *mon ami.*" She kissed him on the ear. "And that day is tomorrow. So this evening is all ours. Best of all, I know what we shall do tonight." She released him and clapped her hands. "The cinema." She laughed.

"The cinema? You know they've just started showing real films again. French films. American movies. But they were all made before the war. How many times can we see *The Wizard of Oz*?" He struggled to stay on track.

"A walk in the Tuileries, then?" she teased as she patted his stomach. "What would you like to do?" She tilted her face to him, that knowing little smile playing over her lips.

"Genvieve. We have seen each other exactly nine times." He practiced patience. "I believe we've visited all of Paris worth seeing." He tried to take the annoyance out of his voice.

"Except Montmartre." Her grin seemed especially mischievous tonight.

"Yes. Yes. Except that. You told me that tonight is the night you will make me dinner. At your place." He swept his lips across her cheek.

"Are you sure, Monsieur Christophe, that you heard me right? I believe I said that *ma mère* will make you dinner." She laughed as she tugged him along the street.

"Your mother? Will she be there?" A scowl crossed Christophe's forehead.

"Wait and see." She led him down the Metro steps.

"So this is where you live?" Even in the twilight, Christophe took in the look of the iron-grilled gate fronting a shabby-looking blue door. Despite the grand-looking gold knocker on the front door, he could see that the building was the most unkempt in the neighborhood. Still, it was a step above most dwellings in Montmartre.

"And this is where we shall have dinner." Genvieve thrust the key into the lock and jiggled the resisting doorknob. She withdrew the key, turned the metal over in her hand, and reinserted the other side. The door opened. "We are in!" she announced.

The room Christophe entered was one big open space with a small kitchen to the side. "Umm." He scanned his surroundings. "You and your mother live here together?" He looked at the double bed against the back wall. A sofa for three sat closer to the door. The room looked as though it had been decorated to serve two purposes—living room and bedroom, but for just one person, or maybe a happily married couple. He had seen many such arrangements in Montmartre, but he had always supposed that *appartements* in the more upscale ninth *arrondissement* would be a little more commodious.

"What meat were you able to get for us?" Genvieve sounded matter-of-fact as she opened drawers and cabinets in the efficiency kitchen.

"I got four chunks of beef, pretty small, but the butcher tells me they will work to flavor a good-sized stew. Did you and your mother just move here?" That Genvieve appeared unfamiliar with the flat filtered into his mind.

"Stew?" She tossed her head. "That will take hours." She walked to him and slipped her hand under his sweater to play with the folds at the back of his shirt. "I'll get our dinner started." She took the package and headed back to the kitchen. "I'll put the meat on to simmer and drop the vegetables in later." She opened three drawers before she extracted the stew pot.

"Genvieve." He couched his words in as much tact as he could muster: "How long have you and your mother lived here?"

"*Ma mère?*" She shot a curious look in his direction. "Oh, no. This is the home of my cousin. She has more fuel than my mother. We will use her stove for tonight."

"That's very kind of your cousin." He looked at Genvieve, who still fumbled her way around the kitchen.

She glanced up as he stared at her.

"Yes, my cousin is very kind." She adjusted the flame under the stewpot, then walked out of the kitchen and encircled him with her arms. This time she pulled the back of his shirt out of his pants as she stood on tiptoes to brush his lips with her tongue.

Taken off guard, Christophe took in a quick inhale of breath as he sucked in her tongue. He felt her fingers creep under his shirt, her lithe fingers strumming up and down his back. A rush of warmth enveloped him. He chanced laying his hands on her hips and maneuvering for the zipper of her skirt, keeping his touch as light as he could. When her body didn't resist, Christophe slid the metal tines open. His hands trembling, he touched the top edge of her panties.

"Mmm." She leaned back as she slid her hands across the skin of his hips to his bare belly. With deft fingers she unfastened the buttons and pulled both shirt and sweater over his head in one move.

His fingers shaking, Christophe pushed her skirt to the floor. He strummed his hands over the curve of her still-covered hips. His knees shook as he stooped to let his hands run up and down the back of her thighs. She wore no stockings. The idea of the delicious feel of nylons covering Genvieve's legs flickered in and out of his head.

"*Mon cher,*" he managed as he kneaded her behind through her panties.

She kicked off her low-heeled shoes and pressed a naked leg against his pants. With one hand, he pulled her hips against his pelvis. He arched her back with the other. His breath roared in his ears as he pushed her sweater up past her brassiere.

"Ah, Christophe…it has been so long…so…" she murmured as she lowered her leg.

He felt her fingers unbuckle his belt. She reached for his zipper, but he stopped her. He unzipped his pants, let them fall to the floor, and stepped out of them. With both hands, he pulled her sweater over her head. Nylon stockings stirred back into his mind and mixed with a brassiere that utterly failed to contain its twin, rounded contents. He pushed the straps off her shoulder. She grabbed one hand and led him to the bed.

"Promise me…" she said, her breath coming in spurts, "…that you will never think ill of me for this."

"Um, nev—" Christophe could not get words out of his throat.

He watched as she reached behind her and unhooked the brassiere. Christophe laid his hands on the garment. In slow motion he eased the white confection down her body as though he were Monet unveiling his latest masterpiece. The sound of his own breathing roared in his ears as he moved the brassiere slowly past an ever-growing mound of round, creamy firmness. The pink of her tits eased into view millimeter by millimeter, the nipples bulging, ready for his mouth. With trembling fingers, he circled her breasts, careful not to squeeze too hard.

"Mmm." Genvieve closed her eyes as her hands lowered his shorts.

His hardness popped against her panties. Flame engulfed him as her fingers played an ever-changing game of stroke-and-squeeze from tip to top of his hardness. Christophe gasped for air as he pushed her panties to her knees. He laid her on the covered bed and climbed in beside her. As he lowered the white panties over her feet, he stared at the thatch of tawny-brown hair. The thumps in his ears came so loudly he could no longer hear Genvieve, though he watched her mouth move, a look of pleasure spreading across her face. He let his fingers twirl in the hair as his fingers searched for the soft spot beneath. He strummed his fingers in and out of her body. She squirmed her body against his.

"Now, my darling. Christophe. Now!" A guttural sound came from Genvieve, though he couldn't be sure if he'd really heard her words.

He kissed her ready nipples, spread her legs with his own, and let his hardness slip inside. He closed his eyes, and the thrust of her body against his took him to a place better than heaven.

CHAPTER 11

Gray smoke from American cigarettes swirled in the air of Le Chat Noir even at this early hour. Not yet ten p.m. and the place was already full. Marie-Thérèse sighed as she looked around the club that had been the heart of Montmartre. Glovia had done her best in the few weeks since the liberation, but the old club was not the Le Chat of 1939. The Germans has seen to that. Glovia's velvet burgundy swags—the ones she hung from the ceiling and cascaded down her walls in luscious folds—had been pulled down and replaced with those dreadful German regimental flags. Now that these, too, were gone, deep zigzagged cracks showed the ugliness of the bare walls. Even Glovia's pride and joy, her upright piano standing on the little stage at the back of the club, looked scruffy and covered with Nazi grime. Marie-Thérèse ran a finger around a gash at the wooden table where she sat. A German saber? Even Gaston's patching could not make it whole. She shuddered and lifted her eyes towards tonight's crowd.

She took a nervous look at the crowd of American soldiers and Frenchwomen as they stomped across the tiny dance floor. The women flipped their skirts, showing their legs in their new nylon stockings while the soldiers taught them the basics of the dreadful jitterbug.

Gaston, standing on the stage of the saloon, blowing Duke Ellington's "Tootin' Through the Roof," did not seem to deter the Americans from their efforts. Frenchmen, who normally groused at the sight of their women in the clutches of foreign soldiers, were mollified by the cigarettes the Americans handed out like advertising leaflets.

"Thanks for letting me get my men settled." Monsieur Lieutenant sat back down at their table. "They can have a little fun. Deserve it. I just don't want them too rowdy. Not tonight." A flash of concern crossed his face.

"I have the nerves for Madame Glovia." Marie-Thérèse swept her eyes over the crowd again. "The first night she open. For many long years."

"Oh? I thought Gaston said her club was open four nights a week all through the occupation. Just had short hours."

"For the Wehrmacht, yes," she answered. "No, I mean open for us...the people of Montmartre. The people of Pigalle. Now we can come and enjoy just like the old days."

He leaned across the table and laid his hand atop hers. "I want this to be a big night, too. For us."

"Um, Monsieur Lieutenant." Marie-Thérèse forced a nervous smile. Lately, this man, with his confusing words, had started to rattle her. "Surely you will play the piano tonight? Glovia will insist."

"Not me." He turned toward the stage, where a trumpet and piano player joined Gaston in rousing the house with the Ellington tune. "These guys are pretty good, even if that song is almost ten years old." He smiled as he turned back to her. "Tonight is not about your Glovia." He scooted his chair next to hers.

"OK, Gaston," an American corporal shouted out. "Let's get to it! Play 'Straighten Up and Fly Right.'"

Gaston smiled as more Americans joined the outcry. The Frenchman launched into one of the three new songs he'd learned from the Americans. His sax took the first bar, and the piano man pounded at the keys, missing several chords.

"Ahh, *man*," wafted out of the crowd of disgruntled soldiers.

"Hey, Lieutenant!" a man with sergeant stripes on his sleeve yelled over the noisy throng. "Help this cat out."

"Not tonight." Monsieur Lieutenant grinned as he shook his head.

"Not tonight? But, Lieutenant, if it ain't tonight, w—"

"Shut up, Washington," Monsieur Lieutenant barked out.

Marie-Thérèse caught a touch of the military in the man. "What does he mean, Monsieur Lieutenant? If not tonight?"

"Tonight you and me are going to enjoy this party." He patted her arm. "I like that dress you're wearing."

"Monsieur Lieutenant," she said as she leaned in closer, "I am no Glovia with the Resistance, and I am not Le Maquis, but the secret I can keep." She moved away when she realized that her lips had almost grazed his ear. "Sorry, *monsieur.* I am a woman who worries about those I care." She bit her lip and wondered why she was making such a chattering mess of herself. "Besides, this dress is the same one I wear for you four times now."

He shook his head. "You caught me." He laughed. "I'm not big on women's clothes—just to notice how good you look in that dress. How good you look in anything."

"*Bonsoir,* my fellow Free French!" Glovia, in full performance regalia, paraded to the stage.

Gaston silenced the trio of musicians.

"This has been one hell of a long time coming." She waited while the French in the crowd howled out their joy and stamped their feet. "They tell me a lot has happened in the outside world since we were last free." Glovia stretched her bare arms out to the crowd. "Tonight we're going to boogie this place down."

French voices screamed their approval as the partygoers clapped American backs.

"Have you enjoyed Gaston and all the old songs?" Glovia, in her tight black skirt with the strapless animal print top, slipped right back into her element.

The French beat out a tempo with their feet.

"She can sure turn on a crowd." Monsieur Lieutenant nodded his approval toward the stage.

For a second, Marie-Thérèse dropped her head and stared at the glass of champagne on the scuffed wooden tabletop of the Le Chat Noir. She took a quick glimpse at the lieutenant and fought down a wave of disappointment. Silly. No matter how honeyed his words to her, he was no match against Glovia, not when the singer was really determined. And tonight, the *chanteuse* looked ready to snare some hapless man.

"I've got a new song for you." Glovia spoke in French. "And one not all that old for you all." She switched to English and flashed her dazzling smile as she shimmied her way across the stage. "Gaston, are you ready?" Glovia climbed on a stool, lifting her skirt to her thighs.

Gaston nodded.

"Mr. Trumpet Player, you ready to hit it?" She moved back to French.

"*Mais oui,* Madame Glovia." The Frenchman bowed himself, and his trumpet, toward the singer.

"Well, that's two out of three." She waited for the laughter to die down in the room. "Now all I need me is a decent piano player." She turned a theatrical stare on the hapless Frenchman at the piano. "And I want"—she whirled around and pointed a finger directly at Monsieur Lieutenant—"*him!*"

"Oh no, Madame Glovia, not toni—"

Glovia in her tight skirt and black high heels teetered off the stage leaning on Gaston's offering hand. She put an exaggerated sway in her hips as she made her slow walk toward the American officer. She stopped every few feet and tilted her head toward the crowd.

"Ain't he the one we want? The one to bring Paris back to life?" Each time she turned to the crowd, she pulled down the leopard top an inch lower over her breasts.

"Don't know what you're saying, Mama, but say it some mo'!" an American private called out.

"Lieutenant. Lieutenant." The call came from an American near the stage and spread fast throughout the room. French voices joined in, stumbling over the American word.

Glovia planted herself in front of Monsieur Lieutenant. She thrust her pelvis at him and did a great imitation of the grunt-and-grind to the hoots of the crowd. Marie-Thérèse shifted her eyes to the floor, a flash of red-hot heat working its way up her chest to her hairline. She appreciated Glovia in full battle gear, she really did. Glovia had paid a heavy price to serve France, and she deserved this moment. But why did it have to be with Monsieur Lieutenant? Marie-Thérèse forced herself to look full at Glovia, who seemed not to notice that Marie-Thérèse was even in Le Chat Noir. Glovia loved to toy with her men. Not in all her days in Paris had Marie-Thérèse ever known the entertainer to be serious about even one of them.

Glovia bent down, her breasts almost tumbling free of the leopard blouse. She grabbed Monsieur Lieutenant's arm and pulled him to his feet to resounding applause. She marched the man to the stage. Laughing, he took his seat at the piano. Marie-Thérèse watched his eyes. Not once did he look back in her direction.

Even through the haze of smoke, Marie-Thérèse could see the sweat pouring down Gaston's face, though the saxophone was now playing quiet backup to Glovia. Monsieur Lieutenant riffed soft runs as Glovia lifted herself onto the piano. She crossed her legs in her tight skirt. Perspiration soaked the leopard top. Neither the crowd nor Glovia seemed to care. Marie-Thérèse peered over the crowd near the open door. The cold November winds could not cool off Le Chat Noir.

"All right, you all. This place has got to close down sometime." Glovia took the towel she held in her hand, swiped her face, and dabbed at her chest. "Madame Glovia's got to get her beauty rest."

"Don't need no rest, sugar. Not as good-lookin' as you is!" a soldier's voice called out.

"One mo', baby, one mo' fo' the road!" another American shouted.

Glovia leaned forward on her perch. She pulled up the leopard top. "You want one more?"

"Give us all you got, sugar!" another voice clamored.

Marie-Thérèse caught the scowl on the face of Monsieur Lieutenant as he glared at the offending soldier. His fingers came off the piano keys. The Americans quieted.

"Here is one from the old days. *C'est pour vous.*" In the smoke-filled room, Glovia's eyes glistened as she opened her arms to the groups of Frenchmen clustered throughout the bistro. "*Pour toi, les patriotes de la France.*"

The room erupted in applause. Marie-Thérèse jumped to her feet. She stared at Glovia. Everyone who really knew the entertainer understood how deeply she loved her adopted land.

"*Il me coûte beaucoup,*" she crooned a cappella. "*Mais il une chose que j'ai.*" She closed her eyes. "*C'est mon homme.*"

A cry of recognition went up from the French in the crowd.

Monsieur Lieutenant, his face mesmerized by Glovia, picked out the tune on the piano. He smiled at the blues song that had swept the American charts in '37. Glovia scooted down from the piano, a smile on her face as she opened her arms toward the Americans.

"*It's my man. It's my man.*"

The soldiers shouted their approval even as the Frenchwomen turned dreamy eyes toward the Frenchmen in the bistro.

"*Cold and wet. Tired, you bet.* I give you Billie Holiday." She leaned against the piano and tilted her head back. "*All this I'll soon forget.*" She shot a look at Monsieur Lieutenant. "*But I love him. Yes, I love him.*"

Marie-Thérèse sucked in her lips as she took her seat. A little waft of a breeze must have made its way through the door, because she felt a sudden chill.

"*Vive La France. Viva la France. Liberté!*" Glovia threw up her arms. "Now go home. It's three o'clock in the morning."

Monsieur Lieutenant took over the microphone. "Yep. That's it. Good night. I've ignored a certain lady long enough."

Marie-Thérèse jerked her head up as Monsieur Lieutenant stepped off the stage and headed toward her.

"I'm sorry about that," he reached her, "but you must admit, that woman can be very persuasive." He took the chair beside her.

"She is a great talent, Monsieur Lieutenant, and is hard to resist."

"Michael." He turned around to face her.

"Michael?" Marie-Thérèse stared into the determined face of Monsieur Lieutenant.

"Yeah. Michael Collins."

"Oh, it is you, Monsieur Lieutenant...you are Michael?"

"Marie-Thérèse, did you know that tomorrow is Thanksgiving?"

"Thanks...*merci*...giving?" A wave of confusion swept over her.

"No, not *merci* giving. Thanksgiving." His laugh lit up his face. "It's a holiday. A holiday back in the States."

"Oh? I never know this *merci*...Thanksgiving. Who do you give your thanks to?" In the background she heard Gaston insist upon closing time.

"Oh, a bunch of pilgrims and Indians, but it's not them I want to celebrate."

"Celebrate? It is a day of celebration?" Marie-Thérèse ran all the Martinique holidays she could remember through her head. None of them involved giving thanks to Indians, and especially not to the Africans who had worked the sugarcane fields all those decades ago.

"Yeah. It's a day we celebrate." He nodded at a clump of American soldiers downing their last cognacs. "We have turkey, mashed potatoes, pumpkin pie." He grabbed her hands. "I'd like to have me one more Thanksgiving meal, Miz Marie-Thérèse, before—"

"Before...Monsieur Lieutenant?" The alarm came out of her mouth before she could control it. She had heard the rumors that some American forces might be called in to give the Germans their final push out of France, and all the way back to Berlin. She had just not allowed herself to think Monsieur Lieutenant would be one of them. Nor, before now, had she allowed herself to think why she cared so much.

"It's this war, you know." He released her arms and leaned back in his chair, putting on an air of fake casualness that rivaled Christophe's at his most guilty. "A guy doesn't know when or where he might get his next Thanksgiving meal." Even his laugh sounded hollow.

"A turkey? Monsieur Lieu—"

"Michael."

"Monsieur Michael. Will a chicken do for your feast?" She laughed at the impossibility of finding a turkey in Montmartre in November.

"You've got to stuff it, you know." He turned to her, his face wreathed in mock seriousness. "With breadcrumbs and sage and cornbread if you've got it. All that good stuff you women know about. And..." He grabbed her wrists as he grinned at her. "I've just got to have me some pumpkin pie. With ice cream, mind you." He wagged a finger at her.

"Monsieur—Michael. You shall have your giving of thanks, no matter if I have to stuff a pigeon with corn kernels and make a tartlet out of sliced turnips." She laughed aloud when his face scrunched up in distaste.

"It's a deal. Sort of." He slipped his arm around her and helped her from the chair. "Tomorrow, at your place."

As they joined the crowd drifting out the front door of Le Chat Noir into the chilly air, Marie-Thérèse looked back to see Glovia surrounded by a group of American soldiers. But the singer's eyes were on Monsieur Lieutenant Michael. And Marie-Thérèse. They reflected surprise.

CHAPTER 12

Marie-Thérèse tucked in the bottom of the white blouse she'd uncovered just this morning at the Les Halles flea market. When she first saw the bargain, she declared it almost new. It had all of its buttons and perfect shoulder pads in its puffed sleeves. She had not detected the one flaw in the garment until a few minutes ago, when she donned the blouse for the first time. The self-covered button in the center of her chest would not properly close, leaving a gap in the blouse where her bra could be seen. Never mind, she would simply use her apron to cover herself through dinner with Monsieur Lieutenant, even though she'd bought the blouse especially for him.

Her stomach fluttered as she condemned herself for her silliness. What real interest could this man possibly have in her when Glovia was so obviously available? Marie-Thérèse checked her watch. Two in the afternoon. The chicken, as scrawny as it was, should be out of her oven in another thirty minutes. The lieutenant was due at three. She peeked again at the austere pumpkin mousse sitting in a bowl of chipped ice she managed to scrounge from the dairyman. Too bad the fellow could allow her only one cup of cream. That she had stirred into a weak imitation of ice cream, sprinkled with a few tablespoons of sugar, rather than into the mousse where it rightfully belonged.

She stepped out of the kitchen and into the bathroom just off the main hall. She took a quick glimpse at her face, debated if she should apply lipstick, decided against it as hopeless, and moved back into her living space. As she passed the photo of Papa, Christophe popped into her mind. Another flutter attacked her stomach. She doubted that her son would be home before the American left. The boy still worked the night shift at the bakery, and too few of his days, when he should have been snug asleep in his bed, were spent in Marie-Thérèse's *appartement*. Then there was Collette, who would not get off from the dress factory for another two hours. She had called out not to expect her until late tonight. The girl had declared that she would be out with friends. Marie-Thérèse only prayed that Martine was one of those friends. It looked as though neither child would be home tonight.

But suppose she needed her children this evening? Marie-Thérèse shook her head in disgust. Just more old woman's foolishness. At fifty, women didn't harbor thoughts of dalliances with men, especially handsome American soldiers who could have their pick of lovers. Her eyes fell on the rosary draped over Papa's picture. She crossed herself and peeked out the window toward the Sacré-Coeur. Certainly such thoughts must be a sin.

The rap on the door came at two minutes after three. Marie knew the precise moment because she couldn't keep her eyes off the clock.

"For you." Monsieur Lieutenant thrust a basket of oranges into her hands as soon as the door opened.

"Oranges? Monsieur Lieutenant, where did you get these?" She hadn't seen an orange in four years.

"Took a little doing, but for the woman who's cooking me Thanksgiving dinner, nothing is too much." He grinned as he stepped inside.

"First, you taste your dinner of thanks." She ran her hands down the front of her apron.

"Smells great." He kissed her on the cheek. "As much as I'm looking forward to the meal, it's you I want to spend time with."

"You will find nothing of interest about me." She hurried to the kitchen, her basket of oranges in tow. "I am an old schoolteacher. Nothing but children in my life." She flushed. Why had she shared that bit of information with the man? She busied herself slicing oranges and making a glaze for the chicken.

"No interest, huh?" He walked over to the photograph of Papa. "A very distinguished looking man. I bet he's got a story to tell." Monsieur Lieutenant turned toward the kitchen. "About you."

Marie-Thérèse splashed a few drops of her dwindling bottle of cognac into the bubbling glaze. "That man...he... he is of Martinique." She kept her eyes on the glaze, hoping that the American didn't detect that she was reluctant to look him in the eye.

"Forgive me Marie-Thérèse. I don't mean to pry." He walked to the half wall of the kitchen. "If you rather not talk about him, that's OK. I just don't buy that 'no interest' stuff." He caught her gaze. "I think you're fascinating."

"Ahh, *monsieur*, that will change when your dinner of thanks is like nothing in America." She forced a laugh that caught in her throat as she poured the glaze over the chicken.

"I have a son, Marie-Thérèse." He watched her as she moved the food to the kitchen table. "Sixteen. Thanksgiving makes me miss him all the more. When his mother passed and I joined up, I sent him to live with her folks." He paused. "You don't look like her, you know, but your heart is like hers." He tapped his chest.

Marie-Thérèse almost dropped the fork she planned to lay on the table. "Monsieur...Michael...I could never...it is you who is special...I thank you so much." She tugged at her apron. "Come and sit."

"You make it all go away, you know. This war...everything." He slipped his arms around her waist.

Marie-Thérèse gasped. She felt his fingers fumble with the tie at the back of her apron. He slipped the garment over her head and sat down.

"Come on, woman. Join me. This looks delicious, but not as good as you in that new blouse."

"He is my papa." She fidgeted with the cutlery to keep her hands away from the offending button. "The man in the picture frame...my father."

"Your father?" Monsieur Lieutenant stared at her as she handed him the carving knife. "Looks white to me." He assessed Marie-Thérèse's face. "But I do see him in you. These things happen. Obviously he was good to you or you wouldn't have his picture." He began slicing the chicken. "I'm glad."

"*Oui.* He was most good to me. The money for Paris. Me and my children."

"How many kids?" He laid chicken on her plate.

"Two, and they are the grown-up." She patted the gray streak in her hair. "You see, I am the old woman."

"That's the second time you've said that to me. I guess I must like my women 'old' then." Before he took a bite, he leaned over and kissed her on the cheek. This time his lips lingered.

Her hand reached for the edges of her blouse. "I have sorrow that you lose your wife. She must have been young."

"Umm." He nodded. "Just forty. I miss her." He started his dinner. "You do make the hurt go away, whether you know it or not." He took a swallow of his wine. "Marie-Thérèse, I told you I don't want to pry. If you don't want to talk about your kids' father, that's OK with me. I just need to know that you're single."

This time the fluttering in her stomach turned to a whirlwind. "My husband? So long ago. He was a Frenchman… You understand? A white man." She stared at slices of dark chicken meat on her plate.

"OK." Monsieur Lieutenant sounded tentative.

Marie-Thérèse looked up at him. She'd known just months after the wedding that the sailor from Marseille only saw her father's money in her. Three years later, he finally grasped that Papa Brillard had no intention of making the husband of his bastard daughter a rich man. Within days, he left her, and his children, for the harbors of Martinique where wealthy Americans waited for someone to captain their yachts.

"Michael, I have no shame for what I do. Was he the man for me? I tell you no." She looked the American in the eye, the fluttering in her stomach gone. "A mistake, he was, but the wife of a French citizen can come to France with no, how you say, fuss? I come to France with my children. Better life for them here than in Martinique."

He reached for her hand and held it against the table.

"I already knew that about you." His eyes scanned her face. "A strong woman who did what she had to do...a shy woman with a soft heart."

"Well, I've never had pumpkin pie...moose...whatever you called it, like that before," he teased. "But it was delicious. Now come sit down here and let's have a real talk." He patted the settee.

Marie-Thérèse took in a breath as she cleared the last of the dishes. She looked over at her couch and grimaced, knowing full well that sitting there was almost the same as perching herself on Monsieur Lieutenant's lap—à la Glovia. She walked over to the sofa and stood a moment. He pulled her down beside him.

"Sorry for all the small talk over dinner." His face turned serious. "I guess there's nothing else to say except to get to it."

"Get to it?" A burst of anxiety shadowed Marie-Thérèse's voice.

"This will be my last night in Paris." He stared at the door. "For a while."

"Oh, Monsieur Lieutenant." She scooted halfway around on her settee to face the soldier. "Yesterday, I fear that...yesterday I hear that...the Americans...they...you...might be on the move to the Germ..." She covered her eyes with her hands. "I don't want this." A wave of fear washed over her.

"Hey. It won't be that bad. Remember, I made it through Normandy." He slipped an arm around her shoulder. "Spending Thanksgiving here with you, like this…well…to think that you tried to make me a Thanksgiving dinner, even if it was a chicken. That's special." He pulled her to him.

"I promise to cook better your Thanksgiving the next time…" She let her body slide against his chest.

"You got a deal. There will be lots of 'next times.'" He tilted her head toward his and kissed her lips.

The feel of his mouth against hers stirred an unfamiliar feeling low inside. She parted her lips and let him caress them with his own. She felt his hand trace down the front of her blouse. His fingers stopped at the middle button. He popped it open and wriggled his hand inside, his fingertips searching for her brassiere. She felt a quickening between her legs—something new. Despite her two children, she had never felt such a thing with the man from Marseille. A flash of heat bathed her face as Monsieur Lieutenant slipped his hand between bra and breast.

"Marie-Thérèse," he murmured, "I want to…"

The click of the key in the door drowned out the rest of Michael's words. She pushed him away just as the door swung open and Collette stepped inside.

"Maman?" Collette stood, mouth agape, the key still in the door.

"Collette, you tell me you have friends tonight." Her heart thumping, Marie-Thérèse arched her back over the arm of the settee, leaning as far away as she could manage.

"I'm sorry, miss." Monsieur Michael brushed his hands down the front of his uniform trousers as he stood and stepped in front of Marie-Thérèse, offering a partial shield. "We haven't met. I'm Lieutenant Collins. United States Army."

"Uh...uh..." Collette stammered. "American. You're an American?"

Marie-Thérèse shifted behind the soldier and deftly buttoned the blouse. She jumped to her feet. "In the house you come, girl." She patted her hands over her mussed hair. "Don't stand there like your mother teach you no manners."

In the back of her head, Marie-Thérèse heard the patois. She remembered. The American hadn't understood a word. She switched back to English. "This is a friend from Madame Glovia's." She put as much bravado in her voice as she could muster.

"Ah, this must be your daughter?" Monsieur Lieutenant turned to Marie-Thérèse. "Yes, I see the similarities. You both have a softness about you."

"The giving of thanks...the dinner...I..." Marie-Thérèse felt her courage fading away.

"Your mother very kindly offered to make an American soldier feel at home." He turned to Marie-Thérèse, his hand on her shoulder. "This woman made me a good, old-fashioned American Thanksgiving dinner. Well, almost." He laughed as he turned back to Collette.

"I see." The girl resurrected her voice as she finally extracted the door key and stepped into the living space.

"I'm afraid I've left you no dinner, Miss... Mademoiselle...?"

"My manners, I forget." Marie-Thérèse waved her hands in the air. "Sorry. Collette, Monsieur...Michael."

"Maman. Maman. My, you *are* the one, aren't you?" Collette's grin brought sparkle to her brown eyes as she shot a teasing grin at her mother. "Well, Mr. American. I hope you enjoyed your dinner."

"Considerably, *mademoiselle*." Monsieur Lieutenant gave a half bow in Collette's direction. "And I hope that someday I will be able to master French a tenth as well as you've so obviously mastered English." He tapped Marie-Thérèse's shoulder. "Your mother has done a masterful job with you."

Marie-Thérèse stood frozen in the center of her living room floor, fuming as Collette smirked.

"Mademoiselle Collette, I hope you will not mind if I bid your mother farewell. I may be…away for a bit." He turned a serious face to Collette.

"Of course." The smirk faded. "I've just come home to change before I go out. You two carry on." She rushed to her bedroom.

Marie-Thérèse laid a hand across her forehead and came away with a perspiration-dampened palm. "Monsieur Lieutenant…Michael…I am…"

"Your daughter is charming, just like you. But I really do have to go. I want one thing from you."

Marie-Thérèse looked toward the hallway. "Monsieur, I have a son, too. He could surprise…"

"Your promise to write me. I don't ask that you do it every day, just whenever you can." He pulled a slip of paper from his pocket. "You can write me here."

"*Oui, monsieur.* I can do that." She took the paper.

"A second promise."

"What, *monsieur?*"

"You will accept my letters when they come. I will write you every day that I can." He stooped to kiss her on the cheek. He shut the door behind him.

"Maman!" Collette bounded from the bedroom, howling with laughter.

"Will you shush yourself? The man just closed the door!"

Collette fell upon the settee, curled her knees to her chest, and laughed until the tears came.

"What you find so funny, my girl?" Marie-Thérèse straightened her shoulders. She was the *mère* after all, and she couldn't allow her daughter to see her so full of embarrassment.

"Maman," Collette gasped for breath. "I never knew you had it in you!" She kicked her heels in the air in glee. "Oh, my God—you almost *did!* Thank the Savior, I got here in time." She doubled up with laughter again. "Or maybe not." She shot a mischievous look at her mother.

"What you talk, you silly girl?" Marie-Thérèse felt the top of her head melt from the flames licking at her entire body. She busied herself washing dishes.

"Thanksgiving dinner, was it?" Collette began to compose herself as she moved to sitting on the settee. "Maman's got a boyfriend. Maman's got a boyfriend." She chortled. "How long has it been, Maman? Sixteen years? No man since my father. Wait until I tell Christophe." She fell back against the settee in fresh gales of laughter.

"You do no such thing! I do a favor for a friend of Glovia, is all I do." A plate dropped from Marie-Thérèse's hand and clattered to the floor.

Collette rose to her feet. "I know what kind of 'favors' Madame Glovia does. Even with the Germans. Yuck!" She walked to the far end of the living room. "He didn't have to go, you know. You two could have finished what you started."

"If I reach you, girl, I teach you to watch your mouth." Marie-Thérèse grabbed the broom as Collette headed toward the door. "You know Madame Glovia sacrifice herself for France."

"Yeah, yeah, I know...Free French and all that." She sobered as she gathered her pocketbook. "Remember, Maman, the way you feel about your American...and that open blouse of yours? Well...that's exactly how I feel about Jean-Michel." She walked out of the door.

Marie-Thérèse heard the laughing all the way to the stairway landing.

CHAPTER 13

Courageux blew on his glove-covered hands in the unheated shack where Alain-Hugo and Panthère sought refuge from the December snows of Alsace.

"We must do this one last thing for France," Courageux repeated. "I know you have already sacrificed a lot."

Their leader, hunched down on the floor, laid that stare on Alain-Hugo.

"Do not question my loyalty to our country." Alain-Hugo glared back. Hadn't he spent almost two years aiding Le Maquis? "But they have gone. The Wehrmacht crossed the border back into Germany last week, and Alsace and Lorraine are free."

"There are no braver men than you two." Courageux nodded toward Panthère, who sat full on the floor, his legs straight out in front of him as he leaned against a stack of explosives. "But we have been asked to make this one last mission."

"They've all been *one last mission*," Alain-Hugo groused. "We have families we want to see."

"Yes, I understand. And you are the only one with a wife," Courageux conceded. "I will not beg you. This is one for your own mind to decide." He leveled his eyes at Alain-Hugo.

"Panthère, are you in with this?" Alain-Hugo slipped his hands under his arms as a fresh blast of snow brushed against the one window in the building.

"I have no wife like you." Panthère kept his eyes on the plank floor. "But I have family that is dear to me."

Alain-Hugo tapped his boot on the floor. He longed to see the tawny-haired *Parisienne* he had married, but what would she think if he deserted France for her arms? For the safety of them all, he knew the group's leader could offer no elaboration on the importance of the mission. Not until they had all agreed. Alain-Hugo would have to weigh his choices.

He turned toward a man soon be revered as a hero of the resistance, though Alain-Hugo doubted he'd be alive to see the adoration of his leader. The sole of his booted right foot burned over the image of his young wife. That little half smile, the way even the black-and-white photo captured the amber of her eyes, the curve of her…"Courageux." His breath left little ice puffs in the air. "Tell me what you want me to do."

The trio's leader hunkered to the floor, acting as if he'd known all along how Alain-Hugo would decide. "I have word that the Wehrmacht is planning a counteroffensive." The man used his finger to sketch out a crude map in the dust on the floor. "In the Ardennes."

"The Ardennes? Belgium?" Alain-Hugo moved closer.

"The Americans have pushed so far ahead that their front lines may be stretched too thin. Our sources say the Nazis are probing for the weakest point in those lines." Courageux paused as he looked from Panthère to Alain-Hugo. "They have found it."

"And what do we do to stop them?" Panthère spoke up.

The shortwave radio squawked. Courageux paused, listened to the transmission, shook his head, and continued. "A German courier, perhaps disguised as a French farmer, is carrying a packet sealed by Field Marshal Rommel himself. Inside is listed the precise point where the attack will occur. The man is to deliver the information to the general in the field."

The trio's leader looked up as the old shack creaked.

"The wind," Panthère declared.

"Mmm." Courageux returned to his drawing, his voice barely a whisper over the howl of the wind. The man's cool eyes darted around the room. "The letter is written in code. The courier carries the key phrase in his head to unlock that code. If that packet is delivered," Courageux slowed his words even more, "the Germans will attack the Americans at their weakest point. And if the Nazis succeed…and the Allied march into Germany is stopped, then the tide of battle…"

Alain-Hugo sucked in a breath and held it. How could he have thought of his own desires, even for a second?

Courageux settled his eyes on each man on his team. "We must retrieve the packet and the courier. Alive."

"Where do we find this man?" Panthère asked, his eyes downcast. "Here in Alsace?"

"And how will we know him?" Alain-Hugo asked.

"His looks we do not know, but we begin here in Alsace." Courageux turned to Alain-Hugo. "That is where you come in."

Alain-Hugo shifted the cap lower over his eyes as he pulled the cart behind him on a road no wider than a goat's path. Up ahead, a farmer carried caged chickens on a pole that lay across both shoulders. In front of that man, almost out of Alain's line of sight in the thicket of woods, another farmer slung a large knapsack so heavy it doubled him over. Alain-Hugo did not turn around to peer at the farmers shuffling through the snow single file behind him, but he smelled the fresh offal of pigs being driven to market in Bergheim.

Courageux had briefed him. Bergheim, a village of half-timbered houses at the foot of the Vosges Mountains, had been kept isolated after the German annexation of Alsace and Lorraine at the start of the war. Now with the Germans on the run, French farmers chanced the trek into the village heart to sell the few crops they had managed to harvest under the watchful eye of the Germans. With the increased traffic, Bergheim made the perfect spot for a courier to slip in and out among the throngs of men moving throughout the area. The close-knit villagers would render curiosity, but not surprise, at the rough-dressed visitors descending upon them.

Alain-Hugo practiced the accent Courageux had drilled into him. The people of Alsace spoke their French with the guttural sound of their German ancestors. Alain had been coached to come close to mimicking them, but the time had been too short for mastery. Courageux had emphasized one other critical piece of information. More than a few of the citizens in Alsace harbored sympathies for Germany.

"*Monsieur*, what carry you in your cart?" the farmer behind him called out as the group of men approached the town meeting hall, where the trading was done. "You have it covered so well." The pig farmer slapped one of his three pigs back into line as the men trekked into the hall.

"The better not to bruise the contents." Alain-Hugo lifted a corner of the burlap covering his cart.

"Ah, you carry the wine from Colmar." The farmer grinned. "I have made the journey from Lorraine."

Alain-Hugo nodded as he stepped inside the meeting place and chanced a closer look at the farmer behind him. The man blended in well with the crowd in the unheated room, though his accent sounded more like the French of Lorraine than the German of Alsace. Probably not his man.

Courageux had warned him. The courier could be in Bergheim, or he might not arrive for days, or he might have heard that Free French had been dispatched to intercept him. Alain-Hugo stripped the burlap from the bottles. He mimicked the movements of the other farmers. Why had Courageux given a Parisian, a man who'd never been on a farm in his life, this critical role?

"What have you there?" a big man speaking German-accented French demanded.

"Wine. From Colmar." Alain-Hugo detected no flaw in his own pronunciation. He looked away as he assessed his questioner. Alsatian, he concluded.

"What year, *monsieur*?" the fellow, in his worn jacket, inquired. "I cannot sell a young wine."

"Forty," Alain answered, his accent perfect.

"You think that was a good year?" the man asked.

Alain-Hugo looked the man in the eye. Could he be the courier with his trick question? A yes answer to the German victory year could indicate Vichy support, but a no response in this area, with its mixed loyalties, could be just as treacherous.

"The year is what you believe it to be, *monsieur.*" Alain-Hugo fought back a quick wave of panic. His attention had lapsed for a second, and he swallowed the practiced trace of his guttural German. He picked up a bottle and held it out to another prospective buyer. "Make me a good price." He slipped his accent back in place.

The second man reached for the bottle, traced a finger over the label, and looked at Alain-Hugo.

"Did I hear you say forty?" The man eyed the freedom fighter with suspicion. "This bottle does not appear to have been long in the cellar. Where did you say you come from?"

"Ferrette." Alain-Hugo answered with the Alsace village name Courageux had supplied.

"Imagine this. I too am from Ferrette." The second man let out a strained chuckle. "I think I do not know you."

Alain was ready. He shot back, "I do not know you, either. And most of the wine houses in the area I know, though I must admit, my family owns none of them."

The man held up his hands, the skin underneath his nails stained purple. "I think your family has no workers in any of them, either." He stared at Alain's calloused but purple-free hands. "*Monsieur,* I think I take your bottles of burgundy. Come, we make the deal." He nodded his head toward a heavy-looking oak-planked door at the back of the hall.

Alain-Hugo put on his most stoic face, though his heart raced as he followed the man. Part one of the plan had succeeded. He'd been identified as a spy. Now, did he have the courage for part two?

"*Monsieur,* I ask you again. Where do you come from?" The Alsatian straddled a chair, his arms resting on the back, his eyes leveled at Alain-Hugo. The purple-fingered one stood just to the right of the wood column supporting the roof.

"*Monsieur,* have I not made it clear? I come from around Ferrette." Alain-Hugo made a fuss struggling against the ropes squeezing his chest tight against the wood column. His eyes swept over the room once more. Three men were in the locked pantry besides himself. The Alsatian, Monsieur Purple Finger, and a silent figure guarding the door. At least there were no guns in sight. Yet.

The punch came fast and hard from Monsieur Purple Finger. The blow snapped Alain's head back against the wood column. A surge of pain ran down the back of his neck.

"I most respectfully ask you from where you come." The Alsatian arched his back.

"Ferrette."

This time the blow came straight to his stomach. Alain-Hugo doubled over as far as the ropes tied around his chest would allow, the pain gripping him. Monsieur Purple Finger stepped back.

"*Monsieur,*" Alain-Hugo gasped, "the ropes, and the fists, are unnecessary." He winced as the knots binding his wrists against the column cut into his skin.

The Alsatian raised himself from the chair and walked toward him. Before Alain-Hugo could react, two more blows pounded at his face. Blood poured into his mouth from his nose and dripped from the gash on his forehead. His chest strained against the ropes. If he could just flick away the veil of blood covering his eyes. He watched as the Alsatian pulled the Mas 35 from under his shirt. Alain-Hugo had hoped for a Luger.

"*Monsieur*," the tormentor began, "my patience is thin. You have never sorted a grape, nor stirred a vat in your life. What do you want of us here in Bergheim?" The gun glinted gray under the lightbulb suspended from its single ceiling cord.

"To sell my wine." Alain stuck to the plan.

The barrel of the gun swept slowly over Alain's groin.

"Now, *monsieur*. I will have my answer. You can give it to me now, or bit by bit." He jammed the barrel of the gun hard between Alain's legs. "Or I can take bits and pieces off you until you do."

"*Non, non, monsieur*." Alain struggled to stay with the plan. "I will tell you what you want to know."

"T'is time." The Alsatian eased the pistol away.

"I steal the wine!" Alain-Hugo cried out. He heard the gun cock and saw it move to his head.

"You choose," the Alsatian narrowed his eyes. "First, I shoot off your ear or, if you prefer, your fingers…your toes? In the end, I get to this." He jammed the pistol harder into Alain's groin. "Which will it be?"

Alain's heart raced. Thoughts of his wife flooded his head. The room swam. The plan was working, but would he be around to celebrate its success?

"I…I am not…from Ferrette. Not from Colmar." His breath came in spurts. This time, his struggle against the pain in his lungs was no pretense.

"*Monsieur.*" Exasperation poured out of the Alsatian's mouth. He circled the gun over Alain-Hugo's body. "Choose," he ordered.

"Free French. I am Free French. Don't shoot."

"I knew it. That accent could not be Alsatian." The man with the gun turned toward a shadowy figure in the far corner. "What shall we do now?"

"*Warum sind Sie hier?*" The German stepped out of the shadows. He walked toward Alain, grabbed the cord holding the lightbulb, and shone the light into his eyes. "Why are you here?" he repeated in French.

Alain squinted against the light. "To get the Wehrmacht out of Alsace."

"The Wehrmacht has left. A week ago. Why is your information so old? And where are your partners? You Free French always travel in threes." The German's French was atrocious.

"In Colmar." Blood trickled into Alain's right eye. "We got word…the Gestapo…counter operation to train insurgents in Alsace…to keep Alsace…German." Though speaking was difficult, he had managed to get out most of the speech Courageux had trained him to say. He prayed that he would live to see the next step in the plan.

"Alsace will always be German. If that is all he knows," the German looked satisfied as he turned toward the Alsatian, "then shoot him."

"No, *monsieur.* I have more!" Alain screamed out just as the big oak door rattled off its hinges and blasted into the room.

Waves of pain pounded into Alain's ears. The space filled with black smoke smelling of sulfur. The lightbulb did a wild dance before crashing to the floor. Chunks of plaster broke loose and struck Alain in the head. He struggled to stay conscious. He felt the body of the Alsatian fall across his lap. Something heavy thudded across the floor. Was it Monsieur Purple Finger? The sound of gunfire blasted throughout the room.

"Panthère, make sure these two are dead," Courageux ordered. "Untie our compatriot. We will use the ropes on the Kraut, here."

"Umm." Alain-Hugo spit out plaster from his mouth. His throat felt clogged with dust. "That was a bit close… wasn't it? Almost too much dynamite." Grit filled his mouth and settled between his teeth.

"I had to wait for the right moment." The figure of Courageux filtered in and out of the dust, and Alain's head.

He felt hands untying his feet while others freed his arms. The room still spun. Sound faded from his ears. Somewhere in the distance, Courageux's voice tried to tap back into his ears.

"Get him to his feet," Courageux ordered someone. Panthère? "Let's get this Nazi back to the cabin."

"You've been out for a while." Panthère adjusted the bandage around Alain's head.

"Did we…is he…did we get it? The packet…the…" Alain-Hugo's tongue filled his mouth and refused to work properly. He tried to raise himself on his elbows, but the move shot a sharp pain from neck to shoulder and he fell back onto the cot. Before he closed his eyes, he saw the empty space on the cabin floor where stacks of explosives had stood just days before. A gray courier's packet lay at the feet of a bound and gagged German, the enemy's Mas 35 in the hands of Courageux.

CHAPTER 14

"Marie-Thérèse, is all this fuss worth it?" Glovia lay on her chaise longue, her eyes covered with a cloth Gaston had dipped in lavender oil.

"You are right. I should not trouble you with my problems. Not now, when you're working every night of the week. Even tomorrow—Christmas Day." Of course, it was worth spewing out her troubles, if just to make herself feel better. But Marie-Thérèse kept that certainty to herself as she sat in Glovia's study.

The *chanteuse* slid the cloth off one puffy eye and peeked at Marie-Thérèse. The seven-nights-a-week grind had taken its toll. Only the low lighting at Le Chat Noir preserved the singer's reputation as a beauty.

"Now, sugar." She switched to English. "Don't get me wrong. I know you only want what's best for your girl." She slipped the cloth back over her eye and tilted her head even further back. "Gaston!" she called out. "You back with that ice yet?"

"*Non, madame.* He is still not here." Marie-Thérèse peered through the open door to the hallway. "I suppose I am wrong to fret over my Collette, Glovia."

"Of course you're not wrong, honey. It's not about how wrong you may be, it's all about you worrying yourself sick over it." She tapped the cloth. "Marie-Thérèse, in all these weeks you been coming here talking about your daughter's boyfriend, what is so wrong about the man—except that he's white?"

"Ah, *madame*, uh, Glovia." Marie-Thérèse stumbled. She'd already told Glovia about her own disastrous marriage to a white Frenchman. What else did Glovia need to hear? "It's just that...that...Collette is too young for such a match." She pounded her conclusion home.

"Didn't you say she was almost twenty-one? Hell, I was married to old man Johnson when I was fifteen." Glovia flung the cloth to the floor. "Now that was *real* hell."

"Fifteen?" Marie-Thérèse exploded. "Was he a white man?"

"In Mississippi?" Glovia howled. "All I'm telling you, Marie-Thérèse, is to let your girl make up her own mind. Don't hold this man's being white against him. This world's got bad colored men in it, too. My Mr. Johnson was an old-fashioned black man straight out of the heart of Mississippi." Glovia laid her head on the rolled arm of the chaise. "My pa, damn his soul, thought my marrying Mr. Johnson would be the greatest thing to happen to a poor black girl since emancipation. The clown owned a funeral parlor, you see. Richest colored man in Greenwood. And you know the best part my bastard of a father told me?"

"Clown?" Marie-Thérèse tried to conjure up the image of the glamorous Glovia married to a circus performer. "*Non.* I cannot guess."

"Mr. Johnson had already sowed his wild oats." Glovia stretched her neck. "Shouldn't abuse me more than two or three times a month. That's the lie my pa told me. Said the old fool just needed to set his eyes on a young gal every now and then to keep his juices flowing." Glovia screwed up her face as though she wanted to spit. "More like two or three times a *day*, and my Lord, was he rough. And forget me saying no." She spoke to the carpet.

"Oh, Madame Glovia." Marie-Thérèse left her chair and started toward the singer. She had to admit that her Frenchman husband was no match in the disgust department for Mr. Johnson.

"Girl." Glovia held up a palm. "Sit yourself down. I didn't tell you all that to make you feel sorry for me." She removed the cloth and turned her face to Marie-Thérèse. "Let me ask you a few things. Go on, get back in that chair." Glovia pointed.

Marie-Thérèse nodded as she resumed her seat. She'd turned to Glovia because Collette's head was hard, and Christophe couldn't be bothered. Gerard was hopeless. Martine, no help. Marie-Thérèse had run out of options.

"Does this man...what's his name?" Glovia groaned as she readjusted the cloth.

"She tell me Jean-Michel." Tired of struggling with the English, Marie-Thérèse lapsed into patois.

"Does Jean-Michel drink too much cognac?" Glovia took the hint and returned to French.

"She does not bring him to my house, but I think no."

"Does the man have a job?"

"She tells me he works at the bank in the ninth *arrondissement*."

"Bank, huh? Does he have a wife?"

"*Merci, non!*" Marie-Thérèse couldn't contain her shock.

"Is he as old as Methuselah?"

"Methuselah? No, Glovia. He is but twenty-six."

"Does he have children?"

"Of course not, *madame.*" Why the questions worthy of the Gestapo?

Glovia slid the cloth down to her nose. "Was he a *collabarateur?*"

"If he was that, I would have turned him over to the authorities myself. And cheered when the rope was strung around his neck." Marie-Thérèse shook her head for emphasis.

"One last thing." Glovia kept her eyes free. "Does he beat your daughter?"

"Never do I see the bruise on her." Marie-Thérèse slapped her hand against the armrest of the chair. "And believe me, I look for all these things."

Glovia struggled upright. "Do you see where I'm going? You got nothing against this guy except he's not part black." She squinted at Marie-Thérèse. "Girl, you've got to come up with something better than that."

"But he will break my girl's heart!" Marie-Thérèse cried out.

"Maybe. But that's up to her to figure out. Not you." Glovia went silent as the front door opened and footfalls quick-stepped down the hall.

"But—"

"Thank God, Gaston. Bring that ice over here," Glovia commanded.

"The ice? Yes, of course, Madame Glovia." Gaston shot a quick look at Marie-Thérèse, a burlap-wrapped small chunk of ice in his hands.

"What's with you, Gaston?" Glovia inquired as she reached for the burlap.

"Uhh." Gaston shot another look toward Marie-Thérèse.

"What *is* it, Gaston?" Marie-Thérèse moved to the edge of the chair. "What's happened? Collette? Christophe?" Bile rushed to her throat.

"Oh, *non, non*, Madame Brillard! Your children are safe. As far as I know." He turned to Glovia, who sat adjusting the cloth over the ice. "The news…is not…"

"*What* news?" Marie-Thérèse and Glovia spoke out in unison.

"The shortwave radio. The Americans call it the 'Battle of the Bulge.'" Gaston looked at Glovia. "It's the Ardennes forest, Madame. The Americans are surrounded by Germans. The American general…Patton, I believe, is trying to reach them."

"What are you saying, Gaston?" Glovia put the ice-packed cloth back over her eyes. "Are we in danger of losing the war or something? Are the Nazis re-taking Paris?" Glovia did not sound worried as she lay back on her longue.

"No, *madame*. That's not it." He blew out a deep sigh. "The Americans that we know…our friends…many of them are in the second armored infantry…the piano player…"

"Piano player?" A knot quickened in Marie-Thérèse's throat as she stared at Gaston. "Not Monsieur Lieu— Monsieur Collins?"

Gaston turned back to her. "I think they call themselves the 'Red Ball Express.' The shortwave says they are driving supplies through enemy lines to reach the trapped Americans. Very dangerous."

"Oh." Marie-Thérèse clutched her purse. She fumbled the lock open and laid her hand against the last letter she'd received from Monsieur Lieutenant just this morning. Her hand shook.

"Lieutenant Collins," Glovia clarified. "Gaston, can you get a hammer and crack this damn ice? It keeps sliding off my face." She handed over the cloth.

"Of course." Gaston started for the door, stopped, and turned to Glovia. "I look forward to the day that Lieutenant Collins returns to Le Chat Noir. He was...he is a great player." He headed toward the kitchen.

"What you got in that purse?" Glovia inquired as she tapped her forehead with her palm.

"Nothing. Something. This morning..." Marie-Thérèse scooted to the edge of her chair. "Madame Glovia, where is your shortwave? Will they have more news, you think?"

"About this Bulge business?" She cast a curious eye on Marie-Thérèse. "You sweet on Lieutenant Collins?"

Marie-Thérèse felt the flush cover her chest and burst out on her face.

Glovia grunted her way to sitting. "Sugar, I can see that blush from here. Where was I when all this was happening?"

"A friend. He...*merci*...I mean thanks day..." Marie-Thérèse shook her head in surrender.

"Well, I'll be damned." Glovia placed her bare feet on the floor but jerked them back in the chill of the room. "What's that in your purse?" She pointed again.

"A letter, Glovia. Just a letter." Marie-Thérèse felt her spine stiffen. She was regaining control. "Monsieur Lieutenant and I...we are friends. I fix him dinner for his holiday."

"You made the man Thanksgiving dinner?" Glovia laughed. "Well, I'll be double damned." She squinted at

Marie-Thérèse. "You know, I hadn't all the way given up on that man for myself. Not yet."

"We are friends. He is someone to write..." Marie-Thérèse hurried her words. "Once he comes back, I'm sure it is you he will want to see..." She jumped from the chair. "Oh, Glovia, how dangerous is this Bulge battle?"

Glovia rocked back on the chaise. "My. You two *are* friendly, aren't you?" Surprise edged her voice.

"I just want him alive!" Marie-Thérèse cried out as she stroked the letter still in her purse. "I know who I am, Glovia. I am not beautiful and I have no talent, but for too long I forget that I am a woman. Monsieur Lieutenant reminds me of that every minute."

"Gaston will show you where we keep the shortwave." Glovia lolled her head over the rolled arm. "And, Marie-Thérèse: no matter how old we get, nor how ugly we may be, every female ever born likes to have a man remind her that she's a woman. Don't worry. Our soldier boy will come back to us."

CHAPTER 15

Christophe slipped the francs into the cash drawer. Almost two days' pay, but chocolate came dear. And this torte had to be the finest. The *boulangerie* only made two a day, and those were for the American market. But today was Saint-Valentin, and he had talked the owner into baking five. He reserved one for himself, at a discount price, of course.

Their celebration would have to come early in the day because Genvieve worked the dinner shift tonight. He debated going home to the *appartement* for a few hours' sleep and then meeting Genvieve at the cousin's place for one of their twice-weekly visits. Maman had mellowed, at least on the Collette front, and these days every encounter with his mother didn't end with her presentation of an outrageous scheme to rid his sister of Jean-Michel.

As Christophe bid good-bye to the day shift at the bakery, he turned toward the rue de la Bonne. Perhaps Maman would not be home to press her second-favorite subject. Martine. Lucky for Christophe, Maman spent more and more time with Madame Johnson. Collette had told him, in peals of laughter, that their mother had a suitor. Christophe failed to see the humor. He reminded his sister that Maman would see her fifty-first birthday this spring. How could the woman possibly be interested in saying more than a polite hello to any man? Even holding hands struck Christophe as absurd.

He did wonder, though, about those thin letters marked with US APO addresses that kept showing up in the apartment letterbox. Nevertheless, his sister must be mistaken. Maman had probably befriended a young American—a boy about Christophe's age. Despite her bossiness around her own children, Maman did have a good heart. She could not, did not, and would not take a lover. What could have been in Collette's head? Too tired to ponder more, he opened the first door to his apartment building and began to climb the stairs.

As always, Christophe stood under the awning of the butcher shop, five doors down from the apartment of Genvieve's cousin. He hesitated to go inside because he felt obligated to buy, and his francs were far too few for that. But with the snow flurries of February stinging his cheeks, he wished his *petite-amie* would agree to changing their meeting place to the flat she shared with her mother. But, too often, the mother was ill, or there was insufficient fuel for cooking, or… That Genvieve did not want to show him off to her family had pushed itself into his head. But he had moved that topic aside in his excitement over the beguiling woman.

Genvieve stepped off the Metro, her face pale and drawn. "Sorry I'm late." The sky streaked gray and threatened a full snowstorm. "What do you have there?" She pointed to the bakery box.

"For later, *mon amie*." He pulled up the collar of her winter coat. "This makes no sense. You travel from your mother's house over here to the ninth to meet me. We spend a few hours at your cousin's apartment, then you head back to the Boulevard to work. You are out in the cold much too long."

"You worry too much, Christophe." She fumbled for the key as they approached the door with its fancy dolphin-shaped knocker. "Oh!" She sounded startled as the key jammed in the lock.

Christophe reached over and jiggled it free. "Tell Annette to get that lock fixed."

Upstairs, the cousin's flat felt chilly. Christophe fed the meter for the heat. "On the two days we're here, I'll leave some francs for your cousin so the place can, at least, be warm when we arrive."

"Uh-huh." Genvieve wrapped her arms around her black coat, the collar still covering her ears.

Had she heard him? "Are you all right?" She wore the same strained face she'd worn for at least the last month.

"Of course I'm all right." She pulled an already-damp handkerchief from the pocket of her coat.

Christophe moved to the tiny kitchen and set the bakery box down on the round, two-person table. He moved back to Genvieve and wrapped her in his arms.

"This is Saint-Valentin's." He kissed her cheek. "Our first together." He kissed her other cheek. "To make this day especially sweet, I've brought you something." He twirled her toward the little table.

"Oh." Genvieve leaned her head into his shoulder, her voice muffled. "Christophe."

"Genvieve," he called out. "It's just a torte. I have not brought you diamonds, or gotten you that gallon of Joy you're always prattling on about." He held her at arm's length. "Are you ill? You look drained." He laid the back of his hand against her forehead the way Maman did when she wanted to check him or Collette for fevers. "You don't feel warm."

"Tired. I must be tired." Genvieve broke his hold. She fidgeted with the strings holding the box. "A Saint-Valentin surprise. That's just what I need." A sudden shudder hunched her shoulders. She kept her back to him.

Christophe heard the sound of a stifled sob as he rushed to her. He slipped his arms around her chest. "It's a torte, that's all," he whispered as his fingers moved up to the top button of her coat. "One day I will give you a room full of chocolate cakes. Strawberries. Champagne." He kissed her hair as he flicked open the button.

Her body trembled as she tried to stifle yet another sob. She pressed the handkerchief to her mouth.

He spun her around to face him. Tears welled in her eyes. "Genvieve, my darling." He stared at her. "What *is* it? What could possibly be the matter?" He drew her body tight against his. Her coat, still buttoned across her middle, bunched between them.

She slipped her arms around his neck, stood on tiptoes, and brushed his mouth with her lips. "Christophe, you must know…you must feel…that I love you more than anything. More than anyone." She pushed away and turned her back. "But, you and me, we can't…*mon Dieu!*" Genvieve rocked back and forth, heel-to-toe. "I don't know. I don't know. What am I to do?" Her wail filled the room as she covered her face with her hands. Christophe closed the space between them, his breath brushing her hair.

"Do? What are you to do because you love me? Did I hear you say it? You did say that you loved me, didn't you?" Christophe stared at the back of the black coat as it swished around his beloved's legs in time to...in time to what? Had her trembling increased? "But, *mon amie*, if you love me, then why the tears?" He pulled her closer but released her when the shaking in her shoulders worsened. "You love me. What could be wrong?" He sucked in a breath. "I love you too." There. He'd finally said it.

She turned to face him, slow as though her body struggled against a stiff winter wind. Her eyes, carrying unsettling flecks of fear in them, roamed his face. A full rain of tears coursed down her cheeks. What had he said? Her sobs pushed her body against his. Her face looked as though she'd lost a beloved grandmother. With a quick shake of her head, she pressed her back against his. Sobs wracked her slumped body.

"Leave," finally bubbled out of her throat.

Leave? Could Genvieve have said leave? But why? What awful thing had attacked this woman he so adored? He felt her rounded back stiffen as though a rod had been laid down her spine. Her head lifted and turned to the cousin's cracked kitchen linoleum. "No." The word, barely audible, fluttered into the room. "I don't want you to go. I need you to help me...to help me with this."

"Help you? Help you with *what*?" Christophe tried to turn her to face him. She resisted. "Help you with loving me? That I can do." He forced a smile he didn't feel. The wool of her dark coat smelled of the damp of the weather. Nothing about this moment felt right. "I will help you with anything, my love, but what are you asking?" He hands skimmed over her hips and probed the front of her body as gently as he could. "Are you hurt? Have you fallen? Has something, anything happened? Your mother? Your cousin?" What could be the problem?

With each question thrust at her, Genvieve lolled her head from side to side against his chest, her tawny hair splaying across his jacket.

"I...am *enceinte*."

A rush of blood clogged Christophe's ears, whisking away most of the sound in the room. "You're what?" He pushed her from his chest and whirled her around to face him. His eyes stared down at the black buckles on her work shoes, then climbed up her legs to her knees, where they met the brown of her jumper peeking out from the black coat. He hadn't noticed before. The bottom two buttons were still fastened. His eyes continued up her body to the side of her face. He watched the twitching of her lips. He shook his head to clear his ears. He strained to sort out that raspy sound that had come from her throat. What had been that sound? A word? What single word could bring such misery to this woman he loved so much?

"Pregnant." Genvieve's groan sounded garbled around the edges, but this time it was clear enough.

Pregnant? *Enciente?* Despite the francs he'd added to the heater box, Christophe shivered. The temperature in the room could be no more than eight degrees Celsius—just a shade above freezing. He needed to add more francs to the meter. Get Genvieve warm in this frigid winter cold. That must be what she needed. He struggled to move toward the front door and the meter box, but his legs refused to obey his command.

"Did you say…? Genvieve, I heard…" His throat closed shut. Slow, like a pantomime, his hand fumbled open the middle button of her coat. He pushed aside the coat and inched his fingers around the wool of the dress covering her belly. He rested his hand over the bulge.

"Ohh." Her voice barely a whisper as she slipped her hand over his.

She led his hand in a slow circle around the little protuberance at her middle. Christophe struggled to get more air into his lungs.

Now breaths pounded so fast in his throat that his words exploded into the apartment. "Are you certain?"

"*Oui*," she managed.

"*Oui*? A baby?" Christophe stared up at the still-boxed torte sitting on the kitchen table, the only two things in the room not spinning. "When? How?"

She loosened his hands as she slowly turned to face him. "The doctor says not quite two months."

"Doctor?" Christophe jerked. "You've seen a doctor?" Heavy thumps flooded his chest. "Then why didn't you tell me?"

"Tell you? I was afraid."

"When? When did you see the doctor? Afraid of what?"

She wrapped the coat around her middle. "Last month. But I guessed it before then. Still, I needed to be sure. I was afraid to tell you."

"Last month?" Christophe struggled to run their assignations through his mind. How many? Six, seven, eight?

And each of them delicious. When had she conceived? "You were afraid to tell me? Why?"

She looked down at her cousin's patched carpet. For a split second there was something in her eyes that flashed desperation, worry, and fear. Something.

"Don't you see? I couldn't. I didn't want you to worry."

Christophe felt the muscles in his forehead twist into a tight frown. "Worry? Of course I will worry!"

His legs felt jittery. He had to think. He had to walk. Christophe began to pace around the petite studio, but that was worse. The bed here, the stuffed chaise longue there, a table between the two. No good. Every spot he wanted to plant a foot, furniture blocked his path. He had to think and that meant moving. "The bakery does not pay much." Random thoughts swarmed around his head. He spoke them out loud to make them stick in his brain. "But this war will end soon. Oh, God, medical school!"

"You don't understand." Genvieve's voice sifted into his ears and right out again.

Christophe stumbled around the apartment, adding the kitchen with its cramped table and chairs to his route. "School will have to wait. I can speak to Jean-Michel. Maybe the bank needs clerks with this war almost over." Now the words he spoke out loud started to form themselves into a plan.

He passed Genvieve standing by the kitchen. Was her face releasing some of the tension? Right now he had no time to interpret. It was up to him to perfect the plan for them both—for all three.

"Christophe." The word brushed past his ear with no more force than a gnat.

"Where will we live?" Christophe muttered as he continued his pacing. "Oh, Lord. Maman." He stopped and swung around to Genvieve. "We'll have to tell Maman that we got married in…how many months are you?"

The tears had stopped. Her cheeks still glowed red, but they were dry. "I can't have this child, Christophe."

"Uh-huh." His ears still played tricks on him. It was plain to see and hear that his *amie* had kept their secret too long. All by herself. "It must be somewhere outside Paris, or Maman will figure out that the date is off." He snapped his fingers as the bones of the plan added muscle. "We must convince Maman that the wedding took place in October. Two months, you say? Then September will give us more cushion. Somewhere near…oh, God, somewhere near where, which town?"

She turned her face to him, her eyes bright for the first time this evening. "You will help me, then? To get an abor— to rid me of…?"

Marie-Thérèse's face popped into his head, twisted with disappointment. Could Maman's edict against interracial romance extend to Frenchwomen as well as men? Sound pecked at his ears again. What had Genvieve just said?

"Christophe!" She raised her voice and carefully formed the word as though she were talking to the deaf.

"Right." He heard her better this time. She must have questions. "Maman can't object to a grandchild. No matter what color." He rushed toward Genvieve.

She put out a hand to stop him. "I can't have your child, Christophe."

Something thudded into his chest with the impact of one of General Patton's tanks. "What did you say?" A feeling of stickiness attached itself to his feet. He struggled to move. To no avail.

"It's impossible." Her face was set, composed. No sign of tears remained. Her fingers no longer twisted the handkerchief into a tight ball. "You must give me your help."

"Help?" The word felt like it came out of another throat.

"I have searched for a woman to help me. Better still, a doctor to help me with—I cannot have this child."

Everything Genvieve had said and done these last twenty minutes played out in his head like a motion picture run in slow motion. He stared at this woman. Had he not just confessed his love for her? "I understand." He bit down on his lower lip, berating himself. "You think...you thought I would not stand with you? That I would not be here for you and the baby? That I would desert you both?" The glue loosened his feet. He rushed to her. "I could never do that! I love you and I want to marr—"

She turned her head just as his hand reached out for her face. "I cannot have this child. I cannot have your child." She closed her eyes. There was no sign of a return to tears.

"Genvieve, what are you saying? Are you telling me that you cannot bear my child? Why in God's name would you say that?" Patton's tank moved in reverse and parked square atop his chest. "I...I..." Sound lodged in his throat, but he had no strength to push it into words.

She moved her hand to his shoulder. Her touch felt like a dagger dipped in ice. He shrugged her hand away. "You do not want...you will not have my child?" The words hurt his throat.

"Thank you for understanding." Her eyes brimmed with relief as she brought her hands to her chin. "I have been so worried."

Christophe clamped his jaw shut and willed his hands to remain still at his sides as the frightening strength of the truth pounded into him. She flung her arms around his neck. He felt the padding of her stomach press against his body. He stiffened against the onslaught.

Genvieve pushed back from him, her face quizzical, confused. "You do understand, don't you?"

"Perfectly." He heard the coldness in his own voice. "Maman was right." He fixed his eyes beyond her and straight at the torte box.

"Your *maman?*" Her head shakes caught in the corner of his eye. "You keep speaking of your mother. What does she know of this...of us? You said you never told her about me." Genvieve searched his face.

"All this." Christophe scanned the room that had moved from his own private sanctuary of love to the most drab tenement in Paris, all in the flash of a second. He closed his eyes. Still the light from the lamp with its cracked ceramic base was as bright as the sun. "Always meeting here at your cousin's. Never at your mother's house." It all seemed so clear. So obvious. Why had he been so stupid? He opened his eyes and turned toward her. "Never allowing me to pick you up at Le Poulet Farsi." Each breath pained him. "Now I know why."

"Christophe." Genvieve frowned as she shook her head, her hair falling across her forehead. "*Non, mon cher, mon ami,* you do not know why. Christophe, it is not what you think. I love you so much."

"Love? Not what I think?" Christophe spit out the words.

The flecks of fear that had stained her eyes faded into confusion. She shook her head. Or was that shock he saw on her face? His feet moved like those of a mechanical man at the before-the-war summer carnivals at the Tuileries. He gripped her shoulders. Only her soft grunt alerted him that he squeezed too tight. No matter. Her eyes opened even wider.

"Tell me the truth." The words felt like cold, rough-edged metal emerging from his throat. "I want you to look at me and tell me why you want an abortion. Why you want to kill this child...my child."

"Kill? No, Christophe. I don't want to kill...if only there were some other way, but..." She clamped her eyes shut and sucked in a breath that seemed to come from deep within. "This child cannot be born." She opened her eyes and captured his gaze. Her words were stronger, more certain. "Oh, Christophe. I never intended to fall in love with you. I just wanted, just needed you." Her hands went to his as she tried to loosen his grip.

"You needed me? For what? A diversion? Is that what you wanted? A little bit of fun? Damn me. Damn the consequences. And now this result." Somewhere in the distance he heard the hiss of a troop train puffing its steam through the ninth *arrondissement*. The sound of it matched the words coming out of his own mouth. "And now you've been caught with what you never intended. What you never wanted!" His hands dug deeper into her shoulders. "I know the truth of it." The words stung his throat as he yanked her toward him, then slammed her away. Her hair whipped her face. "You refuse to give birth to a black child."

He watched her lips move as she flung words into the air, but the words were lost in his ears as though she were speaking through meters and meters of wool batting. Thank God.

The pain in his head was too great to bear the sound of her voice. He released her.

"I thought I had already seen the worst time." His voice shook on small gasps of air. "The worst day of my life. The day I went to enlist in the army." He turned his back to her, stumbled over some knickknack or other the cousin had left on the floor near the lamp table. "The radio, the posters, everyone said to enlist. Join up. Save France. Fight the Germans." Bile rushed to his throat. "Every able-bodied Frenchman is needed. If you love France, do your duty. Well, I…" His chest hurt, and he had to swallow another surge of bile. He swung around to her. "I loved France. I was able-bodied. Hell, I was eighteen years old! I went to the enlistment office. I volunteered." The pain in his chest reached right through muscle and tissue to his spine. "Do you know what they told me?" The words mixed with the bile he could not force down, and red-hot, they passed through his lips.

She stood there, his Genvieve, her arms folded just over her belly, rocking back and forth.

"Woman, do you hear me?" His voice burst into the space between them as loud as any bomb. "Do you know what they told me?"

Genvieve raised a face full of shock and surprise to him.

He lifted an accusing finger at her. "The same damn thing you just told me."

She stared back, her lips parted, her eyes staring blankly at him, her head making tiny shakes. "N—n—"

"They didn't want me, you see. Told me only white men could join the French army. That the Africa Corps was the place for me." His jaw clenched and unclenched. "They didn't want me. Just like you don't want…don't want my baby." Christophe laid a hand across his aching forehead. "Because we...the baby and me, are black!" He spit out the word. "But this...what you're saying to me? What you want to do to me is a thousand times worse than what the French army ever did!"

"Black?" Her amber eyes stared at him. "You're telling me the army rejected you because they thought you were black?" Genvieve looked as though air had just been pumped back into a deflating balloon. "And you think that I"—she rubbed her belly—"that I cannot bear this child because...what? Some fool in the army office tells you that you are black? Who is black in your family? Your *maman*? Your *grand-père*? You think I care? I don't care! You think so little of me to believe that I..." She clutched the wadded handkerchief to her throat as the words strangled in her throat.

Christophe stared at her. What was she saying? That had to be the reason. The only reason. "You would rather condemn yourself to hell than bear my child...my black child. You would defy the Church. Commit a mortal sin. All better than delivering a baby into this world who might not have white skin." The words sounded as though they had come from another man's mouth.

Genvieve's face moved from shock to disbelief to hope to disappointment with the speed of a second hand making a half sweep around a clock. "How can you say such things to me?" Anger pushed away fear. "If you were as black as the *Sénégalais,* I would love you. Don't you know that? Can't you feel that? I don't love you for your color. I don't hate you for it, either. Christophe, I love you for *you.* For what you are. For who you are with me." Genvieve's voice rose throughout the small apartment. Her fingers clenched. She ran to him before he could back away and beat her fists into her chest. "How can you say such things to me?" She turned her back to him.

Christophe tried to work his mouth. Words tumbled in his head, jammed into thoughts that fought one another, and nothing came through his throat.

Genvieve stalked to the kitchen and flipped open the lid of the bakery box. "This torte is shaped like a heart." Her voice sounded hollow. "That should mean you love me." She turned toward him, her coat buttoned, her face in profile. "If you believe that of me...that I could not bear your child because you are black, then you could never have loved me." She started toward the door.

"Then why?" The words poured out of his throat. "Why can't you have our child?"

"Because..." Her lips twitched as her eyes fixed on his shoulders. "I am intended for another. That's why." Genvieve inhaled as she turned and walked to the door with its zig-zag crack along the frame. She placed a hand on the door-knob and lowered her head. "I am guilty of many wrong things, Christophe, but loving you and your child is not one of them."

The pain in his chest ratcheted up again. "Another? You are betrothed to another man?"

Her eyes shifted away from his face. "Two years ago. And he has been that long away. Not a word. It was convenient. An arrangement." Her words sounded directed at the still-closed door.

"Convenient? Arrangement?" Christophe started toward her but stopped. "What sort of betrothal is that?"

"My father had just died." She lifted her head. "There was no money for my mother and me. And the Germans were everywhere." Her words were measured. "She...my mother thought it best if there was a man to protect the two of us. She knew the owner of Le Poulet Farsi. His son had watched me grow up." Her shoulders sagged in her dark coat.

Le Poulet Farsi? The son of the owner? Christophe stared at her back.

"He was like my big brother. There to save me from harm. To keep us safe. Both *ma mère* and me." She paused. "I respect him very much as a man. He is very brave. He fights for France." Her voice dropped to a half-whisper. "But I never loved him. Not the way a woman should love a man. With all of her heart." She opened the door. "Only you."

Christophe reached her before she could close the door behind her. He wrapped his arms around her and buried his face in her hair. "*Ma cherie*. An arrangement. A betrothal to a man you do not love. I thought you did not love me because I was...because I am..." He squeezed her to him. "Forgive me, Genvieve. Please forgive me! We will get through this. You. Me. Our child. We will get through this together."

CHAPTER 16

The May breeze creeping through her window carried the smell of the neighbor's cooking cabbage, but Marie-Thérèse welcomed its arrival.

"*Merci,* Christophe. You do the good job with the window." She turned her head toward her son as he tapped in the last nail repairing the vane of the old shutter.

"Maman, hear those bells?" He stuck his head out of the casement window.

"The Sacré-Coeur. Word must have reached them." Her son grinned as he put the hammer back into the toolbox.

"Will the party be as big as the day of liberation?" she asked as she stood at her stove, stirring the peas she had scrounged from her rations into a soup. She turned over the few pieces of chicken simmering on the next grate. "You think the day come soon when we will have proper meat for the pea soup?"

Christophe lifted the gingham skirt covering the makeshift kitchen cabinets and laid the toolbox on a bottom shelf. He turned and grabbed his mother around the waist. "Those bells mean only one thing." He nuzzled her cheek. "This war is over. The peace treaty was signed this morning."

"Boy!" Marie-Thérèse gasped between chuckles. "You squeeze the life out of your *maman.*" She looked at the calendar still tacked to her wall. May 8, 1945.

"Yahoo!" Christophe yelled as he grabbed his sweater.

"You make sure this time that it is Martine you are with for the celebration!" She lifted the wooden stirring spoon from the soup pot and put it to her lips.

Christophe's smile vanished so fast that Marie-Thérèse dripped some of the soup onto her stove before she remembered to return the ladle to its job.

"Maman, I think now maybe you and I should talk."

"About Martine? About the celebration?" She poked the chicken with a fork. "You just make yourself sure that you do not forget Martine this time."

"This isn't about...this is about..." Christophe stumbled over his words as he stationed himself by the front window.

Marie-Thérèse kept herself busy at the stove. What was her son about to tell her? That look on his face already alerted her that the news would not be good. For months now, Martine had not come to the house. When she saw the *Sénégalaise* on the street, only a polite smile and a hello was ever exchanged between the two before the skinny-legged girl made her excuses and departed.

"Maman, what would you think...?" He sucked in his lips. "Now with the war over, the world will soon be right again. The Americans...there will be jobs. Lots of them. Why just last week, Louis-Philippe and I...bread for the Americans..."

"Christophe! What are your words chattering to me about? Talk to me with sense." This was worse than she thought. She added the chicken to the soup pot before the meat had reached its proper degree of doneness.

"I am talking sense. I want to talk sense. It's just that sometimes things turn out a little different from what you first thought. That's why…school…Louis-Philippe…we are thinking of starting our own bakery for the Americans." He took in a big sigh that Marie-Thérèse knew told only half the story.

"You quit the talk about Louis-Philippe and bakeries right now!" She gave the spoon a hard tap against the soup pot, laid it down, and walked into her living room to face Christophe. "What do you say about school?"

"I will go to medical school. I will." His eyes drifted off her face. "Just not now."

"What you say to me? Of course you will become a doctor, and you will begin this very autumn. No matter how hard this war, I did not touch the money I hide for your school. I know it is not much, but it will start you on your dream."

"Stop!" He raised his voice. "I am not going to medical school. At least not right now. I need to work."

Marie-Thérèse felt the blood rush to her head. "What are you talking? Why for you need to work?" Her hand fidgeted with the buttons on her housedress. "Has something happened at the *boulangerie*?"

"I'm getting married."

"You getting yourself what?" Her stomach seized into a knot. "You say marry? I think I sit myself down." She lowered herself onto the settee. Yes, this marriage was right for her son. But now? She couldn't help herself. Her forehead crinkled into a frown. "I tell you what you already know. Martine is a fine girl, but she will wait for you. Until school is done. Then you two shall marry." The knot loosened in her stomach and she started to smile. But why did Christophe look so miserable? "Unless she is…" Marie-Thérèse heard the beats pick up in her chest as the image of a fat belly on the thin Martine conjured up in her head.

Christophe stared at the parquet floor as though an anguished expression could will away scratches. "She's not Martine."

That knot in Marie-Thérèse's stomach retied itself even tighter and worked its way to her chest, spread out, and ensnared her lungs. "Not Martine?" Marie-Thérèse's hands gripped the arm of the settee. "What you say to me?"

"You don't know her, Maman."

"I don't know who? I do not know the woman you say you will marry?" She heard the shrillness in her own voice. "How can this be? Me, your *maman*, and I don't know who is this woman you want to marry? This woman who is not Martine?"

"Not Martine, Maman." His voice rose again. "She is not Martine."

"Christophe. I hear your words." The ties holding her lungs loosened. "But these are words I do not understand. What is wrong with Martine?" Her lungs burst free. "You do not have it in your head that she loves you?"

Christophe sucked in his lips. She watched his chest capture a breath as his eyes grabbed on to hers and held. "Maman," he breathed, "I love someone else."

Marie-Thérèse could hear little cracking sounds in her neck as she shook her head. Even so, she couldn't stop the shaking. "What nonsense you talk? What woman you think you love more than Martine?" She steadied herself as she held onto Christophe's gaze. "When do you love this woman?" Marie-Thérèse slammed both hands to her chest. *Mon Dieu.* The answer burst into her brain. "A Frenchwoman.

A white woman." Her knees wobbled as she moved to her feet. "Where you meet this hussy?"

Christophe straightened his back. "I won't have it, Maman. I won't have you talk against the woman I love. Genvieve is no hussy." When had her boy grown so tall? "She's going to give you"—his mouth opened, then closed, only to open again—"a grandchild."

Had the bombing started again? Wasn't that the rosary swaying over Papa's picture? What else could explain a living room where the walls throbbed in and out in time to the pulsing of her heart? Marie-Thérèse blinked her eyes. Her knees shook and her ears felt claps of thunder as loud as any bombing. That would explain it. Something outside her apartment, something on the rue de la Bonne must have happened to cause her to mishear her son's words. She licked her lips. She'd say the words back to Christophe. He would look exasperated and think her a silly old fool. Like always. "*Genvieve.* You call the woman Genvieve? This woman you say is *enceinte?*"

"Yes."

"*Mon Dieu.*" The ties clamped tight on her lungs again. She reached a trembling hand out to her son. "Christophe. Christophe." Tears puddled in her eyes just as clarity rushed back into her ears. She heard a cat meow three stories below.

"Stop it, Maman!" Christophe's words rocked the room. "Enough of this 'no white mates' for either of your children." He marched over to the photo of Papa. "This man was white." He jabbed a forefinger at the picture. "Your husband was white." The sound of his voice hurt her ears. "One was good. One was bad. Stop judging people by the color of some old ancestor. I am going to marry Genvieve. Not

Martine. If you can't accept that, well…" He stormed to the entry, turned, gave her a hard look, and slammed the door behind him.

Marie-Thérèse stood in the middle of her living room. She heard the peas boiling in their pot. The time had come for a stir, she was certain, but for the life of her, she could not direct her feet into the kitchen. And if, on their own, they did decide to move to the stove, her head showed no signs of enlightening her on what to do once they got her there.

Martine, Collette, Papa, the man she'd married—all swirled in her brain. How could she be wrong? Like dear Papa, she only wanted the best for her children. She pushed one stiff leg after the other into her kitchen. Her hand reached for the spoon. At first she couldn't tell where the thump came from—her heart, her head, or the door.

"Marie-Thérèse," the deep baritone boomed. "You in there?" The thump came louder this time and turned into a knock.

She dropped the spoon onto the stove, barely missing the flame. She knew that voice. Her legs fired into action.

"I am here!" She rushed to the door, afraid to utter his name.

"Well, are you going to let me in or not?" Merriment filled out the baritone.

She flung open the door and reached her arms around Monsieur Lieutenant. "It is you." Her chest touched his. "I am so glad to see you." The tears came.

"Hey." He squeezed her. "I missed you too. OK if I come inside?"

Marie-Thérèse broke the hold. She pressed her hands against her cheeks.

"It's nice to know you're glad to see me. I just didn't know you'd be *this* glad." He grinned.

"It's just that...oh, Monsieur Lieutenant. I'm so glad to see you." She wrapped her arms around him again and kissed his cheek.

He pressed his lips into hers. "Love this welcome."

Her mind flooded back to her. "Oh, Monsieur Michael. I am so sorry for..." She swiped her hands over her cheeks. "I do not want you to see the red eyes on me. Me with the red eyes. It...my Christophe. You know children." She tried to smile, but she was sure it looked more a grimace.

"Don't be sorry." He found her lips again.

She laid a hand between them. "How long you here? In Paris, I mean. Back from the Ardennes." The smell of the chicken-flavored soup assaulted her nose. "I have food. Not grand, but—"

"Slow down there, girl." He sniffed the air. "Whatever's in that pot smells like the best thing that's come my way since Thanksgiving." He tapped his uniform pocket. "I've got a two-day pass. Two whole days. Just for us."

She moved toward the kitchen. Even with her back to him, she could sense him stiffen in confusion.

"What is it, Marie-Thérèse? I know you're glad to see me."

She turned back to him. "Of course I am." She laid both arms across his shoulders. "But if you just arrive, I have the thought that you go first to Madame Glovia's." She shifted her eyes to the medal on his chest as she stalled for time to dig herself out of her befuddlement.

"Glovia? Why would I go there? It's not her I've written every night. It wasn't her I was thinking about every time

I rounded a curve in the road and worried that a Gerry might be waiting to take a potshot at me and my truck. I just prayed I'd live long enough to see you again."

She touched the medal, a wave of warmth working its way down from her face. "I worried me big—I worried a lot when the news come about the trapped Americans. You save them, yes? You and General Patton. Christophe says…"

"Bastogne. Well, maybe the general had a little bit to do with it, but yeah, the Red Ball Express came to the rescue." He laced his hands around her waist and looked into her eyes. "You sure did keep me going in the rough times."

She found his mouth and drew his lower lip into hers. More than the May breeze from the hill at the center of her neighborhood warmed her body. She felt his hands stroke her hips. She laid her face against his neck. She flicked out her tongue. She had never wanted to taste a man's sweat before.

"Let's dance," he murmured as his hands cupped her hips. "All the way to your bed."

A song played over and over in her head as she two-stepped him down her hall. Where had she heard it before? Not from Glovia, she was certain. Maybe from her early days in Paris. No. The sound came from the far away and the long ago. From her own *mère*. A song of love. She backed him into the door leading to her bedroom. She nudged the door open with her leg. He pushed her into the tiny cubicle and against the edge of her bed. With nowhere to maneuver, she stumbled and fell back. Monsieur Lieutenant landed on top of her.

"Mmm," carried on Michael's breath as he slipped open the buttons of her housedress.

Even her extra thirty pounds felt light when he lifted her to push the dress over her head.

"Mons...Michael...I have little practice for this."

He kissed her lips as he unhooked her ancient brassiere.

She tried, and failed, to keep the garment close to her chest as he tugged it off and tossed it to the floor.

"Oh my Lord." Her words filtered in and out of the pounding in her head. Had she spoken at all? She closed her eyes as her serviceable underpants slid past her knees and over her feet.

Her eyelids flickered open and closed in the room lit only by the moon coming through the skylight. She felt his bare chest against her naked breasts. "Oh, *mon Dieu*," she moaned as her nipples rubbed against the coarse hair on his chest.

She felt his mouth, his lips, his tongue, his fingers explore every inch of her body. She tried to lie still, just as she had endured with her Frenchman husband, but her body refused. Each touch, each kiss, each suck burst through her body, screaming pleasure. Her knees spread wider. His body slipped between them. With his every thrust, she answered back twice as hard.

"Gaah..." Only sound came, when she wanted words. "*Oui. C'est parfait. Seigneur Jésus. C'est parfait.*" Words she didn't mean to say poured out of her mouth. Something deep, deep inside, hiding for fifty years, broke free and flooded her soul.

CHAPTER 17

"For a girl with little practice, I'd say you did all right." Monsieur Lieutenant laid his lips against her cheek as the *Bateaux Mouches* drifted under the Pont Neuf. "Better than all right."

"I do not know. I did not mean…" Marie-Thérèse looked down at the river, the flush of her cheeks in contrast to the gray waters of the Seine. "I do not know who that woman was."

She sensed the other passengers around her, many of them couples. They snuggled together, exchanging kisses just as she and Michael did. She leaned against his chest, her ears drinking in the sound of the church bells pealing joy after four long years. At last, victory in Europe.

"This is the oldest bridge in Paris." Marie-Thérèse lifted her eyes to the upcoming bridge, still flashing bits of gilt despite the neglect of German occupation.

"You come here a lot, do you? Should I be jealous?" The teasing in his voice washed into her ears.

"Oh, hundreds of times." She chuckled. "Look at this body." She rubbed her hand over her ample stomach. "Every man in Paris falls at my feet, waiting in line to sweep me onto a boat ride down the Seine." She leaned in close to his ear. "For wild lovemaking."

"I know all about that body." He didn't bother to whisper. "And let me tell you this: I like what I see. I like what I touch, and I especially love what that body can do." His breath warmed her ear. "From now on, just you and me on this river, and under this…this bridge. What did you call it? The pontoon noof?"

"I will teach you French yet." She rubbed his chest. "The Pont Neuf. I think that means New Bridge in your language. And yes, I have come here many times, and with many, many males." She shot him her best impish grin.

"Males? What kind of males?" A bit of the teasing left his voice.

"Why, young ones, for sure." She waited for his reaction, and laughed when he failed to conceal his puzzlement. "My students. I take them to see the river and all the monuments." She sighed. "Do you know that many of my children have lived in Montmartre all their lives, and yet they never sail this river? Never climb the Tour d'Eiffel? Not even visit the Louvre?"

"That's what comes from living in a big city. Now, San Francisco's a different story. Much smaller. I think I've seen just about everything there." He frowned. "Nope. I guess not. Haven't been across that new bridge yet. We call it the Golden Gate." He looked at her. "Marie-Thérèse, that's a sight I want you to see one day. With me."

"*Oui*, Monsieur Lieutenant. I shall book passage to your San Francisco from Le Havre this very afternoon." She snuggled her head into his chest again. "First class, of course." She shut her eyes and reveled in the sound of Monsieur Lieutenant's breathing, the smell of his skin, the crush of his body against hers. A rush of pleasure floated over her. When was the last time she'd had this much fun?

"No." Michael interrupted her reverie. "I'm serious. I really do want you to see San Francisco. It's a little bit like Paris. Montmartre, really. I don't mean all the churches. I mean the hills, but especially the people. Nobody pays a black man all that much attention here. Not in Pigalle. San Francisco's no paradise, mind you, but a colored man can get away with a lot more there than in the rest of America. I guess that's because there's not that many of us."

"Ahh. In Paris, Monsieur Lieutenant, you are an American, and Paris loves its black Americans."

"Well, it's good to be loved somewhere. Don't get me wrong. Colored folks aren't loved in San Francisco, but back home, I can do more than shine shoes. Do you know what I'm saying, Marie-Thérèse? A black man can make something of himself there. Make a decent life, a good life for himself and his family." He watched the boatman steer the bateaux into its docking place. "San Francisco. I think you'd like it."

"I think I like it, too," she mused.

"Marie-Thérèse, I want you to give some serious thought about San Francisco...seeing it, I mean. And me."

The boat bumped into its mooring.

CHAPTER 18

Maman and her old-fashioned ideas. Christophe stepped off the Arc de Triomphe Metro platform. The clock showed three. This was not one of the days he was scheduled to meet Genvieve, but between the war's official end and Maman's morning tirade, he had finally found his answer.

Le Poulet Farsi was still two blocks away. He would have enough time to refine his latest strategy to free Genvieve from her unwanted engagement. Thank God, the restaurant owner and Genvieve's future father-in-law was none the wiser. Genvieve's loose dresses and big sweaters covered what little bit of her belly that showed. Even these nearly three months had not been time enough to adjust to Genvieve's forced betrothal. Best not to dwell on it. Concentrate on their future together, even if Genvieve had rejected all of his previous plans as unworkable. Christophe looked up at the sky. It was that uncommon blue that was Paris in May. That blue that declared all problems, no matter how impossible, could be solved. Maman always told him that there was a softness about the Paris sky, nothing like the glaring, sharp-edged light of Martinique. There it was again. Maman and her old-fashioned ways. But today, she was his salvation.

He stepped across the street, jostled by a fresh crowd of jubilant celebrants. He couldn't tell his mother about the complication, of course. She would never understand

and would use it as fresh ammunition to prattle all the more about Martine. Martine—more a good friend than a lover. He could never imagine himself married to her, just as Genvieve had no future with the man chosen to be her mate. With just steps to the café, Christophe shook his head to clear away images of Maman and Martine and focus on Genvieve.

Every seat but two at Le Poulet Farsi was taken. He rushed ahead of an arm-in-arm couple reading the day's signboard at the restaurant entrance.

"May I serve you, *monsieur?*" The waiter stood, paper and pencil in hand.

Christophe pasted on an attentive face as he glanced at the menu handed him by the white-aproned man. He chanced peeks at the six tables. Genvieve was not outside.

"A coffee, *garçon.*" Christophe spotted her just as she stepped through the doorway, carrying a full tray.

"*Café, monsieur?*" The server waited, a look on his face that dared Christophe to order only coffee.

"A moment, please. But you may bring my coffee now." Out of the corner of his eye, he watched Genvieve. Her ashen face told him she had spotted him. Christophe buried his head in the menu.

"A *café* before your meal?" The waiter looked as though Christophe had just hurled a great insult at the chef.

"Now," Christophe insisted.

"I have dinners to serve. I will give you time to prepare a proper order, *monsieur.*" The waiter stalked off.

Christophe tilted his head to beckon Genvieve. She shook her no and held up one finger as she mouthed "one hour."

"Never, *never* come to Le Poulet Farsi without first asking me." Genvieve hissed her first words at him as soon as they boarded the Metro heading to the ninth *arrondissement.* "You may be recognized."

"Recognized?" Christophe retorted. "I've only been there one other time. You've made certain of that."

"I told you, Christophe, about my...I thought you understood. It just isn't good for you to be seen."

"That's why I had to talk to you." He tried to reassure her with a calming smile. "I know what we have to do."

Her face flashed curiosity, then a strange look of resignation. She stepped ahead of him as the Metro pulled to their stop.

"Genvieve, why aren't we married?" He looked at her stomach. "You're five months now. I know you're barely showing, but your betrothed's father is going to become curious soon enough. And now that this war is over, the Free French... Le Maquis...they will all return home." A lump cluttered his throat, and he reminded himself of the need to hurry.

Genvieve's hand shook as she turned the knob on the door to her cousin's apartment. The door pushed open without a key. "I am afraid for my mother. Without the good will of *monsieur,* she and I will have no way to survive." Genvieve pulled back the curtain of the *appartement* window. The stucco wall of the building next door greeted her. "Push the door closed."

Christophe jiggled the knob. "Your cousin hasn't fixed this lock yet?" He grunted. "Hear those bells? They are ringing all over Paris. You know what they mean, don't you?"

She turned a wan face to him.

Christophe gathered her into his arms. "*Mon cher*, they mean the world will be free again and our lives are about to begin." He brushed his lips across her hair. "Genvieve," he said as he hugged her to him, the little bulge rubbing against his body, "I understand about your *maman*. That you don't want life to be difficult for her. Surely the owner will not take his disappointment out against your mother."

She pushed away. He watched her strain to put on a smile. "Christophe. The most important thing…I want you to know that I love you. Only you, now and always. It is possible that…oh, I wish there were some way to—"

"That's just it, *ma belle*. That's why I had to see you today." He walked her to the bed. "It is a bit complicated, my darling, and it will take a little bit of doing, but you are right. There is no more time." He sat her on the bed. "But there is a way."

She laid her hand over his, tears welling in her eyes. "I fear we have precious little time left for anything."

He brushed her hair from her face and kissed her eyelids as he lowered himself beside her. "It's a bit tricky, but my mother holds the answer."

"*Votre mère?*" She clutched his hand as though he'd lost all reason.

"Yes, my mother. The first thing we have to do is get married. Then…" He felt her fingernails dig into his hand.

"Christophe, we've talked about all this before." Her exasperation was plain as she shook her head. "I've told you marriage is impossible because we can only post marriage bans here in Paris where we live. We can't just go off to a village somewhere and get married. We have to marry where we have legal residence."

"Yes, Genvieve. I know the law. That's the beauty of my new plan. We will marry at the registry office in our home city, a place outside of Paris." He grinned his satisfaction at his own cleverness.

"And how will we manage that? Christophe, we are both residents of Paris. I was born here."

He leaned her head on his shoulder. "But who's to say we haven't moved outside of Paris?"

"Who's to say?" She pulled away. "With the Germans here, no one could move without everyone knowing. Anybody who knows us will know we still live in Paris."

"Maybe. And the Germans are out of France for good." He leaned close to her ear, his body shaking with suppressed laughter. "But tomorrow, you and I will marry outside of Paris. In Giverny." It felt oh-so-good to have finally come upon a solution that was foolproof.

"Giverny? Tomorrow?" she sputtered. "You think we can get married in Giverny tomorrow? But, Christophe, that is impossible. We are not residents of Giverny." She shook her head with so much certainty, he couldn't help but laugh out loud.

"But Louis-Philippe's sister is," he teased. "She's a resident of Giverny." He knew he should end his beloved's consternation. Just a minute more to revel in his own success. He tapped his sweater pocket. "You've heard me talk of Louis-Philippe?"

"Louis-Philippe? Your coworker at the *boulangerie*? So what if his sister lives in Giverny? How does that help us?"

Whenever she got excited, Genvieve's amber eyes sparked shades of burnished gold like the sun setting on a smoke-filled late November day over the Sacré-Coeur. He loved those eyes, but not the confusion building in them. "Louis-Philippe's sister gave me something." He stroked his sweater pocket again. "Well, not exactly her, but a coworker of a friend of hers. Anyway, I…"

"Christophe!" Genvieve commanded. "What have you done?"

He heard the note of panic in her voice. Had he drawn out the teasing a bit too long? He slipped his fingers into the sweater pocket and withdrew two official-looking, wallet-sized cards. "My darling, that's why it's taken me so long. I thought about this plan early on, but I couldn't make all the pieces fit. That is, not until a few days ago. First, I had to scrounge up enough ration coupons to pay, but…" He paused, waiting for Genvieve to throw her arms around him. After all these months, he was finally about to marry the woman he loved!

"What?" Her voice stuck somewhere between a croak and alarm.

The smile left his face so quickly, his cheeks hurt. "Here." He held the cards out to her, his fingers clutching the edges of the precious documents. "Identification cards." He waited for those eyes to dawn appreciation. Instead he saw only growing distress. "You and I are now official apartment dwellers in Giverny. See the stamps? Don't they look official? That's because they are. Sort of." He waited for the good news to register on his beloved's face.

Genvieve swept her eyes from Christophe to the two cards and back again. "Giverny? Marry? Tomorrow?" Blood seemed to drain from her face, leaving her skin the color of old parchment.

He had indeed teased her too long. "No. Not tomorrow, but in three days' time." He noticed she refused to take the identification cards. "First, we take the train to Giverny. Then, with these two precious pieces of paper proving that we are legal, if short-term, residents of Giverny, we get our license at the registry office. Two days after that and we are married. Of course, the ceremony won't take place in a church, and that will kill Maman, but that can come later." He forced a smile. His plan was foolproof, wasn't it? But why wasn't Genvieve shrieking with joy?

"Not in the church?" she said, her voice as drained of color as her face.

That must be it. How could he be so thoughtless? Pregnant or not, every woman longed for a proper wedding. A wedding in a church. "I know it's not what you want. What you deserve. I swear, my angel, I will make it up to you. We will be married in the church one day, the grandest church."

"No!" Her voice came out a shout. "I mean, that's not necessary." She reached her arms around his neck. "All I want is to be with you. I do not need a church. I do not need to be married." She laid her face into his chest. "Let's just leave Paris. You and me. As soon as possible. Let's go to Giverny."

"You don't want a church wedding?" He stroked her hair. "I understand that you are afraid of the father and his wrath." Something nagged at him. He brushed it aside. His wish to tantalize Genvieve with the truth had backfired. Badly. "Yes, *mon amie*, we will leave Paris. On the morning train." He tilted her face to his. "And what do you mean, you don't need to be married? Of course we will marry, because it's all fixed. Our problem...I've worked it out." He rubbed her stomach. "Besides, Maman will want a marriage. With a baby on the way, she'll have no choice."

Genvieve shot a curious look at him. "Your mother? She doesn't know about us."

"I told her this morning."

"*Mon Dieu, non!*" Genvieve screamed the words into his ear.

"It's all right," he soothed. "She forced it out of me, but it was all for the good. That's when I finalized my plan. Don't you see?"

Genvieve shook her head frantically, tears streaming down her face. "I see disaster. I see...oh, Christophe. Your mother will track me down. She will tell everyone about me." She threw herself into his arms.

But instead of happiness, her body shook with fright.

"Of course she won't. We won't tell her we're getting married until after the deed is done. She already knows you're pregnant, and she will just be grateful that her grandchild won't be born a bastard. When I show you to her, along with our marriage certificate, she will soften."

"Soften?"

"That's the beauty of my plan. The final piece came to me this morning. Maman has put money aside for my schooling for as long as I can remember. If I tell her that I can go to medical school right now, she will give me the money."

"Why would she do that? How does that help us?" She trembled.

"Martinique. I will tell her that I can live more cheaply in Martinique, especially with a child on the way. I can attend university there."

"I don't understand." Tears rolled down her face. "You will go to Martinique without me?"

"Of course not. We will go together. You and me. There is no medical school on the island, but the university is a start." He caressed her back. "In four years' time, you, me, and our child can return to Paris. It will be easier for me to get into medical school then. I'll already have a university degree."

The furrow in Genvieve's brow deepened. "I don't need Paris. I don't need to come back. How long before we can go to Martinique?"

"We can set sail for Martinique as soon as shipping resumes. With the war over, that will probably be in the next sixty days."

"Sixty days? But that is too long. I will be showing by then!"

"No, no. My friend, Louis-Philippe, has said that we may share his studio for the next two months until we can book passage. He lives in the eighteenth."

"Live with your friend in the eighteenth where no one can find us? Get passage money to Martinique from your mother?" She lifted her eyes to him. "Can this really work?"

"You must never doubt me, my sweet." He slipped her shirt over her head, her bare breasts tumbling out.

She pressed her body into his.

CHAPTER 19

"Papa. Papa." Alain-Hugo returned his father's bear hug. "It's so good to be back home."

"Wait till I tell your mama. She will make sure all Paris celebrates your homecoming." His father hugged him once more. "Everyone. Everyone!" the old man called out to the crowded restaurant. "Come and see. My son, my Alain-Hugo, has come home!" Tears streamed down his face. "Victory in Europe, they call this May eighth. My son, my Alain, is the reason we celebrate that victory. I can now tell the world. My son is Free French!" His father planted another kiss on his cheek.

"Papa." Alain-Hugo tried, and failed, to break his father's tight hold. "I don't want all this fuss. Everybody fought for France. You, here in this restaurant. The others…"

"Le Poulet Farsi? Fight the Nazis? Oh yes, I swing my chickens by their feet at the Germans." Papa finally released him. "Knocked more than one of them out cold, too." The burly man laughed. "I forget myself. Food. You must be hungry." Papa turned in the direction of several servers coming toward the reunion. "Charlot, Eduard, Jerome, get my boy some dinner. Pile it on!" he bellowed.

Alain-Hugo watched his father bustle to the kitchen, turn, and head back to give him one more hug.

"It looks the same. Better really." Alain-Hugo glanced around the family restaurant as he broke away from Papa's latest grip. He rubbed his three-day growth of beard. He wished he had shaved and changed out of his three-days-worn clothing, but he had been in too great a hurry to come home.

"Sit. Sit." His father tapped one diner on the shoulder, confiscated the man's chair, and ensconced Alain-Hugo.

Except for a few more gray hairs and a deepening furrow line between his eyes, Papa had changed little. The man still took charge of everyone and everything. It had always been so. Alain looked at the restaurant where he had spent most of his growing up years. Even with just the six outside tables and the twelve inside, with Mama's recipes and Papa's cooking, Le Poulet Farsi had provided a decent living for the family. Paris had never looked sweeter.

"Papa." He laid a hand on his father's white shirt. "If all of Paris hasn't already heard you shout out my name, I'd like my meal served by..." Alain-Hugo looked toward the kitchen. "She is here, isn't she? My Genvieve?"

The lines burrowed deeper into his father's forehead. The old man wiped his hands over his apron, then wiped them again as he spotted one of his cooks. "Étienne, hurry up with that chicken." He turned back to his son, a smile fighting, and losing, its place on his face. "Your mama has concocted the most delicious sauce for my rosemary chicken. It—"

"Isn't she at work today?" A flush of concern flooded Alain's chest as Papa talked on. He stared at the waitstaff—all of whom he'd known for years. His wife was not among them.

"She, umm, has not been herself lately." Papa stared at the top of Alain's head.

"Not herself? Has she been ill?" What was his father not telling him?

"No, not really ill. Just a bit…a bit…" Papa's face flushed pink. "Alain, my boy, you have been through so much. First, I want you to eat. Then—"

"No, Papa." He jumped from the chair and headed toward the kitchen. "Genvieve!" he called out.

"She is not here this afternoon." His father showed a halfhearted smile. "Your wife has been a bit anxious. A worry over you."

"Worry over me?" Alain stared at the tiled floor. "I didn't want anyone to…"

"Of course you didn't. It's just this war." His father shook his head. "Your mama and I try to keep Genvieve's mind off what might happen. The dangers. We all worried." He paused. "War times are hardest on the young. Your mama and I, we went through the Great War. We knew the difficulties, the fear, the doing without, but your wife…"

"Did you say she was gone for the afternoon? Where did she go?" Alain-Hugo looked around again.

"After D-Day, it only got worse." His father sobered. "The Germans were desperate. Jumpy. Everything rationed. Less food. More arrests. Strict enforcement of the curfew. It was bad. Until liberation day—the twenty-fifth of August. We… your mama and I could see the strain on your wife's face. When she talked about spending time with her cousin—just two afternoons a week…we could spare her from the restaurant. And if that helped settle her mind, well, we thought it might be a good idea."

"Genvieve is away from the restaurant two afternoons a week?" Alain looked at his father. The photograph of his wife burned through the sole of his shoe. "With a cousin? What cousin?"

"I don't know which one. But when Genvieve said it was important to visit, we realized that your wife's worry over you was not good for her health. She had been a little sick."

"Sick? With what?" Alarm surged in his chest.

"Not really sick, mind you. Just a nervous stomach. I told your mama it came from too much worry. She still gets her fidgety moments, but she is much better now. I thank God."

"Did you say twice a week? With the cousin?" he repeated.

"Alain-Hugo, your wife needed the change." His father stepped out the back door. Alain followed. "I am not a praying man, as you know, my son. But I knew every moment of every day of the danger you were in. My own belly acted up. I crossed myself every time the bells at the Madeleine church called out." He made the sign of the cross. "Things were very bad here in Paris. Not like what you faced out there, but bad."

"Papa, I know you suffered. All France suffered, but if I hadn't joined the Resistance…"

"My son, hear my words: You did what was right. I know that. Genvieve knows that. But sometimes your Mama and I, we forget that your wife is still a girl. What was she? Twenty-two when you married?"

"I know she was young, Papa."

"So much younger than you. Your next birthday, you will be thirty-three, yes? Would you have married her if it hadn't been for this war?"

Jerome stepped to the door, a large platter of food in his hand. He marched toward Alain.

"Take it to the table." Alain-Hugo waved a hand at the middle-aged man who was like an uncle. Any other time he would have kissed the fellow on both cheeks. But the news about Genvieve... "I'll be there soon."

Jerome nodded.

"I married her to protect her, yes. I knew she was young and hadn't quite finished her growing up, but after her father died, she was alone. Just her and her mother. It was better that we married."

"Marrying you was the best thing for her. You helped settle her down, and it was time for you to have a wife. That's why I agreed when her mother suggested the marriage." He lowered his voice.

"Yes, I married her so she wouldn't be alone with the Germans here. But, Papa, I love her. I loved her then and I love her now. I didn't want to leave my beautiful wife, but I had to do what was right. There could be no life for any of us if France stayed under Vichy rule."

"And there is no braver man in all France than you." He laid his hand on Alain's shoulder. "But it is hard for a young bride to understand why her husband would leave her bed after such a short time. Even to save France. That's why your mama and I agreed. It was best to let Genvieve cry her tears to another young voice who could understand her sadness better than two old people."

"Of course." Alain-Hugo rummaged through his mind. "Strange. I only know of one cousin she has ever talked about, but we never went to her place. And I've only seen her once. She worked in a shoe store," he mused. "When is Genvieve coming home?"

"Oh, she is never gone later than curfew."

"Ten o'clock? Curfew is at ten o'clock." Alain-Hugo winced as he stared at his father. "Papa, my wife walked alone at night on streets patrolled by Germans?"

"Of course I don't allow this. I meet her at the Metro station and walk her back to the *appartement*."

"Sorry, Papa. I've been gone a long time. It's just that Genvieve is young enough to take foolish chances." His last meeting with his wife flashed in his head. "She begged me not to leave her."

"Go. Eat your dinner." Papa's face was wreathed in smiles again.

Alain nodded. "Genvieve had no way of knowing I was returning today. Of course she wants to spend time with other young people." If only he knew the cousin's address.

CHAPTER 20

Christophe held Genvieve in his arms as the afternoon light faded. He smiled as she reached out a lazy hand to raise the crumpled sheet to her body.

"*Non.*" He shook his head. "I like to see you naked. Especially now." He leaned over and kissed her belly.

"But not for long." She poked him in the ribs and giggled. "Soon, I will be too big to do this." She gave him her best coy smile.

"I want that day put off until the last second." He marveled at her body. The baby filled out the parts on her that had been a little too thin. He desired her now more than ever.

"You won't want me in a few weeks," she teased.

"I will want you when you are as big as a watermelon." He laid a hand on her breast.

"When we get to Martinique, you will want a slender woman. One who can wiggle her hips at you. By then, I'll be barely able to waddle." She turned her body into his and lifted one leg over his hips. "A few more hours and we are on our way to Giverny." She sighed as her leg squeezed him closer to her.

"In three days' time, you will be Mrs. Christophe Devereaux Brillard," he breathed.

"Martinique. So far away from Paris." Her body tensed as she rose on one elbow. "You are sure your friend will allow us to stay at his place until we can book passage?"

"I'm sure. Of course, I have to pay him something, but I can do that from the money from Maman."

"Your mother?" Genvieve raised full up on one hand, her leg sliding off his body, her face deep in shadows from the wall-facing window. "You promise not to tell her where we are?"

"How can I do that? Maman will insist we stay with her. At least until we sail for Martinique." Christophe frowned. Convincing Marie-Thérèse that a return to the family birthplace was a good thing was not going to be an easy sell. "I'll just tell her we're staying with a friend."

"She won't try and visit, will she?"

"Well, of course she will. I'll ask her to keep our whereabouts to herself."

"No." Genvieve's voice carried the sound of panic. "She mustn't know where we are. Promise me, Christophe, promise me."

"Of course." He felt her body trembling. "If you're that worried about the owner of Le Poulet Farsi finding you, I won't tell Maman." He kissed the tip of her nose. Why was she so worried? "I'll arrange for her to see you someplace else. Maybe at her friend's house." Maman's friend, the American singer. Ensuring Madame Glovia's silence might be an even greater challenge. Still, the woman had worked for Le Maquis right under the noses of the Germans. Literally. She had the talent and skills to keep a secret as well as extract one.

"As long as it is far away from the ninth *arrondissement*."

"You've got it." There was no need to further upset Genvieve. It was not argument he sought right now. "I'll find a place far enough away so that Maman can see you without raising questions. Now let's forget about her, Le Poulet, your betrothed, his father, everything, everyone, except this." He ran his hand along her thigh. "Concentrate on becoming my wife." He pulled her back down to him.

"Enough of this wife talk." She pushed her hand between their two bodies. "Make love to me now." Her hand made little circles on his stomach, moving lower.

Somehow, the orange glow of sunset found its way into the little studio through the dirt-speckled window. Christophe closed his eyes and reveled in the ecstasy of Genvieve's touch. He shivered as her hand stroked him into her body.

CHAPTER 21

It had taken some doing, but Alain-Hugo finally had the address, or rather, the building description. An iron grill covering a blue door with a dolphin for a knocker. Door much fancier than the building, the greengrocer had announced. Alain repeated the phrases over and over as he walked the streets surrounding Genvieve's old neighborhood. He tugged at the scratchy navy blue sweater his mother had knitted for him months ago—a mother's talisman to ensure her son's safe return home.

Iron grill with crude lilies worked into it, Alain suddenly remembered. Crude lilies? How could he have forgotten that detail? Annoyed, he slapped at his thigh only to feel the outline of the boning knife he still carried out of two years' habit.

Blue door, dolphin for a knocker, crude lilies, Alain repeated. He had met the cousin only once. Babette, Nanette, something. The greengrocer couldn't recall her name either. Alain had no clear memory of the plain-looking woman. Unmarried and in her late thirties, what sort of "young talk" could she share with Genvieve? On their one meeting, at the home of Genvieve's mother, Babette-Nanette had struck him as quite dull. The woman mentioned that she lived only two blocks distant and near a butcher shop. His mission, now, was to locate those two blocks.

Of course, he should have waited until ten o'clock tonight and surprised Genvieve at the Metro. But after two long years, four extra hours felt like an eternity. He'd had difficulty describing the cousin to the local shopkeepers. With the bare-bones description of her as a brown-haired, timid spinster who fancied dark, ill-fitting clothing over her plump body, he'd finally hit pay dirt with one of them. The man remembered a woman who wore ugly shoes though she worked in a shoe shop.

Now as Alain-Hugo walked down the rue Choron, he looked carefully for the building where the greengrocer swore he had delivered cabbages to the cousin. It was on the bottom floor, the portly man had assured him; otherwise he would not have troubled himself. After all, *mademoiselle* was not alluring enough to risk a stair-climbing heart attack. The greengrocer had laid a sheepish grin on Alain as he hinted that he clung to the hope that *mademoiselle* would soon realize that he was her best, if not her only hope for... diversion.

Could that be the building? Alain stopped short. There stood a gate, its grilled ironwork formed in the crude shape of a lily. And yes, it did cover a blue door. Alain-Hugo stepped closer. There, on the door, a brass dolphin. A smile crossed his lips as the handle on the gate turned despite, or maybe because of, the rusted keyhole. He stepped inside and looked to his right. The *appartement* house only contained three apartments on the bottom floor, and *mademoiselle*'s studio was by itself, to the right, the greengrocer had explained.

Alain-Hugo felt the increased beats of his heart. Two long years. Not that long without a woman, of course, but none of them had been his wife, his Genvieve. He tried to imagine the surprise on her face when she opened that door. He walked softly across the rose-patterned carpet. He didn't want to spoil the surprise. Within ten feet of the door with its peeling paint, he stopped. Were those sounds coming from the *appartement*? Twittering laughter, groans, heavy sighs, grunts. What was that? He frowned. Damn greengrocer. So smitten with the unlikely prospect of an afternoon dalliance, he had misdirected Alain. This was obviously not the cousin's apartment.

Alain-Hugo looked down at the rug, some holdover from twenty years ago, no doubt. He walked to the opposite side of the entry and stopped at the first of the two apartments on his left. Alain rapped a knuckle on the door. No answer. He tapped louder. Should he call out and spoil the surprise? "Genvieve?" He tried to disguise his voice. No answer and no sound. Alain-Hugo moved to the second door. The carpet here had been worn to the weft. Not at all what the greengrocer described.

Alain tapped the second door. No sound and no answer. He called out again. Nothing. He shook his head. How many blue doors with fancy brass dolphin knockers could there be on the rue Choron? Never mind, he had to find Genvieve. Even if he had to knock on a dozen doors.

He stepped back into the street. He walked to the corner in both directions. No other blue door. He crossed the street and repeated the process. As he surveyed the neighboring houses, only one reflected the burgeoning moonlight—the blue door with the brass knocker. He had to go back in. Maybe the greengrocer, and he himself, had been wrong. Nanette-Babette might have a lover after all. He had to find out.

Alain stepped back through the dolphin-adorned door and turned to his right. Before he had traveled four steps, he heard the unmistakable sounds of a rapidly approaching climax. He swallowed hard. What should he do? Only Nanette-Babette knew the whereabouts of his wife, but to interrupt at such a time was beyond indelicate. He faced the door. Should he attempt another polite knock?

"Oh my God, Christophe. Yes. Yes! That's it."

Alain-Hugo's hand froze in midair. That voice, that strangled guttural sound...it carried a familiarity. He tried to shake new reason into his head. Of course, Nanette-Whoever's voice would resemble Genvieve's. They were cousins after all.

"Uhh. Uhh." An urgent male voice this time.

Alain laid his hand on the doorknob. His mind could not tell him why, but he gave the brown knob a twist. The door inched open. He fought to get his brain to sort out what his eyes saw. A naked man with pale gold skin gyrating atop a figure with the slender legs of a woman. White legs encircled the man right above his hips. White arms wrapped around the man's humping back. Alain-Hugo blinked his eyes to trigger his sleeping brain. That's it. That little bow in the legs. He knew that bow.

"Genvieve?" The word forced itself out of his throat. The sound felt like ice cutting the inside of his mouth. "Genvieve!" he screamed.

The man's body arched in a great leap as the woman under him rolled out. A head full of hair covered her face. Alain stood rooted just inside the door as he stared at the hair. Light brown, the color of caramel. Sun-lightened strands threaded their way through the caramel. He knew that hair.

"Genvieve! My God!" Alain-Hugo rushed to the bed, pushed the naked man to the floor, and jerked the woman to her feet.

The hair fell from the woman's face. Eyes wide enough to take in the whole of eternity stared back at him. The mouth, with its smudged lipstick, fell open. Her full breasts jiggled as she trembled before him, her arms beating the air at her side.

"Genvieve! Genvieve!" Alain-Hugo shrieked. "He's hurt you. He's hurt you!"

The woman's eyes blinked back. Her face flushed, but then turned ashen white. Somewhere in his head, Alain thought he heard another sound. A male sound.

"Genvieve." The sound made words. "Are you all right? Who...who...?"

Alain-Hugo whirled around. The naked man had climbed to his feet, the evidence of his crime still apparent. Alain lunged across the bed and tackled him. They both went down in a heap. Blows to and from the man came at rapid speed. There was blood, but Alain couldn't tell from which one. He heard the other voice. Her voice.

"No! No!" Genvieve screamed. "Stop it!"

Alain had the man around the chest, but his own body was in a headlock. Blows kept coming and going.

"Alain. Wait. Wait. Please..." Her voice faded.

He heard a thump. The man loosened the headlock and Alain-Hugo scrambled to his feet. The intruder tried to follow, but Alain delivered a blow to the fellow's groin.

The man doubled over. Alain rushed to his wife. Genvieve braced herself against the wall, her knees bent, perspiration pouring off her body. Her breasts heaved with each breath she struggled to take; her belly poked out.

"My darling, I'm sorry!" Alain cried. "I am so sorry this has happened to you." Alain felt unfamiliar tears rushing to his eyes. He took off his sweater and slipped it over Genvieve's nakedness.

Her eyes widened as she looked over his shoulder. "Chris—" Fear flooded her face.

Before Alain could turn he felt the man's arm around his neck, squeezing. With one hand, Alain-Hugo tried to pry the arm away before it was too late and he blacked out. He remembered. His hand slipped into his trouser pocket, fumbled for the knife, and slipped it from its sheath. The tempered steel flashed silver.

"Nooooo!" Genvieve's scream was long and keening. "Christophe, he has a knife!"

Alain-Hugo brought the weapon up swiftly and laid it across the golden skin. Blood spurted from the sliced arm.

"Aww!" the man yelled as he released Alain. "Who the hell *is* this?" The man grabbed at his wound.

"Who the hell are *you*?" Alain regained his feet. He pointed the knife at the man. "Genvieve," he said, keeping his eyes on the intruder, "this man...this..." He swallowed as he stepped closer to the man, the knife steady in his hand as it had been so many times when he faced the Germans. "This man has attacked you." His throat felt dry. "But...but..."

Calmness. Coolness. That's what Courageux had taught him in times like this. Let your eyes and ears take in everything. Give your brain time to take in smells and sounds.

Then you will be able to better assess where danger lies. Assess and take action.

"Christophe?" Alain-Hugo spoke out as the man stood dripping blood, still naked, and oddly protective of Genvieve. "You called him Christophe." He waited for her answer.

"Alain-Hugo..." Words strangled in her mouth.

The man with the wounded arm looked past Alain and his deadly knife, straight to Genvieve. "Alain-Hugo? Genvieve, you *know* this man?"

"Know me?!" Alain-Hugo shouted. "You raping bastard, you've just attacked my wife, and for that, I'm going to kill you." Before he could advance a second step toward the golden-skinned man, he felt a woman's body jump on his back.

"No! No!" Genvieve screamed. "Christophe, get out. Get out now!"

The man stood there. All evidence of his previous activity had long since evaporated. His face drained of its golden tones. He worked his mouth, but no words came out.

"Genvieve." Alain tried to shake her off his back. "Who is this man? How do you know him and how did he come to...to ra—attack you?"

"Wife?" The word came out of the man's mouth on a strangled whisper. "You..." The man raised a finger to Alain-Hugo. He seemed oblivious of the knife still in Alain's hand, pinned to his side by Genvieve's knee. "You are...you must be..." He cast a confused look toward Genvieve, who dug her fingernails deep into Alain's shirt.

"Go. Go." Sobs accompanied his wife's pleas as she laid her head into Alain-Hugo's neck.

Her tawny hair brushed the side of his clean-shaven face. Shaved just for her. Alain-Hugo's brain marched itself slowly into formation. He took his free hand and jerked Genvieve from his back. His head threatened explosions with the thoughts pounding through it.

"You." He pointed the knife at the man—Christophe. "Get your clothes and go."

"Please. Please. Please." Genvieve was on her knees, the blue sweater covering her to mid-thigh. "I need to...I will explain."

"Your betrothed?" The man stared. "Genvieve? Is this... is he...?" The man stood there.

"Listen to her!" Alain-Hugo shouted as he walked over to a pile of clothing and kicked them to the bleeding man. "Take these and get the hell out of here."

"Never!" the man shouted. "I'll never leave her alone with you and...that." He pointed to the knife.

"You think...you believe I would hurt her? Get the hell out of here. Now!" Alain-Hugo dropped the knife on the floor within Genvieve's reach. "Now, no knife. Get out and let me see to my wife. You hear that, you bastard? My wife!"

The man gave a slow shake of his head as he used his foot to retrieve his clothing. He stooped and gathered it in his arms. He backed toward the door. "Genvieve, are you sure?"

She nodded her head yes, her hair falling over her face, covering her eyes.

The man stepped through the door and closed it behind him.

CHAPTER 22

Thank God, nothing stood between him and the wall.

Christophe closed his eyes, his hand still on the brown doorknob as he leaned against the wall outside the apartment. He stared at the carpet. The faded pink of the patterned rose now glistened dark red. Or was that blood? His blood? Despite the support of the wall, he felt his knees weaken. They refused to hold him up and he slid to the floor. Christophe stared at the clothes he clutched, now smeared with blood. His blood.

Sound coming through that closed door beat into his ears. Her voice. Genvieve's. "Alain-Hugo, you surprised me."

Now the man spoke, his voice gurgling in his throat: "Genvieve, who was that?"

The pain in Christophe's sliced arm finally reached his brain. He winced and reached for his trousers. Somewhere in a pocket lay the folded handkerchief Maman insisted a gentleman always carry. He pulled out the square of white cloth and wrapped it above the cut. The effort drained his strength. He laid his head against the wall. What was happening? The man, that man. Who was he? Genvieve's betrothed? Her husband? The woman…his Genvieve. No.

"You're home. You're alive." Her voice. "I hoped for so long. Then I doubted. Months, years, and nothing. I missed you."

The man's voice. "Who was that? How do you know this man? He...he called out your name." The voice stammered shock. "And you called him Christophe. Who is Christophe?" The man's voice arced louder. "He can't be a waiter at the restaurant. Papa would never hire such a...and what are you doing here with him?" Panic eased its way around the voice. "In your cousin's apartment. Why is he here? With you. Tell me. Tell me, please."

The sound of footsteps marching across the room assaulted Christophe's ears. To go back inside or not? He slipped a foot into his trousers.

The man again. Genvieve's betrothed. No. Her husband. "This man...he must be your cousin's paramour. Nanette. Babette. I forget the woman's name. The two of them are lovers, right? Nanette and this Christophe. You came here to visit her, your cousin, at the apartment, and he found you here alone." Dread filled the core of the voice. "Then...this *enfoiré*...this bastard raped you." The man's intake of breath was audible even through the closed door. "Genvieve, my darling, my love, my wife, tell me that's what happened."

Wife? Christophe winced. The man's words hurt more than the agony in his arm. Thump. He heard the sound of a body being pulled to its feet. A gasp. Was it Genvieve? Christophe eased himself to standing and fastened his pants. He stared at the brown knob on the door.

"I...don't...know...what...why..." Genvieve's voice barely carried into the hallway. Was she being shaken?

"You don't know why? You don't know what?" The man's voice rose. "But you do know that he is Nanette's lover." Was the man pleading? "He is Nanette's lover, yes? He found you here instead of her and attacked you!"

Breaths caught in Christophe's throat as silence, seconds long and thick as fog, seeped out of the room. Now was not the time to don his shirt.

"Genvieve." The man's voice again, but this time it had dropped low in his throat, lower still as though it came from the center of his gut. "In the name of God Most Holy..." the sound of the man's heavy breathing flowed underneath the shut door, "tell me that you did not let...swear to me that you did not allow that man...did not permit him to...to..." Panic vanished from the voice only to be replaced by tear-threatened cries of pain.

Christophe let out a breath as he reached for his shirt. A vise clamped over his chest.

"I didn't..." Hoarseness almost kept the sound of Genvieve's voice away from the door. "It just...I was alone. I didn't..."

"You didn't?" The man's voice flashed out hope. "He did rape you then? He is Nanette's lover? What I saw...what I heard was not...you with him. It was him. He turned on you. He raped you." A sigh heavy with sorrow escaped from the man. "Wherever he's run, wherever he hides, I'll find the *fils de pute*...the son of a...and kill him."

"No!" Genvieve's scream shook the room. "You don't understand. He didn't..."

"He didn't?" The man's voice climbed two octaves. "No? Yes? Which is it, Genvieve? Did that man attack you or not?"

"I didn't...he didn't..."

"You didn't *what?*" The cry of an animal with a limb caught in a trap burst through the door. "You didn't wait for me? You thought I wouldn't survive the Germans, is that it? You thought I would make you a young widow? A woman free to take a new lover?"

Christophe heard the sound of heavy boots pacing the room. "When we married, I knew you didn't love me all the way, but that was to be expected. Love takes time. A young girl like you does not always know what is best for her. It takes…" The man's voice caught in his throat, his words matching the pacing of his boots.

Alain-Hugo. A name filtered into Christophe's brain. His name? That's what Genvieve had called him. Christophe squeezed his eyes shut as another wave of light-headedness sucked him into its grasp.

Sound gurgled out of Alain's throat. "But you didn't even wait to get word of my death before…"

"I didn't want you dead!" Genvieve's cries rocked the room. "I wanted you to live. To come home. Back to Paris… back to your family…to your mama. To your papa. I never meant for this to happen."

The slap resounded through the door. Christophe braced himself against the wall. The vise in his chest tightened around his thudding heart. "My Genvieve," he whispered as tears stung his eyes. "No," he spoke into the empty hall. She had never been his. Never.

"You were gone so long. Not a word. Nothing." Her words poured out.

"Not a word? Woman, are you crazy? To get word to you would have put your life in danger! Yours and everyone around you. Oh, my God." The sound of the man crumpling to the bed washed into the hallway.

"Alain-Hugo, I worried day and night. I could feel myself dying under the strain." Her sigh was long and drawn out.

"Just for one day. That's all I wanted. Just a day...an hour... five minutes to feel young again. To forget the despair, the fear, the worry, the..." She seemed to run out of air.

The taste of Christophe's salty tears washed into his mouth and mixed with the gush of warm blood flowing over his lips.

Her soft voice floated under the door. "I know...Alain-Hugo, you are a good man. I was prepared to love you. When you came back I promised myself I would learn to... but the weeks turned into months and the months turned into years and...I'm sorry."

Had she slipped to her knees beside him? Christophe stepped into his shoes. His arm throbbed. His chest hurt, and his head reverberated with hammer blows.

"You would learn to love me? Love me and not him? You cannot possibly be in love with him."

"You are my husband, Alain-Hugo." Genvieve's voice regained control.

"That's it? I am your husband. And what are *you*, Genvieve? Just what are you now?" Anger etched deep into every word. "Surely not my wife." Silence gripped the room for several seconds. "Do...you...love him?"

Christophe pushed away from the wall, holding his wounded right arm bent tight against his chest. He struggled to the entry and away from that damned door. Whatever Genvieve answered, he didn't want to hear.

CHAPTER 23

Sweat popped out on Christophe's forehead as he made his way off the Metro, though the early May evening carried its usual chill. Celebrants in high spirits pushed passed him to enter the train car.

"Victory! Victory!" A stranger clapped him on the shoulder.

Christophe braced himself against the pain. Lucky it had been his left shoulder. He clutched his wounded right arm tightly against his chest. He would have to walk two full blocks, and those only if he could first manage the stair climb to street level. His head felt woozy. Could he make it? He slipped his left hand under his jacket and tugged at the handkerchief tied just above his elbow. He pressed the jacket tight against the wound. How many more steps?

He couldn't go home, for sure. What could he tell Maman? Collette could help, but she spent most of her time with Jean-Michel these days and wouldn't be at the apartment. Even though it was his night to work, the *boulangerie* would ask too many questions. He had too few answers. He stumbled as he stepped off a curb. An ancient taxi whizzed by with just a foot to spare. His eyes glazed as he stepped up on the pavement. Christophe struggled to keep his feet under him. There was the house. Her house. Just a few more steps.

"Martine. Martine." He struggled to find the breath to call out her name as he kicked the door.

He heard scrambling inside, latches being undone, the knob turning.

"Who…" The door opened. "Christophe?" Martine's face looked puzzled. "What are you doing? Oh my God."

His knees failed him. Christophe used the doorframe to brace himself. "Martine," he whispered, "I need you."

Martine's face turned pale underneath the brown tones of her skin. "My God, Christophe. What is it? Come in. Come in." She grabbed at his right arm.

Christophe felt his feet ease out from under him. The door and Martine disappeared.

At first, her voice came from a great distance through darkness. He blinked his eyes, and tiny shafts of light entered his world. Martine's face filtered into view. The one thing that made her almost pretty, the to-the-soul clarity in her dark brown eyes, was absent. "Ohh," he managed as he looked around at his surroundings. He lay sprawled on Martine's worn, green settee.

"What's happened to you?" Martine yelled as her fingers lifted the jacket. "Mary, Mother of Jesus!" she exclaimed. "What…what?" Fright shone from her eyes.

"A wound…a knife…can you help?" He tried to sit, failed, and slumped back into the settee.

"A knife wound? You've been stabbed?" Martine jumped back when she pulled the jacket away. "How?" She squeezed her fingers shut, opened them, and tackled the bloodied handkerchief. "Wait." Martine ran toward the back of the apartment.

Christophe looked around, grateful that Martine's parents were not at home. But they wouldn't be. Both immigrant parents worked the night shift at the factory. Martine scurried back with the emergency kit all Parisians had secreted away. The Germans could be depended upon to let a Parisian die in an emergency.

"Here. Take this." Martine poured a small amount of the carefully hoarded brandy into a glass and handed it to him. "Drink that down." She made swift work of untying the handkerchief.

"*Merci*," Christophe managed.

Martine opened the emergency kit and removed the alcohol. She took a square of gauze, dampened it, and dabbed the cloth on the wound.

"Ahh." Christophe fought a scream. "More brandy," he croaked.

Martine poured a half glass more. She unrolled adhesive tape and cut it into strips. She squeezed the edges of the cut together and laid a line of strips across the slice.

"Now for the infection." She spoke more to herself than to him. She splashed more of the alcohol over the wound.

He couldn't fight it. His scream erupted into the room.

"It can't be helped, Christophe!" Martine proclaimed as she checked the strips. "Now, this." She reached for a brown sack, tied at the top.

The item resembled nothing Christophe had ever seen in an emergency kit.

"What is that?"

"For the infection. Special roots from Senegal. Ground up. My mother says my African grandmother used it all the time back in Dakar." Martine mixed the powder with iodine and doused the concoction over his arm. "Worked every time, too."

"More brandy, please. I promise I will replace it."

"Uh-huh. Christophe, you've been in a fight. It's not just your arm. Your nose is bloody, your lip cut, bruises every-where. What happened?"

"Martine, I need just a few hours' rest. I'll be all right, I know I will."

"Oh, you'll get some rest all right. Let me make up this stew." She opened another mysterious packet. "It has restorative powers. Both my *grand-mères* swore by this one. I'll get you out of here before my parents come home in the morning and take you to your *maman*." She cocked her head toward him. "Why didn't you go there in the first place?"

"A fight. The celebration. You know, Victory in Europe Day, and all that." He ran out of breath.

"No, no." Martine shook her head. "You've never been in a knife fight in your life, and you've been in plenty of crowds. This is something else." She walked to her kitchen. "What I want to know, Christophe Brillard, is why did you come to me?"

CHAPTER 24

"Baby, I've gotta tell you something." Monsieur Lieutenant sat on the edge of her bed as he laced his boots. "I guess there's no easy way to say this."

"Collette has come home?" Marie-Thérèse's heart quickened as she stared at the skylight. "And found us like this? *Mon Dieu.*"

The sky was still dark. She had willed herself to awaken half an hour before sunrise and Christophe's return from the bakery. Last night, Collette had announced, in tones loud enough to alert the entire *appartement* building, her intention to spend the night "with friends." Marie-Thérèse and Monsieur Lieutenant would be alone all night. Had Collette changed her mind?

"No. It's not Collette." He reached for his shirt as he turned to face her. "She's not here."

Marie-Thérèse squinted at the watch on his wrist. "Your clock tells me it is not yet six. No Christophe until closer to seven." She propped herself up on a pillow. "What do you have to tell me?"

"It's not about your kids." He slipped a button through its opening. "I knew it was coming. I even volunteered to stay after my unit…" He laid a hand on her cheek. "Oh, Marie-Thérèse, I really don't want to…"

"You're going home. Back to America." She stared at Monsieur Lieutenant. She'd prepared herself for this moment. When his letters turned serious, she knew they, and he, wouldn't last forever. She just hadn't thought he would be lying beside her when she had to face the inevitable. She promised herself she wouldn't cry when the end came. After all, she'd been the lucky one. What other fifty-year-old woman had been loved so well these past months? And by a man inviting enough to attract Glovia Johnson.

"My unit shipped back last week. I told the Colonel I could stay here and help with the mop-up. But now, with VE Day..." He leaned over and brushed her lips with his. "I got my orders yesterday morning."

"Yesterday? You didn't tell me." She blinked back tears and berated herself. She was far too old to cry. "Monsieur Lieutenant," she forced gaiety into her voice as she sat up, clutching a corner of the sheet, "you go back home. Enjoy your son." She stopped and willed away that catch in her throat. "Enjoy..." She lost her battle. The tears flowed.

He pulled her into his arms and stroked her back. "That's just it, I can't enjoy a thing without you." He mashed her breasts against his chest in the tightness of his hug.

"You will. You will." Sobs shook her body. "You have your son. You have your San Francisco. Soon, you will find a wom—" She grabbed him around the neck. What had happened to her plan?

"That's what I want, too," he murmured in her ear as he clung to her. "Find a woman...a good woman."

A fresh torrent of tears rolled down her cheeks. Her brain flashed condemnations at herself. She'd so often

193

practiced this moment. She had to stop this foolishness. Now. "Of course that's what you want. A good woman." She loosened her grip. "And you have left me satisfied for a life-time." The tears threatened again, but she bit down on her lip. "If you please, I will keep your letters."

"My letters?" He grinned. "You're going to have quite a stack since I'm going to write you two a day from now on."

"Write me more? Monsieur Lieutenant, please no." Marie-Thérèse blinked her eyes shut. She could make her-self say good-bye without complete humiliation. Just barely. But hearing about his exploits in America...that she could not do. "At least, no writing, right now. I think it best if we say our *adieux* here. Right now."

"*Adieu?* Good-bye? Well, just for a while, darling. I don't know how long these things take. I talked to the colonel last week and he said the paperwork could take awhile."

"What paperwork?" Marie-Thérèse fingered the sheet at her chest.

"You know, the stuff we have to sign to get you to America. Something about a morals clause. All kinds of stuff that doesn't apply to me or you."

"America? Me?" She felt her lower jaw go slack. "What do you say?" She wasn't sure if her mouth had just spoken French, English, or Martinique patois.

"I'm doing a bad job of this, huh, baby?" He smiled. "OK. I know I'm getting ahead of myself, but here goes." He slipped off the edge of the bed and dropped to one knee. "Now, I'm not as young as I used to be, but I'll give this bended knee thing a shot." His smile broadened.

"What do you do?" Marie-Thérèse dropped the sheet as she sat upright in bed. Her breasts lay bare. "What..."

"Oops." Michael laid out a fake grimace. "I better get up and get that picture of your father. I guess I have to ask his permission, too." Monsieur Lieutenant laughed as he looked at her face.

Marie-Thérèse guessed she must be a sight worthy of laughter. There she sat, naked to the waist, her mouth open and her eyes bulging, wondering what this man she loved so desperately was about to do. "Permission?" She reached for the sheet.

"I need yours first." He sobered. "Marie-Thérèse Brillard, will you do me the honor of...of thinking about becoming...my wife?"

Marie-Thérèse's inside clock told her it was still too early for dawn, but light bathed the room. Monsieur Lieutenant Michael Collins's face shone. She'd watched his mouth move. Her ears heard sound come out of that mouth. Her brain had even written that sound into understanding in her own mind.

"Wife? You...you...want me...to think...to?" Why couldn't her brain let her answer?

"Woman, will you think about marrying me or not?" He laughed aloud. "I'm not going to push you. I know we haven't known each other all that long. But I do want you to think about it." He grimaced. "Uggh. My knee is getting stiff down here."

"Think about...you want me to think about getting married...to your knee? You?"

Michael titled his head while his lips twitched. "Well, the general idea is to marry all of me, not just my knee." He reached into his shirt pocket. "Double oops. No wonder you're acting so surprised. Here." He held out a ring.

195

"Monsieur…Michael, that is a ring. Rings are for young girls. My Collette. Christophe's Martine."

"Well, this one's a 'think about it' ring." He grunted his way back to the edge of the bed. "Take it, woman. That diamond cost me two whole months' pay."

"Pay? You want me…me, Marie-Thérèse, to…to ring me…to think…you?"

"Well, something like that. You don't handle surprises very well, do you?" He grinned. "Marie-Thérèse, what I want most in this world is you with me in San Francisco."

She heard the banging on the door before she heard the voice.

"What? Who? Is that you, Christophe?" Marie-Thérèse stared at the lieutenant, who turned a puzzled face back to her.

"Madame. Madame Brillard. It's me. Martine. Please let me in."

What was Martine doing knocking on her door at six thirty in the morning? Marie-Thérèse stared at the lieutenant, the diamond still in his hand.

"You want me to see to it?" He looked as puzzled as she felt.

"No!" Marie-Thérèse shouted. "My *peignoir*, Michael."

"*Madame*, if you could hurry." Martine's voice was urgent.

Marie-Thérèse struggled into the see-through nightie. She had no time to search for the matching gown that Michael had given her. She hurried to the door and slid it open.

"Maman, don't say a word." Christophe stood in the doorway, his left arm draped over Martine's shoulder. "There's been a small accident, but with some sleep, I'll be all right." His voice sounded drowsy, drugged.

"An accident? What sort of accident? At the bakery?" Marie-Thérèse stepped aside as Martine tried to marshal

Christophe into the apartment. "Michael? Michael!" she screamed out, her heart doing flip-flops.

"What's happened?" The American bounded out of the bedroom, saw Christophe, and snatched him from Martine's shoulder.

"I've cut my arm is all." Christophe tried a wan smile. "At the bakery. I just need rest."

"I gave him a sleeping potion. That's why he's a bit wobbly on his feet." Martine nodded her head to her words.

"A sleeping potion?" Marie-Thérèse looked from Christophe to Michael to Martine and back again. "What were you doing at the bakery?"

"Maman, mmm, perhaps your old robe. I'm fine." Christophe leaned on Michael.

"I'm getting you to your room." Michael aimed Christophe down the hallway.

Martine removed her jacket and laid it across Marie-Thérèse's shoulders. "Here. Slip this on."

"Oh. Martine, I don't care about any of that. What's happened to my son? What sort of accident?"

"Here's some more of the powders I got from my kit. Just keep slathering this on the wound. And this one." She managed to hold out a grungy burlap bag without taking her eyes off some spot at the top of Marie-Thérèse's living room window. "Two tablespoons in a cup of chamomile tea. I've got to get home before my parents return." She hurried through the open apartment door, slamming it behind her.

Marie-Thérèse rushed to her son's bedroom. Michael already had Christophe on his bed. As she approached, Monsieur Lieutenant closed the door between them.

"Give us a moment here, babe," Michael called out.

"But…" she protested.

"Give me a second, hon. I just want to check the wound. You can come back in a minute."

Marie-Thérèse fumbled with Martine's jacket, threw it to the floor, rushed to her bedroom, and pulled out her serviceable flannel robe. She heard low voices coming from Christophe's room. She hurried back and flung open the door.

"I don't want Maman to—" Christophe's head jerked when Marie-Thérèse plunged into the room. "Maman." His words were slurred.

"What don't you want your *maman* to do?" She stepped toward his bed, only to be blocked by Michael.

"Your boy's asked for some more brandy. Let's get it for him." Michael grabbed her arm and steered her into the hallway. He closed Christophe's door behind them.

"*Non. Non. Je dois voir mon fils, mon…*" In her worry, she'd spoken French. "I must see Christophe. How bad?" Tears muddled her English.

"Let's step away from the door and get that brandy." Monsieur Lieutenant steered her into the kitchen. "I think this is where you keep your liquor." He pulled back the gingham skirt from the shelf.

Marie stood in the center of her kitchen floor, her eyes darting between Michael, her stove, and the burlap bag in her hand. She watched Michael retrieve the glad-to-see-you-again gift bottle of cognac he'd given her yesterday morning.

"Honey, your boy's going to be OK." He pulled the stopper and poured a half glass.

"Michael. Michael? Christophe?" Marie-Thérèse squeezed her fingers. "What's happened?"

"Look, I don't want you to worry yourself, and I don't want you to worry the boy. This was no bakery accident, but you don't need to know any more than that." He looked at her clutched fists. "Did I hear that girl talk about some sort of powders? Don't know if they'll work or not, but I can get my hands on some medications from the medics back at the base."

"You have medicine? To help Christophe?" Her mind clicked into gear. Marie-Thérèse remembered where she kept the chamomile. She turned on the flame under the pot. "There are things he doesn't want me to know?" She looked at Michael.

"It's about a woman, of course. Look, Marie-Thérèse, I commanded a whole platoon full of twenty-two, twenty-three-year-old guys. Remember, we spent two years in England before D-Day. With these kids, it's always about a woman." He poured water into the pot. "A scuffle here. A scuffle there. Sometimes a fella gets a little the worse for wear, and your boy's got a cut on his arm. He'll have a bit of a scar, but his arm's going to heal just fine." He hugged her.

Marie-Thérèse let her body melt into his arms. She closed her eyes and let her mind drink in relief.

"Now, here's what I want you to do." His voice soothed. "It's not your boy's arm you need to worry about. You've got to help your son get over a broken heart. And *that* you've got to do without too many 'I told you so's.'"

She looked up at him and stroked his cheek as fresh tears formed.

"Now, I'm going back to the base and pick up the supplies. Not sure I can get back here, Marie-Thérèse." His face saddened for an instant. "If I can't do the job myself, I'll have a courier get them to you, but your boy will have them by this afternoon."

She nodded her head. She knew what came next. "When do you leave, Monsieur Lieutenant?"

"Tomorrow." He stroked her face. "That's the end of my two-day pass. Say my good-byes in Paris, then ship home."

"Tomorrow," Marie-Thérèse repeated.

Michael reached into his shirt pocket. "Take care of your boy." He took her hand. "And this ring." He slipped it into her left palm and kissed her.

CHAPTER 25

The gauze covering his forearm drifted in and out of his vision like a white curtain. Only it was much too thin and let in too many images. He wanted wool. Deep. Thick. And dark. Christophe clamped his eyes shut. That was worse. He opened them to stare back at the fresh dressing Maman had applied to the wound before she left for work. To look or not to look? It seemed to matter little. Each throb in his arm brought everything back to him as fresh as last week. The apartment...that room where...

He reached for the glass of chamomile tea Maman had left for him on the kitchen table. He squinted an eye at the gingham-covered shelf. Only one bottle of cognac left from the four the American had sent over as his good-bye present to Maman. A bottle on the kitchen shelf, and a half-filled one hidden under his mattress.

"She's gone. Finally." His sister announced Marie-Thérèse's departure, as their mother's footsteps clattered down the staircase.

"Close the shutters, Collette. The sun hurts my eyes." Christophe glanced down at his right arm laid across the kitchen table. He ran his hand along the fresh gauze.

"Nonsense. You've been cooped up here for a week now. That army medic Maman's paramour sent over says you're fine to go back to work next week."

His sister's forced brightness had long since grated on his nerves. "I don't need you to babysit me. I don't need Maman always hovering. I don't need that damn medic telling me when or why I should go back to work." Christophe slapped his arm against the table, and a stab of pain grabbed him. "Damn it! I don't need any of you!" he shouted, jumping from the chair. "Will you get it into your head that I want to be left alone?" He started toward the hallway, but Collette blocked his path.

"Christophe, you've got to come back to life. I know you won't tell Maman what happened, and you didn't tell Martine, but you can tell me." She stood there, waiting.

"Nothing happened. Damn it. I had an accident." He glared at his sister. "Get back to your man. Your Jean-Michel."

"But he is why I need you back in this world. I have to talk to you." She kept her eyes trained on him. "I want my big brother to help me."

"Help you?" Christophe felt the bile rushing to his throat. "I can't help anybody." That face filled out his mind again. Her face. Genvieve. He clutched his stomach with his good hand and blinked.

His sister's image brushed away that other one. Genvieve. But Collette's eyes reflected disappointment and worry. She wanted help. He couldn't help anyone. There was a time when he would have leaped to Collette's aid. He had sided with her when their mother was being her usual impossible self about Jean-Michel. Then, he had been able to do anything. Not now. He laid a hand on Collette's shoulder and gave her a gentle push. He plodded by her toward his bedroom.

"I know this trouble is not about Martine." She raised her voice as she followed close behind him. He could feel her breath on his neck. "Your girlfriend thinks it's about another woman."

"Shut up, Collette." He lowered himself onto his bed, careful of his injured arm. "Please, please, if you want to help me, bring another cognac." Anything to get her out of the room.

Darkness and liquor had been his only solace these past seven dreary days and bleak nights. He had no interest in the world or anything in it. Christophe wanted his mind to blank away every image. He settled on his back, his left arm covering his eyes.

"No more cognac." Collette lowered her voice. "I can't honestly tell you I know how you feel." Silence filled the space between them for long seconds. "I never want to feel that much pain. I'm so sorry for what's happened." Sniffles cut off her words.

Christophe lifted his arm enough to peek at his sister. "No, I'm sorry, Collette." He clenched his eyes shut. He was in hell. But his sister shouldn't be. "What about Jean-Michel?"

He felt Collette sit on the edge of his bed. "I think Maman has softened."

"Umm," Christophe managed.

"I mean since the American…"

"The American? He's gone back home. Maman is out in the cold, too."

"No. Just the opposite. Whatever that man said, or whatever he did, it's worked miracles on Maman. She's almost human now. For months she hasn't given me the Martinique evil eye every time I step out the front door." Collette leaned toward him, careful not to jostle the bed. "I think he's soft-ened her up. That's why I…we…now is the time for me and Jean-Michel."

"The time for?" Christophe tried to maintain his inter-est, but he yearned for solitude and the hidden cognac.

"Christophe, Jean-Michel and I…we want to post the banns this Sunday. We want to get married."

"What?" Christophe raised himself in the bed, putting weight on his right arm. "Uhh." The pain caused him to fall back against his pillow. "Jean-Michel…he's proposed mar-riage to you?"

"Of course, to me." A little smile played across Collette's lips.

"But he must know that you are…"

"You sound just like Maman," Collette shot back, some of the old fire in her voice. "He knows I've got an African grandmother. From Martinique. I've even pointed Maman out to him. She didn't see him, of course." Collette giggled.

"But what of his family? His parents? What do they say about him marrying a girl from the West Indies?"

"You *are* Maman Number Two!" Collette jumped from the bed, hands on her hips. "*They* think I am what I am. Like Josephine Bonaparte. I've got a French father and a French grandfather, after all."

"Do they know about Maman? How difficult she really is?" Christophe eased himself to sitting, favoring his right side. "Collette, you aren't…you aren't…?"

"I'm not what?" She stared back at him.

Christophe licked his lips. The image of Collette with a swelling belly had burst into his head full force. "You are not *enceinte*, are you?"

He heard the gasp and saw her eyes widen at the same time. "*Mon Dieu, non*. Maman would kill me if she...oh, no, no, no."

Christophe's head threatened to burst with the image of the full belly on Genvieve. A full belly. Caused by him. Bile piled up in his throat and refused to leave.

"Christophe, what is it?" Concern marched back onto Collette's face. "I'm not...oh my God." She dropped to the bed.

Christophe read his sister's face. She reflected the shock, surprise, and pain he had felt these past days.

"That woman, the one Martine thinks is your new woman...*mon Dieu*...it's true! You do have another woman, and she...she's pregnant." His sister made a sudden move toward him and stopped. She shook her head. "Oh, Christophe, what happened?" Collette turned toward the bedroom door, nodded when she saw it shut, and looked back at him. "You've got to tell me, Christophe. If there's a child, you've got to tell me, now."

She had always been his baby sister. It had been his job to look after her. On the boat sailing from Martinique to Paris, when the four-year-old got too close to the open stairways in steerage class, he had been the one to pull her back with the strength of his six-year-old arms. Christophe felt unwelcome tears forming. He had always been the big brother, and now...

"I can't." He could barely whisper.

His little sister took his right hand and held it between her two. "Yes, you can. This is what this is all about." She waved one hand over his bandaged forearm without touching it. "It's not about the cut. The American medic said it will heal without a problem. It's about a woman and your baby—" Collette jerked her hand to her mouth. "Oh my God. I'm going to be an aunt. And Maman…" Collette started to laugh.

"Stop it. Stop it!" The pain in his chest cut deep. "Nobody's going to be anything because she's…she has…"

The man's face, Genvieve's face, the flash of the knife, all paled beside that word. That one word coined straight in hell. *Husband.* How could he tell Collette? How could he tell anyone?

"No, I won't stop it," Collette insisted. "What's happened? Why aren't you elated?"

"It's too complicated. You would never understand."

"Complicated? She…Christophe…" Collette sat stock-still on his bed, her eyes staring hard at him. "This woman isn't married, is she?"

He pressed in on his eyes until they hurt. No good. Spirals and streaks of light carried her image with it. Genvieve. He lifted his left hand and stared at his sister. His throat clogged dry, his eyes moist. He managed a tiny nod.

"*Mon Dieu.*" She laid her head on his chest and patted at his heart. "Christophe," her voice choked with tears, "we've got to make this right."

His left hand stroked her hair just as he'd done when the arm fell off her rag dolly when she was seven. "There's… there's no way." He shut his eyes and tried to will the darkness to overtake him.

She pushed up from him. "Christophe, if this child is your blood, then we must *find* a way." Collette looked and sounded as though she had come first in the birth order.

He shook his head. "I don't know. I don't see…"

"You're sure this child is yours?" Collette's voice took on the down-to-business tone of Maman's. "Not the husband's? You're sure?"

"I'm sure." The picture of the man swirled in his head again. Christophe struggled to mouth that dreadful word, but no sound emerged. He swallowed. "He was away months…years, perhaps. With the Resistance. I didn't know. I can't be sure."

"You're not sure of what? You didn't know what?" Collette cocked her head. "That he was with the Resistance? Two years and this woman never told you that her…oh my Lord." She paled beneath the tan tones of her skin. "It's not the Resistance. She never told you that she had a husband!"

"Not until that night." The words scratched his throat.

"So that's it." Collette tossed her hair. "I've got to see her. Talk to her. How could she…how…?"

"No!" Christophe shouted. "I don't want that. I don't want you anywhere near—"

"But the baby. Your baby. My niece. My nephew. Maman's…"

"Especially no Maman. I don't want her to know about the husband." Christophe sat up in bed. "Don't you see? It's best this way. I have no claim on Gen—on the woman or the child. If her husband takes her back, then…" A throbbing light stabbed just behind his right eye and thrust Genvieve's face into his head.

"Christophe?" Collette wore a look mixed with puzzlement and fright.

Genvieve. She had forced her way into his head again. But this time she brought something different: her mouth formed his name. A spark, but more a plea, swam in those amber eyes. Did she want something more of him?

"Ahh...what?" That the words had escaped his mind and into the space between him and Collette struck him when he looked at his sister.

"Christophe?" She drew out his name in a low, soft tone—the same one Maman used whenever he'd fallen off his bicycle and cracked his head.

"Collette, stay out of this." He couldn't focus on Collette right now.

Suppose, just suppose, the husband refused to take her back? Perhaps Genvieve was calling out to him. Calling him to help her. Did she...could she want him and their baby, after all?

He measured his words as air forced its way into his lungs again. "Let me sort this one out." Christophe blinked, and the light behind his left eye disappeared. Along with the darkness he'd sought just a few seconds ago.

CHAPTER 26

Marie-Thérèse smelled the cinnamon a half block from the *boulangerie*. Cinnamon, a spice she hadn't enjoyed since before the Germans devastated Paris. She had francs enough for a treat for Christophe. Not that a cinnamon croissant was going to save her boy. That was her job, and she was on her way to do just that. She'd already queried Martine, and though the girl had played closed-lip, Marie-Thérèse had sorted out that woman involved was that Genvieve. Questioning Collette had yielded nothing, and Christophe had lain in bed all these last seven days and nights, looking like death flapped her wings especially for him.

She approached the open door of the bakery. Her answer lay somewhere inside that building, and she was determined to drag the truth out of Louis-Philippe.

"Madame Brillard?" Louis-Philippe stood in the bakery's back room, his apron smudged with red stains, his arms covered with a light dusting of flour. They were alone.

"Close your mouth, Louis-Philippe. Don't you think I know you've been sneaking to my house every day to see my Christophe? I leave for work and you are in." The patois slipped in and out of her words as she held up the hand-rolled cigarette the young ones made and smoked. "My son does not roll the ends of his cigarette papers like this." She shook the evidence in his face. "Only you."

"*Oui. Non.*" Louis-Philippe's eyes darted around the room. "Madame Brillard."

"No. You don't get out of this place until you tell me what I want to know." She stood flat-footed in front of the back door leading to the alley. If the boy tried running through the front, she would scream loudly enough to alert the customers of an assault.

"But, *madame*...I know nothing." He shook his head so fast, Marie-Thérèse was afraid his white baker's cap would fly to the floor.

"Oh, you know a lot." She advanced on the hapless boy, who was at least four inches shorter than her son. "Start by telling me where I can find this woman."

"Woman?" Louis-Philippe looked close to fainting. "Martine? You mean Mar—" He bobbed his head faster than the rat-tat-tat of a German gun.

Marie-Thérèse grabbed a baguette of freshly baked bread and tapped it on the flour-covered worktable. "I'll start by breaking this bread, then I'll go to the strawberries there. I'll smash every one under my feet. Then you tell your boss how you ruined his tartlets for the entire day. Now where is she?"

Louis-Philippe blanched almost as white as the vat of flour standing next to the worktable. "No. Please, *madame!* I need this job. I only went to see Christophe because... because..."

She broke the baguette in half.

"Oh, please no, *madame*." He reached for the colander of strawberries standing on the counter by the sink, about to be washed.

Marie-Thérèse swept the container from his hand. She tipped it to the side. One strawberry fell to the floor. "Where do I find this Frenchwoman?" she demanded.

Louis-Philippe clasped both hands together. "I worry about Christophe. We've worked here together for the whole four years. The whole time the Germans…"

She tipped two more strawberries to the floor.

"All right. All right, *madame*. Christophe, it's just that he…he doesn't want…" A quick flash of relief flooded the baker's face. "He'll tell you, Madame Brillard! I mean, Christophe wants to tell you himself." He reached out a hand for the colander, a hopeful smile on his face.

Marie-Thérèse dumped half the strawberries on the floor. She lifted the sole of her shoe over a clump of berries.

"*Madame!*" Louis-Philippe screamed. "Genvieve. Her name is Ge—"

Marie-Thérèse dropped her shoe onto the strawberries and ground them into the floor. Red juice squished out and spread in a widening circle. "You fool. I already know that tramp's name. Where can I find her?"

"You know her name?" Louis-Philippe sounded unbelieving.

"Are you planning on making strawberry crêpes today or not? Because if you are, I suggest you hurry up and tell me what I need to know before I have to leave for my Metro train."

Louis-Philippe looked resigned. "I did not know Christophe had already told you. Then, I suppose…"

"Louis-Philippe!" Marie-Thérèse barked. "I also know that the woman is *enceinte*."

A fresh wave of surprise washed over the baker's face. "He didn't know, you see. He wanted to marry her." He looked at Marie-Thérèse. "Of course, he knew there might be a few…difficulties. That's why I…"

Marie-Thérèse struggled to keep the surprise off her own face. If she could bluff Louis-Philippe into telling her what he thought she already knew, then maybe she could get her answers. "I only wanted what was best for my son. Marriage to a Frenchwoman, well, you know that might be difficult, eh, Louis-Philippe?" She softened her tone.

"Not to Christophe. He was all set to marry her." The boy turned earnest eyes on Marie-Thérèse. "He didn't even know until last week, that day when he was stab—got hurt. The guy just walked in. Just like that. Christophe and Genvieve, they were…they were…well…" Louis-Philippe's face reddened as he suddenly occupied himself dusting the flour off his arms.

Marie-Thérèse felt her stomach and her heart do their thump-gurgle dance again. She nodded her head at just the right angle she thought would convince Louis-Philippe that he was repeating old news. She practiced her next words in her head. They had to be just right.

"My poor boy," she began. "How should he know that Genvieve had another lover? My poor boy."

"I wish to God that's all this guy had been." Louis-Philippe shook his head as he babbled on. "Can you believe she didn't tell him? Her pregnant and everything. Christophe had no idea the woman had a husband. Of course, she—"

"Husband?!" The word flew out of Marie-Thérèse's mouth. "The French one had a *husband*?" Horror broke into her head. "My Christophe never knew the woman had a husband?"

"I thought you…you told me you knew." Surprise matching her own swept across Louis-Philippe's face.

"Where is the slut? You tell me now!" Marie-Thérèse stomped every strawberry she could reach.

"Near the Metro stop at the Arc de Triomphe!" Louis Philippe screamed as he dropped to his knees and scrambled to save what errant berries he could.

"What street? What street!" she yelled.

"I don't know. I swear, *madame*, I do not know. But she works at a restaurant. I think it's called the Farsi something. It's two or three blocks from the Metro stop." He scooped ten strawberries to safety.

Marie-Thérèse reached into her purse and withdrew a franc note. She tossed it on the worktable. "Go buy some more strawberries. I'm late for work."

CHAPTER 27

"Maman, have you been listening to me?" Collette cocked her head toward their mother. "It's all right with you if Jean-Michel and I post the banns this Sunday?"

Christophe took a bite of the vichyssoise Maman had prepared for dinner. He didn't question why his sister wondered if their mother had heard a word the girl had spoken. The woman had not taken her eyes off him for the past hour. No wonder. Louis-Philippe had visited him and confessed. At first Christophe had lashed out at his coworker, but in recent days he had refined his options. Perhaps Maman could be helpful after all.

"Post the banns, you say?" Maman frowned, but continued to focus on him. "Christophe, this is your first night back to work. Do you think you should return so soon?"

"Maman!" Collette demanded. "I'm getting married!"

"Of course you are." Maman might as well have said, "Pour another glass of Chenin Blanc." He was sure his mother hadn't quite finalized her plan either, but she was clearly working on something. Was Marie-Thérèse Brillard going to be a help or a hindrance in his plot to get word to Genvieve?

Christophe looked into his mother's face. "If your daughter is marrying in ten days, Maman, shouldn't you be talking about wedding things?"

"What you say?" She finally turned to Collette, who sat before her barely touched bowl of soup. "Of course your sister will not do the marriage in ten days. Time I have to have to do the planning. The dress..." Maman drifted off again.

"Maman, I don't *want* a dress. Not a wedding dress, anyway. We just want to get married." Collette stared at her mother, then at Christophe. She shrugged her shoulders in bewilderment. "Maman, you did hear me, didn't you? I want to post—"

"I hear you, girl." Marie-Thérèse stood and walked to the stove to refill her bowl. "You want to marry." She shot a pain-filled glance at Christophe. "To marry your Frenchman. But this you cannot do until I have the time. It must be right, you see." She dropped the ladle back into the soup pot. "Collette, you have something else to say to me to make you want to hurry this wedding?"

Collette looked toward the ceiling. "No, Maman. I am not pregnant."

Marie-Thérèse's sigh could be heard throughout the little kitchen.

"That's one in the good column," Christophe muttered.

Maman walked to the table, bowl in hand, and took her time looking over her children. "Both of you be in the 'good column' soon enough. Now, Collette, you want to marry your Frenchman, what can your *mère* say? But it must be right. You hear me, girl? It must be right."

"How long will that take?" Exasperation piped through Collette's words. "Why can't we just get married without a big fuss? We'll go to the Palais de Justice, do the job, and have the wedding in the church later on. Maybe in August. Or September?"

"Slow yourself down, missy. You tell me you want to marry your Frenchman. I tell you I cannot stop you." Maman set her refilled bowl on the table, but stood over her daughter. "This does not mean that I hand my girl off to any Thomas, Richard, or Henri without a care in this world. Like a sack of soiled rags with no value. This I will not do."

"Maman! I am *not* a sack of soiled—"

"If marrying the man she loves makes her happy, Maman, how can you say such a thing?" Christophe protested.

"I get to you next, Monsieur Brillard." Maman was back in full force. Despite his misery, Christophe smiled. Maybe he would let Maman in on his plan, or at least the part where she might be some help. "Yes, Maman." He sipped his soup to keep from smiling.

"Now, back to you, missy. You will post no banns until I talk to the parents." She sat down at the table. "Yes. Me. I speak to the *mère* and to the *père* of this Jean-Michel. I am from Martinique, as are you. We do not give our daughters to just anybody, Frenchman or not. And nobody, no one, takes my daughter from me like she was the trash." She placed her hand beside Collette's cheek. "You are a special girl, and I will be sure that you go only to a special family. Now, on your way." She grabbed Collette's bowl. "On your way to your Jean-Michel. Tell him what I say. Shoo." She waved her daughter away from the table.

Collette jumped up and kissed Marie-Thérèse on the cheek. "*Merci*, Maman. *Merci milie fois.*" Collette skipped out the door.

"Now for you." Marie-Thérèse turned on Christophe.

"I won't be as easy as delaying the posting of banns, Maman. I know you spoke to Louis-Philippe."

"Has that boy the brains to make the strawberry torte? He tell me very little more than what I already know."

Christophe pushed aside his empty bowl. "I've got to get word to her...to Gen—"

Marie-Thérèse put her hands to her ears. "I don't need to hear the name of the woman who do this to you. She—"

"Maman, I know what's happened. I feel it here." He patted his chest. "And here." He touched his arm. "What I don't need is you talking against her. She made a mistake, I guess. That's just it, Maman. I don't really know what happened. And I need to find out."

Marie-Thérèse laid her hands over his right arm. "I know you hurt in more than this arm. While I don't understand this woman, I know she carries your child. That counts for everything. You don't know what she wants. I don't know. First, we must find this out."

"I know that, Maman. I have to get word to her. To Genvieve." He waited for his mother's reaction.

Marie-Thérèse sucked in her lip, started to roll her eyes, and stopped. "I think my head into almost bursting on how to reach this woman. That ninny, Louis-Philippe, tell me that she goes to a restaurant near the Arc de Triomphe. A place called Farsi something. You tell me the place and I get word to this woman."

"That's just it, Maman. Who can get word to her? Not me. I'll be recognized."

"For the love of God, of course not you. The danger is too great. At first, I think myself, but no. A restaurant off the Champs-Élysées does not have many customers with brown faces like mine. The husband would get the suspicion."

"Uh-huh. Then I thought of Louis-Philippe, but I don't really think he's up to the task. And Collette won't do either."

"You two look too much alike," Marie-Thérèse mused.

She rested her hand on her chin. Christophe smiled when he realized that he had done the same thing. He and Maman were thinking too much alike.

Marie-Thérèse's face brightened. "I think I know how to do this thing. She will give me the help, I know she will."

"Who?"

"Why, Madame Glovia, of course."

"Madame Johnson? What does she know? Maman, you haven't talked about me to the entire neighborhood, have you?" A wave of shock swept over him.

"I don't have to do the talking. The whole neighborhood already knows you have the trouble with the woman. They just don't know all the details. Now hear me, Christophe."

"I don't know, Maman." He shook his head.

"Well, you will know soon enough, my son. Madame Glovia sweeping into a restaurant on a fancy street will cause no brows to raise over anybody's eyes. They will think it an honor to have an American *noire* at their tables. They will make no connection to you." Maman smiled as though she had worked out the details of the peace treaty all by herself.

"Maybe, Maman. Maybe it just might work."

CHAPTER 28

Alain-Hugo busied himself with the inventory list. Le Poulet Farsi was out of fresh cream, low on tarragon, and sugar was at a premium. He glanced to the main room of the restaurant where Papa folded the napkins Mama had starched and ironed last night. Where else could he place his eyes? Perhaps he could check the chickens roasting in the oven, but Jerome, hurrying between shredding breadcrumbs for the stuffing and keeping watch over the ovens, needed no help. Edouard, already finished with the mousse and desserts for the lunch service, had ferried his creations to the box filled with fresh ice. Alain-Hugo looked down at his list again. He recounted everything three times. There was only one thing left undone. How many potatoes to order. And only one person could answer that. And her, he could not bear to see.

"Will that bushel be enough for tomorrow as well?" he called over his shoulder without turning around. Every time he looked at her, his eyes went first to her middle, and his own stomach dropped to the floor.

"Only enough for the lunch crowd. And then we will need more," Genvieve answered him as though everything was normal.

Alain clamped his eyes shut. Even her voice sparked pains between his eyes. Two weeks now, and his misery had only gotten worse. The tightness in his stomach worsened, and he started toward the main dining room. He would help Papa place the napkins.

"Alain-Hugo." Her voice spoke barely above a whisper, but it sounded like the crack of a whip in his ears. She sat on a stool, a bushel basket of potatoes on the floor beside her, a mound of peelings sitting atop the trashcan.

He turned his back. He said nothing. What was there to say? He'd cried in his father's arms. He'd put on a brave face for his mother. They knew the truth of his pain. What was there to say to her? He had survived the Nazis for *this*?

"Alain-Hugo," she raised her voice, "if you won't speak to me, then I will talk to you."

He watched Jerome and Edouard stop in mid-activity. Both shot cautious glances at him, then redoubled their efforts at looking busy.

"Get out, you two," Alain-Hugo ordered. "I'll watch the chickens." He stood in the doorway as the two workers scrambled past him.

"I cannot change the past, Alain. What do you want of me?"

He took in a deep breath. No words came, and if they had, he didn't trust himself to deliver them to her.

"You and your family have banished me. I'm here." She pointed to the pile of potato parings. "In the back room. In the kitchen peeling carrots and potatoes. But this I cannot do forever. What do you want?"

He whirled around to face her. "What do I want of you?" The words burst out of his throat on a whirlwind. "I want you to be the decent girl I married! I want you to be the woman I left when I went to fight with the Resistance. I want you to

220

be the woman whose picture I carried with me for two long years." He heard the cries in his own voice and sucked in a breath. "Why do you think I joined the Resistance?"

She sat there, saying nothing.

"For you." All the air seemed to have left his lungs. "For you, Genvieve. For you. All I could see, all I could think was to keep you safe from some German...touching..." He clamped his eyes shut. "All I wanted, all I expected, all I dreamed about, prayed for, was you, my faithful wife, waiting for me to return home alive." He heard the cracking of his own voice. He clamped his eyes shut. "But for you, that was too much for me to want."

"If I could take away your pain, don't you think I would?" She sounded too calm, too steady.

"If it is my pain that frets you, a pain that you bemoan only because it has put you in the kitchen like a scullery maid, then why, in the name of God, did you not think of that, my pain, before you...?"

She stood and took several steps toward him. He lifted his hands in front of him. "Don't. Don't you come any closer. You disgust me."

Genvieve dropped her hands to the oversized blue dress his mother had stuck on her to cover the evidence of her sin. That bulge at her middle was plain for him to see. And Jerome, Edouard, and Peter. Soon, every regular customer who took a seat at Le Poulet Farsi would know the cause of that bulge. And every one of them could count. Alain-Hugo closed his eyes, but the faces of the customers crowded out everything else. Smug faces. Scandalized faces. Pitying faces. He snapped his eyes open. He couldn't bear it.

"I understand." Now she looked contrite, her eyes staring at her hands. Hands resting just below that big belly. "You are right. I have done a horrible thing." She looked up at him, her eyes brimming with tears. "But I swear I did not plan it. I waited two years...two long—"

"Two years? Two *long* years, and then you gave up on me?" He spit out the words. "Are you telling me that after two years with a husband away risking his life, every wife in France turned herself into a whore?"

Genvieve staggered back as though he'd struck her. He clenched and unclenched his fists.

"I..." The tears spilled down her cheeks. "You think that of me?"

He pointed at her belly. "Can you deny the proof?"

"Alain." Her voice came out as soft as a summer breeze. "I do not want to cause you any more pain. I know that I have failed you as a wife." She swallowed several times. "I will not protest when you ask...that you will want...I know you will want a divorce." She looked up at him, her eyelashes wet with tears.

"A divorce?" He raced to her side and grabbed her by the shoulders. "You slut! What more are you going to do to me? You have disgraced me, my father, my mother, my entire family with...with..." He bumped her hard in her stomach with his open hand.

"Alain-Hugo!" Her eyes widened with the same terror he had seen when he slashed the knife over her lover's arm. "Don't. It's a ba—ba—ba—"

He watched her hair fly back and forth. He heard the little pops in her neck as her head whipped to and fro. Only the sound of Genvieve's stuttering voice finally registered in his ear. He clamped his hands down hard on her shoulders to stop from shaking her more. He released her, but the blue dress had pulled even tighter against her middle. Before he could stop himself, he slapped her across the face. She stumbled against the stool. He grabbed a handful of dress and forced her into the basket, her arms and legs flailing, scattering potatoes across the floor. He swept a pile of peelings over her head.

"You're worth no more to me than…than that peck of potatoes!" he shouted.

"What is it? What is it?" Papa rushed into the back room, a stack of unfolded napkins in one hand. He grabbed Alain-Hugo. "No, no, my son, you must not! Not here." He looked into the main room. "The customers will arrive soon." He glared at Genvieve, who sat doubled-up in the basket.

Alain-Hugo turned from the sight and reached for the napkins. "Here, Papa. I'll fold these." He struggled to control his breathing.

"Yes, yes," his father answered. "You take care of the diners. It's almost arranged. In just one month." Papa patted him on the shoulder and cast a disapproving glance at Genvieve.

"One more month?" Alain-Hugo asked as he watched Genvieve wriggle her way out of the basket. "Papa, look at her! Can we wait one more month?"

Papa glared at his daughter-in-law's struggles as the dress hiked above her knees. "No. No." He lowered his voice. "In one week," he said, shooting another look toward Genvieve, "they will leave for Toulon. It is almost all arranged. Three weeks there and then…"

Alain-Hugo kissed his father on both cheeks. "*Merci*," he whispered.

"I take that one to the train station myself." Papa turned a sympathetic face toward him. "Not you. You won't have to look on her again. Not until..." He nodded his head toward Genvieve's belly. "After the deed is done, then you will decide."

"What...what are you talking about?" Genvieve struggled to her feet and held a hand over her stomach, a trickle of blood oozing from her nose. "Decide what?"

Papa glared at her. "This will be the best for everyone. Thank God we have family in Toulon." He turned to Alain-Hugo. "Family that will keep their mouths shut."

"Toulon?" Genvieve pressed, alarm pouring from her voice. "What family? What will be best for...?"

"I would think that you would not want the world to know about your disgrace." Papa walked to her. "This way, only a few will know the truth." He leaned in close. "And they know how to keep silent."

Genvieve turned a frantic face between Papa and Alain-Hugo. "What do I have to do with Toulon? I have no family there."

Papa grabbed her by the shoulders. Genvieve winced.

"Now you listen to me. You will get on that train in one week's time. You will go to Toulon until they are ready for you. Then..." He released her.

"She'll be showing for all to see by then, Papa." Alain let his eyes drift to her belly. "When is that bastard due, anyway?"

Fresh tears flooded Genvieve's face as she rubbed her stomach.

"Your mama thinks September." Papa turned to Genvieve. "Do you even know yourself?" he grumbled.

"I'm...I'm five months," she stumbled. "But I will wear big dresses and stay back here in the kitchen for another month. I'll be fine. I know I will. I won't need to go to Toulon!" Genvieve pleaded.

"Oh, you'll go, all right." Alain-Hugo looked out into the main dining room. The first of the lunch crowd had arrived. "Do you think I want all Paris to know what you've done to me?"

"That's why..." She turned from Alain-Hugo to Papa. "They will know in September. That I had a baby." She brightened. "I know. I'll tell them that you came home in disguise and...and..."

Papa's laugh lacked any sign of mirth. "I don't think so, my girl."

The din of the first seating set up in the main dining room. Papa walked past Alain.

"Let me see to them. Tell her the rest." He stepped through the door.

"What rest?" Genvieve frowned. "Alain, don't you see, you won't want this child! It is best if I...I know you agree, if you file for the divorce."

"You are thick-headed, aren't you? No wonder you couldn't stop yourself from spreading your legs." He glared at her. "You're right. I don't want your bastard child. And I don't want you."

"Then you will consent? You will give me the divorce?"

The muscles in his face objected to the smile he forced onto his lips. "Is there no end to your sins? There will be no divorce in this family. I will not be excommunicated from the Church."

"But the baby—you refuse to raise him as your own. Will you change your mind in time?"

"Hell no." He heard the voice of Courageux in his ears. When faced with the greatest danger, let all feelings go. And act. The pain in his head left. "I will tell you this once, so listen carefully. You will go to Toulon in one week's time. You will remain there until the nunnery has a place for you. Three to four weeks. There you will give birth to that…that *thing*." He pointed at her stomach.

"Oh no, Alain. There must be another—"

"Do you want to hear this, or do you want to be surprised when it happens? I suggest you keep your mouth shut."

She stared at him with those amber eyes. She kept silent.

"After the child is born, it will be taken by the nuns. They will raise it in an orphanage. One that is not their own. One that you will never know about."

Her scream rocked the room. The din in the dining room shushed. Papa walked to the door and shut it.

"Please. *Please*, Alain," Genvieve gasped. "No. No."

"Oh, there is more. You will stay in Toulon. We'll tell everyone here that you are caring for my mother's elderly aunt. Oh, I'll trot you out for the major holidays, but other than that, I don't want to look upon your face ever again." He turned toward the door just as Papa pushed it open.

"Alain-Hugo!" Papa's face lit up as though he'd forgotten all about Genvieve. "She's here. One of them has just come to Le Poulet Farsi. And she wants to place a big order!"

CHAPTER 29

The sound of animated, curious voices carried from the dining room into the back of the restaurant. Alain-Hugo peered out from the kitchen. Almost every one of the eighteen tables was filled. Some heads swiveled toward the outside eating area where the six tables sat.

"Who, Papa?" Alain asked. "Who is here, and what kind of an order does she want?"

"I'm not sure of the name, but Jerome declares she is from Le Chat Noir." Papa nodded his excitement. "A famous singer from before the war!"

"The singer from Le Chat Noir?" Alain repeated. "I remember going there." It felt good to smile again. "About ten years ago. Yes, she was quite good. Outstanding, really."

Papa stepped around him and headed toward the roasting chickens. "She wants Le Poulet to cater one of her soirees." He turned to his son. "A big one! I'm not sure we can accommodate such a party."

Genvieve patted her face with a wet cloth.

"When, Papa? When does this woman want this done?" Alain asked.

"Next week. She said next week." Papa tapped a hand to his chin. "But I forgot to ask the day, because I'm not at all sure..."

227

"You stay with her." Alain jerked his head toward Genvieve. "I've just told her to ready herself for Toulon. See that she stays here, and I'll talk to the *chanteuse*...Madame Glovia, that's her name." Alain grinned, pleased that he remembered the name of the American *émigré* after a decade. He walked through the main room and grabbed a pad and pencil. At last. Something to keep his mind off...off... He stepped outside and spotted her immediately.

"Madame Glovia." Alain-Hugo congratulated himself again. It had been ten years, after all. Long before the Germans marched in. The room had been dark and smoke-filled, and she, with her golden skin and green eyes, had been the most exotic woman he'd ever seen.

This afternoon, in the harsh light of late May, he saw the lines on her face and the puffiness under her eyes, but not one whit of her glamour had disappeared. "And you are?" She turned on that smile.

He returned her greeting with a little bow. "I am Alain-Hugo. You just spoke to my father."

"Ah, yes, the charming gentleman. Will I be working with him or you?"

The foxtail she wore around her neck was not new, but what *Parisienne* could afford new furs these days?

"I would be happy to serve you, Madame Glovia. When will you want this food?" He smiled as she twisted in her seat, revealing a nylon-stockinged knee.

Alain looked across at the man who sat to her right, a big Frenchman who sent a definite signal that he did not appreciate Alain's attention to the older woman.

"Next Tuesday." She tilted her head. "One week from today." She held out a hand toward the man, who popped a cigarette into his mouth, lit it, and handed it to Madame Glovia. "My soirees are always on Tuesday nights."

"Very good, *madame*. How many guests will you have?"

"Oh, honey, I never know that. I just spread the word to my friends and they show up if they can. Of course, my place is always packed." She puffed on the cigarette as she scanned Alain-Hugo from top to bottom. "I bet *you* didn't spend the entire war serving chicken dinners here, now did you?"

"Ahh." Alain stumbled. "No. I was not here."

Madame Glovia leaned back toward the man sitting next to her. She kept her eyes on Alain as she lowered her voice. "See, Gaston? I can always tell who the heroes of France are." She took another puff and left the red imprint of her lips on the cigarette.

The man's scowl deepened as he stared at Alain-Hugo.

"Now let's get down to business." She sat up, pulled down the hem of her skirt, and stubbed out the cigarette. "I know you will do a perfectly fine job feeding my friends, but I have some particulars I need to be sure of. My purse, Gaston."

"Of course, Madame Glovia." Alain watched as the muscular fellow handed over the black leather clutch.

She pulled out several sheets of paper and handed one to Alain-Hugo. "Now, this is what I will require. But first, take me to your kitchen."

"Into the kitchen, *madame*?"

"Yes. Into the kitchen." The *chanteuse* sounded matter-of-fact, as though her request was as normal as ordering an after-dinner coffee. She stood, walked past Alain, and headed toward the main dining room.

The man she called Gaston pushed back his chair and laid an arm on Alain's shoulder. "*Madame* has her little quirks. It will be a big order. It's best to let her have her way."

"Of course." Alain-Hugo led the group inside.

"Seven, eight, nine." Madame Glovia pointed her red-polished nail. "I see you're used to serving a big crowd. Forty, fifty people at a time." She glanced outside to the six tables, then back to the main dining room. "Now take me to the kitchen."

"Are you certain? The kitchen, it is not as orderly…but of course, it is quite clean! We are a—"

"That's what I intend to see." She brushed him aside and headed toward the closed door.

She swung open the door and swept into the back room. Papa stared open-mouthed. Genvieve looked confused, the side of her face swollen and reddened where he'd slapped her. Speckles of blood from her nose dotted the blue dress.

"May I…can I be of assistance?" Papa stuttered.

"It's all right," Alain-Hugo assured. "Madame Glovia here wants to place an order for twenty-five dinners." He looked down at the paper she'd handed him. "And she wants to make sure our kitchen can accommodate that many."

"Of course. Of course." Papa beamed.

Without an invitation, Madame Glovia canvassed the room, checking the ovens and running a gloved finger over the worktable. She stopped in front of Genvieve.

"Who is this?" the star demanded.

"My wife." Alain-Hugo spoke before he remembered. His stomach churned again.

"Can she serve?" The singer scanned Genvieve. Her eyes lingered on her face.

"Other than being clumsy, of course she can." Papa forced a laugh. "She's just tripped over that stool there. Haven't you, Genvieve?"

His wife looked from Papa, to him, and back to the American. "Of course," she whispered.

"Good. I've got my staff all lined up, by the way. But I want someone from this place, one of you who knows about this food, to come help out. And I want a woman, don't I, Gaston?"

"Yes. *Madame*'s guests prefer female servers," the big man answered.

"Next Tuesday. My house. Here's the address." She pressed the sheaf of papers into Genvieve's hand. "Food for thirty...and send this one." She pointed to Genvieve. "She'll fit right in with my guests."

Papa shook his head. "I'm sorry, Madame—er, *madame*, but this girl, she cannot, she will be...uhh."

"You got another woman working here?" The singer flashed annoyance at Papa. "I don't see another woman."

"No," Alain-Hugo interrupted, "she is the only one. But we have an excellent staff. Jerome, Edouard, Peter. They've been with—"

"Eight o'clock sharp. And I want that girl, or no deal." Madame Glovia swept out of the room, the head of her fox fur lying clamped across her shoulder. Gaston followed.

CHAPTER 30

"Yep. You'll do just fine. *Real* fine, in fact." Monsieur Crawford circled Marie-Thérèse like she was on the auction block.

Marie-Thérèse cast an anxious look at the front door. Seven thirty. A half hour until the caterers arrived from Le Poulet Farsi. And here was Morgan Crawford, standing in Glovia's study, acting like she was a trick elephant in a circus.

"What do you say, Marie-Thérèse?" He took a step back and studied her.

"I say no. That's what I say, Monsieur Crawford." She tried to walk away from him. She had to find Glovia.

He blocked her path.

"You know you come too early anyway," she chastised.

"Tut-tut, as they say in England. I can never come too early to one of Glovia's shindigs. Besides, I wanted to talk to you." He surveyed her like he was measuring her for a dress. "Yes. You would be perfect." He grinned. "In fact, I insist."

"No, Monsieur Crawford, I tell you again. I will not pose for you in the...without any...with no clothes on."

"How about for my apprentice?" he persisted. "You'd be perfect sculpted in bronze. A goddess. You've got just the right proportions. Big, rounded hips. A sturdy trunk. Breasts that overwhelm the eye." He drew her figure in the air. "Rubenesque!"

"No thank you." She scurried around him and made her way down the hall when the knocker on the front door sounded.

Marie glanced around for Gaston. She suspected he was in the salon wrestling with tables. "I'll get it!" She hurried to the door.

Monsieur Jimmie Lee looked through her in what passed for his best greeting. He did wait until she stepped aside before he plunged through the door. He headed straight for the salon. "Another early one," Marie-Thérèse muttered under her breath as she fingered the diamond ring suspended from her neck on its silken cord. And still no food. She hurried to the kitchen. No Glovia. She checked the study, only to find Madame Mabry sprawled on the settee, with Monsieur Crawford polishing his latest brass in the opposite corner.

Marie-Thérèse hurried to the closed door to the bedroom and, with the briefest of taps, walked in on Glovia.

"Marie-Thérèse?" Glovia looked up from her dressing table where she painted rouge across her cheeks. "I told you, I don't want you to be the one letting the restaurant people in this house." She turned in her boudoir chair. "You haven't been answering that door, have you?"

"Uh…well…I am just so anxious."

"We've been over this, Marie-Thérèse." Glovia put on her patient voice. "Me, you, and your boy. Stick to the plan. You two have got to lay low. Stay out of sight until I make sure the girl is here. The girl, and not that husband of hers. If he comes and sees you, he just might put two and two together. I want that fool to come up with five, not four." She turned back to her primping.

Marie-Thérèse paced the bedroom, her stomach fluttering. "Are you sure she got the note?"

"I put the damn thing in her hand myself." Glovia started drawing lines over her eyelids.

"But suppose the husband saw you. Suppose…"

"I gave her a bunch of papers with the dishes I wanted cooked. The note Christophe wrote to her was all folded up. I made sure I put that one underneath the other papers, and she stuck them all in her apron pocket." Glovia picked up another pencil and stroked lines around her lips. "Believe me. She knew I slipped her something for her eyes only."

"Are you sure it was the right girl? Suppose—"

"How many pregnant Genvieves could there be working at Le Poulet?"

"But what if—"

"Marie-Thérèse, quit it." Glovia held a string of pearls against her neck. "Now you and Christophe stay out of sight in the alley until I can make sure the girl is alone."

"You said she had been beaten. Suppose—"

"I'm telling you, Marie-Thérèse. No more." She dropped the pearls and picked up a necklace with an emerald center stone. She laid it against her neck. "Now get outside before the caterers get here."

CHAPTER 31

Sweat popped out across Christophe's forehead as he stood in the alley behind Madame Johnson's apartment house. He looked up at the sky. Eight o'clock and the sun still shone. But of course it would. It was early June.

"Maman, stay away from that door. Suppose one of them opens it and spots you?"

"Me? This man, this devil who hurt you, does not know me. Besides, Glovia told that one he is not to come tonight." Marie-Thérèse did not leave her post. She was close enough to hear every word spoken on the back porch, but not inside the house or the kitchen.

Christophe went over the plan again. If Madame Johnson had succeeded and actually gotten his note to Genvieve, and if Genvieve agreed to talk to him one last time...if she wanted to talk...if she loved him, and not her husband...Christophe clamped his eyes shut. He had run every possibility through his head so many times, so many ways. Right now, he felt his head might explode.

"Shh," Marie-Thérèse hissed. "I think I hear voices."

"Maman, I haven't said a word." He walked to the alley door, careful to stay close to the building and out of sight. His mother pushed him behind her as she busied herself with the trashcan.

"What are they saying?" he whispered. "Who's in there? Oh, let me have a listen."

"No!" she commanded in a half-voice. " I think...I hear... yes. It's Gaston."

"Gaston? Madame Johnson's bodyguard? I don't care about...who else, Maman?" His chest tightened. Should he run inside? Did Genvieve need him? "Who else do you hear?"

"Glovia for sure. I know American when I hear it. And voices I do not know. But it is difficult. If only I could slip inside. Hide in the pantry."

"Is it a man or a woman's voice?" Worry collided with impatience.

"I think it is a low voice." Maman held her ear against the door, one hand on the knob.

Christophe grabbed at his mother's dress to stop her from moving inside. Why did she insist upon putting herself at risk? The man with the knife could lash out at anyone. Even at an old woman. But especially Genvieve. Thoughts that fought with one another rolled over in his brain again. He tapped the throbbing between his eyes. Genvieve. Had she lied to him on purpose? Or could she actually love him? When he thought about it, she had saved his life when she jumped on the husband's back. He had to know the truth.

The back door flew open, striking Maman a glancing blow on the forehead. Madame Johnson's man stepped out; his eyes widened when he spotted the pair.

"Gaston, what—?" Maman began.

The big Frenchman laid a finger to his lips and jerked his head toward the pantry as he shut the door. He grabbed Maman by the shoulders, turned her around, and ushered the two down the alley toward a wrought-iron gate, six doors away. As Christophe quick-stepped behind Gaston, he spotted a short flight of stone stairs leading to a neighbor's basement.

"What is it, man?" Christophe's heart pounded. "Has she come? Genvieve. Is she here?"

With one hand, Gaston sat Maman on the top stone step. With the other he motioned Christophe to grab one end of a blue planter box holding a profusion of trellised flowers.

"But—" Christophe protested.

Gaston stooped down and put his shoulder against one end of the heavy box. His eyes, peeking between a red geranium and a white rose, signaled silence and a plea for help. Christophe grabbed the other end of the container, and together they shoved the plant in front of the iron gate, blocking the steps from the view of anyone meandering outside of Madame Johnson's back door.

"There," Gaston huffed. "This will give you some screening from curious eyes. You both must wait here until one of us can signal that it is safe to come into the pantry."

"How long will that be?" Christophe whispered, squatting on the step next to Maman. "I can't just wait here!"

"I understand." Gaston crouched behind the makeshift screen. "The woman is here. She looks terribly frightened. And…"

Frightened. The word pounded in Christophe's head. He struggled to stand only to be pulled down by the Frenchman.

"That will not do, *monsieur.* Two men have come with the girl. One is the man who waited on us at the restaurant. The owner's son." Gaston leveled his eyes at Christophe. "He is called Alain-Hugo, and he is the husband."

"*Mon Dieu,*" Maman blurted.

The bodyguard laid a hand over her mouth. "There are two of them. A 'Jerome' has come with the husband." He looked at Christophe. "They are both in the kitchen."

"With Genvieve?" A wave of nerves jangled Christophe's body.

"Yes, but Madame Glovia is with her. You two are to stay here. Out of sight. Now I must go." Gaston made his way to Madame Glovia's just as the back door opened. "*Monsieur,* may I help you pack up something?" Gaston's voice rose as he approached the man who had just stepped through the back door.

"The lady, your boss, says this party might last until two or three in the morning."

The man's features were obscured by the blinding rays of the quick-setting sun, but Christophe recognized the voice. He shot a warning glance toward Maman as he executed a slow shift to better his view of the fellow. He peered through the foliage at the man. The shoulders, and those arms, he would never forget. There stood Genvieve's husband. Christophe clenched his jaw as he willed himself to wait for Gaston's signal.

"Yes. *Madame*'s parties often last till near dawn." Gaston kept his back to the screened hiding place. "What time did *madame* suggest you return?"

"Come back?" The light of a cigarette in the man's hand flashed in the dimming light. "Eleven." Christophe watched the freedom fighter in silhouette. The man lifted an arm to his face. "Surely your guests will have had their fill of food by then." The man spoke in measured tones. "Isn't that when the serious liquor gets served?"

"Eleven?" Gaston paused. "Perhaps midnight might be better."

The cigarette went to the man's lips. "Eleven."

"As you wish." Gaston opened the back door. "We will see you back here then."

"No," the husband's voice rumbled in the alley. "I'll just wait here. Jerome will wait in the front." The man stepped to the middle of the alley, stared long seconds at the trellised screen, then turned to survey the opposite direction. "My wife has an early train to catch."

"Train, *monsieur*?"

"Yes. A train." The man stared at Gaston. "Why do you ask?"

"Then I shall make sure that your employee does not overtire herself if she has a journey tomorrow." Gaston stepped into the pantry and closed the back door behind him.

"Hmm." The man settled himself on the curb and took another puff of his cigarette.

Christophe watched Maman wrap her arms around her chest. The sun had disappeared over an hour ago, and the June night air carried a hint of chill with it. He reached over and rubbed her bare arms. His own knees ached from crouching so long. The sound of a trombone drifted out of Madame Johnson's open windows. The *madame*'s voice, raised in song, could be heard, though Christophe did not recognize the tune. Mrs. Johnson crooned in English something about a sentimental journey home. During the past hour, the husband had taken turns sitting on the curb and pacing to and fro before Madame Johnson's back door.

"Ahh." Maman let out a little sound as she jerked to attention at the crack of the back door opening.

"Hey, Jimmie Lee." An American voice. A woman. "Don't this fresh air feel good?"

Christophe shot a questioning glance at Maman.

"Madame Mabry and Monsieur Hudson," Maman whispered back, her eyes filled with surprise.

"You got a cigarette on you, Jimmie?" The woman's voice. Madame Mabry.

Christophe used a hand to sweep away the foliage and widen his glimpse into the scene unfolding six doors up the alley. There in the doorway stood a tall figure of a thin American *noir*, and a woman wearing a dark-colored dress stretched tight over her more-than-ample backside. The woman peered in the direction of the husband, a few steps away in the alley.

"Hey, baby, I didn't see you there." Madame Mabry thrust her hips forward and slunk up to the resistance fighter.

Christophe watched as Alain-Hugo shook his head in confusion. Genvieve's husband acted as though he spoke no English.

"*Pardon, monsieur,*" Madame Mabry trotted out her poorly executed French. "What are you doing out here?" She laid an arm over Alain-Hugo's shoulder and rubbed her body against his. "Hey, Jimmie Lee. We got a new one over here." Her laugh sounded drunken.

Maman tapped Christophe on the back as she tried to get a look. "Monsieur Hudson never comes in the alley. Never." She was emphatic.

"*Non, madame.*" Alain-Hugo sounded confused by these Americans. "I am not a guest. I am the help."

"Hell no!" Madame Mabry's voice boomed. "Glovia don't believe in that. White folks here. Black folks there. Gentry on one side, the help on the other." She stretched on tiptoe and kissed Alain-Hugo on the cheek. "Been too much of that shit, if you know what I mean."

Christophe watched as Alain-Hugo pushed the woman away.

"Oh, you don't swing that way, huh? Jimmie Lee, get on over here." She beckoned the skinny man.

Maman found her peephole in the vegetation. Christophe heard her chuckle. "That one is not doing all that much acting, you know." She tilted her head in the direction of Madame Mabry.

"*Égalité.*" The skinny man's voice doubled his size. "The cobblestones where stand the feet." He brushed Madame Mabry aside as he confronted Alain-Hugo.

Even in the darkness, Christophe could make out the scowl on the American's face. "Count each one, nice and neat." The monotone filled the cobbled street. "Hold your face to the rain. Hear their pain. Move your feet." Monsieur Hudson clamped a bony hand on Alain's shoulder and began marching him up the alley and away from the trellised hideaway.

"I...I'm sorry?" Alain-Hugo shook his head as he protested his forced walk.

Christophe watched as the husband tried to pull away, but Monsieur Hudson squeezed tighter and pushed the man forward. That poet was stronger than he looked.

"That's it, Jimmie Lee," Maman coaxed. "That's it."

"Baby," Madame Mabry called after Alain-Hugo, "just go with it. He's a poet. A famous one, and one of Glovia's best guests. You best keep him happy if I was you."

"Paris, your cobblestones tell the truth of your tale." Jimmie Lee continued his relentless march—now five houses distant, Alain-Hugo in tow. "Paris, you say no to your poor. Paris, you show your black colonists the door. Paris, your *égalité* doth fail."

Maman pushed her palms together in a silent clap. She nudged Christophe and nodded her head.

"Wait, Maman." Christophe laid a hand across her arm as he stared at Madame Mabry.

The woman signaled "wait" with one finger. Christophe peered around the shrubbery. They both looked up the alley. Jimmie Lee and Alain were almost at the corner, now ten houses distant. The American woman gave the signal to Christophe. He crouch-walked to the deeper darkness of the side of the buildings and inched his way toward the back door. Madame Mabry stood in the street, singing. Any noise he happened to make would be masked by that God-awful voice of hers. Christophe cracked the door open and slipped inside the room-sized pantry to face Gaston. And Genvieve.

CHAPTER 32

"Christophe!" The cry crawled out from deep within Genvieve's throat. She took a step toward him, her eyes brimming with tears. "Thank God, you're all right."

"Hurry!" Gaston urged, as he left the back door open a crack.

Christophe looked back. He could see Madame Mabry still staggering along the alley. In the distance, he could hear Monsieur Jimmie Lee keeping up his distraction, with Maman still safe in her hiding place.

"No more than five minutes," Gaston announced. "I'll be right inside the kitchen." Glovia's man closed the pantry door between the two. Christophe sucked in a breath when he turned to face Genvieve.

"Christophe," she strained, "I was so frightened. Alain is so angry." Tears splashed down her face. "He wants to… Christophe, can you help me?"

"Help you? You want my help?" Now that he looked at her, a torrent of anger rushed at him. "You are a married woman. How am I to help you?"

"No. No. Christophe. Your note—" She batted her hands in the empty air. "You said you wanted to talk, to hear me explain."

"I've changed my mind. What can you possibly say to me? You let me"— Christophe swallowed hard—"you let me fall in love with you." He struggled to quell the shaking in his body. He felt his own tears forming and fought them back. "Genvieve...Gen..." His voice cracked.

"Oh, *mon cher,* you must believe...you must understand. I didn't mean for this to happen. That day of liberation on the Champs-Élysées, I'd never felt so alive. First freedom, and then you stepped into my path." She rested her hand over his right arm as she tilted her face up to him. "You turned to look at me. What I saw in your face made me shiver. You looked at me as though I were the most special person in all this world...that being with me felt even better than having Paris free. No one, no man, had ever made me feel like that before."

"You think I've forgotten that day?" Christophe tapped his chest. "It's here. Stamped right into my heart. We all lost a little bit of our minds that day. All of us. The sun never shone brighter. The bells of the Sacré-Coeur never sounded sweeter. And I had never seen a woman so beautiful." The sweet pain of memory flooded back.

"Yes! Yes! That's what I felt for you, too." Her eyes glistened. "Christophe, please believe me. That day, I wasn't looking for anything. I had nothing planned. But that moment when you carried me to safety and out of the crowd, that evening in the bistro, the way I felt when your hands stroked my ankle...

"Then, there we were, standing on the Tour d'Eiffel, looking out at all the city. Just the two of us, you and me, with Paris below. It felt so like a dream." She bent over and kissed his injured forearm through his sleeve. "So right."

Christophe gulped in air and swallowed hard. "But it wasn't right, Genvieve. Not for us." He looked at this woman he loved, and felt his chest squeezing shut. "You were…you *are* a married woman. Why didn't you…?" His voice cracked again as he shook his arm free. "Why couldn't you tell me before I fell…before it was too late?"

"I tried, Christophe. I really did. A thousand times I almost said the truth. But something always…the time was never right. You were so happy. I was so happy! I told myself it was all right to laugh again. Nothing that felt this good could ever be wrong." Her words ran together. "I knew it. I could sense in my heart what I felt for you had to be all right with God. No loving creator would ever want any of his creatures to spend endless months stumbling through life more dead than alive. Even Saint Mary Magdalene would grant me permission to feel something *live* here in my heart." She searched his face. "And then, it was too late. I'd fallen in love with you." She stared at the pantry floor. "After that, I couldn't bring myself to tell you the truth. I was afraid."

"You were afraid? Afraid your husband's family would find out? Find out how you deceived everyone?"

She shook her head, her hair hanging limp. "Afraid I would lose you." Her amber eyes shone at him. "I knew that if I told you the truth—that I was married—I would lose you. And by then, I was…I *am* so in love with you…I couldn't bear to have you hate me."

"Did you think I would never find out? Never discover the truth?" A fresh surge of anger swarmed over him. "When we met, you knew the worst of the war was over. It was the day of liberation, in the name of God! The Germans were on the run. It was just a matter of time…months, maybe weeks for all you knew…before your husband came back."

She ran a hand through her hair, the knots catching at her fingers. "Don't you see? I couldn't think! I couldn't allow myself to think about a future.

"And no, Christophe, the war was *not* yet done. Le Maquis was still fighting, and who could know for sure what the future would bring?" She reached both arms out to him. "I couldn't bear another second of the uncertainty. If Alain came back, if he survived, I thought it best if I just made an excuse to you and disappeared. I couldn't bear to hurt you by telling you the truth. Sometimes, in the back of my mind, I thought maybe, for you, I was just an infatuation. You would get over me."

"You knew better than that. Get over you?" Christophe's laugh caught in his throat. "I'll never get over you."

She walked to him, her lower lip sucked in. "Nor I you." She laid her head against his chest. He felt her arms encircle him, her hands clutching into his shirt. "Christophe, I must tell you good-bye."

Her words cut into his soul. He held his arms stiff at his side. "So you have decided." His lungs felt deflated. "After all your pretty words, you've made your choice. You're going back to him…your husband."

She released him and took a step back. "Never. I would never choose him over you." Her eyes flamed. "I've asked for, pleaded for, and begged for a divorce."

"A divorce? You asked for a divorce? But divorce is a sin. You would do that for me?"

"I would walk the halls of hell for you." Genvieve's arms clutched her blue smock. "He is sending me away."

"What?" Christophe struggled to shake understanding into his head. "Where? When?"

246

"Tomorrow. To Toulon. Oh, Christophe." She rushed to him.

"Toulon?"

"In the morning." She lifted her head from his chest and turned red-rimmed eyes toward him. "On the train, but there is much worse."

"I won't allow you to go. I won't." Christophe slipped his arms around her shoulders.

"The child, our baby…" Fresh sobs racked her body. "Alain-Hugo will give him to the nuns as soon as it is born. I'm never to see our son again. Nor Paris…or you."

He pulled her closer. "No. No. We will not lose our child." He looked into her face. "I bless you for believing we have a son."

"Sen-ti-men-tal jour-ney and the boat is sail-ing home." Madame Mabry's off-tune voice cut through the pantry from the alley. But the lyrics had changed.

Christophe pushed Genvieve behind him and peeked out the door. The American continued her exaggerated swagger and her singing. "The boat is sail-ing home, right now." She shot a quick look at Christophe. "Ho-me, home, away from ho-me. Hide away, Hide a-way n-ow. Oops."

She dropped to her knees just as Christophe heard the droning of Monsieur Jimmie Lee.

Christophe rushed to the kitchen door. "Gaston. He's coming back. Where can we hide?"

Gaston spilled out, grabbed Genvieve, and pushed her into the kitchen. He nodded to Christophe. "Here. In here."

"But Genvieve?" Christophe's eyes darted from alleyway to the shut kitchen door.

"No time." Gaston gestured Christophe toward a wooden barrel, labeled "Cabernet."

Together the men pushed aside the container. The bodyguard made quick work of loosening the nails holding a section of the floorboards. Alone, he lifted a two-foot square section from the floor. Madame Mabry's voice caught in his ear.

"Jimmie Lee. And Mr. Kind Frenchman!" the American woman called out from the alley. "I seem to have gotten myself on this damn ground. I betcha these old cobblestones came up and smacked me right in the behind. Could you two be gentlemen...well, maybe not you, Jimmie Lee. It's got to be you, baby. Jimmie Lee don't do no heavy lifting."

"Here," Gaston hissed at Christophe. "Get down. This is Madame Glovia's hideaway. Room for her best champagne, caviar, her Luger, her Mas 35. And one person. Down you go."

Christophe scrambled into a hole smelling of old dust and cobwebs. He looked up just as Gaston lowered the fake floorboard over his face. He heard the rumbling of the wine barrel settling over the trapdoor.

Christophe shuddered in the tiny space, grateful that he was not claustrophobic. In the pitch darkness, he stretched out an arm and ran his fingers over the roughness of hundred-year-old bricks. His hands tapped along the wall, touching dozens of wine bottles. He probed the floor with his foot. More uneven bricks. His foot stabbed at something hard. He squatted to the ground and patted the brick floor with his hands. Something metal greeted his touch. Christophe ran his fingers along a long, slender, steel cylinder. He scooped the object into his hands. And felt the trigger. He held the Free French weapon of choice in his right hand—a Mas 35.

"Tramp the truth of the cobblestones down." The sound of Mr. Jimmie Lee's footsteps seeped through the planked floor of the pantry. "Keep away the evil of suppression with a hidden frown."

"Of course, *monsieur*." Alain-Hugo's impatient voice cut through the poet's recitation. "Where is my wife?"

Christophe tensed. His hand clutched the handle of the gun.

"She is tidying the kitchen, *monsieur*." Gaston's voice drifted to the hidden cellar.

"Baby, I got another song for you." Madame Mabry must have made her way inside. "I'll sing it to you in French this time."

"*Non, madame.* It is time for us to leave." Alain-Hugo's voice. "I will have Jerome help my wife finish up. Please have *madame* ready my fee."

"Of course, *monsieur*." Gaston's voice drifted down from a spot almost directly over Christophe's head. "But as you can hear, Madame Glovia still entertains."

Christophe heard the sound of feet moving rapidly across the floor.

"Just one more song, baby." Madame Mabry's high heels clicked along, but not before Christophe heard the sound of the kitchen door opening.

He snapped open the gun and ran his finger around the bullet chamber. The weapon was fully loaded.

"Genvieve!" the husband's voice called out. "Jerome will pack the rest. We're leaving."

"Now?" Genvieve, more distant, answered. "There is more food…"

"Jerome will...Genvieve, why do you want to stay?" Alain-Hugo's voice carried a whiff of accusation.

"Food is for the masses. Food..." Mr. Jimmie Lee.

"Look. Enough of this." Anger from the resistance fighter reached down to the hiding place. "You. Go tell your boss that we are leaving. Now." Footfalls stomped around the room. "Genvieve, have you been crying? Here? Who have you been talking to?" More accusations.

"*Monsieur*," Gaston kept to his spot near the sheltering barrel, "I do not wish to be rude, but I find your behavior unacceptable."

"Baby, just one..."

"No, *madame*." Alain-Hugo's voice came out in a cold condemnation. "You get back to your party, and take this buffoon with you. As for you..." The sound of feet leaving the area.

Gaston's measured tone filtered into the cellar. "I am sure that the evening has tired *monsieur*. After all, Madame Glovia has placed a very large order with your establishment. I am quite certain that *monsieur* would like the good name of his father's establishment to continue."

Christophe stroked the trigger on the Mas 35.

"It would be best if *monsieur* left now. His man may accompany Madame Genvieve home when her duties are complete. Perhaps in an hour."

"You dare interfere with my wife? Why? Who is at this party? Genvieve!" The sound of scuffling feet invaded the hiding place.

Christophe felt around for something to stand on to boost himself out of the hole. There was nothing.

"No. No. Please, Monsieur Gaston." Genvieve's voice. "My husband is right. I have overworked myself, and I do have a journey tomorrow." She paused. "I think we should go."

"Now you want to leave?" The sound of boots drifted closer to the barrel. "What's in that?"

"*Madame* is not accustomed to having her private wine stock inspected," Gaston, his breathing heavier, explained.

"Well, I want a look," the resistance fighter snarled.

"If you want me on the train to Toulon tomorrow, I suggest you take me home to pack now." Genvieve's voice sounded stronger.

"*Madame*, are you sure?" Gaston asked.

"Please thank Madame Johnson for her kindness. I am glad her party has been a success. But I do have the journey to Toulon in the morning." Footsteps. Genvieve's footsteps, walking out the back door. Heavier footfalls followed.

Christophe stretched his hands to push at the fake floorboard. He could not budge it. The barrel stood in the way.

"Stay where you are a few more minutes." Gaston, his voice softer now. Had he knelt closer to the hiding place?

"But Genvieve," Christophe whispered. "She's gone with that monster."

"I think, maybe, the Free Frenchman has a weapon with him. Perhaps the same knife that he used on you. Maybe even a gun. If his suspicions were too aroused, I was afraid he might use either."

At last he wrestled the barrel aside. Christophe pushed open the floorboards, and the pale glow from the single lightbulb shone down upon him in the hole. Gaston's white face appeared above him. The bodyguard reached down to help him out.

"I'll go to the train station in the morning."

"Monsieur Christophe, from what I see and hear tonight, I do not think that a wise decision."

CHAPTER 33

"Sit yourself down, Christophe. This pacing will not help."
Marie-Thérèse felt like pacing herself, but that would not
keep her son safe.

"Yeah. Take a load off." Madame Glovia stood by the
étagère and poured herself a drink. "Brandy, anyone?" She
waved the decanter around her study still shrouded in midmorning shadows.

Christophe walked past Glovia, moved on to Marie-
Thérèse, and paced past Gaston.

Gaston unfolded the train schedule. "The train for
Toulon pulled out two hours ago."

"I should have been there. I should never..." Christophe
quickened his walking.

"Honey, settle down. Glovia's got a headache, and I don't
need you moving around me like blurred lightning. Going
to the train station was a bad idea anyway. Facing this guy
square on was going to get you nothing but dead, and your
woman, gone. Remember, the law's on his side. She's his
wife." Glovia swirled the brandy in her glass as she walked
to her settee. "Now, Christophe, tell me how you want to
play this thing."

"*Non!*" Marie-Thérèse protested. "Glovia, his head is
worse than yours. He cannot 'play' anything. His heart

cannot let him think clear right now. My boy does not understand the danger he is in."

"Oh, Maman," Christophe groaned. "I know Madame Johnson's right. The husband was getting suspicious. I have to think of Genvieve."

"That woman." Marie-Thérèse placed her hands over her eyes. "She brings terrible trouble to us all."

"Marie-Thérèse!" Glovia arched an eyebrow as she pointed the untouched brandy snifter in her direction. "We don't need that right now."

"Would everyone stop fighting over me!" Christophe barked. "Genvieve has been taken to Toulon. And that bastard plans to keep her there. Forever. I've got to get her back to Paris."

"Yeah, that we know." Glovia set her glass on the floor. "Now, the question I have for you is…how?"

"How?" Christophe took another circle around the study. "I'll leave for Toulon tomorrow." Christophe turned a questioning face to Madame Johnson.

A vision of Christophe's mangled body flushed through Marie-Thérèse's mind. *"Non-non."*

"And what will you do when you get there?" Glovia queried as she shot a "keep quiet" look at Marie-Thérèse.

"Do?" Christophe licked his lips. "Madame Johnson, last night, when I was in your cellar, I spotted a Mas 35…then there is the Luger."

"Oh my, no!" Marie-Thérèse ignored Glovia's waving hand. "I tell you absolutely no."

"OK, Marie-Thérèse," Glovia interrupted. "Enough of that. Seems to me the first order of business is to figure out where in Toulon this girl is being taken, then—"

"A nunnery." Christophe stopped his pacing. "She mentioned being sent to a nunnery to wait for the baby. Then the husband…" Christophe's face reddened.

"Well, it can't be all that hard to figure out where this nunnery place is." Glovia picked up her glass and raised it to her lips. She peered over the rim. "How many nunneries they got in Toulon? Marie-Thérèse, you're into this church stuff, why don't you go to the Sacré-Coeur and ask one of those priest fellas for the name of a nunnery in Toulon. Then we'll get somebody down there." She turned to her bodyguard. "Gaston?"

"How long is all this going to take?" Christophe demanded.

"Has *monsieur* a better plan?" Gaston asked. "One that will not bring harm to himself?"

"I'm not afraid of him. With that Mas 35…or maybe even with the Luger…"

"Won't be no Lugers." Glovia shook her head. "No Mas 35, either."

"Enough of this gun talk!" Marie-Thérèse moved to her feet and faced her son. "Tell me, Christophe, if you take the gun, find the husband, and shoot him, then what? How will that get you your Genvieve?"

She watched him work his mouth to answer, then shake his head.

"Christophe." Marie-Thérèse leveled her "listen-to-your-*maman*-for-once" face at her son. "If you take the gun, and this Free Frenchman has his own…you be the one dead. Then what good are you to your child?" Marie-Thérèse walked over to her boy. She laid a hand over his injured arm. "If this is the woman you want, then you know your *maman* is with you. But the way to get her is not with the gun."

Christophe dropped his head.

"Let's go with what we've got." Glovia rolled the brandy glass over her lips. "Christophe, you find a friend willing to go to Toulon. Talk to those nun women."

"Whoever goes had best hurry," Christophe broke in. "The baby is due in September."

"I go to the Sacré-Coeur and speak to a priest now." Marie-Thérèse headed toward the hallway and the front door. First, the priest. Discover the location of the convent. And then, Martine.

CHAPTER 34

Marie-Thérèse stood outside the dress factory door. She and Collette had been very careful not to alert Christophe of their plan, though for the last forty-eight hours he had hounded every person he knew to take action. Only Louis-Philippe had agreed to travel to Toulon. Bless him. But enlisting the help of the good-hearted but dull friend of Christophe's was almost as bad an idea as carrying the Luger.

Marie-Thérèse looked at the brass-faced clock over the front door of the little factory. Five minutes till *dejeuner*. She tried to swallow back her impatience as she awaited the midday lunch break.

"Maman!" Collette beckoned from the shadowy interior of the small brick building on the rue de Cambon.

Marie-Thérèse rushed to the factory door.

"I think I've talked her into coming outside for a bite of lunch, but I'm not sure." Collette stood holding an armful of white, black, and pink fabric.

"You *think*? Collette, we have too little of the time to waste on your thinking. You go back and make sure Martine comes outside. To me."

"Oh. Oh. I've got to go, Maman! The supervisor spotted me. I've got to rush this fabric over to Madame Chanel.

Even though she's in official retirement, she still drops by to dabble in fashion."

"I know this already. Stop your chatter and hurry." Marie-Thérèse nodded as Collette turned and raced down the hall. Martine was their best, and only, hope. While Christophe and Gaston sparred over enlisting a male spy, Marie knew that would never work in a building full of man-shy females. It had to be a woman. A young girl. And Collette, with her almost look-alike coloring to Christophe, would never do.

"Madame Brillard?" Martine's voice cut through Marie-Thérèse's pondering. "Have you come to join Collette for lunch?" The girl looked puzzled. "You don't usually..."

"The school year has ended." Marie-Thérèse grabbed at the first explanation that popped into her head. "I thought I would come to celebrate."

Martine turned a skeptical eye to her. "Madame Brillard," the girl looked up and down the cobblestoned street, "Collette has worked here for three years." She settled her gaze on Marie-Thérèse. "You've never had lunch with her before. What is the problem with Christophe?"

"Oh, *mon Dieu!*" Marie-Thérèse cried. "I know my boy has not done right by you, but he is in such, such trouble. Only you can help."

Martine's deep brown eyes darkened as she shook her head. "From that night he came to me with the cut on his arm, I knew Christophe had troubles. And I knew they were about a woman." She sucked in her cheeks. "But, Madame Brillard, I am not the one to help."

"Yes. Yes, Martine, you are." A wave of panic swept over Marie-Thérèse. If not this girl, then in whose hands could she trust her son's life? "This help only you can give. *Only you*." She clasped her hands together. "This Frenchwoman has clouded my son's eyes. For now. But when these troubles are over, then he will see—"

"No!" Martine shouted into the summer air. "He *won't* see. At least, not a brown, plain girl like me." She turned and started toward the building.

Marie-Thérèse rushed after her, tugging at the sleeve of Martine's sweater. "Oh no, Martine. Such nonsense talk will not get you out of what you must do. You see this face?" She jabbed a thumb toward her own cheek. "You think my Christophe does not love the brown face of his *maman*? You think he spend two years with you because he thinks you are plain and ordinary? You must do better than that, my girl, to get out of your duty."

"Madame Bri..." Martine, standing in the doorway, sputtered. "I only meant...my duty...what do you think I can do?"

"Go to Toulon."

"Toulon?" Martine shook her head. "Why would I do that?"

"This woman, the one who carries my son's child, she has a...a husband."

Martine's jaw hung slack. Had she been in Martinique, a fly would have found an easy resting place. The girl's eyes widened. "A baby?" Martine staggered back. Her face looked as though it had been struck by a fist in an iron glove. "Madame Brillard, what are you saying?" Martine's eyes bored into Marie-Thérèse.

"I think I tell you. If not me, then maybe Louis-Phillipe? I think you know already...this woman...this Frenchwoman, she carries Christophe's child."

Martine's blinks came so fast, Marie-Thérèse wondered if a swirl of dust had caught in the girl's eyes. The
Sénégalaise's head bobbed. Marie-Thérèse flashed on the
memory of the palsied boy she sometimes saw at the flea
market.

"Madame Brillard," her voice sounded strangled, "you're
saying to me that Christophe's woman is…is pregnant?
Oh my God." Martine swayed before Marie-Thérèse. "No,
there's more. Worse! She…Christophe's new woman…has
a *husband*?"

Marie-Thérèse grabbed the tall girl and pulled her
down to her chest. Martine's trembling cries shook both
their bodies.

"*Non. Non.*" Martine pulled away from Marie-Thérèse,
her eyes red. "Christophe would never…I know him." She
sniffed in air. "You are right, Madame Brillard. I do know his
soul." Her voice cracked. "The Christophe I know, the man I
know, he would never have an affair with a married woman."
Tears rolled down her cheeks. "There must be some mistake.
Christophe would never…never…not if he knew."

"But of course, my boy did not know. She, this
Frenchwoman, she never told him. Not until it was too late."
Marie-Thérèse shook her head.

"Too late?" Martine's muddy eyes bored into her. "You
mean Christophe didn't know about the husband until she
told him about the child?"

"Oh no. That one did not tell my son about the husband
even then."

Martine's eyes searched Marie-Thérèse's face as though
she were looking for some clue to make sense out of her
words.

"It was the husband. He found them together." Marie-Thérèse watched a fresh wave of shock roll over the girl's face. "Not till then did my Christophe know the truth."

"Together? And the husband discovered them like that? Mother of God!"

"Martine, I know I ask a great favor of you. Could you, would you, travel to Toulon?" Marie-Thérèse held her breath as she watched the *Sénégalaise*.

The girl's knees wobbled. Martine took a forward step to catch her balance. Now her eyes glowed the blackness of coal.

"Martine, I beg of you. Help my son. Go to Toulon. Speak to the nuns."

"Nuns? The sisters?" Martine's body shuddered.

"The husband has banished her from Paris. Will you go?" Marie-Thérèse raised her voice. Martine seemed in a trance. "The woman has been taken to Toulon, to a nunnery there. My boy, my Christophe, wants her back in Paris. If you don't go, he will go himself. And that could be very dangerous."

Martine blinked her eyes. Was she awakening? "That night," she began, "the cut on Christophe's arm. He put it there, the husband, didn't he?" Martine's eyes refocused.

"And my boy came to you." Marie-Thérèse prodded the girl's memory. "In his heart, it will be you in the end. Always you, Martine."

"No, *madame*. I know you want it, but it will not be me." Martine jumped to life. "Christophe has not asked for my help, has he?"

Marie-Thérèse felt the scream erupting from her throat. She struggled to push it back and failed. "Me. Marie-Thérèse

Brillard. I ask for your help. My boy will die if you don't give it to him."

"Madame Brillard, I would help you, but Christophe…" Martine clenched her hands as she puffed her cheeks in and out. "Why does he want the wife of another man?"

Marie-Thérèse patted Martine's shoulder. "He doesn't. Oh, in his head, at this moment, he thinks he wants this woman. For now. But that will pass. That I promise you. It is the child he really must have." Marie-Thérèse patted Martine's hand. "If I go, if I travel to Toulon, will you come with me?"

"I…I don't know what I can do. Christophe has made his choice. The Frenchwoman and their child…" She squeezed Marie-Thérèse's fingers. "But I don't like to see you this unhappy. I will take the train. I will sit with you. But that is all I will do."

"Tomorrow? Can we leave tomorrow?" For the first time in more than a week, Marie-Thérèse felt a glimmer of hope.

"Saturday. After work. But don't tell Christophe." Martine's tears had dried.

CHAPTER 35

The train rocked the tracks as it made its way alongside fields of yellow sunflowers, patches of new summer grass, and mind-soothing lavender. Marie-Thérèse looked beyond Martine, whom she had given the widow seat she coveted, to the rolling hills of Provence. Half-timbered houses, stone cottages, and the occasional chateau on a distant hillside drew her attention from the dialogue she had carefully worked out in her head. Now she had to say her speech to Martine.

"*Billet, s'il vous plaît.*" The conductor walked the length of the second-class car.

Marie-Thérèse reached into her tapestried carpetbag and extracted two tickets. She pulled out the pink and gold boudoir pillow Glovia had loaned her for the occasion. "Here you are, *monsieur,* and how long to Marseille?" She put on her cheeriest smile as she held out the two tickets.

"One hour, *madame.*" The conductor looked down at her ticket. "And then another two after you change trains in Marseille." He returned the clipped ticket to her.

"Martine." Marie-Thérèse nudged the girl, who was making good use of her seat with a view. "Before we reach Toulon, I want you to stuff this in your underpants." Her eyes peered around the train car before she nudged the small pillow onto Martine's lap.

The girl turned to her. "*Madame?*"

Marie-Thérèse moved in close. She scanned the train car once again as she tried to sort out the descriptions Glovia had given her of the husband, the man's father, the wayward Genvieve, and the restaurant workers. Any one of them could be on this train, and she couldn't afford to arouse suspicion.

"Madame Brillard." Martine's insistent voice cut through Marie-Thérèse's planning review. "You want me to do what with this pillow?"

Marie gave one more quick look around the train car. Now she leaned her shoulder into Martine's. She picked at the girl's heavily pomaded, tufted hair, her lips almost close enough to whisper in Martine's ear. "A middle-aged woman with a brown face will not be believed at the nunnery." She looked around again. "The husband was in the Resistance. If he asks questions, he could sort out that I might be the *mère* of Christophe."

"You want me to wear this thing in my underwear?" Martine prodded. "What for? I will look preg—oh, I see. You *want* me to look *enceinte*. That's absurd. The husband will be just as suspicious of me."

"I hope you will not see the husband. Just the sisters. And they will take you for a poor black girl in need of redemption. No need for suspicion."

"And you want me to do such a thing?" Martine pushed the pillow back toward Marie-Thérèse. "I know I agreed to come along, but...no!"

"I know what you said, girl, but now is the time for you to do the action. Now wear this pillow when you talk to the nuns." She pushed Glovia's pillow into Martine's lap.

"*Mon Dieu!*" Martine raised an angry voice to Marie-Thérèse. "I will do no such thing. *You* speak to the nuns!" She pounded the flat of her hand into the pillow.

Marie-Thérèse shook her head. "Don't you think I would do that if I could? Who would believe that a fifty-one-year-old woman would come in secret to deliver a baby?"

"Oh." Understanding flooded Martine's eyes. "Now I see. I'm to be pregnant, and you hope I will meet up with Christophe's...his Frenchwoman at this nunnery." Martine's eyes sparked. "Why in the hell would I want to do that?"

"To pass her a note." Marie-Thérèse hid her surprise at the girl's outburst. She gestured to the carpetbag. "Don't worry, I write the note, not Christophe. And you will not have to speak long to her. You give the paper and then you tell the nuns that your heart cannot do it. You will marry the father."

"Madame Brillard." Martine shook her head. Her greased-down hair did not move. "No."

No matter how much Martine frowned, Marie-Thérèse was determined to coerce the girl into action. "The note will tell her, the Frenchwoman, to make her way to..." Marie-Thérèse scrambled in the bag for another scrap of paper. "Here. See. This park."

Martine turned her head back to the window. Marie-Thérèse heard her labored breathing.

"Madame Brillard," the words struggled out of Martine's throat as she kept her eyes on the passing scene outside the train-car window, "who helped you with this ridiculous scheme?" She swung back around to glare at Marie-Thérèse. "Once this woman gets to the park, *if* she gets to the park, then what?"

"I meet her there, of course. We take the public transportation to the train station. You will go back there yourself, *sans* the pillow, of course. Then we all catch the train back to Paris." Marie-Thérèse exhaled, glad that she had unburdened herself of the plan that had taken her two days to perfect.

Martine's head shook so much, Marie-Thérèse wondered if the train hadn't hit a particularly rocky stretch of track.

"And what does she do, Christophe's woman, once we all get back to Paris? Live with you and Christophe?" Martine's voice rose over the din of the train engine. "You think I want to help with that? The woman is an adulteress, for the name of God!"

Marie-Thérèse put a finger to her lips and darted her eyes around the train compartment. "Once in Paris, Madame Johnson will sort it out."

"I can have no part in such an insane scheme. We'll all be condemned to hell."

"If it helps my Christophe, then I will be the first to dance the cancan in hell." Marie-Thérèse crossed herself. She'd forgotten. She left Papa's rosary at home.

Martine clamped her lower teeth over her upper lip. Her forehead furrowed into a frown much too deep for a girl not yet twenty-four. "Madame Brillard." She drew out the name. "Does Christophe even know that you are here?"

"Uhh." Marie-Thérèse scrambled for an excuse and cursed herself because one refused to present itself fast enough. "Christophe...he cannot be here. It is best if I solve this problem for him." She turned a hopeful face to Martine. "It is a mother's duty."

Martine slammed back against the train seat. She slapped her forehead with her hand. "I must be absolutely out of my mind to do this." She turned to Marie-Thérèse. "If I burn in hell for helping an adulteress, I will insist that the devil push you in the fire first."

CHAPTER 36

Alain-Hugo stared at the golden figure of Jesus hanging on the wall behind the head of Mother Superior. The nun scribbled notes on a slip of paper between making clucking noises and sending condemning looks in Genvieve's direction. It was the backdrop to which the three-dimensional figure of the crucifixion was affixed that mesmerized Alain. The deep red background pounded the truth of his pain into his heart. Red, the color of blood. The child his wife carried was not of his blood. The misery that had settled within him these past weeks squeezed his heart again.

"*Monsieur.*" Mother Superior looked up from the mahogany desk, the best piece of furniture in the private study. She pushed her glasses back onto her nose. "Let me see if I have all the information correct."

Alain-Hugo, sitting in the austere office, forced his eyes to focus upon the sister. Her face, as pale as that swath of white covering her forehead, provided the only contrast in her costume of head-to-toe black. She sent a rush of pity toward him, but it was not sympathy that Alain wanted. He felt his back tighten in the thin-cushioned chair on which he sat. Out of the corner of his eye, he caught a glimpse of Genvieve seated to his left. To look at her directly pained him. He grabbed the armrests and scooted his chair away from his wife. He twisted his back to her and stared at the Bible on Mother Superior's desk.

"*Monsieur*?" Mother Superior frowned.

"Of course." Alain-Hugo pulled himself back from his misery. "I'm sure you have it all there."

"It is an unusual circumstance, *monsieur*." She removed her glasses and trained her eyes on Genvieve. "We don't have many husbands who come to us. Nor many married women…" She touched the small crucifix hanging on a gold chain from her neck. "Very few married women wish to give away their babies."

Genvieve's sigh was audible, but at least her tears had dried. These past days, Alain had struggled to shut out her pleadings.

"I want the child given to a decent family, you understand." He pursed his lips as he sought the head nun's eyes. "Just not a family in Paris. I wish no harm to the child."

"These are difficult times, *monsieur*. Even with the war over, very few country families have the means to support another mouth." Mother Superior slipped her hands into the sleeves of her habit and sat back in her well-padded leather chair. "We find that we have the most good fortune with boys. Placing them in monasteries for the redemption of their souls." She turned to Genvieve. "Pray that your child is male."

"*Non*." Genvieve straightened in her chair. Her face flashed hints of defiance. "No. I do not wish this child placed in a monastery. He must go to a family…and he has done nothing to need his soul redeemed."

"Oh, *madame*, we have all been born in sin. Surely you do not presume to know the heart of God?"

"No. Of course not. Yes," Genvieve stumbled. "I only meant that—"

"In any event, what you ask is difficult, but not impossible, unless..." She unfolded her arms and leaned across her desk toward Genvieve. "This child is legitimate, is it not?"

Genvieve dropped her head as though she had been punched. Mother Superior arched an eyebrow and turned a questioning face to Alain.

He cleared his throat. "There has been a...I was away... the Resistance."

"All France blesses you, my son." Mother Superior made the sign of the cross. "Now, tell me of this impediment to a legitimate birth."

"While I was away there was an indiscretion." Alain-Hugo swallowed. He fought to keep his face impassive. "I wish no harm to the child, though it is not..."

Mother Superior's exhale ricocheted off the walls. "I see."

Alain-Hugo turned to Genvieve, whose body seemed to shrink into her hard-backed chair under the withering condemnation of Mother Superior.

"And I want my wife to remain here, at the convent until after the..."

A knock came softly at the door behind him. "Mother Superior, may I see you for a moment?" A younger sister stuck her head through the door. She wore the habit of a novitiate. "The birth appears imminent, and the doctor wishes to speak to you."

"Please excuse me." Mother Superior nodded to a Bible on her desk as she moved toward the door. "*Madame*, I suggest you read this. And *monsieur*," she clamped a sympathetic hand on Alain-Hugo's shoulder, "we shall offer special prayers for you tonight."

The golden Christ figure, with its blood-red background, drew Alain-Hugo's attention again. He wasn't sure how many seconds passed before the sound of Genvieve's voice finally poked into his brain.

"I ask you again," she said, her voice low, almost muffled, "let there be a divorce."

In his two years with the Resistance, he had never known the impact of a blast from a Luger into his body. Now he understood what that flesh-searing blow must feel like. He swung around to Genvieve. "How could you speak of...that word in this, the house of God? I've told you before that there will never be a divorce."

"You cannot even bear to look at me, Alain-Hugo." She turned in her chair to face him. "And when you do, it is with such hatred." She twisted the handkerchief. "How can you keep me as wife for the next forty or fifty years if you cannot stand the sight of me?"

Alain looked back at the figure on the wall. "I will pray for the strength to do what I must."

"But will you pray for the strength to forgive?"

He turned back to her. "What you did...your betrayal can never be forgiven." The bile rushed to his throat.

"You have stopped loving me." She held those amber eyes steady on him.

Alain-Hugo dropped his head. "Love?" He looked into her face. "You have killed all the love I once had for you."

"I am sorry for that, Alain-Hugo. I truly am. But what will you do with me—a wife—when you find the woman that you *will* love?" She leaned toward him in her armless chair. "And you will love again."

"What will I do?" Alain shook his head. "What will I do if I find a woman I can trust? I will love her with all my heart and soul."

"And what of me? Your wife."

"You?" He was puzzled. "You will remain a wife. Here in Toulon."

"Alain-Hugo, you cannot make me stay in Toulon. No more than you can make me stay here at the convent." She shook her head. "I will not be a prisoner."

"A prisoner? Is that what you see? I am giving you the opportunity to redeem your soul! To save what is left of your name." The bitterness bit into his tongue. "I offer you salvation. How dare you refuse—"

Genvieve shook her head. "I will do as you say." She turned a composed face toward him. "Alain, I know how important your family's name is to you. How you want to avoid scandal. I will help you, if you promise me one thing."

"You dare bargain with me? Look at you!" His voice rose. "Your crime is right there in front of you."

"That may well be." Genvieve flashed a face at him that would have rivaled that of many of the women in the Resistance. "I can make this episode easier for you, or very difficult. What I want is simple."

"No divorce."

"I understand. All I want is your promise that this child will be given to a family in Paris."

A wave of white-hot anger burst into his chest. "To your lover? Never!"

Her face looked impassive, her tone sounded cool. "I understand that, too. No, the child will go to a family of your choosing in Paris. If they require money to keep my son, I will supply that. I only ask that I be able to see my child occasionally."

Alain-Hugo stood and closed the short distance to the still-seated Genvieve. He towered over her. "And you will then run straight to your lover?"

She returned his glare for several seconds, then looked at the crucified Jesus on the cross.

"If I agree, Genvieve..." A dozen thoughts paraded through his head. His father. His mother. The restaurant. His friends. "I want three things from you."

She turned back to him.

"You will remain here at the convent until you give birth. You will give the good sisters no trouble. And you will never see your lover again." He bent down close to her face. "I will kill him if you even try to contact him." He stood back up. "And you, after that."

He watched her swallow, but the steadiness of her gaze had returned. "I must be allowed to see the baby at least twice a year."

"I guarantee no more than once, and you must never reveal that you are the mother."

She swiveled in her seat and looked again at the crucified Jesus. She clasped her hands in prayer. He watched her mouth the words of the rosary. And he wondered: Was it true? Could a woman guilty of such a great sin actually be redeemed?

"I will do as you say," she whispered just as Mother Superior turned the handle on the door.

"That's all settled," Mother Superior announced. "*Monsieur,* may I suggest that *madame* go with Sister Margaret-Adele to the mothers' dayroom while you and I finish the paperwork?"

"That will be just fine." Alain-Hugo turned back to Jesus hanging on the cross. Had he done the right thing?

CHAPTER 37

Christophe watched the figure of Martine in her gray dress with those sprigs of embroidered flowers sprinkled down the front. He had seen the garment on her often enough these last four years, but why did it suddenly make Martine look six months pregnant? Christophe leaned in closer to the stone facade of the Toulon train station.

And then he had his answer. Maman.

There she stood, instructing Martine just as though the girl were one of her own children. Christophe recognized that "I-won't-take-no-for-an-answer" expression on Maman's face. His mother was never going to change. That's why he'd decided just to agree with her when she insisted that he stay in Paris and out of Toulon. Maman had enlisted Madame Johnson, and almost every other person she'd ever met, to keep him away from Genvieve. It was not going to work.

He'd had little difficulty piecing together the tiny slips of the tongue from Collette, Louis-Philippe, and even Maman herself. But Maman had one trick he hadn't predicted. When he followed her to the D'Orsay train station this morning, he'd been stunned to see Martine there. But the frown on his friend's face told him that Martine had not come along willingly.

Now here the two women stood in the mild June afternoon with a soft breeze from the Mediterranean sweeping the air clean. Christophe watched as Maman pointed Martine in the direction of the Sainte-Maria Majeoure. From his own map, he knew the Convent of the Magdeleine stood just behind the bomb-damaged church. He tapped his fingers along the length of the unfamiliar fake mustache he had glued to his upper lip this morning. Mercifully, it still held tight. He watched Martine trudge up the street. If Maman followed, he would have to reveal himself before he wanted. He could not have his mother put herself in harm's way more than she already had. He watched Marie-Thérèse turn off the street, walk past a small park and step into the nearby café, and settle herself at one of the inside tables by the window. Christophe managed a smile of relief. Maman would pay no attention to an anonymous priest walking along the street a half block away. Now all he had to do was discreetly follow Martine.

As his old girlfriend walked past the cathedral with its blasted-out walls, Christophe remembered underground news of the ferocity of the battle for Toulon when the Africa Corps, with its Senegalese troops, had liberated the city last August. He'd felt a surge of pride for the Africans though he'd rejected being counted among their ranks. He watched Martine approach the convent. Though she must have hated this assignment, she carried herself with that steady, quiet courage he admired most in her. She must have come from warriors.

Whatever Maman had schemed just might work with Martine's help. He had to admit that a seemingly pregnant girl walking into a nunnery known to help unwed mothers was a masterstroke he wished he had come up with. He kicked at the ankle-slapping priest's cassock he wore as he glanced behind him. The little café was too distant for him to get a look at his *mère*. Despite her meddling ways, she did have a good heart. He blew a kiss in her direction. He felt almost giddy. He would soon rescue Genvieve.

Christophe adjusted the unfamiliar *soultane*, checking that he'd buttoned the garment correctly. He fumbled with the black biretta and pulled the three-ridged hat lower on his forehead. But that only left more showing of the black toupee he'd stuck under the biretta. Christophe recited the results of his research to himself: The Order of the Brothers of Saint Thomas the Beloved. Founded in Aix in 1261. Devoted to growing special flowers from which the dyes used in tapestry making were extracted. Aix. 1261. Special flowers. Colored yarn for tapestry.

Martine pulled the rope on the gong announcing her arrival at the gated front door of the Convent of the Magdeleine. Just a few feet behind her, Christophe grimaced. He'd almost forgotten the most important part of his cover story. The reason for his visit to the good Sisters of the Madeleine. Orphan children. Boys to be raised at St. Thomas…to work in the fields of flowers. Christophe had to convince the Mother Superior that he was the rare exception in the order. He, himself, had not been born at the Convent of the Magdeleine, nor turned over to the reclusive monastery to work as a lifelong indentured servant.

"You have come to repent your sins against God." A robust-looking nun peered through the locked iron gate at Martine. Speaking what she must have taken as obvious, she pointed a finger at Martine's middle. "I see that your sin is great."

The girl bowed her head and executed a perfect little bow. "Oh, Sister, if I may speak to the Mother Superior. I am in need of such help."

"Humph." The nun placed two pudgy hands on the grill-work as she inspected Martine from head to foot. "You are not American. You are African." Had she just condemned Martine to Purgatory?

"No. Yes." Martine showed the first signs of stepping out of her assigned role. "I mean, my grandmothers were African; my grandfathers, French." Martine squared her shoulders.

The nun cast a skeptical look at the girl. "And the man with whom you sinned?"

"Sinned? Oh yes, of course, Sister. I have sinned." Martine dropped her head and stared at the cobbled courtyard.

"Well?" The nun tapped her fingers against the iron grill. "Was he French or African?"

Martine's shoulders jerked. "Oh, yes...he was...is a Frenchman."

Christophe stood far to the side of Martine. He wished he could get a better look at her face during this perform-ance of a lifetime. Despite his worry, he felt a flash of amusement. Ahh, Martine had her moments. He remem-bered how they'd walk, stone-faced, past the German sol-dier patrolling their street, and with the man's back to them, they'd whistle "Le Marseillaise" just loud enough to make the guard wonder. Christophe corrected himself. It would never do for a priest to smile at the misfortunes of a wayward girl.

"A Frenchman? I suppose we should count the angels' mercies for at least that." The sister rattled the gate. "The Convent of the Madeleine is most fortunate to have those of good heart who will take in a bastard child."

"Bastard chi—?" Martine slipped again. "I do understand, Sister. I beg of you to help me. Help me cleanse my soul."

"Not that many of your kind cares about such civilities." The sister grudged Martine a head shake. "But I see that you do recognize your sin."

"Civilities..." Martine caught herself. "I do understand, Sister, I do." She lifted her hands in prayer.

"Very few of you *noires* seem to understand the gravity of such an act." The nun dropped her hands into the folds of her robe. "We have almost no one who cares to take in an *enfant noir*. They fear the child will grow up with the low morals of the mother, you see." She turned to walk away.

"Wait, Sister!" Martine raised her voice as she reached a placating arm through the opening in the grillwork.

Christophe stepped forward. He called out to the retreating nun. "Ah, Sister, I see that I do not have to ring the gong."

Martine turned shocked eyes toward him. "Chris—?"

He squeezed her arm, hard. "Christian charity is what you seek, my daughter."

Martine stood transfixed as the nun turned at the commotion. She walked back toward the gate.

"Father?" She examined him. "You are of the order of St. Thomas the Beloved. How may we help you?" She bobbed her head.

"I am Father Sebastian from St. Thomas, yes. We seek your good services. Three boys this time."

"I do not...forgive me, Father. You are not the usual one who comes to us from St. Thomas." She looked more confused than suspicious.

Christophe breathed a sigh of relief as he nodded toward Martine. "No, I am not. Recently, five years ago, I came to St. Thomas from the monastery of St. Andrew. In the Pyrenees. We are an order of silence." Drat. Why hadn't he prepared more? Suppose Mother Superior asked him some little detail he hadn't uncovered?

"I did not think you could be one of ours. A bit of the Spanish in you, is there?" She took in the look of Christophe's golden skin.

The biretta and toupee were working. He hoped his light brown eyes would allow him to pass as a close-enough white Frenchman. "God called me to do His work at St. Thomas."

"Of course, Father." She unfastened the keys from her waist and unlocked the door.

She cracked open the gate to allow Christophe entry and swung it closed before Martine could walk through. Christophe turned to a startled Martine.

"I can see the sin of this girl." He spoke to the nun. "Allow her entry. God knows that the Sisters of the Madeleine hold special pity for this, one of their most unfortunate."

"Well…" the sister mused. "At least the father is a proper Frenchman."

The Mother Superior looked harried as she rushed toward Christophe. Martine trailed behind him and the plump nun.

"Father, I had no word you were coming." Her reddened hands pulled at the sleeves of her habit.

"Oh? Monsigneur Andre-Bartholomew informed me that he had written to you." Christophe reached under his cassock and extracted the forged note from the pouch at his waist. "And he has also sent his requirements in this." He handed her the note, praying that the wax seal he had affixed bore a reasonable resemblance to the one he'd observed at the Sacré-Coeur.

Mother Superior made quick work of ripping open the envelope. She glanced at the note, flushed, and turned to Christophe. "I'm sorry to be so ill-prepared, Father. We shall accommodate you, of course."

"Oh, don't fret on my account." Christophe pulled out his most benevolent smile. "Care for whatever duty you have scheduled."

"Well...I..."

"Perhaps while I wait, I could assist this young woman here." He jabbed a thumb in Martine's direction without looking at her. "Maybe this poor unfortunate might meet other girls in her same state of fallen grace." He sighed.

"Meet the others?" Mother Superior peered around Christophe and the big nun to take her first good look at Martine. "Oh dear, I'm afraid that we don't usually accept her kind."

Christophe reached into his cassock and removed *grand-père*'s rosary. "All the more reason that God's poor fallen creature should take every comfort she can from those who have repented their sins. Have you other young women here who have thrown themselves on the mercy of the Heavenly Father?"

Christophe sensed Martine stiffening. Nerves, no doubt, but he was too close for her to give away their plan now. He made the sign of the cross. "It would be a Christian kindness to allow her to see others who once lived her same life of degradation. I suppose I could make time to counsel the girl."

"That would be a sainted kindness, indeed. But not necessary. I doubt that her sort—"

Christophe made the sign of the cross again and mouthed, "Forgive her, Father."

Mother Superior blushed as she cleared her throat. "Sister Margaret-Adele, take the father and," she chanced a glimpse at Martine, "this unfortunate sinner to the mothers' room." She folded her hands as she addressed Christophe. "I am sorry, Father; if only I had not misplaced the note from your monsignor, I would have…as it is, I must return to my meeting with a father…a husband, actually."

"A husband?" Christophe caught himself. "Do many husbands seek to place their wives? Oh, I see. Married men sometimes have their indiscretions. We must pray for them, too."

"Oh, no, no, Father." She leaned in closer to Christophe. "It is the wife this husband has come to place with us. It is she who has created the…the indiscretion." Mother Superior made clucking sounds with her tongue. "Truly scandalous, really. I'm not sure all the praying in the world will save that one."

"Mother Superior." Christophe added a disapproving edge to his voice. "God can forgive all if we pray hard enough. I insist that you allow me to see her."

Mother Superior turned to her assistant. "Take him to the *Parisienne*. Maybe he can do something with her."

CHAPTER 38

The coffee slid down Marie-Thérèse's throat. She closed her eyes and savored the deep flavor of the drink as she sat in the little café. How long had it been since she'd tasted real coffee? Oh, she supposed Glovia had some at her disposal, but the woman never served it during her soirees. That was the time when the liquor flowed. On those rare mornings when Marie-Thérèse stayed overnight, she always left hours before Glovia even cocked open one eye, and Gaston prepared coffee only for Madame Johnson. Marie-Thérèse looked out at the distant waters of the Mediterranean and rubbed her arms in the warmth of a June day in Toulon.

Coffee and magnificent scenery. That's where she had to keep her focus. She must remain calm awaiting Martine's return. A dozen times this afternoon she had been ready to follow Martine to the convent. What if something happened to the girl? Marie-Thérèse would never forgive herself. Then reason pounded into her head. What harm could come to the mulatto even if her ruse were discovered? Martine would be safe. Christophe, back in Paris, would be safe. Marie-Thérèse breathed a sigh of relief.

It was short-lived. The Frenchwoman. *She* would not be safe, and Christophe would never forgive his mother if something happened to her.

Marie-Thérèse moved to the edge of her seat. She had to get to Martine.

No. She sat back down and rummaged in her tapestry bag. There they were.

She pulled out the packet of letters the *facteur* had delivered to her mailbox just yesterday. They came to her in batches, though the dates showed that they were written on consecutive days. She understood. It took military mail a long time to reach Paris from America. The letters—his letters—did much more than soothe her.

"*My Darling*," they all began. She retrieved the first one from the pack. Each written by Monsieur Lieutenant. He told her of the winding down of the war in America, how good it was to be back home, the excitement of a fresh start. Americans fretted over their other war—the battle in Japan. But Monsieur Lieutenant assured her that he would be safe. The Pacific fight was one for the American navy. In each letter, he reminded her of his parting gift— the ring, and his promise to love her forever. He told her to take her time considering what he asked of her. He would not expect his answer until the whole war was over.

Marie-Thérèse sighed as she fingered the diamond ring that had taken two whole months' pay of an American army officer. She kept it around her neck, even when she was sleeping. She answered each of his letters, usually that very same day. But she included only the most general things about Christophe. So far away, how could Michael Collins do anything to help her son in this current predicament? She refolded his letter and returned the packet to her bag. Where was Martine?

CHAPTER 39

"The mothers' dayroom is around this corner, Father," the big nun announced.

Christophe followed her down the long hall, Martine behind him, the heels of her shoes clacking like pistol shots with each step she took. As he watched the broad back of the nun lead the way, he scrambled to snap together bits and pieces of his plan. Despite his disguise, he needed to take care not to catch Genvieve unaware. Others could be watching. To his right just across from the dayroom, he spotted a small, darkened room, lit only by sparse candlelight. Was it a chapel?

"Ah, Sister, this is your place of prayer? Allow me to better prepare myself in here." He took a step toward the chapel. "I must cleanse my soul of any condemnation." He looked at the nun. "For judgment is mine, saith the Lord."

"As you wish, Father."

"Take this poor unfortunate inside." Christophe gestured toward Martine.

Martine sent a glare in his direction. The big nun had already turned toward the dayroom door. Behind the sister's back, Christophe mouthed to Martine, "Prepare Genvieve." Martine sent a second glare his way. She followed the nun into the dayroom and, mercifully, left the door ajar behind her. Christophe breathed out a sigh of gratitude. Martine was one smart woman. If he strained, he could hear what was said in the mothers' room from his position in the chapel.

Christophe stepped into the chapel, where two candle stubs cast a paltry light onto the altar. He knelt at a spot steps inside the door...the best and safest place to allow him a view through the cracked door of the dayroom. He clasped his hands in prayer. He chanced a look toward the mothers' gathering place. Martine had done her job. She stood just inside the doorway.

"There's no need for you to sit apart." The big nun's sharp voice carried the short distance from dayroom to chapel. But who was she speaking to? Martine wasn't answering.

If only Martine could manage two things: get rid of the big nun, and keep that door open.

"You'll be staying with us for a while," the sister continued. "Make yourself comfortable. You may as well mix with the others. Like you, these poor girls have lost their way." Her voice lowered and Christophe strained to hear. "But you are a married woman. Thy sin is surely greater." The swish of the nun's robes reached Christophe's ears. "As for you," Mother Superior added as Christophe watched, "I fear we cannot accommodate your needs." Was she speaking to Martine?

"If I might have a bit of a look, Sister." The girl had regained her acting skills, and they sharpened by the second: "Just to know that there are others who have who have strayed through their own weakness gives my soul comfort." Martine's acting improved by the second.

"I will pray for your salvation."

Christophe caught a swirl of black in the dayroom door-way. He grabbed his *grand-père*'s rosary and repeated the Stations of the Cross just as the big nun appeared at the Chapel door.

"Father...oh, forgive me." She stopped in the hallway. "I do not mean to interrupt your prayers, but I must attend to Mother Superior. I shall be no longer than fifteen minutes." She pounded down the hall.

Christophe eased off his knees and moved just inside the open chapel door. Close enough to hear snatches of conversation, but discreet enough not to rouse suspicion should he be observed.

Martine no longer stood in the doorway, but her whispered voice caught his ear: "Are you Gen...?"

"What?" Genvieve's voice. Clear, and too loud.

Christophe held his breath. He had to depend upon Martine.

"*Madame*," Martine tried again, "a priest wishes to speak to you. I suggest you listen to what he has to say."

"A priest? Who are you? How do you know my name?"

"*Madame*," Martine's rushed, soft voice, "I know that you are a sinner like me. Yet we both may find salvation if we listen with our ears and keep our mouths closed."

Christophe took two steps into the hallway, looking first in the direction where the big nun had disappeared. He moved to the far wall and inched his way toward the open door of the dayroom. He heard only the subdued voices of Martine and Genvieve.

"Perhaps *madame* would accompany me to chapel?" Martine. "We could pray together for our salvation."

Christophe was about to step inside when she asked, in a louder voice, "May we go to the chapel, Sister?"

Sister? How many nuns were in the dayroom? And how many were on guard? Christophe rushed back to the chapel.

"Neither one of you has officially signed in as yet." A new voice, with the accent of Provence, reached his ear. "I'm sure prayer is much needed for both of you. But you," the voice raised, "you will be assigned to us as soon as your husband completes the forms. No more than ten minutes in chapel, please."

"*Merci*, Sister." Martine's gladdened sound.

Christophe repositioned himself in the chapel's shadows.

Martine walked into the room. "All right. Here she is." A curious Genvieve followed.

"My sister, I have come to save you." Christophe spoke out of the gloom. Adrenaline flooded his chest.

"Father..." Genvieve blinked as she peered at him through the semidarkness.

Christophe checked that he stood well within the shadows cast by the half-open door.

"I am in need of confession...I..." Genvieve cocked her head. Her words stopped in her throat. She stared at him. "Father...I...that mustache." Her eyes widened. "The hair." She pressed a hand to her mouth. "Christophe, is that you?"

Martine stepped outside the chapel and eased the door shut. Christophe could see the creeping shadow of her feet underneath the door.

"What? How...? Oh!" Genvieve threw herself into his arms in the near blackness of the room. Her hands traveled his body. She patted his chest, ran her fingers along the contours of his face. "Oh, *mon cher, mon* Christophe."

He reached his hands around her bulging middle and stroked her back, his heart pounding. "Genvieve." He breathed in the scent of her hair as he moved his lips down the side of her face. "*Mon amour.* I can't tell you...I thought I'd lost you. Forgive me." He buried his face against her neck, the toupee inching backwards, the mustache knocked slightly askew. "Oh, Genvieve, forgive me. I tried to tell myself...I forced myself to believe that I could live without you. But that I can never do, no matter what." He brushed her lips with his.

"*Mon cher.*..that on your lip?" she breathed as she stroked the sleeve of his cassock. "Your arm?" She pushed back the sleeve and brushed her lips over the healing wound. "I love you so very much." Her voice cracked.

He pulled her closer, the roundness of his child in its mother's belly pushing against him. He felt her body suddenly stiffen in his arms. She laid her hands against his chest and pushed away.

"What are you doing here?" Genvieve trembled. "Dressed like a priest? Christophe, you shouldn't...you can't be here!"

Even in the dimness, he could see confusion, denial, belief, and resignation ride across her face.

"Hurry." He reached for her arm. There was no time to explain. "I will get you and Martine out of here."

She jerked her hand away. "Martine? That girl...who is...?"

"A friend. Never mind her. We must hurry." He put his hands on her shoulders, turned her around, and propelled her toward the door.

"But where, Christophe? Where do you take me? Back to Paris?" She pushed her weight against his hands. "Don't you see? That won't work!"

He laid his hands against her back and marshaled her to the door. He reached around her body and laid a hand on the doorknob.

"No!" She raised her voice. "We'll be discovered in Paris. Don't you understand? Alain-Hugo has powerful friends." She turned to face him. "Dangerous friends. Comrades from the Resistance." She blocked his hand with her body.

"I'm not afraid of the Free French. You and I will go on with our plan. Immigrate to Martinique."

"Martinique." The word eased out of her mouth in slow motion. "No." She shook her head. "Alain-Hugo will not give me a divorce, but he will allow me to see the child... our child...if I..." Her breaths came in quick spurts. "If I..." She swallowed. "I need these three months to convince him, convince Alain-Hugo to change his mind."

"Hurry it, you two!" Martine's urgent whisper through the door. "I can hear people coming down the hall. Mother Superior, the nun, and a man's voice I don't recognize."

"Just stay there, Martine." Christophe spoke through the closed door. "And follow whatever I do." He turned back to Genvieve. "You get back to the dayroom and I will come for you later."

"No, Christophe, I beg you! Let me handle this. I have three months to convince Alain to give me a divorce...to set me free. Let me have that time. Then we...you, me, and our baby, we can all be together."

"Genvieve. Three months? I can't wait three months."

"You must trust me. It is the only way." She put a finger to her lips.

Voices drifted down the hall and congregated beyond the chapel door.

"You must go." She whirled around to face him, her back to the door. "Now."

"Now? Without you?" He pulled her into his arms. "I cannot do what you ask." The voices moved closer. Christophe heard Martine tap a heel against the closed door. "What of Mother Superior? And your—?"

Genvieve broke his embrace. "Christophe, if you love me, you must let me handle this for all of us."

"But...I can't just leave. Mother Superior..."

"Why do you stand there, girl?" Mother Superior. She could only be speaking to Martine. "If you need prayer, go inside."

"Father is in there...with the woman. You know, the other new one. I did not want to disturb." Martine played her part well.

"That would be your wife, *monsieur.*" A solicitous Mother Superior paused. "Stand aside, girl."

The door was flung open, and the chapel brightened with the bit of light filtering into the room from the hallway.

"Father Sebastian?" Mother Superior asked. "Have you finished your prayers for this woman?"

Christophe stepped into the shadows and dropped his head. He altered his voice. "Prayer giveth redemption."

"Father?" The husband peered past Martine. The *Sénégalaise* stood just beyond Mother Superior, inside the doorway. "I appreciate your help with my..." The man squinted into the dimness. "Do you come to this convent often, Father?"

"Father," Martine interjected, stepping in front of the husband, "will you pray for me, too?"

"It's...been...arranged." The sound of the husband's staccato voice punched into the chapel. He tried to maneuver around Martine. The *Sénégalaise* held her ground.

"You will stay here until the birth." The husband addressed Genvieve without looking at his wife. He stretched his neck over Martine's head and peered deeper into the shadows. He took a step toward the figure behind the door, bumping Martine.

The girl did not move.

The husband cast a curious look at Christophe. "Father, have I seen you here before? You look fami—"

"And you've kept your promise?" Genvieve laid a hand against the husband's back. "The child will go to a family and not a monastery?"

The man recoiled and glared down at Genvieve. "That priest," he said, gesturing past her, "has he been helpful?"

Christophe held his breath and fixed his eyes on Martine's shoes. Suppose the husband sorted out that women six months pregnant did not wear high heels? Sweat beaded his forehead.

"No one can be helpful to me until I know that you will keep your word." Genvieve sidled between her husband and Martine.

Now Christophe had two women shielding him from view.

The husband's eyes narrowed as he strained to see around the women. The husband laid his hands on Genvieve's shoulders and pushed her against Martine. Martine took three steps back, moving closer to Christophe. In his hiding place, Christophe sucked in his breath as his eyes darted around the tiny chapel. If the man threatened harm to Genvieve, what could be useful as a weapon? The husband tightened his grip on Genvieve, but she gripped his wrists.

Martine whirled around and grabbed the sleeve of Christophe's cassock. "Come pray with me, Father." She fell to her knees, dragging him down with her. "Pray with me here, please, Father. I don't feel worthy enough to approach the altar."

They kept their backs to Genvieve and the husband. Christophe lowered his head. The candle stubs flickered. If he had to, he would grab the candle and jam the flame into the eyes of the freedom fighter.

"When I make a promise, Genvieve, I keep it." The husband spoke, his voice icy. "Remember well the promises I have made you. Know that I expect you to keep your own."

His eyes on the sputtering candles, Christophe sensed Genvieve move between him and Alain-Hugo. Christophe turned his head just enough to catch a glimpse of the pair as the husband grabbed Genvieve by the shoulders and moved her ahead of him through the chapel doorway. "Father, once I've settled my wife," Alain-Hugo's words echoed in the chamber, "I would like a word with you."

"Of course." Christophe muffled his words.

"Perhaps prayers with the Father will allow you to forgive me." Genvieve's crisp voice cut through the room.

With his eyes staring at the small gray tiles on the chapel floor, Christophe heard Genvieve turn and stalk from the room. He clenched his fingers under the sleeve of the cassock as his ears strained to take in every bit of noise. Martine's uneven breaths caught in his ears. He heard low grunts and garbled sounds caught in the throat of Alain-Hugo. Christophe squeezed his eyes shut to better hear. The candle stub burned even lower. The air in the room vibrated as the husband turned away and marched after Genvieve.

Christophe's ribs hurt from holding his breath. With Martine beside him, he slowly forced air into his lungs. Could Genvieve be right? Did the husband hate her so much that, maybe, he would release her from her marital vows? Could he trust this man with Genvieve? Still, she sounded so certain. Three months, she had begged. Could he allow her that much time?

"Father Sebastian." Mother Superior's voice cut through his thoughts. "Sister Margaret-Adele will show this young woman out the back gate. I am afraid that we cannot find a proper placement for the child of a…a *noire*. Not in these difficult times. When you have completed your prayers."

"Ten minutes, Mother." Still on his knees, Christophe kept his head low as he spoke to Mother Superior. "And I, personally, will lead this woman to the front gate. You needn't come for me. I will see you in your study in fifteen minutes. Now, if you please, I will lead this soul in prayer."

"As you wish. Christian charity requires that I have a basket of food prepared for this girl to take with her." He heard Mother Superior walk out of the chapel. He tracked the squeaking of her rubber soles down the hall.

The big nun closed the door behind them. Christophe signaled silence to Martine as he counted to sixty. He turned and took a quick peek at the light filtering under the door. No shadows. He gestured to Martine to remove her shoes. In three minutes, the two slipped out of the chapel and made their way down the maze of hallways to the locked front gate. He boosted Martine to the top of the fence. She pulled the pillow from under her dress and used it to cushion her body against the pointed tips of the fence railing as she scampered over. Christophe followed. He had to trust Genvieve to make things right. With Mother Superior and with the husband.

Martine, running barefoot and clutching Madame Johnson's pillow, led the way back to Maman.

CHAPTER 40

"Stand still, girl, before I stick you with this pin." Marie-Thérèse pulled another pin from the cushion attached to her wrist. "Stop your fidgeting, Collette."

Marie-Thérèse shook her head. Her daughter was testing her nerves over this wedding. She smiled to herself. Thank God for Collette and her happiness. It kept her mother's mind off Christophe and his impatience. Yes, her son had agreed to wait three months until the birth of his child before retrieving the Frenchwoman. And here it was July—already three days after Bastille Day. One month down. Only two to go. Yet Christophe still fretted.

"Collette." Marie-Thérèse raised her voice, more to keep her daughter in line than to chastise the giddy girl.

"I still can't believe you gave your approval to Jean-Michel's family." Collette laughed again. "It was worse than the Inquisition. I thought the day would never come when Marie-Thérèse would find a family worthy enough to marry the granddaughter of Papa Devereaux, the saint of Martinique." Collette's cheeks flushed with another peal of laugher. "You even grilled the grandparents. You even hinted they were worthy of being your in-laws."

Every time the child laughed, she pirouetted on the kitchen chair where she stood in the satin slippers she would wear on her wedding day, allowing the raw edges of her dress to swirl in uneven lines around her ankles.

"I say no such thing." Marie-Thérèse felt a twinge of annoyance. "At least, not to their faces. You want a wedding dress with a crooked hem?"

"I've got a wedding dress that's pale pink instead of white. Why should I care if the hem is crooked?" Collette stamped her foot in feigned disdain.

Marie-Thérèse jabbed the pin lightly into the back of the gown, nipping Collette in the hip. "Ungrateful girl. Your boss give you this fabric for just a few francs. And she even throw in the sketch she make."

Collette settled down and executed a slow turn as she stood on the chair. "Madame Chanel is not my boss. She's officially in retirement. Just likes to keep her hand in the business. Besides, she gave me this fabric only because the dye lot for the silk came out pink instead of white. I'm surprised at you, Maman. You want everyone to think your daughter is not a virgin on her wedding day?" Collette smirked.

"The things you say..." Marie-Thérèse jabbed in a second pin.

"Ouch!" Collette cried out in mock pain. She convulsed in laughter again. "And yes, Maman, Madame Chanel did allow me to use her sketch for my dress—but only because I found it discarded in the trashcan."

"Hmm. A dress by Coco Chanel. I wonder if *madame* will ever un-retire? She could make a name for herself someday."

Collette bent forward and kissed the top of Marie-Thérèse's head. "If she does, I will tell the world that you, my very own *maman*, were the one who made the pattern from one of her sketches and stitched this dress just for me."

"Hush yourself, girl. Your Jean-Michel will love you in whatever you wear."

"Yes, he will love me, no matter what." Collette tilted her head to the side. "And what about your Monsieur Lieutenant, Maman?"

Marie-Thérèse ignored her, but her hand fumbled underneath the neckline of her housedress. Michael's ring felt warm against her skin.

Collette executed a quick turn on the chair, snagging one of the pins on the chair back, undoing part of the hem.

"Now look what you do!" A blast of heat flashed over Marie-Thérèse. "You talk such silliness when what you need to think is your wedding day."

"Mine is in four weeks. And when is yours?" Howls of Collette's laughter rang around the apartment. "Maman's got a *petit ami*. Marie-Thérèse Brillard's got a boyfriend!"

Marie-Thérèse ripped the pincushion from her wrist and flung it on the kitchen table. "Why your mother should care that you get married next month, I don't know." She shook her head as she stalked to the window and swung the casement open wider. The warm July air did little to relieve the furnace-hot heat drenching her.

"What's all this laughing about?" Christophe opened the front door. "Have you heard some news?" He looked hopeful.

"I'm getting married!" Collette announced as she stepped down from the chair. "That's good news. Or did you think Maman was making me another go-to-work dress?" The girl laughed again.

Christophe smiled. "No. It's just that—"

"Your sister is one silly girl," Marie-Thérèse turned to her son, "but this is her time for happiness." She stroked Christophe's cheek. "Your time will come. You'll see."

Christophe shook his head. She had to admit that the boy had made a remarkable effort to sound cheerful in the face of his sister's joy.

"Oh, Christophe." Collette sobered. "You will be the one to give me away, won't you?"

"Me? Collette, I don't think I could face a wedding right now."

"I know I ask a lot." She hung her head. "Perhaps too much." His sister lifted troubled eyes toward him. "If you think it best, I can speak to Jean-Michel. We can postpone the wedding until September. Maybe October."

Christophe gathered his sister in his arms. "You've been an awful bother to me for twenty-one years. And now you expect me to wait two more months to get rid of you?" He held her at arm's length. "And let that dress turn even pinker with each passing day?" He forced a laugh. "What would the neighbors say? Of course I'll give you away." He released her as he looked over at Marie-Thérèse. "And the sooner the better."

Marie-Thérèse smiled as she picked up the pincushion. "Go. Take off that dress. I do the best I can with that wreck of a hem you make for me." She picked up her sewing basket as Collette raced to her bedroom.

"Maman." Christophe moved in close to her. "I think we almost have a deal." Her son grinned.

"Deal?" Marie rummaged through her sewing kit for the thimble. "What sort of deal?"

"Remember, Maman, I told you." He looked down the hallway toward Collette's closed bedroom door. "I didn't want to say anything in front of Collette. All she has on her mind is this wedding."

"And that is what we all must think about these next weeks. Collette will have the perfect day." She patted his face. "Then we make the plans for you."

He shook his head. "That's just it, Maman. We don't have to wait until Collette's wedding." He whispered in her ear. "Louis-Philippe and I talked to the Americans. They have all but guaranteed a contract for baked goods."

Marie-Thérèse frowned as she pulled out the thimble. "Christophe, what do you talk? What baked goods?"

"Oh, it will be small at first. We can't possibly supply all the American needs, but we can deliver bread and about a dozen cakes and pies to them every day."

"Oh?" She held the thimble aloft. "How you cook these bread, cakes, and pies when you have no oven?"

"Well, Maman." Christophe shot a quick look toward her kitchen.

"Oh no you don't."

"It won't be perfect, Maman." Christophe clasped his hands together. "But it will work. Louis-Philippe will do some baking in his mother's kitchen. I'll do the rest here. And the two of us will get the goods to the army base in Louis-Philippe's cousin's car. It will work."

"Slow down, Christophe. You go too fast."

"Maman, I can't slow down. I'll only have to use your kitchen until Genvieve and the baby come home. Then we'll move close to the Americans. You know we can't stay in Paris. I'll use the kitchen in our new place. I'll—"

Marie-Thérèse set the thimble on the table. "You hurt my ears, Christophe." A pain knotted itself above her eyes. "My son, you know I will go to my grave doing everything I can that is good for you." She laid a hand on the side of his cheek. "You know this is true, don't you?"

"Of course, Maman." He removed her hand and walked into the kitchen. He opened the oven door. "I can bake three loaves of bread at a time in here, and if I start at midnight, I can complete over a dozen."

"Christophe." She followed him into the kitchen. "It is not about the bread you can bake. Nor how many *gateaux* you prepare. You plan this new life." She laid both hands on his cheeks, making sure his eyes did not drift away from hers. "And I want you to have this good life. But the woman, this Genvieve, is not yet divorced."

"But she will be." Christophe laid his hands over his mother's. "She will convince the husband. And from what I saw at the convent, he does want his freedom."

"To divorce is to be excommunicated." She tugged on her son's cheeks. "If this divorce takes the time it might, I want you to wait with the patience. I only say this to you because your head must be clear with this woman."

"Maman, you do worry too much. Genvieve will not rest until he agrees to give her a divorce."

Marie-Thérèse dropped her hands and stared at the kitchen chair where Collette had just stood. "Christophe, I must say this to you." She turned to face him. "I know you believe you love this woman, and I—"

"Maman, don't start that Frenchwoman stuff again!"

"That is not what I must say to you. I don't care anymore that she is French. I do care that she will be a divorced woman. Outside of the Church. Will you do one thing for your *mère*, Christophe?"

The boy stepped back, a skeptical look on his face. "I will not give her up. Never."

"And I never ask that of you. Not now. But I do ask that you let her get her divorce."

"Well, yes."

"And you will not be her lover until she does."

"Maman, that's ridiculous!"

"For your soul, I ask this, Christophe. When you fall in love with this woman, you do not know she is married. Now you do. If you become the lover of a married woman, you will be…" Marie-Thérèse swallowed. "Give thought to your child. You do not want your son to be called the child of… of adulterers."

"That's enough, Maman!" Christophe shouted.

"What have I missed?" Collette, dressed in her blue housedress, bounded out of her room carrying the wedding gown.

"Ask your mother and her old-fashioned ideas." Christophe stalked out the door, letting it slam behind him.

"Maman? What have you done now?"

"You pay your brother no mind. Soon he will see that the sense I speak is right."

Marie-Thérèse took the gown from Collette. She sat down on her settee and slipped the thimble on her finger. She prayed she was right.

CHAPTER 41

"Gaston's out arranging for the flowers." Glovia smeared cream over her face as she sat at her dressing table. "He knows where we can get a few more bottles of Veuve Clicquot. What time does that clock say? I've got to get to Le Chat Noir early tonight so I can start sprucing up the place. Just one more week and you get your big wedding, Marie-Thérèse."

"Just past four." Marie-Thérèse wondered why Glovia didn't break down and get herself a pair of glasses. The woman's eyes seemed to be getting worse. "Glovia, this is very good of you. Having the wedding dinner at your club."

Glovia shrugged. "My wedding gift to your daughter."

"So generous a gift! Jean-Michel's family offered to pay, yes? You could have let them at least share, no?"

Another shrug. "Wouldn't have been the gift I wanted, then."

Marie-Thérèse's mind drifted to the letter in her purse. Did she dare talk to Glovia about it? Madame Johnson might think it too trivial, and then... "Glovia, who will play the piano at the wedding party?"

"Oh, the cat we've got now will do, but nobody plays like that American. You know, the one who was sweet on you." Glovia swung around in her boudoir chair. She arched one just-drawn-in eyebrow. "Marie-Thérèse, you heard from that American? Name was Michael Collins."

"Uhh." Marie-Thérèse felt the flush work its way from chest to hairline.

"Honey." Glovia stood from the chair, clad only in her lacy underwear and black *peignoir.* "What you been keeping from Glovia?" She laughed.

"Madame Johnson." Marie-Thérèse stared at her purse.

"Well, I know this guy had a big ole thing for you. You sweet on him, too?"

Marie-Thérèse threw her hands in the air as she stepped over to Glovia's bed. She sat down on its plushness. Something in her head prodded her to get up—she had no business being there—but she could only think about the letter in her purse.

"I guess you just answered me." Glovia sat down beside her. "Honey, you ought to be tickled pink. That was one good-looking cat. Fancied him myself for a while there."

"He wants to know. Now," Marie-Thérèse blurted.

"Run that one by me again, sugar. Michael Collins wants to know what?"

Marie-Thérèse pulled the letter from her purse. Her hand trembled as she unfolded and refolded the thin pages. "He wants me…" She lowered her voice. "He tells me…oh, Glovia, I don't know what to do! Collette will be the new bride next week, but Christophe…he is in such a fix. I cannot leave him."

"Leave him?" Glovia questioned. "Leave your son to do what? What are you trying to tell me?"

She turned to Glovia, adjusting herself on the mattress. "Monsieur Lieutenant…he tells me he will be out of the army...discharged in September." She squeezed her hands together. "By October he will be back in France. A private citizen."

"Hey. That's good news! You know, that man can always have a job at my club. Can't nobody beat him playing that piano."

Marie-Thérèse closed her eyes. Her heart pounded. Should she tell Glovia the rest? "Glovia, I am not you," she began. "I am not a woman that a man comes halfway around the world to...to pursue."

"Pursue?" Glovia leaned in closer, her eyes wide. "Michael Collins is coming back to France for you?" She fell back on the bed, laughing. She kicked her feet on the floor, the black pompoms of her slippers bouncing. "What do you mean, you're not a woman a man would pursue?" She rose up and gave Marie-Thérèse a hug. "Looks like you got *something* he wants. So what are you fretting about?"

"Him. Monsieur Lieutenant. Michael. He wants to come back to Paris and...and marry me. Then we go to America." Marie-Thérèse shook her head. She couldn't believe she had gotten words out of her mouth that her head could not accept as true. "Me. He wants to marry me."

"Yeah. OK." Glovia looked puzzled. "By the looks of you, I'd say you want to marry him, too." Glovia stood and reached for the floor-length green sequined number she would wear this evening.

"Of course I want to marry him! I just can't believe...I just didn't know that such a thing could happen to a woman like me, especially not at this time when I'm so...so old."

"Old? Men, especially French men, like a woman with some seasoning on her." Glovia dropped her *peignoir* and slipped into the gown. "Besides, by October, November, when this guy gets here, your kids will be settled. Or close to it. And it'll take a lot of time to get the paperwork done for the marriage. You being a French national and all." She fastened the gown and headed toward the door. "Bring yourself on in to my study. Let's break out the champagne."

Marie-Thérèse paced as she waited in the study for Glovia to fill her champagne flute. She wished the woman were right about her children. Especially Christophe.

"To you and Michael Collins." Glovia lifted the glass high, just as the front door opened. "That you, Gaston? We're in here. Marie-Thérèse's got a blockbuster of a story to tell you!"

Marie-Thérèse took a sip of her champagne as an ashen-faced Gaston walked into the room—staring directly at her. Out of the corner of her eye, Marie-Thérèse saw Glovia casting curious glances between the butler and her. The bubbles caught in the back of Marie-Thérèse's throat and refused to budge. She coughed to clear her voice. Gaston's face blanched white. The archway where the man stood suddenly tilted.

"Gaston," Glovia's voice arched in alarm, "you look like you just saw death."

The man worked his mouth, but no words came. He kept his eyes on Marie-Thérèse.

Marie-Thérèse fumbled for the armrest of a chair. A palm frond bushed her cheek. Whatever this man had to tell, it was awful, and it was meant for her. Something damp splashed over her foot. Was it her champagne? Marie-Thérèse turned to watch Glovia's stricken face move rapidly between herself and Gaston and back again.

Marie-Thérèse turned to Gaston. His jaw wobbled. He cleared his throat. Still, no words.

"Hell, Gaston," Glovia commanded, "spit it out!"

"Madame Brillard," the words whispered out on a reed-thin waft of air, "please sit."

Marie-Thérèse fell backwards into the chair. Was it Monsieur Jimmie Lee's favorite? "Christophe? Collette?" Her chest threatened to split open to make room for the thumps inside.

"No, no." Gaston came alive. He bounded across the room and knelt beside her. "Your daughter, she is safe. Your boy is safe, *madame*, but..." Gaston looked down at the patterned carpet.

"What the hell is it, Gaston?" Glovia looked as frozen as one of Monsieur Crawford's bronze sculptures.

"Your boy, Madame Brillard, your son has asked me, and almost everyone else, to help him get information about the woman."

"Yeah. Yeah," Glovia urged as she clutched her flute.

"I've asked a friend to frequent Le Poulet Farsi. He goes there every week. The staff...the workers...they got to know him a little bit. Enough to not watch every word they said around him. Today...today when he went, he saw...he saw..." Gaston reviewed the entire pattern of the carpet again.

Glovia slapped his shoulder. Marie-Thérèse reached out a soothing hand.

"Gaston, you may tell me. I will be all right." She stroked his shoulder.

He looked up at Marie-Thérèse. "The place...Le Poulet Farsi is draped in black."

"Black?" Glovia raised her voice.

Marie-Thérèse clamped her eyes closed. The memory, dark and desperate, rolled up from her stomach to her chest. Her lungs forgot to take in air. Pictures. Dear Papa, his face as white as his finished sugar. Smells. Cane juices caramelizing as the giant cooking vats boiled the extracted liquid into sugar crystals. She knew. She just knew. Darling Maman hadn't complained at all. She stood there in Papa's big factory kitchen just outside Fort-de-France, overseeing the workers as they tended the bubbling liquid, capturing the molasses for dear Papa's rum. Darling Maman had simply laid a hand to her perspiration-soaked forehead. Declared her head hurt in the one-hundred-ten-degree heat of a Martinique July, and dropped to the tile floor. Marie-Thérèse knew, just knew then and there, that Edith-Chantal Le Mère, black paramour of Monsieur Devereaux, would never rise from that floor. At age forty-seven, and in the space of five seconds, darling Maman was dead.

"*Mon Dieu*," Marie-Thérèse barely heard her own soft words, "my poor Christophe."

"What?" Glovia called out. "Gaston, what are you trying to say? What's happened? Has someone died at the restaurant? The father?" Glovia eased back onto the longue's cushions, frowned, hunched her shoulders, and sat up straighter. "Is it that bastard of a husband who's dead?" She fumbled for her cigarette case.

Gaston shook his head. "No, not the husband. Nor the father."

"The mother? Why are you looking like somebody stole your sax?" Glovia twittered a nervous laugh.

Gaston sucked in his cheeks. "It is...perhaps a brandy for Madame Brillard?" He nodded toward Glovia's *étagère*.

"How?" Marie-Thérèse gripped the armrest of the chair. "How did...how did it...?" Her champagne flute dropped to the carpet with a thump, dribbling out the last of its contents.

Gaston turned his face to her, his eyes searching for... for what? Signs that she would scream? Faint? That other time, she'd just stood there on the terra-cotta tiles in her father's factory as though sugar juices had solidified her feet to the floor, while all around her, panic.

"They say it was an accident."

Glovia's eyes flitted from her to Gaston and back again. "Accident? What are you two talking about?"

"Perhaps the brandy first, *madame*. Please." Gaston.

It was happening again. Marie-Thérèse felt like stone. "I don't need brandy. Tell me. Is it Collette or Christophe?" She'd heard him tell her no the first time, or had she?

"No, no, *madame*. It is not your children." Still, Gaston's voice sounded apprehensive.

"Then, then what...who?"

"Hold on, sugar. Maybe Gaston's right." Glovia stood and moved to her liquor cabinet. She poured brandy into three snifters.

Glovia handed two of the glasses to Gaston. The woman drank half of her own in one gulp. "OK." Glovia clutched her nearly empty snifter. "Out with it, Gaston."

Gaston lifted the brandy glass to Marie-Thérèse. That other time, while Papa wailed his grief, one of the servants tried to calm him with rum. Another pressed a glass into her thirteen-year-old hands. She didn't want liquor then, and she didn't want it now. Someone was dead. If not her children, then it had to be...who else could cause Gaston such misery in front of her? But liquor wouldn't help. It could not make the pain that would soon be Christophe's go away.

Marie-Thérèse laid a hand over Gaston's. She leaned forward in the chair. "Tell me."

Gaston swallowed all his brandy. He ran his tongue over his lips. "She was with the old woman...the aunt of the husband's mother."

"Oh my God." Glovia jerked and the last of the brandy sloshed in her glass. "What she? Who?"

"With an aunt?" Marie-Thérèse ignored Glovia. "What was an old woman doing at a convent for unmarried pregnant girls?"

Gaston wrapped her hand around the snifter and held tight. "I don't believe it happened at the convent. My spy only heard that it happened in Toulon. Nothing about a convent."

"How?" The liquor felt warm beneath Marie-Thérèse's hand.

"A...a German Luger."

"A Luger?" Two voices battered her ears. Marie-Thérèse looked over at Glovia, who stood with her mouth open and shock in her eyes.

Quick bursts of air flooded Marie-Thérèse's chest, bringing the sting of pain with it. "That's a Nazi gun." She dug her nails into Gaston's hands. "How, where, did she get such an awful thing?"

"They…the people at the Poulet say it was the husband's souvenir from the war. From a German he killed. They say she was cleaning the weapon." Gaston stared into her eyes. "It went off and the bullet struck her in the forehead."

The light faded in Glovia's study. Marie-Thérèse reached out to welcome its grayness. A noise battered in her ears like a long, low moan that went on forever. Was it Glovia? Was it her? Like that other time. Then, the sound had been high-pitched and keen, and when it finally came five days after darling Maman, Marie-Thérèse hadn't recognized the tone as her own until dear Papa squeezed life back into her with beats from his own heart.

She flickered her eyes open to find Gaston fanning her while Glovia laid a damp towel over her forehead. The Frenchwoman—her Christophe's Genvieve—was dead, and with her, his baby. Marie-Thérèse's grandchild. Dead. How was she ever going to tell her boy?

CHAPTER 42

"*Requiem aeternam dona eis, Domine.*" The priest, in his funeral vestments, began the Requiem Mass for Genvieve. The hard bench of the Madeleine church made Marie-Thérèse's hips ache. Like always, she translated the Latin words into French and muttered them to herself. "Grant them eternal rest, O Lord." She tightened her grip on Christophe's left hand. Her boy sat still as stone in the back row of the old Paris church. Dozens of candles flickered off his still face, casting shadows that showed the depth of his shock. Marie-Thérèse looked beyond her son to Collette, who clutched Christophe's right hand.

"*Quam olim Abrahae promisisti et semini ejus.*" Make them pass over from death to life, as you promised to Abraham and his seed. Marie-Thérèse tried to follow Christophe's gaze in the cavernous sanctuary. Mercifully, rows and rows of mourners obscured the casket at the front. But Christophe seemed to be looking into nothingness. She squeezed his hand again. And as it had been since that awful time three days ago when she broke the news, her son sat as quiet as one of the carved marble angels in the Madeleine vestibule.

"*Sanctus, sanctus, sanctus.*" Holy, holy, holy. Gaston, in the row just behind Christophe, turned his head to look for straggler mourners. Gaston was flanked by six burly friends. Glovia had called them all "music lovers" who wanted to support Gaston as he paid his respects to an acquaintance of Madame Glovia. Marie-Thérèse knew better.

She had done a good job of keeping her eyes away from the direction of the front row. With so many mourners—surely almost all patrons and friends of Le Poulet Farsi—seated between her pew and the front of the church, she could not see the husband's family. Fifteen minutes ago, Louis-Philippe had stood watch at the entry to the Madeleine. He gave the signal for Marie-Thérèse and her party to enter by a side door only after the husband had been seated. She clamped her eyes shut and prayed that Alain-Hugo did not know that her son was among those paying respects to his dead wife.

Christophe would have it no other way. In the days leading up to the funeral, he would not, could not, believe his Genvieve was gone. She'd promised him, he repeated over and over: they would be together. Christophe declared he must attend the funeral although he believed the rites, too, could be as much a lie as talk of an accident. Genvieve could not be dead. She had escaped from the convent and gone into hiding, Christophe reasoned. She would get word to him when it was safe. Marie-Thérèse kept her eyes shut and prayed. Let them all get through this service without a confrontation between Christophe and the husband.

"*Benedictus qui venit in nomine Domini. Hosanna in excelsis.*" "Hosanna in the highest," Marie-Thérèse repeated as Glovia slipped a look at her. Marie-Thérèse turned to her left. The entire row was filled with American *émigrés*. On her right, Monsieur Jimmie Lee sat at the end of the row. Monsieur Crawford was next to him. Glovia reached for

Marie-Thérèse's other hand as she sent a silent inquiry about Christophe. Marie-Thérèse mouthed the words, *No change.*

Glovia had insisted that Gaston come along that awful day. She said Marie-Thérèse was in no shape to break the news to her son without her family surrounding her. Marie-Thérèse remembered the tears she'd finally shed as Gaston rounded up Collette, Jean-Michel, and even Louis-Philippe. They'd all stood there, in her living room, when Christophe entered. He had read the horror in their faces before Marie-Thérèse could get out a word. He'd planted his feet on her scratched floor, ready for battle. Shaking his head, he'd called them all liars. Genvieve, she couldn't be dead. Preposterous. He accused her, his *maman,* of one last plot to keep him away from the Frenchwoman he loved. He'd shouted. Christophe even took a swing at Gaston in his fury. He'd grabbed the rosary from Papa's picture and fallen to his knees. His screams filled the *appartement* as he pulled the beads apart one by one.

"*Agnus Dei, qui tollis peccata mundi, dona eis requiem.*" Lamb of God, who takes away the sins of the world, grant them rest. Marie-Thérèse squeezed Christophe's hand. No response. That day, that awful day, her son had vowed vengeance against the husband. Why would the freedom fighter have an amateur like Genvieve clean his gun? The husband hated her. That was why she had run away. The funeral was just a ruse to cover the family's embarrassment. Gaston had been the one to get through to Christophe, though they all had pleaded with the boy to accept the truth.

This was no accident, Gaston had declared the next day. His spies overheard whispered conversations at Le Poulet Farsi. Although the husband's family presumed the staff did not know, every one of them was well aware that Genvieve had been pregnant before Alain-Hugo's return from the war. They even knew that Genvieve wanted a divorce, and that her husband had refused. Gaston had faced down Christophe in Marie-Thérèse's living room and told him what he'd heard. The woman—Genvieve—had not run away. The husband had taken her to the aunt's house for the weekend, for one last round of talks before he decided the fate of the unborn child. The talks had not gone well. When the husband insisted that the sham marriage continue, she—Genvieve—committed suicide. It was the husband's mercy, Gaston declared, that the family fabricated the story of an accident. A death by suicide would never be allowed either a Mass or a burial in sacred Catholic ground. The family lied for the Christian repose of Genvieve's soul. That was when Christophe turned to stone.

"*Requiem aeternam dona eis, Domine.*" Grant them eternal rest, O Lord. "*Et lux perpetua luceat eis.*" And may everlasting light shine upon them. The priest readied to end the Mass and Holy Communion. Marie-Thérèse heard a commotion at the front of the church. She suspected the family was marching past the closed coffin. She felt Christophe's fingers tingle to life. He squirmed in his seat.

"Aggh!" The cry gurgled from deep within her boy's soul. Christophe moved forward, then attempted to rise.

Marie-Thérèse and Collette tugged hard on his hands to pull him back into his seat in the pew. Christophe broke free and trod on Collette's foot as he headed toward the aisle. Monsieur Crawford placed both feet against the back of the pew in front of him to stop Christophe's passage. Monsieur Jimmie Lee Hudson stood, blocking the aisle.

Jimmie Lee's eyes reflected animation as he shook his head at Christophe. Gaston rose and reached for the back of the boy's jacket. One of the music lovers grabbed Christophe in a bear hug.

"I've got to see her!" Christophe's cry rang throughout the sanctuary. "To know if it's true!"

The priest stopped in mid-word. Marie-Thérèse heard more commotion at the front. Another music lover wrestled Christophe into the seat vacated by Monsieur Jimmie Lee. Gaston made his way to the aisle and stood just behind Christophe, a hand gripping her son's shoulder.

"*Et lux perpetua luceat eis. Cum sanctis tuis in aeternum, quia pius es,*" the priest resumed. And may everlasting light shine upon them. With your saints forever, for you are merciful.

The mighty organ of La Madeleine began to play as the recessional began. Glovia laid her arms around Marie-Thérèse's shoulders, hugging her close. Even so, Marie-Thérèse could not stop her trembling. The black-robed priest led the recession, sprinkling incense as he intoned the old words for the dead. A man and woman a little older than herself walked paces behind a man dressed in a black suit. Marie-Thérèse's heart skipped two beats. The husband. Alain-Hugo. She broke Glovia's grasp, pushed Collette aside, stumbled over Monsieur Crawford, and reached Christophe as he broke free of Gaston. The gray coffin, borne by eight pallbearers, glided down the aisle. Christophe reached out a hand to touch the top.

The husband stopped; the rest of the mourners nearly stumbled into one another. He faced Christophe. "I remember you." Alain-Hugo's tear-free face stared at Marie-Thérèse's son.

"And I, you." Christophe moved his right hand in slow motion toward the top of the metal casket.

The husband looked from Christophe's hand to the coffin, and back again. He held his face stiff as he raised an arm to block Christophe. Marie-Thérèse noticed two men behind the husband. Gaston and his music lover friends surrounded Christophe.

"My friends have come to pay their respects." The husband spoke in tones that felt as cold as the marble columns outside the Madeleine church. "Courageux and Panthère. You may have heard of their reputations."

Christophe stared into the husband's eyes. He didn't blink. Inch by inch, he lowered his hand below the husband's blocking arm. "And here are my friends." He nodded to Gaston and the six music lovers. Christophe's fingers snaked below the husband's outstretched arm. He brushed the top of the casket. His eyes never left the face of Alain-Hugo.

With deliberate slowness, the husband reached into a jacket pocket and retrieved an envelope. He handed it to Christophe. "This is for you." He nodded his head toward the coffin. "From her. Let this business be over." Alain-Hugo waved the procession on.

As the recessional moved outside into the humid August air, Marie-Thérèse watched Christophe slump into the waiting grasp of Gaston. She heard a soft, strangled sigh from her boy, and no more.

CHAPTER 43

Marie-Thérèse clung to Glovia as Gaston and the music lovers walked Christophe out a side door of the Madeleine church. In the front of the building, she pressed against a wall as she and Glovia watched the pallbearers lift Genvieve's coffin into the hearse. The family climbed into automobiles parked nearby.

"Come on." Glovia flapped at the short black dress she wore as perspiration stained her underarms. "Let's see what that note's got to say."

"Ohh." Marie-Thérèse's heart still pounded. In her fright, she had forgotten the envelope the husband handed to Christophe. She hurried Glovia around the corner.

Christophe stood surrounded by Gaston, the music lovers, and the American *noirs*. Miss Mabry spotted Marie-Thérèse. "Says he wants a private place to open it." She waved to Marie-Thérèse. "Gaston says we got to get out of here. Now."

Marie-Thérèse rushed to Christophe's side. "Here, we step back into the church. The family has gone. Come with me." She tugged on the sleeve of Christophe's only suit.

Her son nodded and followed her into a small room off the main sanctuary. Light from one of the three high domes poured into the space.

"I turn my back," she volunteered. "You read the note."

Marie-Thérèse stared at the statue of Mary Magdalene in the vestibule. The sainted companion to Jesus was being escorted to heaven by two marble angels. She heard the sound of paper being pulled from an envelope. She waited long seconds, fingering Papa's re-strung rosary.

"I can't...I won't believe...Maman," Christophe's choked voice called out. "Genvieve would not do this. She said...she promised..." Soft sobs drifted through the space.

Marie-Thérèse turned around. She willed her hands to her side. Christophe needed these moments with his own feelings, not hers. He finally looked at her with reddened eyes.

"I don't know, Maman. I don't think I..." Tears coursed down his cheeks.

"Take your time, son. This is not something you must share with your *mère*. Not until you are ready."

The paper shook in Christophe's hand. He crumpled the single sheet into a ball, then smoothed it out. "No, Maman...I mean, I can't read it. You read..." His voice was swallowed in tears.

She took the paper from his trembling hand.

Christophe. It is no use. Alain-Hugo will never give me a divorce. I am sorry that I must take this way out. It is for the best. Let this business be over. Genvieve.

Marie-Thérèse stared at the handwritten words. She looked at her son, who held his eyes closed.

"How could she?" His words were garbled in his throat. "I don't believe it. I can't believe it. She promised me we would be together, the three of us." He sobbed. "I should have taken her out of that convent when I had the chance! I should never have allowed her to stay, no matter what she said. I should have known!" Christophe slammed his chest with his hand. "The husband would never give her a divorce. Why did I believe she could change his mind?"

Marie-Thérèse pulled her son close. "The pain you feel, I will never know," she whispered in his ear. "I only know my soul and the soul of your sainted *grand-père* break for you." She rocked him in her arms. "And from the core of this mother's heart, I am so, so sorry."

"Madame Brillard," Gaston called, peering into the antechamber, "we really must leave this place. Now would be a good time."

Marie-Thérèse pulled out her black-edged handkerchief and wiped Christophe's face. Then she wiped her own. "Of course, you are right, Gaston. We go now, Christophe." She slipped the letter back into his hands.

Outside, she watched Gaston and the music lovers settle Christophe into a car that sped down the Place de la Concorde and turned onto the Place Vendôme. Glovia headed toward a car door held open by Monsieur Crawford.

"Come on." She quickened her pace. "Let's get out of here. Gaston's taking everybody to my house."

Marie-Thérèse rushed to catch the entertainer. She pulled on the short sleeve of her dress. "Glovia, I don't believe it."

"You don't believe what?" Glovia stopped just feet from the car and Monsieur Crawford.

"I read the note."

"Oh? What did the thing say?"

"Do you know any woman who writes in a square hand? I've taught school here in Paris for almost seventeen years. I've seen all kinds of handwriting. Squiggles I can barely make out. Penmanship so good it could win prizes." Marie-Thérèse shook her head at Glovia. "I know without looking when a girl writes her words on the paper. And I know when the marks come from a boy. I know when one copies the schoolwork of another. That letter did not come from a woman."

"Marie-Thérèse," Glovia soothed, "you're taking on a bit too much, you know." She patted Marie-Thérèse's cheek. "Honey, you just need some rest. This has been quite a strain."

"This was no accident."

"Yeah. That's what Gaston said." Glovia rummaged in her black purse for her lipstick. "What kind of a fool would point the barrel of a gun at her own head when she was supposed to be cleaning the damn thing?" Glovia twisted off the cap of the lipstick tube. "But this penmanship idea of yours is a little farfetched, don't you think? Maybe the girl just couldn't write."

"Madame Johnson, I know you have not had the children, but—"

"I almost had me one once." Glovia looked past Marie-Thérèse and up to the top of the Madeleine church, then looked into Marie-Thérèse's eyes. "I killed it."

"You kill your child? How? Why?" Marie-Thérèse cocked her head. "Let me ask you this, Glovia. Did you love the father?"

"Love? Mr. Johnson? I told you. I hated that old man's guts." She snapped the cap back into place.

"Is that why you didn't want his child?" Marie-Thérèse looked directly into Glovia's sunglass-shielded eyes, though she sensed the American would give anything not to face Marie-Thérèse at this moment.

Glovia's words carried on the sigh slipping out of her mouth. "I was sixteen."

Marie-Thérèse leaned in closer to hear Glovia's words over the street traffic.

"Sixteen, but I knew better. He was the richest colored man in town, but he sure had me working in his funeral parlor doing all the grunt work. I knew I shouldn't have done it. Knew it was dangerous. He sent me to get the embalming fluid. It was on the top shelf, you see. I pulled out the ladder. Went up four rungs." She looked down at her patent-leather shoes.

"Yes?"

"The jar of embalming fluid was bulky. Kind of heavy. It dropped off the shelf and hit my shoulder. I slipped off the ladder." She tried a wan smile on Marie-Thérèse, but tears filled her eyes. "I was six months. Started bleeding heavy. The baby died."

Marie-Thérèse gathered Glovia into her arms. She rubbed the taller woman's back. "That's what you feel, Glovia." She held her at arm's length and peered into her face. "Loss. You feel like you were cheated. Yes, you hated the man who was the father." She gave a little shake to Glovia's shoulders. "And no, you didn't want to be pregnant with his baby." She patted her cheek. "But even after thirty years, you still cry over that lost child."

Glovia pulled out her own handkerchief and dabbed at her eyes as Monsieur Crawford sent an anxious look toward the pair. "God knows I do."

"But what if you loved the father? Would you ever, on purpose, kill the child of the man you loved? Even if things got so bad with yourself? Wouldn't you move the heaven and the earth to keep his baby...your lover's child alive?"

The woman stared back at her, and slowly shook her head. "Not an accident. Not a suicide. Marie-Thérèse, are you saying what I think?" Glovia's tears dried.

"This is no suicide. He kill her. The husband...this Alain-Hugo. He pull the trigger himself. He shoot Genvieve with the Luger."

Glovia clamped her hands on Marie-Thérèse's shoulders, ignoring Monsieur Crawford's increasingly frantic looks. "Now, see here, Marie-Thérèse. You can't say a thing like that in front of Christophe." She shook Marie-Thérèse. "You hear me?"

Marie-Thérèse laid her hands over Glovia's. "But it is the truth. My son has the right—"

"Good God, no!" Glovia shouted. "That boy's in bad enough shape. If he thinks that the woman he loved was murdered by her husband...good God Almighty!"

"But—"

"No buts about it." Glovia dug her hands deep into Marie-Thérèse's shoulders. "You know as well as me that if Christophe thinks that girl was murdered, he'll go after the husband."

"*Mon Dieu,* I don't want that!" Marie-Thérèse tried to squirm away from the fingernails digging into her shoulder.

"You think the girl was murdered. Maybe yes, maybe no, but that's something we can't have your son believing. He's got to think it was a suicide."

"But Glovia, you didn't see him. First, he prays she is alive. Then he must accept that she is gone. And now you ask that he believe she took herself away from him on purpose."

Marie-Thérèse sucked in her lip. "No. I cannot bear this much pain in my boy. He blames himself."

Glovia smoothed the skirt of her black dress. "Let me put it to you this way, Marie-Thérèse." Her voice calmed. "You can have a son who goes through life blaming himself for the death of his girlfriend—wondering what he could've, should've, might have done different. I admit that's not a good place to be." She played with the tube of lipstick in her hand. "Or you can tell him what you think—his woman was murdered by her husband—and have your boy dead within twenty-four hours, at the husband's hands. It's up to you."

Marie-Thérèse covered her face. "You know I have no choice." She peeked between her fingers at the columns of La Madeleine. "I only pray that I have the strength to keep the truth from my Christophe. Always."

CHAPTER 44

The smell of the sea, even this far from the placid blue-green waters of the Caribbean, always reminded Marie-Thérèse of Martinique. But a snap of a breeze off the Atlantic forced her to snug her sweater close and reminded her that she was not in the sunshine-warmed Caribbean any longer. Instead, she stood on a dock in Le Havre where an early October wind called for a light jacket. She had not yet glimpsed Monsieur Lieutenant, one of a handful of civilian passengers among the merchant mariners pouring off the *Ile de France*. Roped off in another area were hundreds of American soldiers awaiting transport home on the one-time luxury liner, now converted troop ship.

"Have you spotted him yet?" Glovia made her way through the crowd, dressed in a smart yellow outfit that had to be new.

"Not yet," Marie-Thérèse answered. "He said there would be very few real passengers getting off the ship. The traffic is almost all one way. To America."

"Yeah. Yeah. Soldiers going home. Don't worry. Gaston will locate him. Who'd you leave with Christophe?"

"Collette. Then Louis-Philippe will get him for work."

"Well, at least he's still going to work."

"But Glovia," Marie-Thérèse shook her head, "Louis-Philippe says Christophe does his job, but he speaks to no one. He is like one of the machines…a thing with no feelings." She rubbed a hand across the bodice of her dress. "I don't know which is worse. Seeing him cry out his pain, or watching him act like he is already dead." She felt her always-present tears threaten to overflow.

"He still blaming himself?"

"Until he knows the truth, he will always blame himself." Marie-Thérèse bit her lip.

Glovia shot a quick glance at Marie-Thérèse and shook her head.

"But you do not see!" Marie-Thérèse's voice rose. "Glovia, you do not know what he is like. When he is not at the *boulangerie,* he never leaves the apartment. He sleeps hours and hours. And the minutes when he is awake, he takes my kitchen chair and sets it in front of the window. He sits there and stares. Nothing but staring out at the rooftops of Paris." Marie-Thérèse clenched a fist to her mouth. "He says not a word." Her voice strained out. "Not to me. Not to Collette. Not to anyone. I am so worried. More than worried. Oh, Glovia. I fear that he might…that he could do harm to—"

"Baby!" The voice called out from a throng of milling merchant marines.

Marie-Thérèse turned to see a grinning Gaston and a handsome, tan-faced man in a natty, American-style, blue pinstriped suit. She stared. "Monsieur…Michael?" A sudden burst of excitement erupted from that place she supposed had died three months before.

The American cut through the crowd and swept her into his arms. Marie-Thérèse melted into his embrace, relishing the strength of his arms as he squeezed her close to his heart. The moistness of his lips covered her face and mouth. Suddenly the gray sky over Le Havre turned an uncommon blue.

"Don't tell me you didn't recognize me in my civvies?" Monsieur Lieutenant teased. "You look good in that dress." He kissed her again.

"It is the same dress you've seen a dozen times!" she called out in her rusty English. A rush of pleasure swept over her. Where had that forgotten feeling come from?

"Afternoon, Miss Glovia." Michael nodded to the entertainer. "That offer to play piano at your club still good?"

"Sugar, you bet it is." Glovia grinned her best toothy smile. "Welcome back to France."

"The honor, she be great," Gaston tried out his almost nonexistent English. "New music from America?"

"The latest from the Hit Parade." Michael grinned his thanks. "And the best in rhythm and blues." He turned to Marie-Thérèse and gave her another hug. "Now you fill me in on Christophe and Collette." He sobered. "That's what I'm here for. You and your kids."

The tears spilled onto her cheeks as she took his arm and laid her head against his shoulder.

"Gaston, grab that bag," Glovia commanded. "We can just make that afternoon train back to Paris if we hurry."

"And your son, Monsieur Lieutenant. How is he?" Marie-Thérèse snuggled against Monsieur Lieutenant in the first-class compartment Glovia had so generously secured for their trip from the harbor.

He kissed the top of her head. "I know how much you're hurting, baby. About your boy. I'm taking my kid back from his grandparents. I hope that's all right with you?" He squeezed her shoulder. "Didn't know how much I'd missed that boy until I got back home. Went to his high school graduation. Almost cried."

"You are his father, and it is a blessing when a father wants to be with his children."

Glovia cleared her throat. "Me and Gaston are going for a quick bite." Glovia tapped the bodyguard on the shoulder, and the two left the compartment.

"Now that woman knows discreet." Monsieur Lieutenant put out a weak smile. "I got all your letters about Christophe. That was a rough deal. He getting any better?"

A wave of trembling washed over Marie-Thérèse. She shook her head. "Michael, I do not know what to do. I try crying with him. I try praying. Talking about her. Not talking about her. I try everything. Nothing works."

Michael wrapped her in his arms.

"Sometimes I think," she crossed herself, "I think he plans to join her. Genvieve. He might…he could…" Marie-Thérèse buried her head into his shoulder. The rough wool of his jacket scratched her face. She burrowed even deeper and closed her eyes, struggling to brush away her worry.

"We'll just have to come up with some plan to get him off the suicide thoughts, now, won't we?" He sounded so certain.

For the first time in three months, she wondered if she could let another person into her heart to help her protect her boy.

Marie-Thérèse waved good-bye to Glovia and Gaston as she opened the front door to her *appartement* building. She led Monsieur Lieutenant up the three flights of stairs. At her door, she reached into her purse for her key.

"Michael," she whispered. "Christophe...he may not say anything to you. He doesn't speak to any of us. Not anymore. Please don't be offended."

He patted her shoulder. "Let me handle this, Marie-Thérèse."

She opened the door. Collette, in the kitchen washing up the supper dishes, turned a wan smile toward the new arrivals.

Did he eat tonight? Marie-Thérèse mouthed to her daughter.

Christophe sat with his back to the door, his face to the window. He made no effort to turn to greet the guest.

Collette shook her head no.

"Christophe," Marie-Thérèse began, "I told you. Today I go to pick up Monsieur Lieutenant from Le Havre. He's come for...for a visit."

"Hey, Christophe." Michael waved a quick hand toward Christophe's back before he turned to Collette. "And you are much too young to have that deep scowl on your face." He approached her. "Your mama tells me you've postponed your wedding."

Collette shot alarmed looks toward Christophe's back. "I...we...Jean-Michel and I think it best," she whispered.

"Hmm. I understand." Michael had not lowered his voice. "We don't do the formal one-year mourning thing in America either. Not anymore."

Marie-Thérèse put a finger to her lips. Why was he saying such a thing? Didn't he know that Christophe could hear?

"I've got a son. Only seventeen, but still, he's a boy, so I don't have to worry about planning a big wedding. Is that what you want, Collette? A big wedding with all the trappings? Or do you just want to be with the man you love?"

Confusion flooded Collette's face. The soft sound of a body shifting position caught Marie-Thérèse's ear. She turned from her daughter toward the chair at the window. Christophe sat in profile. One eye was fixed on Monsieur Lieutenant.

"Collette." Christophe's voice came out a croak. He cleared his throat and tried again. "Marry Jean-Michel. I want that for you." He looked down at the floor.

"What?" Collette's voice ended in a high note of surprise.

Monsieur Lieutenant dropped his suitcase to the floor. "I don't expect your sister wants a big wedding. I don't believe any of you are feeling like a party right now. I've been studying how this marriage business works in France." He slipped a quick look at Marie-Thérèse.

She shot frantic glances between her son and the man she loved. She felt torn between the two. Why was Monsieur Lieutenant talking about such things around Christophe? She had banned all talk of weddings, parties, lovers, any- and everything that could drive Christophe deeper into his misery. Marie-Thérèse looked at her son and suddenly realized. Her boy had just uttered more than a simple yes or a plain no for the first time in three months. He had actually entered a conversation. A short one, but still he had spoken to a living human being. She turned, openmouthed, to Michael Collins.

"What they tell me is that here in France, it's a simple deal. The couple heads off to city hall when they want to get hitched. A place called *mary...marria...*?" Monsieur Lieutenant spoke in that casual American way as though everything, and everyone, in her apartment was normal.

"*Le Mairie*," Collette offered.

"Yeah. That's where they make the job legal. No muss. No fuss. No church needed. You don't even need a minister or a priest." He looked at Collette. "But I suppose that's what all young brides want. A fancy church wedding."

"No," Collette blurted. "I just want to marry Jean-Michel. I don't care about a dress or the ceremony in the church." The girl turned a questioning face to her mother and then to Michael Collins. "You think I really could...we should...?" She sent a hopeful glance toward Christophe.

Marie-Thérèse swallowed as fresh tears threatened. She hadn't seen her daughter's face this hopeful in months. A pang of regret swept her heart. In trying to save Christophe, had she sacrificed Collette? Before the thought could fully register, Monsieur Lieutenant pulled her into his arms.

"Kids, your mama here has been a bit worried." He looked at Christophe, who returned his gaze. "I know you must be going through hell. My own wife died four years ago, but that was nothing compared to what's happened to you. I miss her, and in some ways, I guess I always will." He sighed. "Christophe, what say we let your sister get married?

She'll always be here for you. But this way, you'll have a new brother to bolster both of you up."

"Of course, I want my sister's happiness." Christophe spoke slowly. "And Maman's. Make it soon." He stood and walked to his room. "I don't think I can be bolstered too much longer."

Marie-Thérèse turned a face mixed with fear and hope to Michael Collins.

The silk sheets Michael had just presented her slipped over her naked body as he slid his knee between her legs. She closed her eyes and let the joy of his touch pour into her. The little quivers that sneaked up when she wasn't expecting them washed her mind clean of all thinking. There were his hands. Large, strong, but with the gentlest fingers. They caressed, stroked her breasts, played with her most personal parts. Thinking galloped out of her brain—all those worries that had fretted her since July. Gone. What to do about Collette and the wedding? Gone. Christophe. He must be saved. Gone. Michael licked his tongue around her nipple. Her mind retreated into itself, grateful to be at rest, at last. Now it was her body's turn to take control. Marie-Thérèse pushed her breast farther into his mouth. He sucked it in, and the shivers raked her body. Somewhere in her head, a message tapped through. They were alone in the *appartement.* No other sound in her ears except her own moans and Michael's breaths pouring warmth down her chest, her belly, lower. A sliver of heaven wrapped itself around her and made her want to call out the Savior's name. Michael moved inside her, and her whole body shifted into spasms of starts and stops. She dug her knees into his hips as the pleasure train roared on.

"*Seigneur Jésus!*" screamed that strange voice that sounded nothing like her own as her hips rose off the bed.

"Marry...me!" His sound burst through the room. "I love you!" sprang out of his mouth on one powerful grunt.

For long seconds, she lay under Michael, her mind and body bathing in the perfume of him. She ran her hands over his hair as bits and pieces of her mind reemerged. "For that, I do anything." Her breaths began to pace themselves into a normal rhythm. "I do anything you want."

More seconds ticked by. "Prove it." Almost no air carried his words as he rolled to his back. Michael stretched out an arm and gathered her next to him.

"Oh, Monsieur Lieutenant." She reached for the silky top sheet. "I think I like that."

"I think..." He panted as he turned a sweating face to her and touched the cord holding the ring around her neck. He slid the diamond to the front and held it against the hollow at her throat. "I think you *do* like..."

She smiled at him.

"I...want..." He took in deep breaths. "Damn, woman!" he managed. "You take my breath away." He smiled as he clutched the still-attached ring in his hand.

She placed her hand over his.

"I know you like this." He ran his hand over her belly as his breathing slowed. "But I want you to prove that you love me." He tugged on the cord holding the diamond.

"Michael. Monsieur Lieutenant. I could never feel like this if I did not love you so much." She stroked his chest.

"Then wear my ring." He fumbled for the knot holding the cord in place.

Marie-Thérèse pulled the crumpled sheet to her chin. Her mind burst out of its prison.

"Don't you know, Monsieur Lieutenant, that what I want is to marry you? But I cannot."

He laid a hand over her mouth. "Don't let those words pass your lips, Marie-Thérèse. I know you love me." He undid the knot. "And I know why you're hesitating."

"Of course you do." She leaned on one elbow as she broke away. "If there was any other way, Monsieur Lieutenant… any other way, I would marry you tomorrow."

"Never in this life would I want to go through what your son is going through." He slipped the ring from its cord. "But I do know what it's like to lose someone you love."

Marie-Thérèse dropped her head and laid a hand on his shoulder. "I know you love her, your wife, very much."

Monsieur Lieutenant lay on his back, his arms reaching toward the ceiling, the diamond ring sparkling off the lights of Paris seeping in through the skylight. "I did. I loved her with all my heart." He sat up in bed.

Marie-Thérèse scooted her back against the headrest.

"I never thought it could happen to me again." He looked at her. "I thought miracles only happened once, if at all." He played with the ring in his hand. "But damn if I didn't get me two miracles." He took her left hand in his. "Marie-Thérèse, I love you in a different way from her, but I love you every inch as much. You are here. Deep in my heart. You will always be here. I want you to take this ring."

Her hand trembled in his. "Oh Michael, I want to. I want to!"

"Listen to me, Marie-Thérèse." He stroked the third finger of her left hand. "What I'm telling you is that love can come around a second time. With the right person." He looked toward the skylight. "God above found you for me. I was dead without you." He twirled the ring over her fingertip. "Just like Christophe."

"Christophe?" Marie-Thérèse jerked her hand.

Michael held it fast. "There is a woman out there for your son. A woman who will love him with all her heart. A woman who, like you, will make the worst of his pain go away. A woman, like you, Marie-Thérèse, who can make him want to live again. If you can, find your boy such a woman." He slipped the ring on her finger.

Marie-Thérèse stared down at her hand. Little glimmers of light from above caught the sparkles and sent showers of hope into her heart.

CHAPTER 45

The priest intoned the last of the Mass. Marie-Thérèse took care in slipping Papa's rosary back into its silk pouch. As she stood from the pew in the Sacré-Coeur, she covered a yawn. A Mass that concluded at eleven o'clock at night had never been her idea of refreshing a soul. At that hour a soul needed rest, not more praying. But no matter. Monsieur Lieutenant had been right two nights ago. She had to find a woman for Christophe. Of course, she hadn't told Michael that she already had a good prospect in mind. Martine.

As departing congregants moved out of the cathedral, every door opening reminded her that she'd made the right decision. Best wait to surprise Martine inside the building rather than outdoors, where the *Sénégalaise* could skip away before Marie-Thérèse could complete her business. Marie-Thérèse followed two other parishioners as they made their way along the pew to the church aisle. As the others headed for the great cathedral doors, she stopped at the end of the row. Better to wait for Martine here.

When she slipped into the sanctuary just after ten, she'd taken her time to adjust to the gloom. Then she'd spotted her. Martine, sitting near the front. Marie-Thérèse secreted herself in the rear. Let Martine say her prayers without interference. Cleanse her soul. Then the girl would be ready to do what she must.

Marie-Thérèse certainly had enough of her own prayers to offer. Standing at the end of the pew, sheltered within the gloom of the Sacré-Coeur, she looked to the far corner of the cavernous hall and at the statue of St. Mary of the Sacred Heart. The marble, in need of a good steam cleaning, stood there in half-light. Marie-Thérèse strained to look at the saint's face. Mary had been a mother. She would understand. Marie-Thérèse had not been wrong in her assessment of her son's feelings for the Frenchwoman, but just in case her words could be misinterpreted in heaven, she fingered the rosary pouch as she looked at the sainted Mother.

More parishioners from the front of the sanctuary moved down the aisle toward the door. Young men. Young women. Smiling behind their whispers. Happy. No more Germans. No more war. Only a bright future. They could have, should have been her Christophe. Marie-Thérèse swallowed to dampen her dry throat. Did she need to rehearse her speech to Martine one more time? There could be no mistakes. She peered toward the altar again. The willowy form of Martine moved down the aisle three pews from where she stood.

The girl startled when she saw her. "Madame Brillard? What are you doing here? I didn't expect…you never attend late-night Mass."

"No, I never come at night, but Collette tells me that you young people often prefer the last service."

"Uh-huh." Martine shot a nervous glance toward the cathedral door. "Madame Brillard," she stared at the mosaics on the floor, "I am sorry about…" Her words drowned in her throat.

Marie-Thérèse pulled a handkerchief from her purse. "It is a hard thing for us all," she murmured.

Martine shook her head. Her hot-combed hair that reached just to her ears did not move. "No. You don't understand." Martine wiped her nose with Marie-Thérèse's handkerchief. "Sometimes…some days…I did want her…" Tears puddled in the girl's eyes. "Christophe's woman. I did want her to…d—"

Marie-Thérèse grabbed Martine's shoulders. "We both know the Frenchwoman, God bless her soul, was not the woman for Christophe." She gave the *Sénégalaise* a little shake. "In time, my boy would have found out that truth."

Martine's head wagged back and forth as the tears slid from her dark eyes. "But…he loved her, and I…I wanted her dea—" She made the sign of the cross.

Marie-Thérèse tightened her grip. "You wanted no such thing. You could see as well as anyone with eyes that this woman could not make my boy happy for always," she soothed. "Look at me, Martine. You did not wish that woman dead. I know this because it was you who went to the convent to help him rescue her."

Martine glanced down at Marie-Thérèse. "That's just it. I didn't. Rescue her. Maybe part of me was hoping that we… me, you, and Christophe would fail."

"You hoped no such thing." Marie-Thérèse held the girl at arm's length as she looked into Martine's eyes. "Yes, you knew this was the wrong woman for Christophe. I know that, too. But her dead, you never wanted this, because you, Martine, have a woman's heart."

Martine blinked, but the trembling in her lip continued.

"You knew that his pretend love with her could not last, and in time, his eyes would clear." Marie-Thérèse stroked the girl's shoulders. "Men can have their eyes clouded by many things."

Martine pressed the handkerchief to her eyes. "A woman's heart?"

"Not every woman has the patience to follow her woman's heart. To take the time to understand a man." Marie-Thérèse reached a hand under Martine's chin. "Men sometimes have their heads turned by a pretty face. Sometimes the man thinks all he wants is her bed tricks to excite him. Men are not like us. They are afraid to die old and alone. Sometimes men fear to take the chance to follow their hearts, and they settle for what is safe."

"But... not Christophe."

"A woman who truly loves the man—with her woman's heart—knows that this thinking cannot last. A pretty face will wrinkle. Bed tricks without love grow tiresome. Settling for secure will not fill his heart in his last days." Marie-Thérèse stroked the girl's chin. "One day, the man will see the truth. And then he comes back to the one who knows his real heart."

Martine stared at Marie-Thérèse. Did she think the old woman was speaking gibberish? "But Madame Brillard, suppose, by that time...by 'one day,' it is too late?"

"Now you talk the foolishness. Christophe sinks himself in sadness. He blames himself for the...accident." She released Martine and looked at the floor.

"Madame Brillard. I know. Everybody in Montmartre knows. It was a suicide."

"And for that, he blames himself." She looked up at Martine. "Now he sits quiet all day, but I know his mind is whirling. Telling him over and over, 'If only...if only.'"

"I'm so sorry." Martine sighed. "I've been too ashamed to visit Christophe. I heard that he was in an awful state. I knew I should have come, but I was afraid that he would blame me." She sighed again. "I let Christophe down. It's true." Her voice talked to the ancient tiles of the Sacré-Coeur. "Suppose just my being there, at the convent in disguise, and then running away without her. Suppose that angered the husband enough to refuse her the divorce?"

"You think I don't wonder this too? The plan was mine. Not yours. Not Christophe's." Marie-Thérèse clamped Martine's face hard between her hands. "But it was the plan that could have freed her...at least for a little while. It was her, this Genvieve, who made the decision. She tell Christophe to go without her. Not you. Not me. She know more about this husband than all three of us. What the husband do, what she do, was her own choice." Marie-Thérèse steadied her hands. Now was the time she needed every fiber of her strength. "Martine, there is no more that you can do except pray for that poor girl's soul. But for Christophe, there is something that only you can do." She had maneuvered the *Sénégalaise* as best she could. Now she had to convince her.

Martine looked up. "You know I will do anything for Christophe."

"My boy thinks nothing but dark thoughts. If he keeps this up, he will take it into his head to join Genvieve." She stared into Martine's eyes. "But I know, here in my heart," she thumped her chest, "that my son will get past these dark days. He will want to live if he has something…someone who thinks he is the most special person in the world."

Martine nodded her head as she fixed her eyes on the marble Mother of Jesus. "He has you. He has Collette."

"Not his *maman*. Not his sister." Marie-Thérèse spoke softly. "My Christophe…Martine, he needs you."

Martine's mouth opened. She stared at Marie-Thérèse. She cleared her throat. "Me? Oh no, Madame Brillard. Not me. Never me."

"Yes, you. Because he loves you."

A lopsided smile played across Martine's lips. "Christophe does not love me. I am not the one for him."

"You do not listen, girl. He was in love with her, this I know." She leveled her gaze. "But it is you he loves." She laid a hand over the girl's heart. "In here. Only now, he feels too dead inside to know it." She grabbed Martine's wrists. "Give him time, Martine, and you will see. When this pain is over, you will see that it is you he will turn to."

"How long will that take? A year? Five? Ten?" Martine's voice spilled over the sanctuary. "I can't, I don't *want* to wait until I am an old woman to have Christophe finally realize that it is me he really loves."

"And if I tell you that it will take twenty years, will that make your life easier…happier?"

Martine, owl-eyed, looked at her. Her jaw wobbled, but no words came.

"For the rest of your life, you will love only Christophe. You know this is true. You may take another man for your husband, but he will be the wrong man. And you and he will always know the truth of it."

Martine clamped her teeth over her upper lip.

"Even if it takes my son thirty years to come to his true feelings, you will always only love him. I have something to ask of you, Martine."

Martine stared at the cracked tiles of the Sacré-Coeur.

"You know what I ask, and you know why I ask. Because it is best for Christophe…and for you."

"Madame Brillard." Martine spoke to the floor again. "I don't know if he's ready."

"Not today. Not tomorrow. But he will do what I ask of him by month's end. You must agree to do your part. You are ready. Marry my son."

CHAPTER 46

The pungent comingled scents of rosemary, thyme, and turmeric pummeled through Glovia's kitchen and into her hallway. Marie-Thérèse sniffed in the aroma of *parmentier* with duck. The foie gras and the truffles were already laid out on serving platters scattered throughout the kitchen. Glovia had even provided extra tables to line her hallway. There the staff from the Montmartre Café set tureens of *roti de boeuf, épinards,* and *pommes au gratin.* Everything was ready. Almost.

Marie-Thérèse started up the hall toward the study just as Glovia made a quick exit out of the salon carrying a bouquet of apricot-colored roses and a Limoges vase. She stopped when she spotted Marie-Thérèse.

"I know what you're going to say, and the answer is no. I don't think this is too much." Glovia tried to slip past her.

"But Collette does not want a big party. And Christophe…"

"Has the boy come yet?" Glovia asked as she stepped into the bathroom.

Marie-Thérèse clasped both hands to the bodice of her new rose-colored dress.

"I guess that means no." Glovia handed the roses to Marie-Thérèse and began filling the vase with water. "Stop your fretting. He'll be here. Didn't he promise Collette?"

"Yes, I know he promised to come here for the celebration, but Glovia, if it looks too much like…"

"A party?" Glovia retrieved the roses. "Look, Christophe said he'd make the wedding cake for his sister. If he said it, he'll do it." She cast an accusatory glance at Marie-Thérèse. "If you ask me, he would have gone on down to the courthouse, too, if Collette had asked."

"Oh no. Collette wanted no one there for the marriage. Not Jean-Michel's family. Not even me."

Glovia headed toward the salon carrying the flowers in the cobalt-blue vase. "The girl got married down at the justice place, and the least I can do is host this little gathering to honor the event." She looked over her shoulder at Marie-Thérèse. "You notice I didn't call it a party."

Marie-Thérèse followed Glovia up the hall. She took another fast look at the front door, especially at the fill-in butler, Mr. Jimmie Lee Hudson. As they approached the salon, someone rapped on the door with the lion's head. Jimmie Lee took his time ambling to greet the new arrivals. Marie-Thérèse tried to disguise her stare at the guests. No Christophe.

"Mr. Jimmie Lee," she asked the makeshift butler as Glovia ushered guests and flowers into the salon, "you will tell me right away if Christophe arrives, won't you?"

"Look into the depths of your soul, and the bright side shall make you whole." Jimmie Lee turned to open the door for Miss Zaidie Mabry.

"Hey. That music's divine." Zaidie kissed Marie-Thérèse on one cheek. "Now, it ain't jazz, but that piano sure is mellow." Zaidie handed a wrapped gift to Marie-Thérèse as she put a hand on her hip. "I hear tell your piano man is back from the States. Baby, he sure can play." She sauntered into the room just as Gaston's saxophone blended with Monsieur Lieutenant's rendition of a song Michael swore was America's latest hit.

"Monsieur Jimmie Lee, if you see…" Had she just asked him that?

"A heart can harbor thoughts that are dreary and blue, and a heart can give truth to thoughts that are good and true. Which will yours be? Trust and see." Jimmie Lee turned back to his door-opening duties. No Christophe.

Marie-Thérèse followed the music coming from the salon. Michael looked up as she entered and gave her a twinkling smile. She raised her left hand to her mouth and wiggled her third finger. His grin broadened.

Though it was just six o'clock, early December darkness had already fallen over Paris. A trombone player joined the group stationed in front of Glovia's window. The room swarmed with people. Monsieur Crawford held court in a far corner as Jean-Michel's family gawked at two of his big-breasted bronzes. As usual, the artist explained each cleft and dip he'd put into his creations. Marie-Thérèse looked around two stout guests as she tried to spot Jimmie Lee, only to be greeted by a Chanel-gowned Collette. Marie-Thérèse clamped her hand to her mouth, and her worry drifted aside.

"My girl!" She felt the tears forming. "You look like the angel you have always been."

"Angel? Maman, you always told me I was your devil child." Collette, her hair in unstraightened waves, laughed. "Maman, I am so happy!"

"I say no such thing." Marie-Thérèse pretended to bristle. "Not too much?" She smiled back at her teasing daughter. "I tell Glovia no sliding across the piano, not too much showing the leg, the bosom, and no naughty songs. I don't worry about the music, because Monsieur Lieutenant will take care of that."

Collette, in her pink-tinged gown, with apricot-colored roses sprinkling her hair, leaned over to kiss her mother. "Maman, I want you to marry that man. Your Monsieur Lieutenant." She looked toward the piano. "If only... Christophe." She sobered.

"No. No. Today is all for you and for your happiness. I take care of mine soon, and as for your brother, we will all pray." She caught Jimmie Lee looking at her. What had he said about trusting her heart?

Jean-Michel walked up and whisked his bride away just as Glovia directed the servers from the Montmartre Café to circulate their trays.

"Come on in here with me," Glovia ordered.

Marie-Thérèse followed her into the bedroom. Glovia closed the door. A wave of panic brushed over Marie-Thérèse.

"Christophe? Has something happened?"

"Not Christophe. Quit your worrying about him. The kid's young, he'll bounce back. No, I've got something to show you."

Marie-Thérèse's heart steadied and picked up the two beats it had skipped. "Collette is collecting lovely gifts. I put them all in the study." She turned to leave. Christophe should have been here twenty minutes ago.

"I got a letter," Glovia announced.

Marie-Thérèse stopped and turned. "A letter?"

"From my sister in Mississippi. Well, actually from the New York City post office. Seems like my sister wrote the damn thing in 1941 from Greenwood. Something about trouble getting mail to France during the war." Glovia grinned.

Marie-Thérèse shook her head. "A late letter?" she puzzled.

"He died in thirty-five." Glovia's grin broke out full across her face.

"Died? Who died in thirty-five?"

"Mr. Johnson, that's who the hell who. The old bastard keeled over. My sister thinks he had to be ninety-four," Glovia prattled in English as she rushed at Marie-Thérèse. She gave her a hug so strong it lifted the heavier Marie to her tiptoes. "You know what this means?" Glovia let her go and stamped her feet as she did an impromptu dance around her bedroom.

Marie-Thérèse had never seen Glovia so giddy. The strain over Christophe had affected them all in so many ways.

"Hallelujah, Lord!" Glovia cried out as she tried out the shimmy she'd promised to curtail for Collette's wedding reception. "The old bastard's dead. The old bastard's dead!" Glovia's voice grew louder and louder. "Hallelujah, he's dead and buried. Moldering in the cold, dark ground." She slipped into singsong. "Burning in hell."

"I know he did wrong to you, Glovia." Emotions tumbled inside Marie-Thérèse. She was glad for her friend, but was it right to celebrate the death of another human being? Well, maybe an evil one. "I am glad you are free."

"You got that right, girl." Glovia went back into her foot-stomping routine. "That's just it. I am free. I never divorced the bastard. Couldn't. It was me who ran off with another man. I'd a been accused of adultery in a divorce case. Couldn't do it." She took in a big sigh and fell back onto her bed.

Marie-Thérèse dropped down beside her. "Now I understand." She pulled Glovia into an embrace. "I am happy for you."

"Not as happy as you're gonna be when I tell you the rest of the news." She jumped to her feet. "Come on with me." Glovia sprinted into the salon.

"Everybody. Everybody! Listen up!" Glovia began in English, but when she saw the confused faces on the family of Jean-Michel, she switched to French. "This is a happy, happy day." She stood between her grand piano and Gaston, who lowered his saxophone to look at her. "This is a song for lovers everywhere." The room quieted. "A song and a toast. Real love only comes after a struggle. Sometimes it takes something awful to bring two people together." She grabbed a flute of 1928 Veuve Clicquot from a passing server. "Like our wonderful Collette and her ever-so-handsome groom, Jean-Michel. A toast."

"To Collette and Jean-Michel!" the partygoers called out in unison as they raised flutes to the newlyweds, who stood beside the piano.

Glovia took a quick sip of champagne. "Other times it comes to those of us of older years." She aimed the champagne glass into the crowd and moved it slowly across the group. "Like my friend Marie-Thérèse over there, and..." she pointed the flute directly at Michael, "the best piano man I ever had. I drink to you both."

"Hear, hear!" Monsieur Crawford chimed in.

"Let's hear it for the piano man!" cried Miss Mabry, not to be outdone.

"And for some of the more hardheaded among us, it may take years and years, but in the end we finally come to our senses." She moved next to Gaston and linked her arm through his. The sax man beamed down at her. "Me and Gaston here." She gazed up at him. "Took me twelve years to get my heart and head together, but I finally did it." She raised on tiptoes and kissed his cheek. "I love this man something awful." She lifted the flute to his lips. "We're getting married."

"Thank Jesus Ah-mighty!" Monsieur Crawford shouted out in an unfamiliar version of English. "It's about time!"

Jean-Michel's family paid rapt attention as their son translated.

Marie-Thérèse felt fresh tears forming. Happiness for Collette and for Glovia. Maybe, someday, even for herself. She looked up to catch a wink from Michael.

"Here's a song a friend of mine just gave me. Brand new." Were those tears in Glovia's eyes? "This is for lovers, especially Collette and Jean-Michel…and Marie-Thérèse and Michael, and…" Glovia's lower lip trembled as she looked at Gaston. "This is for you, baby."

Monsieur Lieutenant ran his fingers over the keyboard.

"*Quand il me prend dans ses bras. Il me parle tout bas.*" Glovia's voice quivered. "Give me a minute, piano man."

Michael nodded as he looked at the new sheet music. Glovia walked over to Monsieur Lieutenant and plucked one of the apricot roses from the Limoges atop the piano. She clutched it in her hand.

"I want to thank Mademoiselle Edith Piaf for this song." She got her voice under control as Michael trolled the black and white keys. "*Hold me close and hold me fast. The magic spell you cast. This is* la vie en rose." She turned her gaze on Gaston, his sax quiet in his hand. She held out the rose to him.

He looked at her as though she were the only woman in the world. Marie-Thérèse glanced up to see Monsieur Lieutenant nodding at her. She rubbed the diamond on her finger.

"*Je vois la vie en rose. Il me dit des mots d'amour.*"

"Madame Brillard." Jimmie Lee's soft tap on her shoulder startled Marie-Thérèse. She turned a tear-streaked face to the poet. What could he possibly want with her?

Jimmie Lee tilted his head in the direction of the hallway. There stood Martine. And Christophe. Memory gripped her chest like a vise. She excused herself through the crowded salon, the guests swaying in time to Glovia's stirring voice. Marie-Thérèse bounded over to her son, who held a large box. Inside, she spotted the *croquembouche*. Her daughter's pyramid-shaped wedding cake had been done up in a colorful profusion of pinks and whites and dusted with gold flecks.

"Christophe!" She tried to kiss her son on the cheek without disturbing the precarious balance of the cake.

"Where is this to be?" Christophe asked as Martine stood, quiet, beside him.

"In the salon." Jimmie Lee motioned a server to help Christophe set up the cake.

"Please just take it. I don't think I can stay." Christophe handed the cake over to the server.

"Oh no. You will not disappoint your sister." Marie-Thérèse sounded firmer than she intended. "You do not have to mingle with the others. Just wish Collette and Jean-Michel your congratulations. But first, you two come into the bedroom with me."

Martine shot a stricken look at Marie-Thérèse. "I'll help with the cake. You take Christophe to the bedroom." She scurried after the server.

Marie-Thérèse ignored her son's head shakes. She planted a firm grip on his wrist, just as she had done when he was six years old, and led him into Glovia's bedroom. She closed the door behind them and stood in front of it.

"Maman, I will try to be as cheery as I can." Christophe walked to the center of the room and turned to face her. "You know that I want Collette to be happy. But it is just so... so difficult."

"You think I don't feel this in you, Christophe? Every day now for five months, I see the hurt in you, but tonight, on your sister's big day, I have something for you."

"Maman, I know you mean well. I know you love me, but I don't...I can't take one more pep talk."

"Who talks to you about the pep? I tell you I have something for you." She reached into the new leather purse Collette had chosen for her at the factory where she worked. Of course, it had been Michael who paid for the extravagant gift. She withdrew a large envelope stamped with the logo of the Bank of France on it. She reached out to Christophe.

"What is that, Maman?"

"Here. Take it. It is rightfully yours."

Christophe stretched out a hesitant hand. He fumbled the seal open and looked inside. "Maman!" Shock echoed around the room. "There must be hundreds…thousands of francs in here." He turned to her, his eyes wide, his mouth open.

"Thirty thousand francs. But you needn't look so surprised. It is the money for your school. I save it all these years." She waited for her words to register. "A new year begins in six weeks. Nineteen forty-six. The first whole year free from the Germans. A new year. A new beginning. Now you can be the doctor you always wanted to be."

Christophe gazed at the envelope, then at Marie-Thérèse. "But that was a lifetime ago. When I wanted to be a doctor." He clamped a hand to his head. "I'd almost forgotten."

"You remember now," she soothed.

"But, Maman." He frowned. "How can I think…study? Not now." He swallowed hard. "It's all too late."

"Why you say this?" She waited patiently for her son's answer. In her head she crossed her fingers. She could not afford a mistake. Now was the time for all her carefully laid plans to be trotted out. So far, so good.

He stared at her as though she'd just had an attack of senility. "Maman, I can't. I just lost the woman I *love*. Genvieve."

"But it is for Genvieve that you must do this thing." Everything inside her seethed in worry; on the outside, she knew she had to be as still as one of Monsieur Crawford's bronzes.

Christophe shook his head in confusion as he clutched the money envelope in his hand.

"My boy, you think your *mère* a fool?"

"Of course not, Maman." His forehead creased even more.

"I know that you blame yourself for her…Genvieve's suicide." She sent up a quick prayer to the Holy Mother for the suicide lie. "Do you believe this woman love you above all others?" She stared straight into her son's eyes, refusing to let him look away.

"Yes, Maman. She loved me." He licked his lips, tried to stare at the carpet, but Marie-Thérèse closed in on him. "There was a time, when I first found out that she was married, that I doubted. But after seeing her at the convent, I knew the truth. She loved only me."

"If that is so, my son…" She pushed Christophe onto the edge of Glovia's bed. Marie-Thérèse sat down beside him. "Why do you think this woman take her life?"

Christophe stared at her. "I don't understand," he murmured.

"Of course you do not. Otherwise you would not put the blame of her death upon your shoulders."

"Maman?"

"A woman who love you would only take her life for one reason."

"He…the husband would not give her a divorce."

"No. That is not the reason a woman would take herself away from the man she truly loves. Herself and their child."

Christophe's mouth dropped open. "I don't…what do you mean?"

"You must take the money I save for you and go to medical school. You must go on with your life."

She watched her son's head tremble as non-understanding washed over his face. He opened his mouth, but no words escaped, though he tried several times.

"You owe that to Genvieve. No woman who loves her man would kill herself and take his child with her if she had any other choice." Marie-Thérèse gripped her son's arms. "The husband give her no choice."

"The divorce?"

"I told you no. Much worse. Think about it. A woman who is *enceinte* would only take her life…commit the suicide…if she believed it would save the life of the man she loved. The husband tells her to end this thing with you." Marie-Thérèse sucked in a breath. This was it…the focus of all her plans to save her son. "Christophe, hear me speak. The husband tell her she must let you go. But that is the one thing she can never do."

Christophe's clouded eyes blinked back at her.

"He, this freedom fighter, he tell her end it or he will kill you. *You*…not her." She licked her dry lips. Her throat longed for a sip of anything wet to wash away the lie. "What choice does this woman who loves you have?"

"Choi…?" The sound stuck in her son's throat.

Marie-Thérèse leaned forward, her voice almost a whisper. "She kill herself to save you. You." Her lungs searched for air. "Your Genvieve understands only what a woman with love deep in her heart can know. With her death, and only with her death, the husband will call this business with you to a finish."

She watched the muscles in her son's face change with the clicking of a clock. Confusion. Denial. Possibility. Probability. Truth. She steeled her mother's body to remain still when the thing she'd prayed for, planned for finally erupted.

Christophe's cry ricocheted around the room. Her boy's face paled. His body shuddered.

Enough. Marie-Thérèse pulled her boy's head to her chest and rocked him as she had when he was a toddler. Her voice murmured a Martinique lullaby in his ear.

Long minutes passed with only the sound of Christophe's sobs and Glovia's soul-wrenching lyrics floating under the door.

"The new year is here soon." She rested her chin on his cropped curls. "Your Genvieve wants you to live your life. She give her life for yours. You must repay her. You will do this for Genvieve?"

"Maman. Maman, I hadn't thought…never thought that…" His words were muffled as his tears dampened her new dress. "Genvieve…gave her life to save mine."

"You cannot doubt what is plain to see. This husband was a man who already use the knife on you. Free French, a hero, I know, but a man skilled in killing." She released her grip as Christophe pushed away from her. "It was her, your Genvieve, who saved you that day. Why you think she would not do it again if she believed you were in danger?"

"Maman." His fingers gripped the money-stuffed envelope. "Genvieve…she gave her life for me." He blinked back more tears. "If that's true, if that's so…" He kept his eyes on his mother. "How can I go on without her? I don't know if I can."

Marie-Thérèse sucked in her breath. She parceled out her rehearsed words with the greatest care. "You will not do this thing alone. Martine will help."

"Martine? Why would Martine…?"

"I do not have to tell you that Martine loves you. Even with all this, she stand by your side." She allowed him precious seconds to absorb her words. "Marry Martine."

Christophe's head jerked. "Marry? Martine? Maman! How could you ask such a thing? Preposterous. I can't. I couldn't."

"You think Genvieve went to her grave wanting you to be a monk? She give her life for you. A life that you owe her now. A life you must live to the best."

Christophe's lips moved, but his words were garbled in his throat. "You're telling me to marry? Me? I'll never marry. I couldn't!"

"Genvieve." Marie-Thérèse drew out the name as she captured her son's eyes. "*She* is the reason you must marry. You say you love this woman. You tell me, your *maman*, that you know this woman's soul. If you do that, if you think that is the true, then look into your own heart and do what you must for her."

She refused to let Christophe look anywhere other than into her eyes, though seconds ticked away. Michael's piano music drifted down the hall, sending its lushness floating through the shut bedroom door. Glovia's voice crooned songs of love to Collette and Jean-Michel. To her Gaston. Finally, Christophe blinked.

"You think...you believe that Genvieve would want me to go on without her? Even marry another woman?" His head shook his doubt.

Marie-Thérèse pulled up that reserve of strength she stored in her mother's heart. She was too close now. "It is not me who must do the think. It is you." She kept her eyes on him. "Ask your own soul. If it had been you who commit the suicide, would you have wanted Genvieve to dry up inside? If you sacrifice your life so she could live, what you think that new life should be like? Misery? Unhappiness? Bitterness? Loneliness?"

Christophe shook his head, the pain of the last five months still there, but something else beside it. Confusion, yes, but also hope.

"But to marry someone else?"

"You doubt the deepness of Genvieve's love for you?"

Christophe's eyes bored into Marie-Thérèse's. Confusion faded. "Of course I don't doubt her love...our love, but marry anybody? That I cannot do."

"I don't tell you to marry anybody. I tell you to marry Martine." She waited. "Now, you think why."

"Martine? We're friends, yes. Good friends." He looked down at the envelope. "At one time we were more than... but now..."

"You tell me there will never be a love like the one you have for Genvieve. Yes?"

"No. Yes. I can't...I won't love another."

"Your Genvieve know of the pain you be in. She sacrifice her life for you, hoping and praying to the saints that you forgive her for what she must do. Forgive her enough to find someone to help you through your agony." She gave Christophe time to take in her words. "Who better to help you than your best friend? A patient woman who loves you. Martine."

Another voice filtered into the room. Was it Monsieur Crawford offering a toast? Christophe stared minutes at the daylight streaming underneath the boudoir door. His body trembled. "She would not want me to be unhappy. I know that." Tears welled in his eyes. "But Maman, marriage? Maybe someday. Not now."

"You know your Genvieve's heart better than me. You tell your *maman* how long does she want your pain to go on? A year? Ten, twenty? You know her best. Would she object if a friend, a woman who was once your lover, turned into a wife? What would your Genvieve say against that?"

Christophe's eyes drifted from the door to Marie-Thérèse's face. He ran his tongue around his lips. "Genvieve…she would say…she would want…" He covered his eyes with his hands. "But what about her? Martine. Does she want to marry me? She knows I will always love Genvieve."

"Martine put her life up to help you. I think she is ready to help you through the pain."

He nodded. "But as a wife? A friend, yes, but a wife?"

"Louis-Philippe is a friend. A good friend. But just a friend cannot do for you what Genvieve wants."

Christophe's voice came out soft and low. "I would be an awful husband, and what if…what if she wants children? I don't think I could bear to have another child. Not after losing my son." He shuddered.

Marie-Thérèse swallowed. She was almost there. "Martine has the patience to help you heal your heart. She will give you all the time you need." She watched Christophe streak his hands down his cheeks. "I know you love your Genvieve, and I know you love your son, though you never set eyes on him." She rubbed the red marks he'd left on his face. "But just as Genvieve wants you to have a wife, she wants you to have another child, another son to give you all his love."

"No!" He raised his voice. "Another son could never replace the one I lost. I couldn't bear to look at another child." He turned away from her.

"He can never be replaced…this son you lose. You will always feel that pain. Here." Marie-Thérèse laid a hand on his chest. "But one day, when your new son looks at you in that certain way that says he puts all his trust in you, his papa, your heart will melt. You will find that you have love to spare to pour into him. In the beginning, you may not understand how this can be true." She stroked her fingers across his brow. "It may take years for this truth to come to you, but one day you will understand. Then you will know that you have always had love enough in your heart for two sons. And for two women. Now come with me. We must find Martine." She stood.

"Maman, I'm not sure. I need a little more time to—"

"Genvieve gave you all the time of her life. I think she give enough, don't you? You owe her the respect of living your life. Of having a woman to love you. Of having a family. That's the gift she give you. Can you reject it?"

Christophe struggled to his feet. The money envelope trembled in his hand. "I'll think about it."

"No more thinking, my son. It is time." Marie-Thérèse opened the bedroom door and headed toward the salon.

Christophe followed.

Monsieur Lieutenant looked up and shot a questioning glance in her direction as he played another new song. She gave him a quick smile as she handed Christophe off to Martine. Glovia nodded her head and continued singing the newest American hit. Something from a Mr. Perry Como. Gaston played saxophone, his eyes never off Glovia.

Monsieur Lieutenant nodded to Glovia's old piano player. Without missing a note, Michael handed over piano playing duties to his backup man. He walked over to Marie-Thérèse and took her into his arms.

"Let's dance, baby."

"*Till the end of time.*" Glovia snuggled against Gaston. "*Long as stars are in the blue...long as there's a spring...a bird to sing...*" She brushed his cheek with the apricot rose.

Safe in Michael's arms, Marie-Thérèse looked around the room. Jean-Michel gazed at his new wife as though Venus de Milo could not hold even second place to her beauty. Monsieur Crawford danced with Jean-Michel's grandma, and Jimmie Lee stepped on Zaidie Mabry's foot more than once. Monsieur Lieutenant gave her a slow twirl around the floor. She battled back tears when she saw Christophe hold Martine at arm's length and begin an awkward two-step. Her world was going to be all right.

"*I'll go on loving you till the end of time.*"

ACKNOWLEDGEMENTS

Let me begin with an apology. I'm sorry Terry Goodman, Senior Acquisitions Editor at AmazonEncore. I'm sorry I treated you like a door-to-door encyclopedia salesman—one peddling low quality books, yet. These days I console myself for insisting that the blinders I'd clamped to my face in 2009, rightfully belonged there. Why would I believe that my manuscript, the work of an unknown, unpublished writer who'd only advanced to round two in a writing contest, could catch the eye of a brilliant editor like Terry—a strong talent at Amazon's new publishing venture? Thank you, Terry, for sticking with me despite the dozens of roadblocks I planted in your path. Without you, neither Page from a Tennessee Journal nor Paris Noire would ever have seen print.

Paris Noire began when a courageous friend shared a painful aspect of his family story. Without his generous heart, this novel would never have been peopled with characters of such dauntless bravery. Thank you, Gilles, for entrusting me with what is so precious to you. I hope I have been faithful to the soul of your history.

A writer puts words to paper. An editor discovers them and leads them to print. But a published work can languish in Book Limbo forever without the right support team. The guidance, direction, encouragement, and downright enthusiasm from the Author Team at AmazonEncore has been spectacular. I truly could not have accomplished even the smallest measure of success without you, Sarah T, Jacque B-J, my publicists, and the entire team. Thank you.

No writer could make much headway without the support of family and friends. Rozelle, you have been spectacular in your efforts to promote my work. I wouldn't be surprised if 75% of San Francisco households are now aware of my books, thanks to your untiring efforts.

Continue what you're doing, California Writers' Club—Berkeley Branch. Your support of fledgling authors through amazing opportunities like the 5-page critique group is the stuff of legend. Thank you Anne, David, Ken, Bruce, Richard, Alex, and all the other members of this fantastic gathering. Your gentle probing and prodding force me to improve my craft.

To my sons Hank and Doug, and daughter-in-law Lidia, I thank you for your unstinting support. To grandson, Andrew, who finally believes that Grandma K can actually make a book from a computer, I thank you. (It's tough to convince a bright four-year old.)

No, it's not yet time for me to thank the Academy but I would like to thank the readers of Paris Noire. You are my greatest support. I hope by offering a fresh peek into the lives of people whose stories may not have been fully appreciated, I have earned that support.

ABOUT THE AUTHOR

After a three-decade career as a pediatric occupational therapist specializing in the treatment of children with physical disabilities, Francine Thomas Howard opted for early retirement. Driven by her desire to preserve the remarkable oral history of her family tree, she began writing down family stories. In the winter of 2009, she entered her grandmother's story, *Page from a Tennessee Journal*, in the Amazon Breakthrough Novel Award contest. Two weeks after the contest ended, Ms. Howard was contacted by AmazonEncore.

Ms. Howard's stories reflect her multiethnic heritage—African, European, Native American. In addition to *Paris Noire* (a tribute to another of her three grandmothers) and *Page from a Tennessee Journal*, Ms. Howard has written *The Sisterhood Hyphen*. She is currently hard at work on a five-book series—Scattered Seed—covering the 350-year saga of three kidnapped noblewomen of Timbuktu.

Ms. Howard resides in the San Francisco Bay Area with her family.